Praise for

DAVID FENNELL

'A truly extraordinary crime novel . . . a gritty, dark thriller with
a serial killer of frightening proportions'
LYNDA LA PLANTE

'I flew through it . . . Tense, gripping and brilliantly inventive'
SIMON LELIC

'Layered story telling'
BRIAN MCGILLOWAY

'Unsettling, fast-paced, suspenseful and gripping . . . Excellent'
WILL DEAN

'A tense-as-hell, high-body count page turner, but a rarer thing too –
one that's also full of genuine warmth and humanity'
WILLIAM SHAW

'Totally compelling'
ARAMINTA HALL

'Fennell's agenda here is the ratcheting up of suspense and
that's done with aplomb'
FINANCIAL TIMES

'An unsettling and twisty ride'
HEAT

'David Fennell more than earns his place at the crime fiction table
with this superb exploration of a psychopath with the creepiest
modus operandi I've read in a long time'
FIONA CUMMINS

'A serial killer classic in the making . . . hooks you in and holds you
tight, right up to the extremely satisfying final page'
SUSI HOLLIDAY

David Fennell was born and raised in Belfast. He left for London at the age of eighteen and jobbed as a chef, waiter and bartender for several years before starting a career in writing for the software industry. David studied Creative Writing at the University of Sussex. He is also the founder and director of the Beyond the Book Festival. He is married and lives in Brighton.

To find out more, visit his website: www.davidfennell.co.uk

You can also follow him on social media:
Twitter: @davyfennell
Instagram: @mrdavidfennell

Also by David Fennell

The Art of Death
See No Evil
The Silent Man

A Violent Heart

DAVID FENNELL

ZAFFRE

First published in the UK in 2024 by
ZAFFRE
An imprint of Zaffre Publishing Group
A Bonnier Books UK Company
4th Floor, Victoria House, Bloomsbury Square, London, WC1B 4DA
Owned by Bonnier Books
Sveavägen 56, Stockholm, Sweden

A CIP catalogue record for this book is
available from the British Library.

Hardback ISBN: 9-781-80418-607-7
Trade paperback ISBN: 9-781-80418-606-0

Also available as an ebook and an audiobook

1 3 5 7 9 10 8 6 4 2

Typeset by IDSUK (Data Connection) Ltd
Printed and bound in Great Britain by Clays Ltd, Elcograf S.p.A.

Zaffre is an imprint of Zaffre Publishing Group
A Bonnier Books UK company
www.bonnierbooks.co.uk

For my sister, Nicky, the light in all our lives.

Mallory Jones Investigates: A Violent Heart

Podcast trailer

Mallory Jones (voiceover): In this series of *Mallory Jones Investigates*, I do a deep dive into the murders of women, victims of the so-called Bolt Gun Killer. I speak to friends, family, neighbours and the police to build a picture of who these women were. I ask why these murders, some stretching as far back as thirty years, have never had the investigation they deserved. Is insidious misogyny within the police force to blame? Did this prevent the capture of a killer who committed multiple murders? It took one person to step forward and take control. A name familiar to listeners of this show, a woman who sees the big picture, a detective with a heart that beats so violently she will stop at nothing until justice is served. Featured in our award-nominated series: *The Girl Who Lived*, *The @nonymous Murders*, *The See No Evil Murders*, and *The Silent Man*, Detective Inspector Grace Archer leads the charge.

MUSIC to fade

Mallory Jones (voiceover): They were women living on the fringes of society. Women living in poverty trying to get by during recessions and enforced austerity. They had rent and bills to pay. Some had mouths to feed.

They were estranged from their families, alone and surviving the only way they could.

MUSIC EXTRACT to fade: The Smiths: 'Half a Person'. Traffic sounds in the background.

Fiona Brooks: Sally and I were best mates. We lived on the same street and went to the same school. We did everything together back then.
Mallory Jones: What was she like?
Fiona Brooks: (laughs) It's nice that people ask that and not obsess about what happened to her. The detective asked me the same question. I liked that about her.
Mallory Jones: Detective Inspector Grace Archer?
Fiona Brooks: Yeah. That's her. I told her the same thing. Sally was funny, and a bit gobby (laughs). She was brave. Much braver than me. I always admired that about her. Oh, and she loved music, especially the Smiths. Which I never understood. They were so depressing (laughs). I was more a Wham! girl.
Mallory Jones: Why did she move to London?
Fiona Brooks: She had lost both her mum and dad in the space of two years. She was left with no one. No other family. The social worker told her she'd have to go into care. That was the last thing Sally wanted. That's what made her run away to London. Despite being only sixteen, she was fiercely independent. She disappeared with dreams of finding a new life in the big city. Poor Sally. I still can't get my head around what happened . . .

MUSIC to fade

Mallory Jones (voiceover): *A Violent Heart* is available to download now from wherever you get your podcasts.

EXIT MUSIC

Chapter 1

Elena

IN THE MOMENT THAT ELENA steps into the man's car she feels a flash of dizziness that disappears almost as soon as it had arrived. It was a strange sensation, like a sixth sense perhaps, or a 'shining' as Marianne might call it, just like the book. She's never read it, but they had watched the movie together, and it had terrified her. She blinks it away and turns to the client, resting her shoulder bag on her lap. He's wearing a PPE mask, which unsettles her. The pandemic has passed, the world is back to normal. Most people are glad to see the back of masks. Obviously, not everyone.

'I've been vaccinated,' she says.

'Best to be safe.'

Elena shifts in her chair, the strange turn playing on her mind.

'Are you OK?' he asks.

She swallows and composes herself. 'Yes,' she replies with a fixed smile.

'You have an accent,' he observes.

Her lips tighten. English people always love to point out that she has an accent as if it was something that made her an oddball. 'Everyone has accent. Even English people,' she says.

'I suppose that's true,' he says, turning on the ignition.

Elena looks ahead, hoping this will be quick. She feels his gaze lingering and turns away, her lips set. Something about this man she can't quite put her finger on. A moment passes and the car has not moved. She looks at him, her brow furrowed.

'Seatbelt,' he says.

She bites her tongue and pulls the belt over her sleeveless blouse.

'I like your necklace,' he says, glancing at the gold half of a heart hanging from the chain around her neck. He switches on the indicator, checks the side mirror and pulls away from the kerb. Elena folds her arms and makes a silent prayer for this to be over soon. Leaving the quiet gloom of St Michael's Street, he turns left onto Praed Street. They pass McDonald's and an Angus Steakhouse, restaurants that she and Marianne would eat at depending on how much spare cash they had. Guilt ripples through her and she feels a creeping cloud of unease. She dips her head in an effort to not be recognised, and wrings her hands. But who would see her? Marianne is the only one that matters and she's at work. Perhaps one of Marianne's friends would spot her in the car and report back. Elena swallows. She couldn't bear to see the despair and disappointment on Marianne's face. Elena has already put her lover through enough. Marianne hated when Elena took to the streets. She especially hated when she got into strangers' cars.

'It's so dangerous, *chérie*! Please stop . . . please.'

They were both hot-headed and had argued, which Elena regretted horribly. But the truth of the matter is the cost-of-living crisis has hit them hard. They have no money for basics, never mind their crippling drug habit. She can't think about any of that right now. She sighs, dispelling the memory and thoughts from her mind in a rapid breath.

The car has become clammy and warm. The windows are closed, the air conditioning is off. Elena shifts uncomfortably on the vinyl seat, which feels a little tacky on her bare legs. It doesn't help she's wearing a short skirt.

'May I open a window?' she asks.

'I'd rather you didn't.'

'It's very warm.'

He frowns, and after a moment, takes one hand off the wheel and switches on the air conditioning.

They drive for ten minutes in a strained silence. Elena thinks about her 'shining' but pushes the thought from her head. Before stepping into the car the man had promised to pay her well. She needs money and this could be a good earner.

'Where are we going?' she asks.

'Somewhere quiet,' he responds, slyly glancing at her thighs.

'Not too far,' she replies. 'I have to get home, so let's be quick, please.'

'Where are you from?' he asks.

She sighs. 'Croatia.'

'Are your family there?'

'Yes.'

'You must miss them.'

Elena looks out the passenger window and doesn't respond. She did not sign up to getting personal with clients.

They stop at traffic lights. Elena has no idea where they are. She notices the man is looking at the track marks on her arms. She folds them over concealing them from view.

'You have a tattoo on your wrist,' he says, easing off the brakes.

'Yes.'

'It's nice.'

She feels her patience thinning, 'Can we just get this over with? I must get home.'

'We're nearly there,' he replies softly, pulling into a parking bay facing an expanse of darkness that she thinks might be a park. She hears pounding dance music and beyond a cluster of trees sees coloured lights flashing from the open window of a tower block flat. She hears voices, laughter too. A party. In this gloomy unfamiliar place, it gives her some comfort that she is not far from civilisation. Elena removes her seatbelt.

The man is looking through the window, no doubt checking that they're not being watched. Usual nervous client behaviour. Elena is eager to move fast. 'OK, let's do this.' She reaches for his zipper, but his hand grabs hers and squeezes hard, crushing her fingers. Icy pain shoots up her arm. She gasps and pulls away, but he is strong; his grip, vice like. Panic and adrenaline set in. With her free hand she reaches behind her and fumbles for the door handle. She pulls it, and cries once more as he yanks her towards him. Confusion clouds her and she does not see, but feels his fist connect with her nose. A horrible crunching sound. Her head slams against the passenger window, the door flies open, and she flops sideways out onto the stony tarmac, her legs still inside the car. Her breathing is rapid. Blood pours from her nose. White dots float in front of her. Her heart is pounding.

Run! She lets out a muffled cry of panic, kicks her way out of the car and scrambles onto all fours. *Trees nearby. Run to them. Hide.*

'Help!' she cries but her voice is swallowed by the thumping music.

She hears the thud of the car door closing and the slow tread of his footsteps approaching. She takes a breath. Trembling, she looks back. He is silhouetted in the gloom of the car park, a dark, malevolent presence. In his hand, he holds what looks like a thick baton just over a foot in length. *Oh my God!* She feels a wet warmth run down her legs.

'Oh dear, look at you,' he mocks.

'Please, don't hurt me ... I ... I won't say anything. I just want to go home.'

He is more shadow than man now, dark as night, and seems to grow in stature as he draws closer.

Elena thinks about her 'shining'. It had been a warning. She should have heeded it. She curses herself and inches back, stepping onto the soft grassy surface. Her life flashes in her mind, a compilation of heartache, loss and pain. All because of men. It seems her lot in life is to be at the receiving end of them and their grubby, ugly penises and fists. Spineless cowards. That's what they are.

He is closer now, his eyes empty of compassion. She sees only death in them. A surge of anger rises inside her, erupting into a fury. She spits saliva and blood on his masked face. The shock and disgust in his eyes give her a spurt of courage, and before he can do anything, she kicks him hard in the balls. He howls and doubles over. Lucky, she thinks, her confidence returning. Elena kicks off her heels, spins around and sprints towards a copse of trees, screaming without thinking where she is going. She keeps running, the dry, uneven surface biting into the soft soles of her bare feet. Glancing back, she sees him searching for her. Elena darts behind a tree and fumbles her phone from her bag, but her fingers are damp with sweat, and it slips through them, falling to the grass below. The screen lights up, illuminating the ground around her feet. She spots a thick broken branch nearby and grabs it, her phone too. The branch is heavy and unwieldy, but it will do as a weapon should he catch up with her. With her other hand, Elena uses facial recognition to unlock her phone. She wants to call Marianne, but hesitates . . . what could Marianne possibly do other than fret and worry? There is no time. She needs the police.

'Hello, which emergency service do you need?' says the operator.

'He's trying to kill me!' she blurts out.

5

'Madam, do you require the police? Are you in danger?'

She hears his thudding footfalls running. Looking across, she sees him charging towards the glow of her device. Mustering all of her strength, she swings the branch hard at his head but he manages to raise his arms and shield himself from the blow. She does not give up and strikes him three times with little impact. She must get away from him. Dropping the weapon, she bolts from the trees, running blindly into the dark.

'Help!' she screams, but her voice is drowned by the music. She's still holding the phone but the call has disconnected. 'Fuck!'

She hears him running behind her, panting, and at that moment, remembers the one person who changed her life for ever. The one person, other than Marianne, she has ever trusted. She holds the phone close to her face and feels herself slowing. 'Hello, Siri!' she says, tears filling in her eyes.

Her phone's digital assistant's cheery voice answers, 'Hello, Elena. How can I help you?'

But then the man has caught up with her and pushes her to the ground with such force that the phone slips from her grasp.

'Siri, call Grace Archer,' Elena shouts.

'Calling Grace Archer,' Siri responds.

Elena hears the phone ringing. She looks up at the man. He uses the baton to smash her phone. The glow extinguishes. Elena's heart sinks. He straddles her stomach and rips open her blouse. Tears pool in her eyes. He places the metal baton on her bare chest. She thinks of Marianne and the life they could have had together. 'I'm sorry, chèrie.' The baton has a trigger at the top. He squeezes it. She hears a loud cracking noise and feels something icy cold penetrate her body. She gasps and shudders as the world darkens for ever.

Chapter 2

GRACE ARCHER KNEELS ON A newspaper by the graveside, bathed in morning sunshine, and with secateurs, trims the overgrown grass and weeds that had sprouted since her last visit four weeks ago. She tosses the detritus into a heap by her side and edges her way around the plot, focusing hard like a seasoned gardener, ensuring the surface is even and immaculate. Satisfied with her work, she scoops the cuttings into a compostable garden bag and sweeps up the remaining waste with a small brush. From her backpack she takes out a cloth, and a spray, which she uses to clean the dust and bird droppings from the gravestone. Rinsing the cloth with water from a bottle, she carefully cleans the gold engraving in the three names: Samuel Jacob Archer, Rosalie Mary Archer, Jacob Arthur Archer. A stirring of emotion ripples through her, a reminder that she is alone in the world. She feels an ache in her chest yet, at the same time, a sense of peace that comes with being at the final resting place of those you love. One of those odd dichotomies.

A shadow darkens her vision, pulling her from her thoughts. Her muscles coil, and she turns. A man carrying a posy of crimson carnations is walking by.

'Morning,' he says.

Archer relaxes and returns the greeting. She scans the grave-yard as is her instinct every time she comes here. At the age of twelve, still grieving the loss of her murdered father, DI Sam Archer, she had bunked off school and come here only to be abducted by her father's assassin, the child serial murderer, Bernard Morrice. Through tenacity, bravery, a burning rage and, let's face it, a lot of luck, young Grace had escaped Morrice's incarceration, charging at him and tumbling down the stairs alongside him in his home. Morrice's neck had snapped in two. She had survived. Justice had been dealt. Still, despite finding a measure of comfort in this holy ground, Morrice's foul presence seems to linger in the shadows.

She feels a vibration in her pocket. Her phone is still on silent mode. Removing her gloves, she takes out the device. It's a call from her partner, caustic Belfast man, Detective Sergeant Harry Quinn. She swipes and answers. 'Morning.'

'Hi, bestie,' says Quinn.

'Bestie?'

'Yeah, you know, like bezzie mates. Muckers.'

Archer smiles. 'Is that what we are?'

'It occurred to me this morning that in all the time we've been working together, we never talk about our muckers. Therefore, I concluded that like me, you're a little thin on the ground with besties. Hence, we must be besties-cum-muckers.'

'That's very presumptuous of you.'

'What can I say . . . Anyway, did you get the message about the emergency meeting at ten o'clock this morning?'

'One minute.' Archer checks her phone. There are no messages, only a missed call from an old friend late last night. 'Nope.'

'I had wondered. Deb from HR sent it. I didn't see your number on the list.'

'Debbie and I are not . . . muckers,' Archer says, mocking his accent.

Quinn chuckles. 'She is Dolores Umbridge to your Harry Potter.'

'Is she the evil one, dresses in pink and has a kitten fetish?'

'That's her.'

'Now that you say that . . .' Archer laughs.

'Anyway, not sure what it's about, but Deb is in Clare's office with Chief Inspector Les Fletcher. Heard of him?'

Clare Pierce is Archer and Quinn's boss. Just over six months back she had been promoted from DCI to Chief Inspector. A dynamic, power-suited, no-nonsense straight talker, Pierce is a fierce governor who worked the system and got results for her team and the investigations she oversaw.

'No. Who is he?'

'Don't know. He's in uniform, pressed white shirt with a basketball-sized belly trying its best to break free. Has a disconcerting gammon complexion.'

'That narrows it down.'

'I'm going to ask around. Make a few calls. Oh . . . that's . . . weird.'

'What do you mean?'

'Flat pack cardboard boxes have just arrived outside Clare's office.'

'What's that about?'

'No idea. Perhaps we'll find out at the meeting. Can you make it?'

Archer checks her watch. 'It'll be tight. I'll finish up what I'm doing and get there as soon as I can.'

'Cool. I'll request a delay from Clare on your behalf.'

'Thanks.'

Archer clears up and deposits everything into a tote bag. She checks her phone and looks at the missed call from Elena. Something niggles at her. It had been two years since they'd spoken, but Archer knew Elena was in a better place and had moved in with Marianne. Everything seemed rosy from her social media posts. She bites her lip. When does social media ever reveal an accurate depiction of real life? She taps Elena's number and calls her for the third time that morning. Once again it goes straight to voicemail. A twist in Archer's stomach. 'Hi, Elena, it's Grace . . . just checking in. Call me back. Bye.'

It takes a slow thirty minutes in an Uber before Archer arrives at Charing Cross. Hurrying to the third floor, she notices a meeting is in progress in the conference room. Debbie from HR is smiling at a large man in his fifties with blotchy skin who is addressing the team. Quinn's gammon-faced Chief Inspector Les Fletcher. Clare Pierce, a thin woman with short dark hair, sits at the table, eyes down, expression grim. As if sensing she has arrived, Pierce looks across to see Archer approaching. She holds Archer's gaze for a moment. Something in her eyes.

Archer knocks on the door and enters. 'Sorry I'm late.'

'Chief Inspector Fletcher, this is DI Grace Archer,' says Pierce.

Fletcher's eyes fix on Archer. 'The famous Grace Archer. Welcome,' he says with a strong Yorkshire accent. He cracks a smile without sincerity or warmth. 'Take a seat, DI Archer; I'm just updating the team on what I expect from them.'

'What you expect from them?' Archer asks.

'Grace—' Pierce begins.

Fletcher interrupts, 'As of today, I will be taking over Chief Inspector Pierce's responsibilities. You and everyone else will report to me. Those that have worked under me will tell you I run a tight ship and have little toleration for many things – sloppiness and timekeeping, to name a few.' He glances at Archer.

She bristles and looks at Quinn. He meets her gaze, eyebrows raised. She notices her colleague, senior analyst and tech guru, Klara Clark, arms folded, a frown creasing on her high forehead.

Fletcher takes a breath, but Archer interrupts, 'Excuse me, why are we only hearing about this now?' Her eyes look from Fletcher to Pierce.

'Something personal has come up, Grace,' says Pierce.

'If you'd have been here on time, you'd have heard Chief Inspector Pierce tell the room that she's taking leave and may be gone for some time.'

Archer glances at HR Manager Debbie Dickson, who watches her with a tight grin.

Archer ignores her and turns to her governor. 'Clare?'

'We'll talk after this,' Pierce replies quietly.

'I'd appreciate that,' says Fletcher. 'Unless there are any other questions, please, all of you, get back to work.'

'Let's go to my office,' Pierce says to Archer.

Pierce closes the door behind Archer and leans on her desk.

'What's this about, Clare?' Archer asks, narrowing her eyes at the flat pack cardboard boxes.

'I . . . I'm taking time out. I had given notice yesterday. I told them I could work for another month, but they wanted me gone sooner. "They" being HR, who miraculously conscripted Fletcher to replace me. He jumped at the chance, apparently. Been waiting for the right opportunity for some time.'

'They can't just force you out like that.'

'I could fight it, but I don't have it in me right now.'

Pierce sits down on the small sofa opposite her desk, shoulders drooping. She looks defeated.

Archer perches beside her, her hands pressed together. 'What's going on?'

Pierce hesitates before answering, 'It's Richard. His Long Covid is getting worse. He needs round-the-clock attention.'

Richard is Pierce's husband of thirty years. He'd been in hospital with Covid for six months during the pandemic. He'd been put into a coma and, to everyone's relief, had come out better, yet like thousands of others, he had not made a full recovery.

'Oh, Clare, I'm so sorry.'

'He's so pathetic looking. It breaks my heart.'

Pierce sits at her desk and rubs her arms, her forehead lined with worry. 'They think it could be months. Or a few years. We've had our ups and downs like everyone, and Lord knows, I have been a shitty person sometimes but the thought of him . . . I just can't . . .'

'Is there anything I can do?'

Pierce shakes her head. 'We should think about what I can do for you.'

Archer is uncertain what she means.

'There's not a lot I can do right now other than advise you to watch your back.'

'My back?'

Pierce's eyes slide across the office to the conference room where Fletcher and Debbie from HR are deep in conversation. 'I've known him for a few years. Some might call him old school. I'd replace "old" with prehistoric. You didn't hear this from me, obviously.'

Archer feels her stomach knotting.

'There's one expression I keep coming back to every time I have dealings with him.' Pierce watches him, her eyes narrowed.

'What's that?'

Pierce turns to Archer and smiles. 'A prize cunt. And that's between us, too.'

A knock at the door. Quinn is looking in. Pierce gestures for him to enter.

'Excuse my butting in. I need to talk to Grace.'

'You two carry on,' says Pierce.

Quinn steps towards Pierce. 'Sorry about Richard, Clare.'

Pierce nods a thanks.

'For what's it worth, I'm going to miss your frank openness and unfaltering willingness to remind me how shit I am.'

'Don't mention it. Anyway, I have every intention of returning, so don't give up on me just yet.'

Quinn grins and opens his arms. 'Give me some sugar,' he says, pulling her into an embrace.

Pierce stiffens. 'Oh God. You know I'm not a hugger.'

'Hush now. Just take the love.'

Pierce wriggles out of his arms and turns away. She takes a paper handkerchief from a box on her desk and dabs her eyes.

Archer and Quinn exchange a concerned look and leave the Chief Inspector to herself. Archer shoots an anxious look back in at Pierce, who is clearly broken. Outside the office the mood on the third floor is sombre, heads are down, buried in computers and phones.

She turns to Quinn. 'What's up?'

'Dixy, the TikTok twat, has been posting videos again.'

Chapter 3

'JUDGING FROM YOUR EXPRESSION, I'M not sure I want to hear this,' Archer says.

Calvin 'Dixy' Dixon is a Gen Z social media cult sensation famous for filming himself playing pranks on the unsuspecting public. In one video, he runs into a synagogue during worship, laughing and speaking loudly in tongues with a baby voice. In another, he gatecrashes a wedding, and when the priest asks if there is anyone present who objects to the union of these two people, he pipes up and shouts, 'I do!' in the same grating voice. In other videos, he gets into the passenger seat of female drivers' cars and professes undying love to them in that voice. He has also run through the halls of a school, banging classroom doors and claiming to have a gun. He's upset many people, and a dozen or more complaints have been made to the police, resulting in multiple arrests. His posts have gone viral, and his notoriety has been covered extensively by the media. His profile was elevated further when he was invited to explain himself on various news shows. He came across as inarticulate and defensive, and refused to apologise by claiming he was not a 'prankster', but a 'content creator'. This made the online Gen Z'ers love him even more. He was creating a brand, and to Quinn's utter disbelief, the arse biscuit, as he had coined him, had a net worth that had risen to over £90,000.

'He's branching out with his content,' Quinn says. 'And doing another of his "Night Terror" videos.'

'I don't even want to think what that might involve.'

Dixy had first come to Archer and Quinn's attention when he released the first of his Night Terror videos. He had broken into the remains of Ladywell Playtower in Lewisham, former home to the Blood of the Lamb cult, and the location of two murders that had brought an end to an investigation Archer had led before the pandemic. Dixy had formulated his own batshit theory about the cult and the murders. To Archer's disbelief, his video had received over fifty thousand views. She and Quinn had caught up with him, slapped his wrist and sent him packing. He was an irritation, much like a hungry buzzing mosquito that refused to fuck off. He was also becoming a drain on police resources.

Quinn takes out his phone and opens up the TikTok app and Dixy's profile. He selects a video with a grinning Dixy, dressed in a Dalmatian-patterned tracksuit standing in a dimly lit room, holding his phone with a selfie stick. The room has eaves and looks in a state of disrepair. Dixy begins to speak in his normal voice.

'I've made a new friend . . .' he says. Cartoon hearts flutter like butterflies on the video. 'I found her lying here all wrapped up in a rug . . .' He pulls a sad face and then grins from ear to ear, his teeth large and white, his eyes narrow, sly and insincere. 'Looks like she's been here for some time. Let me introduce you.' He crouches beside a rocking chair. Archer feels her muscles coiling. 'I don't care what anyone thinks,' says Dixy. 'But we's in love.'

Quinn pauses the video. 'Sick fuck. I've called his number several times and he's not picking up.'

Archer stares down at the screen, not quite believing what she's seeing.

'Let's bring him in.'

They make their way out of Charing Cross police station, hurrying down the stairs and out to the unmarked Volvo on Chandos Place. They drive in silence for a few moments before Quinn breaks it. 'So Chief Inspector Gammon has a douche reputation. Other news on the grapevine is that he's going to shake up the department.'

'Clare doesn't like him much.'

'From what I know the feeling is mutual.'

'She doesn't want to go. Not yet anyway.'

'Did she tell you that?'

'She wanted to stay a bit longer. I've never seen her so vulnerable, so . . . scared. She feels HR and Fletcher are forcing her out.'

'She's in my prayers. Richard, too, obviously.'

Archer shoots him a sideways look, her eyes narrowed. 'Thought you gave up on all that – "hocus pocus", I think was the term you used.'

'Like all Irish Catholics, I dip in now and again when it suits.'

'At funerals, you mean?'

'Weddings, baptisms, communions, confirmations, that sort of thing.'

Calvin 'Dixy' Dixon lives with his mum and dad in a Victorian terrace on a smart street in an upcoming part of South London. The only son of lower middle-class parents, his folks had worked hard in their careers to open up opportunities for him that they never had. Unfortunately for Mr and Mrs Dixon, Dixy's spurt of fame was for all the wrong reasons and had not been in their masterplan. They knock on the front door and wait. No one answers. A second knock, still no answer. Quinn peers through the letterbox. 'No sign of life,' he says.

'They're probably at work,' comes a woman's voice.

They turn to see a woman in her sixties strolling past, pulling a trolley of shopping.

'We're looking for Dixy,' Quinn says. 'Have you seen him?'

'You mean Calvin? No, I've not seen him in a few weeks. Used to be such a sweet boy.'

'Do you happen to know where he might be?'

'I'm afraid not. He comes and goes, like most young people round here.'

'Thank you,' says Archer.

'We should have the parents' number on file,' says Quinn.

'I'll call in and get it,' says Archer.

She phones the office and talks to analyst Os Pike, who looks up Dixy's file and finds his mother's mobile number. He texts it to her.

Archer calls the number and listens. After three rings it picks up. 'Hello,' says Mrs Dickson, a tremor in her voice.

'Mrs Dickson, this is Detective Inspector Grace Archer. We met briefly some weeks back in relation to an incident with your son, Calvin.'

'Oh God. Please tell me he's OK.'

'As far as we know. We'd just like to talk to him.'

'It's about these awful videos, I know. Why must he keep doing them? I'm at my wits' end.'

'I'm sure you are. Could you tell us where we might find him?'

She scoffs. 'If only I knew. He had a bust-up with his father last week and left the house. We haven't seen him since and he's not answering our calls. I'm worried sick and the only way I know he's alive is to check in on the TikTok. Cursed thing. Is he in trouble?'

'That remains to be seen. Have you any idea where we might find him?'

'I heard he's staying with a friend in some apartment on Earlham Street. That's all I know.'

'If you hear from him, please call me immediately on this number.'

Mrs Dixon hesitates before answering, 'Of course.'

'Thank you.'

Chapter 4

ARCHER AND QUINN SPEND THE best part of the day following up on leads and sightings, all of which amount to nothing. They return to Charing Cross and ask tech guru, Klara, to run one of her covert 'no questions asked' scans to find the location of Dixy's phone. To their disappointment, the scan reveals nothing. The phone had last been connected the night before.

It's mid-evening. Archer is in the office alone, working overtime. Her phone rings. It's Klara.

'His phone is back on,' Klara announces.

'Can you see where he is?'

'Not precisely, but he's definitely somewhere in the West End.'

Archer closes her laptop and stands. 'He's staying at Earlham Street. I'm going to head there now. Call me if he's on the move.'

Archer hurries up St Martin's Lane, navigating the theatre crowds in the clammy evening. Her phone rings once more. 'He's on Tottenham Court Road,' Klara says.

'That's impressive accuracy.'

'I created a quick program to alert me when he posts or is tagged on socials. Right now, he's being filmed by small mob of fans.'

'Perfect. I'll call in for back-up.'

'No need,' says Quinn.

'Harry's on the line,' says Klara. 'Thought you could use him.'

'I'm driving into town now,' Quinn says.

'Where are you?' she asks.

'About ten minutes away,' he replies. 'The traffic is bollocks and the pissing air con has just given up. It's sweltering in here.'

'Not much better here,' she replies, her brow moistening. 'I'm going to have to run,' she adds.

She hears the sound of Quinn's siren turning on. 'Sod that!' he says. 'I'm on my way.'

'Stay on the line.' Archer legs it across Cambridge Circus, dodging the tourists taking multiple selfies underneath the giant *Cursed Child* nest statue at the Palace Theatre. She hops onto the road, glancing behind her to ensure she is not about to be squashed by a Routemaster.

'He's on the move,' says Klara.

'What direction?' she asks, panting into the phone as she flies past Foyles bookshop.

'He's still on Tottenham Court Road.'

'Shit,' says Archer, upping her speed.

Moments later, after dodging traffic, she arrives at the neon-lit Tottenham Court Road junction with Oxford Street and slows. Her eyes scan the faces. 'I'm here,' she says breathless. 'There's no sign of him.'

'Look for a gathering of young people with their phones in the air.'

Archer pushes her way through the crowd that thickens like shifting walls closing in on her, sparking her claustrophobia, twisting it into ringing anxiety. Her head spins. 'Shit.'

'You OK?' says Klara, a concerned tone in her voice.

'I'm fine . . . it's just . . . crowded,' says Archer.

'Take a few deep breaths,' says Quinn, who seems to have twigged her predicament. 'I'm moments away.'

She takes three calming breaths.

'He's wearing jeans, a lime green vest and green baseball hat reversed on his head,' says Klara.

Archer stands on her tiptoes and searches the crowd. It takes her a few moments to catch the cap bouncing below the heads of the throng. She had forgotten how short he is. 'Is the cap lime green too?'

'Yeah,' says Klara.

'Is lime green in fashion?' Quinn asks.

'I've got him,' Archer says.

She turns back the way she came, hurrying after him she hears Quinn's siren close by. Archer is bumped by someone weaving through the crowds, knocking the phone from her hand. It falls to the pavement and gets lost among legs and feet. 'Hey!' she calls.

'Sorry,' comes a man's voice from somewhere.

Bracing herself, she quickly crouches down, and snatches it before it is kicked away. The edges are grazed, the glass screen fortunately not cracked.

Quinn is talking but she's not taking it in. At the junction with Oxford Street, she spots Dixy standing at the crossing, waiting for the traffic to stop. On the opposite side is the mammoth stainless-steel exterior of Tottenham Court Tube station tinted red and blue from the large glowing Underground sign jutting out over the thoroughfare. The crowd jostles around her to get ahead. Archer stands on her toes, peering over heads, but Dixy has dipped out of sight.

'Can't see him,' she says, pushing through the crowd. From Oxford Street, she hears the angry blast of car horns. She sees

Dixy dashing across the road, a blue tracksuit jacket in hand, awkwardly dodging oncoming traffic.

'He's in a hurry,' says Archer.

'D'ya think he saw you?' Quinn asks.

'I don't think so, but it's possible. He's going into the Tube station.'

'Fuckballs!' says Quinn. 'I'm not going to make it.'

The traffic stops as the lights change to red. Archer bolts across the road into the forecourt and onto the escalator.

'Stay in the car. Wait to hear from me. I'll call you when I can.'

'But—'

She ends the call and drops the phone in her jacket pocket. Dixy is stepping off the bottom of the escalator. He's not looking behind him and his stride is slower now. Good. He's unaware he's being followed. Archer hurries down the moving steps.

Using her Oyster card, she slips through the turnstile and onto the platform for the Northern Line train heading north. She watches him furtively from the corner of her eye. He's tapping his foot and biting his lip as if he's nervous or excited. Maybe both.

The train whooshes in, brakes screeching to a stop, the bitter scent of oil and fumes choking the confined space.

A confined space.

The walls, the ceiling, the train, the closeness of it all. Her head begins to spin. 'Shit!' She feels a tightness around her chest as a memory flashes in her mind.

At the age of twelve, Archer's kidnapper, Bernard Morrice, had trapped her in a dark pit for weeks. With a grim determination to live, she had clawed her way out of the muddy prison and escaped. The trauma had never left her nor had it quite healed. The phobia for small spaces remained and Tube stations were no exception.

The train doors slide open and passengers spill onto the platform.

Breathe. Breathe.

Archer composes herself. She searches for Dixy, squinting through the horde. She sees him through a grubby window dropping onto a Priority seat in the carriage. It's almost full inside. She swallows. The doors begin to bleep their warning. *Fuck it.* With a deep breath she dives through the sliding doors, squeezing among the passengers, clutching hard the cold steel of the holding pole. Dixy is gazing down at the floor, feet tapping, lost in his thoughts. The train rolls forward and starts to gather momentum. She closes her eyes and breathes steadily, opening them when the train slows and stops at Goodge Street. Dixy remains seated. They stop at Warren Street, Euston, Mornington Crescent and Camden Town with no sign of him alighting. As they approach Tufnell Park, he shifts in his seat and peers through the grubby windows. The train comes to a halt, he stands, and leaves when the doors open. Archer takes out her phone as she steps onto the platform. Dixy is heading for the exit. As she ascends the stairs, her phone signal returns. She calls Quinn and tells him where she is.

Dixy exits left from the station and walks down Brecknock Road, increasing his pace. Archer keeps a safe distance behind him. Several minutes later he turns left onto Pleshey Road, a quiet street with brown brick Victorian townhouses on either side. He slows to a stop outside a property that is boarded up and in a bad state of repair. The houses on either side are numbered forty-six and fifty. A tall wooden fence has been erected to keep people from wandering inside. Danger signs are nailed to boarded-up windows. He looks up at the house as if in awe and then glances around him. Archer darts behind a tree and out of sight. A moment later she peers out. She sees

Dixy's head dropping behind the fence. She waits a moment, listening and looking, but there's nothing.

Her phone vibrates. Quinn is calling.

'I'm at least fifteen minutes away,' he says.

'He's just entered an unused, boarded-up derelict townhouse on Pleshey Road. Number forty-eight.'

'Hope you're not thinking of going in after him.'

Archer looks at the forbidding property. It's narrow and tall, three storeys, with a single round window in the eaves. She's not the superstitious type, yet if she was, she'd turn her back and walk away from what is a quintessential creepy haunted-looking house. A thought occurs to her. Had he caught sight of her just now? She can't be sure, yet she has an uneasy feeling that can't quite explain.

'I'm going in.'

'Grace, wait . . .'

'Something's not right.'

'When is anything ever right? I'll be there asap.'

Archer ends the call and notices a dim light glowing in the round window of the eaves.

Chapter 5

ARCHER APPROACHES THE HOUSE. AT five foot four, the towering six-foot fence is too high for her to climb or jump. She peers into the garden next door and notices a dividing brick wall. It's about four feet high, enough to give her a leg up to quickly scale the fence. The neighbours' curtains are drawn. She passes through the gate, darts through the garden, climbs onto the wall and hauls herself over the fence, dropping onto the overgrown grass and weeds below.

There are steps leading up to the entrance, a panelled door with blistered black gloss. Quietly and cautiously, listening out for a sign of the 'TikTok sensation', or anyone else for that matter, she climbs them. It's a risk following the suspect alone into this run-down, abandoned and, let's face it, creepy Victorian house, but what choice does she have? This could be a perfect opportunity to nail him.

It doesn't look like anyone has lived here in a long time, which is odd. She's surprised it's empty. Properties in North London are snapped up and sell for a premium. Maybe this one has a dodgy history. One that repels potential buyers, forcing them to look much further afield.

At one time, the door had been bolted and padlocked. Yet the bolt is old and rusty and hanging off the wood, clearly forced. She reaches out and places her palm on the door and pushes it open. A creaking sound echoes in the gloomy, cavernous hallway. She waits, listening for the sound of footsteps, or an angry, enquiring voice, but nothing comes. There's a faint lingering smell of ash, as if there'd been a fire recently. There's no light. It's not an option to proceed without something to help her navigate the interior so she takes out her phone and switches on the torch. The walls are blackened. She enters, stepping onto dusty burnt floorboards, grateful that she chose to wear trainers that morning and not her heavy brogue boots. She slides inside and lets the door close quietly behind her. The torchlight is weak, but it's enough to avoid tripping on broken boards or breaking an ankle on a random piece of rubble that litters the floor. Ahead is the staircase and to its right the hallway leading down to the dark mouth of the kitchen. Archer climbs the stairs stealthily, two at a time, eyes upward, scanning the gloom above. Charred wallpaper hangs from the walls like webbing from a long dead giant arachnid. A bitter stench invades her nostrils when she reaches the second floor. Weed. Tinny grime music comes from behind the doorway at the top of a narrow staircase leading up to the attic. The door is half open, a warm amber light glows inside. She can hear Dixy talking. Archer swallows and thinks she should wait for Quinn, to be on the safe side, but then she hears laughing. Is someone there with him? She hears giggling and climbs the stairs quickly.

She pushes the door open.

Inside is a small attic room, with boxes stacked on either side, a lit candle on the top of each. Dixy has his back to her, his jacket lies in a heap on the floor on a threadbare Persian style rug. He's bending over a wheelchair muttering to someone. A wisp of weed smoke rises above his head. His shoulders are shaking as if he's suppressing laughter, his hands thrust deep into his trouser pockets. She hears the wail of Quinn's siren.

Dixy stiffens and looks across at the window where the DS's blue lights flicker in the distance. Dixy starts to blow out the candles. One topples onto the floor, still lit. The room goes dark.

'Calvin,' says Archer, her beam pointing directly at him.

Dixy jumps and turns, mouth open, eyes wide with shock. He sucks in a breath, swallows the tiny remains of his spliff, and chokes.

'Detective Inspector Archer. Remember me?'

He spits out the butt and blinks. She can see he's thinking fast about his next move.

'I just want to talk, Calvin, that's all.'

She glimpses a figure, seated behind him.

'You might have some explaining to do.'

He shakes his head. 'No . . .' But his face contorts into an angry expression and then he charges her. He's fast and agile like a greyhound, and before she can move out of the way they are both tumbling down the narrow staircase, her phone slipping from her hand. She lands on her back with a thud and is winded by Dixy's elbow as it connects with her diaphragm. He's legging it down the stairs and is surprisingly fast, considering he is clearly stoned. Archer pulls herself up, eyes on the attic. Smoke is filling the room. *Is someone there?* 'Fuck!' She grabs her phone and calls Quinn.

'I'm outside!' he says. 'I've radioed in for back-up. They'll be here in two minutes.'

'Dixy's on his way down. He heard you coming so he may try another way out.'

'I'm peering over the fence. He's not coming through here. I saw an alleyway on the GPS map. I'll go on foot after him.'

Archer climbs the stairs, 'There's a fire starting in the attic. I think someone's inside.'

'Be careful.'

'Don't let him get away.'

Archer ends the call. The flames are mercifully small. A thin fog of smoke billows across the room. She can just about make out the figure slumped on the wheelchair.

'Hello, are you OK?'

There's no response.

Archer grabs Dixy's jacket, spreads it over the flames and stamps them out with her feet. Smoke chokes her throat and barrels into her lungs.

'Hey, it's the police.'

Still no response. Perhaps they're unconscious.

Archer coughs, and hurries to the round window, unlatches it and shoves it open. Glorious fresh air spills inside. Down below she sees two officers climb out of a response vehicle and peel a slithering Dixy from Quinn's grasp. Archer waves her hand to ward off the smoke. Covering her mouth to block the smoke, she hurries to the wheelchair and crouches in front of it. She reaches across and touches the person but something is not right. Taking out her phone, she turns on the torch, points the beam through the clearing fumes, and gasps.

Chapter 6

QUINN'S FOOTSTEPS ARE THUNDERING UP the stairs two at a time. She hears him tripping.

'Fuck!' he cries.

Limping and panting, he joins Archer in the attic room. He pauses, silent, taking in the sight before him.

'Holy mother of . . . Norman Bates!'

'My thoughts, too.'

'It's a movie prop, right?'

'I'm pretty sure it's real.'

'I recognise her from one of his videos.'

'Yup.'

On the wheelchair are skeletal remains. Female, judging by the clothes: a stained and ripped faded denim jacket, with badges pinned on it. Beneath the jacket is a dark, stained T-shirt, strings of rosary beads hanging around the neck, a lace finger-less glove on one hand.

'Whoever she is, life didn't end well for her.'

The skull is cracked above the left eye, and there is a dark stain on her chest. Blood.

'Someone did a number on her.'

'I'll start making calls. Get CSI here.'

Archer peers through the window and across the street. In the house opposite a silhouetted figure slips quickly out of sight behind a curtain.

'Someone's eyeballing us,' Archer says.

Quinn follows her gaze. 'We should go say hi.'

CSI are on the way. The house is sealed off and guarded by two wet-behind-the-ears constables. Quinn regards them both grimly. 'Whatever you do, don't set foot inside.'

'No, sir. We won't,' says one of the constables, a burly chap called Barrow. He has a peculiarly small head, which makes his cap look oversized and ridiculous.

'Also, if you hear anything, ignore it.'

'Like what?' Barrow asks.

Quinn shrugs. 'A scream. Or a baby crying.'

'A baby crying?'

'Just ignore it. That's all.'

Barrow looks at his colleague with an uncertain expression.

'DI Archer and I won't be far away. If something happens, we'll come galloping to the rescue. Any questions?'

'Erm . . . none from me,' says Barrow, quietly. His partner shakes his head.

Quinn holds up both hands and crosses his fingers. 'Best of luck,' he whispers to them.

As they cross the road to the watcher's house, Archer says, 'You're a bad man.'

'It's not often I get to have fun in this job.'

They ring the doorbell. There's no answer at first. Quinn presses a second time, a more persistent ring. Archer leans into the door and hears footsteps padding down creaking stairs. The front door opens a crack, the chain locked in place, and a man's round, flushed face peers up at them through thick-lensed spectacles.

'Yes, what is it?'

Archer shows her ID. 'DI Grace Archer. DS Harry Quinn. May we have a quick word?'

'I'm in bed!'

'We won't take up much of your time.'

'I'm very tired. It's been a long day. Can you come back tomorrow?'

'I'm afraid not.'

He hesitates, unsure what to do, before sighing. 'If you must.' He closes the door. Quinn raises his eyebrows at Archer as the chain lock slides across. The door opens, and they smile at him. He's a short, chubby man, around five foot four, dressed in salmon pink silk pyjamas and a blue silk dressing gown. His thin greying hair is combed neatly in a side parting. He looks to be in his mid to late fifties, despite his face being low on the wrinkle scale. Archer thinks he has the preserved look of a chap who moisturises at least twice a day.

'Thank you, Mr . . .'

Tying his robe, he replies, 'Davenport. Miles.'

'It's good of you to see us at this late hour.'

They stand in an awkward silence in the hallway for a few moments before Archer breaks it. 'Is there somewhere we could sit?'

He thinks for a moment, rubbing his chin, and gestures to a room across the hallway, 'Through here,' he says with a sigh and leads them into the living room, a space furnished with an abundance of expensive-looking Gallic antiques.

'Not short of a bob or two,' Quinn whispers.

There's a maroon velvet chaise longue, where he gestures for them to sit. He settles opposite them, gently lowering himself onto a matching sage green chaise longue, hands resting on thighs, eyes sliding from Archer to Quinn and back again.

'Lived here long?' Quinn asks.

'About twenty years.'

33

Quinn glances around the room. 'Are you in the antiques business?' he asks, a wry grin cracking across his face.

Davenport frowns. 'No. I'm in finance.'

'Oh . . . that's nice,' Quinn replies.

Archer says, 'In twenty years, you must have seen a lot of change around here.'

The man shifts on the chaise as he considers his response. 'Like anywhere. People come and go.'

'The empty house across the street had a fire,' says Archer. 'Do you know anything about that?'

'That's right. Last year. November, I think.'

'How did it start?'

'Hoodlums got inside and tried to burn it down.'

'That sucks,' says Quinn.

'Did you see what happened?' asked Archer.

His gaze drops momentarily. 'I saw . . . hoodlums.'

'Hoodlums?'

He folds his arms. 'Yes, three of them. That's what I reported to the police, anyway. It's all in their file.'

'Did you see what they looked like?'

'Not really. It was dark.'

'Were they caught?'

'No. They got away. Police were too busy, I expect.'

'A familiar story,' says Quinn.

'Did anyone else see them?' says Archer.

'No.'

'None of the neighbours?'

'They were sleeping. Except for Mrs Powell at number fifty-two.'

'Did she see them?'

'I don't recall.'

'We can ask her.'

'She's dead.'

'Oh. What happened?'

'It was not long after the fire. She fell down her stairs. She was old. Poor dear.'

'That's sad.'

'Yes, it is.'

'And you're sure no one else saw anything?'

'Quite sure.'

'Are you friendly with your neighbours?' Quinn asks.

'Some. Most I don't have anything to do with. We keep to ourselves. It's London, after all.'

'Tell us about the house across the road,' Archer says.

'What do you want to know?'

'Who owns it?'

'It did belong to Bob Innes. He became ill. Caught Alzheimer's before he had a chance to hand over power of attorney to his family. He's still alive but doesn't have his wits. The family are going through a protracted and angry dispute for ownership of the property. It's very messy.'

'I'm sure. How long has it been empty?'

'Around two years. It's falling apart. It will cost them a fortune to fix it up.'

'Indeed. You may have noticed a kerfuffle outside the house this evening.'

He blinks rapidly and says, 'Goodness. No. What's happened?'

'We were following someone. A man.' Archer takes out her phone, opens up a picture of Dixy and holds the screen across for him to see. 'Recognise him?'

Davenport slides his glasses up his nose, leans in, studies the photo with a frown and shakes his head. 'No. Can't say I do.'

'You've never seen him enter the house opposite?'

'No. Never.'

'Not even on the street or anywhere else?'

'I really don't recognise him.'

Archer nods an acknowledgement, pockets her phone and stands. 'Thank you for your time, Mr Davenport.'

He shows them out and closes the front door, sliding the chain lock into place.

Archer and Quinn walk down his pathway and onto the street. They look at each other.

'He's hiding something,' says Archer.

'I think we'll be talking to Mr Davenport again.'

'I'm going to call it a night.'

'I'm fried.'

'It's been a long day.'

Chapter 7

'WHAT EXACTLY IS IT YOU think my client is guilty of?' asks Dixy's brief, a willowy, thin-faced man called Garvey, with a severe and oddly distracting widow's peak.

They are seated in a room in the basement of Charing Cross police station, ten minutes into the interview.

Quinn does not hold back. 'Let's have a recap, shall we? Detective Inspector Archer and I, Detective Sergeant Quinn, for the record, found Mr Dixon in the attic room of number 48 Pleshey Road, smoking weed and chatting and giggling with the remains of a dead woman.'

'I'll ask again,' responds the grim-faced Garvey. 'What crime has he committed? In your report, you estimate the remains in question belong to someone who has been dead for more than thirty years. Is that a medical opinon?'

'The victim's clothes would suggest—'

'My client is twenty-six years old. I leave you to do the maths.'

Archer bristles, and changes tack. 'Calvin, do you have any idea why we were following you?'

'I have no clue, innit.'

'We've had complaints about your TikTok videos. Your recent content including the fun times you were having with the remains of a dead woman. Do you understand now?'

He shakes his head again, eyes down, mouth in a sulky pout.

'We've been here before, Calvin. Give us a yes or a no verbal response,' Quinn says.

'No!'

'You recall officers visited you twice in the past few weeks, including DI Archer and I, following up with your adventure in what remains of Ladywell Playtower.'

'Can we get to the point?' Garvey asserts. 'What are you accusing my client of?'

Archer grits her teeth and levels her gaze at the solicitor, who is now pushing her patience. She turns back to Dixy. 'The remains of the woman in the attic. Do you know who she is, Calvin?'

'How would I?'

'What the hell were you doing with a dead woman's remains, Dixy?' Quinn growls.

He tuts and sucks his teeth. 'She was just there, man!'

Archer continues with a softer tone, 'Prior to yesterday evening, had you been to 48 Pleshey Road before?'

He takes a moment to respond. 'Yeah.'

'How many times?'

'Twice, innit.'

'When was this?'

'Last Wednesday and the Friday before.'

'What brought you there? After all, it's almost twenty-five miles on public transport from where you live.'

Dixy rolls his eyes.

'You filmed yourself with the remains of the woman in the attic, didn't you?' Quinn states.

Dixy grins and shrugs.

'Do you have any other dead bodies we should know about?'

Dixy sighs quietly and seems to fold in on himself like an armadillo rolling into a ball.

'Calvin, it's OK,' says Archer. 'We know you're not responsible for her death. We just want to know how you came to be in the attic of 48 Pleshey Road.'

After a few beats, he speaks. 'Someone contacted me via a message board on my website. He had seen my videos and offered me money.'

'To do what?'

Dixy folds his arms. 'To burn the house and video it.'

'You're saying a stranger, a person you've never met, offered you money to burn 48 Pleshey Road?'

'Yeah.'

A fleeting grimace darkens Garvey's face.

'What did you say to that?'

'I asked him how much. He said £500. I told him to do one. He came back with an offer of £1,000. I said £1,500. He agreed. I told him to send me the address.'

'Tell us about him.'

'I don't know who is he. Or even if he is a he. He might be a she. I just assumed it was a bloke from his email name.'

'Which is?'

'Napoleon1103@gmail.com.'

'Why didn't you burn the house down?' Archer asks.

'I became suspicious.'

'Of what?'

'Why he wanted to burn it down in the first place. I mean, it's already a shit hole. Insurance wouldn't pay much, if anything. My spider senses were tingling. I knew something was up.'

'So you decided to search the house?'

He nods. 'I found her in the attic rolled up in that rug. I couldn't believe it. This was a dream find. Perfect content for my followers, sick little bastards that they are.'

'Why didn't you report it to the police?'

Dixy shrugs. 'She's long dead. What's it matter?'

Archer sighs.

'Did you speak to this Napoleon character after discovering the body?' Quinn asks.

'Yeah. He emailed me and got right shitty. I told him I'd burn the gaff once I'd had my fun.'

'And what did he say?'

'He lost his shit and told me the deal was off. He was trying to stitch me up. As soon as I burned the house, the police would find the remains and it would come back to me. I'd get sent down.'

'The house belongs to a Robert Innes. Do you know him or anyone in his family?'

Dixy responds with a no. Archer feels they're done with him for the time being. There's little more to be learned at this stage and no reason to keep questioning him any longer. They finish up with some closing questions, before ending the recording.

On the stairwell, as they make their way up to the third floor, they exchange ideas and theories.

'Interesting choice of email for Dixy's client.'

'I thought so too. Napoleon. Who's short, round and has a thing for French antiques.'

'Talk about leaving breadcrumbs.'

'Seems our Davenport is not as clever as he thinks.'

'We'll keep an eye on him. First though, we need to talk to the Innes family.'

Chapter 8

THE FIRST OF BOB INNES'S offspring, Vicky Dunmore, is a medically retired nurse and another casualty of Long Covid. She's secreted in an armchair in the living room of her bungalow, next to a portable breathing apparatus, from which she is sucking oxygen. A plump woman with greying hair, Archer estimates her to be in her early fifties, unless Covid has aged her a decade. Her husband, Dennis Dunmore, insists they wear PPE masks to 'keep the air clean'. A slim man, dressed in beige coloured slacks and a matching sweater.

'Take a pew,' he says, gesturing at a cream leather sofa. 'I'd offer you a coffee or tea, but you'd have to go outside and drink it.'

'We're fine,' replies Archer.

He retreats and stands by a fake white fireplace, the room's focal point, arms behind his back, eyes fixed on his wife. Mrs Dunmore unhooks the plastic mask from her ears and sets it on the arm of her chair.

'Thank you for seeing us at short notice, Mrs Dunmore,' says Archer.

'Dennis said it's about my father's house, but he didn't say any more than that.'

'When was the last time you were there?'

'Before the pandemic. I can't get out much these days, what with my health and all that. Dennis has been there. He went to see the damage after the fire last year.'

Archer looks at Mr Dunmore, who fleetingly meets her gaze.

'Did you enter the house, Mr Dunmore?' Archer asks.

'No, the fire brigade had boarded it up. Too dangerous,' he replies.

'Did you happen to catch up with any neighbours when you were there?'

He shakes his head, muttering a no.

'Not even Miles Davenport, who alleges he saw the vandals start the fire, or Mrs Powell?'

'Dennis is not the social type,' interjects Mrs Dunmore. 'He's quite shy, aren't you, Dennis?'

Mr Dunmore nods his head courteously.

'Miles phoned me,' says Mrs Dunmore. 'We have a catch-up now and again.'

'About the house?' Archer asks.

'That and other things. He's quite the gossip, you know. Fills me in on who's been to the house and what's happening in the street.'

'I bet he's a mine of information,' says Quinn.

'Dennis doesn't like him, do you, Dennis?'

Mr Dunmore shakes his head.

'Thinks he puts his nose too much into other people's business. I suppose he does.'

'What has he told you about the house?'

'He mentioned about the vandals. Couldn't wait to tell me. He also said he saw my brother with some tradesman types.'

'Did he mention anyone else hanging around or visiting the house? A stranger, for instance.'

Mrs Dunmore pauses as she considers her response. 'Actually, nothing like that. If anything, he asked lots of questions about the house itself.'

'Could you elaborate?' Archer asks.

'I suppose he was always tapping for information on when the house was being fixed up. He was just about to start renovating his own place and was looking for recommended builders. I told him I didn't know any and it could be years before we start on Dad's place. My brother and I don't get along, you see. He's a selfish greedy prick who wants complete control of our father's estate. And I won't allow that.'

'That must be hard.'

'Yes. So, are you going to tell me what this is about?'

'Of course. Apologies for not getting to the point. Yesterday we followed a man to your father's house. He had broken in and we found him in the attic with the remains of someone.'

Mrs Dunmore's face pales. 'Oh my good God!' She looks to her husband. 'Dennis, a dead person in Father's house.'

Mr Dunmore shifts on his feet. 'Extraordinary,' he says.

Confusion ripples across her face. 'But how could that be?'

'That's the question we need answering,' Quinn replies.

Archer takes out her phone and shows her a photo of Dixy. 'Do you recognise this man?'

Mrs Dunmore studies the picture and then shakes her head. 'Never seen him before.'

She shows the photo to Mr Dunmore who also replies with a no.

Archer stands. 'Thank you for your time, Mrs Dunmore. I'm sorry to bring this news to you. We are investigating the matter and will keep you up to date with our findings.'

'It's all very distressing. I don't know what to think.'

'We'll figure it out, Mrs Dunmore.'

Stephen Innes manages a large Tesco store in Chiswick. Sitting behind the desk of his office, he leans forward, elbows on the surface, pink pudgy fingers intertwined. 'Is this about the fire last year?' he asks.

'Not directly,' Quinn replies. 'But who knows?'

'Then how may I help you?'

'Mr Innes, we found the remains of a dead body in the attic of your father's house.'

Innes blinks, then frowns. 'But how . . .?'

'That's what we're trying to figure out. When was the last time you were at the house?'

The news has thrown him, and it takes a moment for him to compose himself. 'I was there the day after the fire. But I wasn't inside the house. It had been closed off.'

'Prior to that, when had you been there?'

'Maybe a few weeks before that. Around the thirtieth of October, I think.'

'And what took you there?'

'I wanted to survey the property with builders and get some quotes on fixing the place up.'

'Did you give the keys to any of the builders?'

'No, they never set foot inside without me.'

'Did you go up to the attic room?'

'Yes, we covered every space in the house. Had to.'

'And you noticed nothing unusual, or out of place, in the attic room?'

'No, there were just the boxes filled with old junk.'

'Did you talk to your sister about your plans with the builders?'

44

'We don't speak. We fell out a long time ago. She's a difficult woman. Paranoid, and a hypochondriac. Have you met her?'

'This morning.'

'That's nice for you. Is she still playing the Long Covid card?'

Archer doesn't respond.

'Of course, she is. I suppose you met Dennis, too,' he continues. 'He's the big nasty in all this. Behind that mild-mannered surface is a calculating, controlling bully. He's poisoned my sister against me. Anyway, what does any of that matter? I can't believe a body has been found at the house.'

Archer shows the picture of Dixy. It comes as no surprise that he responds that he doesn't recognise him, nor does he use TikTok.

'Does anyone other than you and your sister have access to the house?'

'Let me think . . . obviously, Dennis has my sister's keys. I have Dad's and a set of my own. No one else, I think.'

'OK. Thank you for your time, Mr Innes. We appreciate it.'

'Oh, wait. I don't know for sure, but before he became ill, I recall Dad mentioning that he'd given a neighbour a set of keys for safekeeping. He'd locked himself out a few times, you see.'

'Do you know which neighbour?'

'Yes. The busybody who lives opposite. Miles Davenport.'

Archer smiles and thanks him.

'You're welcome.'

'One last thing,' says Archer. 'You mentioned the boxes in the attic room.'

'Yes.'

'It might be nothing, but you didn't mention the Persian rug on the floor.'

Innes frowns. 'There is no Persian rug on the floor. Not when I was last there.'

'Thank you, Mr Innes. We'll be in touch.'

The pathologist, Doctor Kapur, presides over the stainless-steel table containing the remains of the body found in the attic room of 48 Pleshey Road. The victim's clothes have been removed, the bones laid out, the pieces placed loosely back together like an elaborate three-dimensional jigsaw puzzle. Kapur holds a chewed biro in his hand that he uses as a pointer.

'The victim is female. Her skull is fractured just above the eyes. One of the ribs just above the heart is cracked. I might hazard a guess and say it has been penetrated with something.'

Archer leans in for a closer look. 'By a bullet, perhaps?'

'Hard to say. There is no indication of an exit wound, either on the bones or clothes.'

'How old do you think she was?'

'Her bones have not fully developed. She was young. A teenager.'

A teenage girl, brutally murdered, her body discarded. Are her family still wondering what happened to her? Could they have seen Dixy's TikTok content on the news and wondered if that corpse was their daughter? *Shit! What a world we live in.*

'We estimated the death to be around thirty years ago,' Quinn says.

'I'd wager 1987.'

'That's impressively precise.'

'Pinned to the victim's denim jacket are various badges. I cleaned the blood away from one. It was cracked and dented but I could make out the picture of a man's head with the word

LISTEN. This badge relates to the 1987 album by the Smiths, *The World Won't Listen*.'

'Very scientific,' Quinn remarks.

'I was ... actually, I still am a Smiths fan. I believe you are too, DS Quinn, from a previous conversation.'

'Yeah, I'm a fan. I know the album well.'

'It made me think of a line from one of the songs ...' Kapur hesitates before continuing. 'In the song, he sings about a girl being sixteen, clumsy and quite shy. She goes to London and dies.'

'"Half a Person",' says Quinn.

'That's it,' says Kapur.

They look at the remains in a collective, respectful silence for a moment. Archer breaks it by thanking Kapur, and as they leave, she makes a call to DC Marian Phillips requesting she do a missing persons search on teenagers from 1987 onwards. 'Harry and I are on our way back to the station,' she adds. 'We'll catch up then.'

'So, two mysteries: who killed her and how did her remains get from wherever they were to 48 Pleshey Road?' Quinn says.

'Pleshey Road's chief curtain twitcher can probably help us out there. He's an easy egg to crack. We need to get him at the right time.'

As they leave the mortuary, Quinn's phone rings. He looks at the screen. 'Excuse me while I take this call.'

He smiles as he greets the caller. An old friend by the sounds of it. Archer catches Quinn's eyes. He looks at her with a grim expression. 'Do you know Elena Zoric?'

Chapter 9

ARCHER'S HEART IS THUDDING AS she slides into the passenger seat. *Please let this be a mistaken identity.* She gathers her thoughts. Why had Elena phoned her two nights back? Had she been in trouble? Quinn finishes up on his call with the SIO at the scene, a DS Lee Parry, giving him the heads-up they were on their way. He starts up the engine and, checking the traffic is clear, pulls out with a lead foot on the accelerator.

'Who is she?' Quinn asks.

'I knew her from my days at the National Crime Agency. Elena had been trafficked from Croatia to London at the age of sixteen. She and several other girls had been brought here by a meat-faced gangster called Fedor Kowalski, and his English wife, Anna. They'd set up several brothels across the South-East offering sexual services to their clients.'

'A tale as old as time.'

'The operation had been a passion project of mine. I worked really hard with Elena to help bring down the Kowalskis' businesses and get them both sent down. Elena and I had become close.'

'Maybe it's not her,' says Quinn, reassuringly.

Archer says nothing. From Quinn's tone she can tell he's not convinced of that himself.

'She called me . . . two nights back.'

'Was she OK?'

'My phone was on silent. I was sleeping and missed it. I called her back a few times the following morning but there was no answer.'

They drive in silence.

Archer folds her arms and stares out the window, her stomach in knots.

They arrive at Annesley Avenue and park outside an unprepossessing block of flats. The windows are obscured with net curtains and a dozen rusted satellite dishes are fixed onto the exterior. Beyond the block, in contrast to the 1980s grim starkness, is a lush green area thick with trees where the Silk Stream, a tributary running from Burnt Oak to Hendon cuts through the estate. They walk around the building and cross the green towards the flashing blue lights of three police vehicles. Curious locals, speculating and gossiping, stand scattered in small groups. Others watch from rear windows of the block. A barrier of police tape manned by two uniforms, surrounds a copse of trees. Beyond them near the bank of the river two people dressed in disposable hazmat suits are looking at the screen of an iPad. At their feet are police holdalls and a valise. One of the men looks across and waves.

'That's Lee Parry,' says Quinn.

Archer and Quinn present their ID to the guards, duck under the tape and make their way towards Parry. He approaches them. Quinn and the other DS shake hands, beaming in a matey fashion. 'Long time,' says Quinn.

'Not long enough,' replies Parry.

'Lee and I worked together for a bit before he left to tackle the big bads in the North-West burbs,' says Quinn.

Archer shakes Parry's hand. 'Grace Archer.'

'Good to meet you. Shall we dive in?'

'Please,' she replies.

'Let's get you suited up,' says Parry, taking two plastic-wrapped disposable suits from a holdall. 'As mentioned, I had one of my team look up Elena Zoric. He found your name attached to her file. I knew you worked with Harry so I gave him a bell. We were contacted two days back, and I stress I did not know about Marianne Boucher's phone call until this morning.'

'Who is she?' Quinn asks.

'Elena's girlfriend,' says Archer.

Parry continues, 'Marianne Boucher spoke to one of my guys about Elena not returning home the night before last. The officer advised her to sit tight, and told her there was not a lot he could do at that stage. Marianne lost her cool and ended the call. She phoned back later and kicked off again.'

'Doesn't sound like he took her seriously.'

'She'd admitted they'd had a row. Plus both Marianne and Elena have records. Small stuff like stealing and possession, so my officer . . .'

'Before you continue with your excuses, there's a dead woman,' Archer replies sharply.

Parry stiffens, glances at Quinn and hesitates before answering with a nod. 'If you're ready, we can proceed.'

They cross the park to the bank of the stream where a white tent has been erected.

Parry gestures towards a copse of trees. 'We found her shoes there.'

Beyond the copse is a car park. 'What sort of shoes was she wearing?' Archer asks.

'Heels . . . I think.'

Archer feels her patience thinning. 'You think?'

51

Parry considers this. 'Erm . . . yeah . . . heels. Black suede.'

'She was brought here in a car,' says Archer. 'They parked in the car park. He attacked her. She ran through the trees and probably kicked off her heels to get away faster.'

Parry clears his throat. 'Yeah . . . that's what we thought.'

Archer scans the area taking in the park and the stream.

Parry continues, 'This morning, a local woman was walking her Jack Russell. It ran down to the river and wouldn't stop barking. She tried to call it back, but it wasn't much interested. She became concerned when the barking stopped. She made her way through the trees to find him and it was then she saw him licking a hand sticking out from the bushes.'

They enter the screened-off area. The remains are shrouded by grass and foliage. Archer sees the hand, fingers curled inwards, protruding from the greenery. She can make out the pale skin of the arm leading to a bare shoulder and a head of long dark hair.

'Christ!' says Quinn, stepping forward.

Archer feels her stomach tightening. She inches closer and sees a half-exposed chest, caked in a pool of dried blood. There's a small hole above the heart. A bullet wound? On the victim's arm is a tattoo. Two foxes running side by side with two calligraphy-style names above them: *Marianne & Elena Forever*. Archer's heart sinks. Also, on her arm leading to the crook of the elbow, are four small scabs. Track marks. Her eyes slide reluctantly to the victim's face. It's bruised with blood on the nose and mouth. Guilt claws at her.

'How'd you figure it's Elena?' Quinn asks Parry.

'We found a purse with photo ID close to the scene.'

'It's her,' says Archer.

Archer notices an evidence marker on the other side of the stream. 'What's there?'

'A mobile.'

Archer takes out her phone, thumbs through her contacts until she finds Elena Zoric. She dials. The call goes straight to voicemail. Elena's answer message starts.

'Hello. This is Elena. Can't take your call right now. You know what to do!'

She ends with a giggle. Despite its jolly tone it's like a voice from the beyond. A darkness clouds Archer's soul. Elena Zoric's story had touched her like no other. Trafficked into prostitution in her teens, she spiralled into a drug dependency, abused and exploited by the monsters who controlled her.

'Did anyone hear anything?' Archer asks.

'Once the door-to-door is complete, we'll know more.'

'You'll let us know when the reports are ready?'

'Of course.'

'Elena tried to call me two nights back, just after midnight. But I was sleeping.'

'Did she leave a message?'

Archer looks across at the smashed phone. 'It seems she didn't get the chance.'

They say nothing for a moment.

Archer breaks the silence, 'I know Elena's girlfriend, Marianne. I don't want to tread on your toes. However, it might be better if she hears the news from me. I can report back to you.'

Parry shrugs. 'Sure. That would be super helpful.'

Archer nods. 'I'll be in touch.'

Chapter 10

I T's A CRUEL IRONY THAT Elena Zoric's home, the one she shared with her girlfriend Marianne Boucher, is little more than five minutes' drive from the location where Elena's body was found. Their house is a shabby Victorian terrace opposite a tyre replacement centre on a drab, busy thoroughfare. Diesel and rubber choke the air. Quinn is peering through the blinds.

'The TV's on,' he says.

Archer bangs harder for the third time.

'Someone's rising from the sofa. Someone with piercings and a spiky barnet.'

'Marianne,' says Archer.

Through the mottled glass, Archer sees Marianne's sturdy figure shuffle towards the door. With a soft French lilt and an admonishing tone, Marianne says, 'You better have a good reason for being away, Elena!'

The glass has played a cruel trick. Archer is the same height, build and hair colour as Elena.

The door snaps open. Dressed in boxer shorts and a vest, Marianne's tired eyes, heavy with black eyeliner, betray an expression of surprise that melts into confusion before contorting into a pallid terror. 'What's happened?' she asks, her voice quiet and shaky.

'Marianne. We met a few years back . . .'

'I remember you.'

'This is my colleague, Detective Sergeant Harry Quinn.'

'Where's Elena?'

'Can we come in?' Archer asks, gently.

Marianne hesitates, studying Archer's face as if searching for answers. And then she retreats into the hallway. They follow her into the living room where she sits on the sofa, in the gloom, eyes never leaving Archer's. The air is stale, the room stuffy, with smells of burger meat and stale beer.

'Mind if I turn a light on?' Quinn asks.

Marianne doesn't answer. Quinn switches on a floor lamp anyway, and presses mute on the TV remote. The room is cluttered and untidy. There's a coffee table littered with fast food bags and empty beer cans. On a wall is a framed photo of Elena and Marianne, cheek to cheek. Marianne is laughing. Elena is smiling. She always had such a pretty smile.

'Is she dead?' Marianne asks, bluntly.

'Marianne, can I get you a drink?' Quinn says.

She seems confused by the question for a moment before answering, 'Coffee. Black.'

'Coming up. Kitchen through here?'

'Down the hallway.'

Quinn exits the living room.

Archer perches on the sofa beside the woman and treads carefully with her words. 'I'm so sorry.'

Marianne's eyes widen, her gaze becomes vacant. 'It was the drugs, wasn't it?' Her head drops to her hands and she begins to sob. From the kitchen Archer hears the kettle boiling and the sound of cupboard doors shutting.

'Someone took her life,' says Archer.

Marianne looks at Archer, eyes blinking, mouth open. Archer slides across the sofa. Marianne crumples and falls into her embrace. 'I'm so sorry.'

She sobs and a moment later composes herself. 'I knew this would happen. I knew it!'

Quinn returns with a mug of black coffee. He hands it across.

'Why do you say that?' Archer asks.

'I told her not to do it. That would we get by, but she wouldn't listen to me.' She takes a sip of the coffee. 'We were short of money.'

'What was she going to do?'

'The only thing she really knows how to do.'

'She was back on the game?'

Marianne nods her head.

'Was she working for someone?'

'I kept asking her, 'cause I don't trust those sons of bitches. But she insisted no. I knew she was lying because she was working at the Chicken House in Praed Street. That's all I know. I swear.'

'The Chicken House?'

'It's what they call it. It's a brothel.'

'Do you know the address?'

'It's above the Southern Fried Chicken Shop.'

'Ironic,' says Quinn.

'Who runs it?' Archer asks.

'A woman. I don't her name.'

'When did you last see or speak to Elena?'

'It was Saturday afternoon before I left for my shift at the bar. When I got home we were going to do some shots . . . and whatever.' Archer glances at her arm. Similar track marks to Elena's. 'It was around midnight by the time I got home, but she was gone. I called her but there was no answer.'

'Did she say where she was going?'

Marianne shakes her head. 'Praed Street, I assumed. She had mentioned she needed money. I told her we would make do and that there was enough at home for us to have fun.' More tears fill her eyes. She closes them. 'We argued and I left the house slamming the door.'

'Did she have friends working at Praed Street?'

'She knew some of the girls.'

'Do you know any names?'

She thinks this over for a moment. 'The only name I recall is April. I don't know her second name.'

'OK. Why did she need the money?' Archer asks, although she suspects she already knows the answer.

Marianne looks down at the coffee mug and folds her right arm inwards concealing the tracks on her skin. 'She was skint. That's all.'

'This could be important in finding out who did this to her.'

The French woman's fingers squeeze the mug.

'She was using. Wasn't she?'

Marianne frowns, her shoulders tighten.

'You were both using,' Archer adds, gently.

'I didn't want to go there again. I never did. But Elena ... she had suffered so much. To look at her, you would see a beautiful, smiling, warm lovely person, who had time for everyone. But after what she'd been put through those years – the trafficking, the beatings, the forced drugs. All of it. She was scarred inside. It felt sometimes that I could do nothing to help her other than get the drugs she needed to forget. We started off small, but then the dependency came and I couldn't afford to pay our bills and the habit. Elena took matters into her own hands and went back to work. That's our story. That's all.'

'I'm so sorry, Marianne,' says Archer.

'I want to see her.'

'That might not be a good idea.'

'Please.'

Archer exchanges a look with Quinn. 'We'll see what we can do.' She takes out a contact card from her jacket. 'Please call me if you think of anything else. If you can't reach me, ask for DS Harry Quinn on the station number.'

She takes the card.

'Would you like us to send some support officers?'

Marianne snorts through her nose. 'What's the point? She's gone.'

Archer looks across at the photo on the wall. 'Do you mind if I take a picture of Elena?'

Marianne nods.

Outside as they make their way to the car, Quinn asks, 'Next stop, Chicken House at Praed Street?'

'Yeah. Let's track down this April. Perhaps she saw someone with Elena.'

Chapter 11

T HE SOUTHERN FRIED CHICKEN SHOP, a poor imit-
ation of its distant Kentuckian cousin, is wedged on
the corner of Praed Street and Norfolk Place in
Paddington. Situated within an ornate, carved-up Victorian
block, the reconfigured ground floor stripped of its period
elegance, it's made up of glass walls looking into a characterless
fast-food restaurant. The floors above retain the original archi-
tecture with rows of sashed windows, some with discreetly
closed curtains, others open, overlooking both roads. A slim
young blonde woman wearing a white T-shirt is on the second
floor leaning out of a window, arms folded, vaping and watching
the world go by.

'I'm assuming the entrance is not through the restaurant,'
Archer says.

'My guess is that backstreet,' Quinn replies, nodding to a
short, covered alleyway connecting two buildings.

'Let's find out.'

They cross Praed Street and walk past the chicken restaurant.
Archer glances through the windows. A young woman with a
long brown ponytail is paying for two large bags of takeaway
food. They enter the alley, which leads them into a courtyard.
There's one large steel door leading to the back of the restaurant
on Praed Street. There are five worn stone steps just behind

the alley, leading up to a second door with an intercom fixed to the wall next to it. They look at each other. 'Bingo,' says Archer.

'Full house!' Quinn replies, pressing the button.

'Perhaps it will be.'

A crackling noise is followed by a woman's voice. 'Who is it?' she asks, curtly.

'Is this the Chicken House?' Quinn asks, scrunching his face, realising this was probably not the best way in.

Archer rolls her eyes.

'Turn right onto Praed Street and you'll see it.'

'Sorry, that's not what I meant. We want to speak to you. We're—'

'Do you have an appointment?'

'No . . .'

'Then go away,' she replies, cutting him off. The intercom goes dead. Quinn presses a second time. The crackling noise again. 'No appointment. No entry!' Before Quinn can speak the line goes dead.

Archer hears footsteps echoing from the alley. She nudges Quinn to step aside. They stand a short distance from the entrance as the young woman from the restaurant appears with the bags of takeaway food. She climbs the steps and presses the intercom. It crackles once more. 'Only me,' she calls leaning into it. The door buzzes open, and she uses her back to push it open.

Archer legs it up the steps behind her, following her inside and into a narrow staircase.

'You can't come in here,' says the woman.

Archer flashes her ID. 'Yes, we can.'

'Why don't you people just leave us alone?' she says and makes her way upstairs. 'Margaret, we have uninvited guests!' she calls.

A broad woman with dark curly hair appears at the top of the stairs, holding a baseball bat like a walking stick. Her face is heavily made up. She looks to be in her mid-fifties and is dressed in a flamingo-patterned kaftan. Archer is reminded of Elizabeth Taylor in her later years.

'Get out!' she says.

Archer introduces herself and Quinn.

'We don't want any trouble. I run a decent business. I've told you lot before. We ain't got no traffickers here. No sex slaves. This is a safe place for young women to earn a living.'

'We're not here for a bust,' says Quinn. 'A raid, I mean,' he adds, fumbling an apology.

The woman called Margaret gives him an impressive withering stare. The younger woman smiles at Quinn and bites her lip.

'Please, Margaret. It's important,' says Archer. 'We won't take up much of your time.'

The woman studies them both for a moment before nodding her agreement. 'Five minutes. And you can call me Mrs Jackson.'

'Mrs Jackson it is,' says Archer. She turns to look at Quinn and silently mouths, 'Bust?'

He shrugs an apology.

'Can't be too careful round here,' says Mrs Jackson. She turns to the younger woman, 'Ginny, give the girls their food.' She turns back to Archer and Quinn. 'This way.' She takes them to an office with two sash windows overlooking the courtyard and entrance at the back of the building. The room has the feel of an accountant's or a solicitor's office rather than the working space of a brothel madam. There are sparse feminine touches but the dominance of an antique leather-topped desk with a brown leather chair assert a patriarchal quality to the room. There are filing cabinets and a stack of files on the desk. She sits at the desk and steeples her fingers together. 'What's this about?'

'Do you know Elena Zoric?'

'We've had some dealings.'

'When did you see her last?'

'On Saturday evening. Around nine.'

'Was she working here?'

'No. Her partnership with us is on hold for the time being.'

'On hold?'

'She's not meeting the required standards for this house.'

Archer holds her gaze momentarily. 'We found Elena Zoric's body this morning. She was murdered.'

Shock flashes on her face at this bombshell, but she remains composed. 'What does that have to with me?'

'She worked here. At the Chicken House,' says Quinn.

'Don't call it that!' she hisses.

'Apologies. But she did work here, didn't she?'

'She had, on occasion, taken a room here when she was short of cash. She was always welcome. She was a sweet, popular girl. I had a lot of time for her. But she had her demons and was using. I saw the tracks on her arm. We all did. I didn't want drugs here nor did I want anyone who has clearly been injecting. It's not good for business.'

'Did you talk to her on Saturday?'

'Briefly.'

'What did you talk about?'

'Nothing much. I refused her entry and reminded her she was banned until she cleaned up her act.'

'Her partner seemed to think she was working here,' says Quinn.

'Maybe that's what Elena wanted her to think.'

'How did she seem?'

'She was jittery, nervous. I asked to see her arms. She didn't want to show me, but she did. She knows . . . knew . . . that I don't tolerate users of hard drugs. I told to her leave. End of story.'

'Is April working today?'

Mrs Jackson frowns. 'She's busy.'

'We'd like to talk to her.'

'Not possible.'

'Let me state a fact, Mrs Jackson,' says Archer. 'Had you overlooked Elena's lack of standards, then she would be alive today.' The madam flinches. 'Respectable business or not, if I have to, I will get an order and bring a dozen officers back here to close this place down.'

Mrs Jackson's jaw tightens at the threat. 'Wait here,' she says, standing.

'Don't mention anything about Elena. Leave that to me.'

She returns minutes later with the blonde vaper Archer had seen leaning from the window earlier. She's in her early twenties, slender and tall, dark roots poking out from under bleached hair.

'Hi,' says Archer.

'Hello,' April replies with a toothy grin.

Archer turns to Mrs Jackson. 'Give us a moment, please.'

Jackson sighs and exits the office.

'Don't mind her,' says April. 'She's one of the good ones.'

'She seems a little uptight,' says Quinn.

'With good reason. The police turn a blind eye to this place, but that comes at a price.'

'What do you mean?' Archer asks.

'Some of our regulars are coppers.'

'Is that so?' says Quinn.

'Yeah. And most of them are arseholes. They treat us like trash.'

Archer feels she should be surprised but isn't. 'I'm sorry to hear that, but that's not why we're here. We have some bad news about your friend, Elena.'

Her face pales. 'What's happened?'

'Her body was found this morning.'

'Oh my God,' she replies, trembling and steadying herself against a filing cabinet, 'Elena . . .'

'I'm so sorry.'

'I . . . I can't believe it. I only saw her on Saturday night.'

'How did she seem?'

April folds her arms, squeezing them into her chest, as she tries to think. 'Fine, I suppose, except she was pissed off at Margaret. She needed money, you see.'

'What did you two talk about?'

'Nothing. I had a client and couldn't hang about.'

'Did she mention where she was going?'

April's brow furrows. 'There was a man.'

'What man?' Archer asks.

'Just some bloke who propositioned her before she came in to see Margaret.'

'Where did this happen?'

'I don't know. We often get blokes hanging around outside. They know who and what we are.'

'Did she say anything else about him?'

'Only that she was going to find him.'

Archer takes out her phone and quickly emails Klara requesting all the CCTV footage from Praed Street and the surrounding areas for the evening of 23 July.

Chapter 12

I**T'S HOT AND STUFFY WHEN** Archer wakes the following morning, Elena's murder foremost in her mind. Sliding slowly out of bed, she makes her way to the bathroom, sits in the tub and washes herself with an old shower hose fitted to the hot and cold bath taps. She can't get Elena's bloodied remains out of her head. Guilt had coursed through her, twisting and knotting her unrested muscles. She bitterly regrets leaving her phone on silent the night that Elena had called. Logic says that had she taken the call, the likelihood is she would not have been able to help Elena. Yet her heart tells a different story. One that concludes with a happier ending. Could she have aided Elena's escape at the end of the line? She sighs as the water rinses over her, warming the growing anger bubbling inside her. Elena had been a fighter. She had endured trafficking, enslavement and forced prostitution. She went on to make a life for herself, albeit a difficult one that ended at the hands of some evil, cowardly bastard.

Archer is dressed and pulling a slice of smoking black toast from the temperamental toaster. The kettle is boiling. She waves the smoke with her hand and opens the back door to let it out before the alarm kicks in. The sun is shining. It's a beautiful summer morning.

Not only is Elena is occupying her head space, so is this house. She tries not to look at the spot on the kitchen floor where she had found her grandad. She still misses him every day. Archer focuses on buttering the charred bread, eyeing it with a distracted and distasteful gaze. The kettle has boiled. Dropping a tea bag into a mug, she pours hot water and stirs in milk. Archer had been here with Grandad on that day. He seemed fine, in good spirits. She left him briefly to pick something up from the office. On her return she found him lying on the kitchen floor. He had died alone without her. She was heartbroken and had never forgiven herself. At the time, she was convinced that one of gangster Frankie White's minions had carried out the promised hit on him in retaliation to what had happened to White's grandson. But she had been wrong. Grandad had died from a stroke, confirmed later by the pathologist. Yet Archer had no doubt the stroke had been triggered by everything White had put them through. In a way, the now-deceased London gangster had succeeded.

She stares down at the toast, frowning, unsure what to make of it. *Pull yourself together.* She rubs her arms.

In 52 Roupell Street, Grandad's presence remains. It almost feels like a museum with his pictures, his trinkets, his clothes, his memories, his lingering smell. He had left her the house in the will, including a modest sum of money, more than she had ever owned in her life. But there was too much history here. It was the house where her father had grown up, and the same home where she had grown up after everything turned to shit. The shit being: 1. Her father, Sam Archer, a Met detective inspector, executed in a gangland killing, and 2. Her father's murderer, a child serial murderer, who had abducted her at the age of twelve with the blessing of the same gangland boss. And 3 – her grandmother's decline and death from the tragedy of losing her only son. Death by broken heart, Grandad had said. This was all history, but the scars were still etched deep and this house – in this quiet, pretty, unspoiled nineteenth-century village preserved in the heart of London – was full of memories and ghosts that were sometimes too painful to live with. And for those reasons, living here was becoming intolerable. Grandad, along with her father and grandmother, would remain in her heart, yet she needed a change. She needed to move on with a fresh start.

And so she'd decided to change everything, remodel the house with the money. Refresh, start a new chapter, brighten it up and bring in some new happier memories, or sell up and move elsewhere. So far, nothing was going to plan. The builders were a disaster. They had torn the place to shreds, ripped it apart mercilessly as if it was a condemned building. In the end she'd fired them, resulting in her living in a building site for weeks.

Her phone rings, pulling her out of her thoughts. It's Quinn.

'Not that I'm pushing you, or reminding you that duty calls and all that, but I thought you might be here already.'

'I'm still waiting for your mate to arrive.'

Quinn's friend, Liam Duffy, was a carpenter, a decorator, a jack of all trades, and the answer to her home remodelling dilemma, apparently. He had recently moved to London from Dublin and was due to start this morning at 8. It was now 8.45 and Archer was unimpressed.

'He just called me. He lost your number.'

'That's convenient.'

'He's stuck in traffic, he said.'

Archer says nothing. She just wants out of the house and the distraction of work.

'Do you want me to pick you up?' Quinn asks.

'I could do with the walk.'

'No worries. See you later, then.'

Archer ends the call. Biting down on the toast, she chews slowly, grimacing at the bitter blend of charcoal and the ubiquitous plaster dust that seems to have penetrated every space, including a sealed loaf of bread. She tosses the toast and the bread into the bin, and swallows a mouthful of lukewarm tea. The cup is gritty with dust that floats on the surface of the liquid. 'What the hell,' she mutters, wiping the grime from her mouth. She begins to pack up when the doorbell rings. Pushing through the dusty plastic sheeting that covers doorways and walls, she opens the front door, trying her best not bristle.

A broad-shouldered man smiles at her warmly. He's of mixed heritage, with pale hazel eyes, full lips and perfect white teeth.

'You must be Grace,' he says, with a soft Dublin brogue. 'I'm Liam . . .'

When she doesn't respond, he adds, 'The joiner and decorator . . . Harry's mate.'

'You're also late,' she replies.

'Sorry. Traffic was a nightmare.'

'Come in,' she says, leading him into the kitchen.

He's looking at her with an apologetic expression.

'I'm late for work,' she says, turning from his gaze.

'Right . . .'

'I'll leave you to it.'

'Where'd you want me to start first?' Liam asks.

She takes a moment to consider. 'How about the bathroom? I'm really done showering with a rubber hose.'

'Sure. Upstairs?'

'I'm sorry?'

'The bathroom. It's upstairs?'

'Yes. Of course.'

'Sorry ... I ... I'll get started.'

'Harry's pinged you my number?'

'He has.'

'Call me if you have any questions.'

Archer turns to leave.

'I have one,' Liam says.

Archer frowns. 'One what?'

'Question.'

'Oh ...'

'Is there a key for the front door? I may need to go out and grab materials or something to eat later.'

'It's on the kitchen table.'

'Grand.'

Archer grabs her jacket.

'By the way, you have something on your face.'

Archer frowns. With no mirror to hand, she takes her phone from her jeans pocket and checks using the camera's selfie option. Across her mouth and chin is a greyish streak. 'Plaster dust,' she says, sighing, and wipes it away with the back of her hand.

'It gets everywhere,' says Liam.

Archer takes her backpack from the kitchen table, swipes dust from the bag and hurries out the door.

'Nice to meet you ...' he calls, but the door is closed, and she is already hurrying up Roupell Street.

Chapter 13

ARCHER CATCHES UP WITH ADMIN before having a quick pep talk with the team and dipping out of the office with Quinn, to avoid the bombastic Fletcher, whose booming mouth, or cake hole as Quinn calls it, bellows across the third floor.

Praed Street is their next stop on the trail of Elena Zoric's last steps. Quinn is driving. Archer sits quietly, staring blankly out at the window, her mind processing Elena's murder.

'You looked tired when you came in this morning,' Quinn says.

'Lousy night's sleep.'

'Elena?'

'Yeah.'

'There was nothing you could have done.'

She knows he's right, but still, the nagging doubt that there was the slimmest of chances that she could have somehow prevented Elena's murder is eating at her. It's a fantasy, but maybe Elena could have put Archer on speaker and she could have reasoned with the killer or demanded he get the hell away from her because the police were on their way.

'You OK?' Quinn asks.

'The only thing I can do is find her killer.'

'About that . . .'

73

Archer looks at him, curious about the tone of his voice.

'I spoke to Parry last night. He called me after seeing our reports. I get the sense he's becoming . . . a little territorial.'

Archer's jaw clenches.

'He'd like us to step away and let him and his team lead the investigation.'

'Has he forgotten that one of his officers didn't bother to follow up when Elena was reported missing?'

'Yeah . . . he brought that up. He wants to make up for it and do what's right, apparently.'

'Does he now,' Archer replies, drily.

They sit in silence for the remainder of the journey, Archer seething at the thought of the opportunity to catch Elena's killer slipping from her fingers.

Quinn bags a roadside parking space in Spring Street. Switching off the engine, they climb out of the Volvo, leaving behind the cool comfortable air con, emerging into heavy oppressive heat. Quinn locks the vehicle, leans against the car and looks at Archer. 'It's crap, I know,' he says.

'It's his catchment. He's the SIO. What can we do?'

'*We* should keep an eye on him and his team.'

'What are you implying?'

'I'm implying we should offer our services and keep our oar in the game.'

'Is this another way of saying Parry's not up to the task?'

'Don't get me wrong. I like Lee, but he's one of the lads. A bloke's bloke. I'm saying, he may not be the best choice to lead an investigation into the death of a young female sex worker. Especially one that took drugs.'

Archer feels herself bristling. 'That's just what the women of London need. Another "blokes' bloke" copper to protect them.' She thinks of the Met's brutal handling of a peaceful women's

74

vigil in Clapham Common last year. A young woman had been raped and murdered by a Met officer. The women had held the vigil for the victim and when they didn't comply with police lockdown demands, the police went in like bulldozers violently hauling frightened women from the gathering, cuffing them and arresting them. The pictures had gone viral. The vitriol against the police had been justifiably harsh. Ironically, the chief commissioner at the time was female, and had displayed no contrition.

'I hear you,' says Quinn.

They stand in an awkward silence for a moment, Archer rattled by the thought of Parry taking over Elena's murder investigation.

'Incidentally, he has an appointment at the mortuary at 2 p.m. today. He stressed there's no need for us to be there.'

'Thoughtful of him.'

'Yeah, *très* magnanimous. I say we could stop by and show our faces. Just to say hello.'

Quinn has a mischievous look on his face.

'Could do no harm,' Archer says.

'I already dropped Kapur a message and told him when Lee arrives not to start without us.'

'Did you now?' Archer says, smiling.

'You know me ... total rebel. Hey, I'm parched. Do you fancy a cold drink?'

Across the street is a Pret. The heat has made her thirsty. 'Good idea.'

Archer grabs a fizzy water, Quinn, an iced coffee. They walk up Praed Street, sipping their drinks, taking their time in the various shops and restaurants, showing pictures of Elena, and asking questions. Out of twenty-two people, two think she seems familiar, but cannot say when and where they've seen her. To Archer's disappointment it seems a waste of almost two hours; however, that changes when they get to the Southern Fried Chicken Shop. A young Spanish server with PABLO printed on his name badge, recalls seeing her sitting in the restaurant on the same night she went missing.

'Is she OK?' he asks.

'We're just making some enquiries. Mind if I call you Pablo?' Archer asks.

He flashes her a smile. 'Not at all. Is my name, after all.'

'Did you talk to her?'

'A little. I flirt some, you know. She's a pretty girl.'

He flashes the smile at Archer again. Quinn chokes on his iced coffee.

'What did you talk about?'

'Nothing. I ask her what she want to eat. That's all.'

Archer holds his gaze. There's something in the way Pablo conducts himself, his male confidence, his unflinching stare and lothario smile that makes her doubt that's all he spoke to her about.

'You have nice eyes. Different colours,' he says. 'Can I get you something . . . spicy?' he says, grinning.

She arches a brow at him. She must be at least a decade older than him. 'That's all you spoke to her about?'

He shrugs. 'I ask her name, and if she's eating all by herself.'

Archer pictures him fawning over Elena and her showing no interest.

'What did she order?'

He thinks for a moment before replying. 'A Diet Coke and some fries is all.'

'Where did she sit?' Quinn asks.

Pablo points to a white plastic table and chair in the corner near the entrance. 'There. She sat and watched the world go by.'

'Did anyone join her?'

'No, she was alone. She was on her phone, though.'

'Talking?'

'No, probably on socials or something. Or texting. I don't know.'

Archer looks at the table and tries to get a sense of what might have been going on in Elena's head. She looks around the restaurant and notices CCTV cameras.

'Oh. Now that I think of it, there's something else,' Pablo says, interrupting her thoughts. 'A man was watching her. His eyes like the hawk. You know what I mean?'

'What did he look like?' Quinn asks.

Pablo takes a moment to think. 'Short hair. A bit fat. When she left, he left too. Did not finish his chilli Korean wings.'

'Is your CCTV working?' Archer asks.

'I think so. You'll need to speak to my manager, though.'

The manager, a pot-bellied man with oily skin called Steve, is happy to oblige. He takes them to a storeroom at the rear of the restaurant that's also home to an antiquated computer, which is wired up to the CCTV. Fortunately, it appears to be in working order.

'It doesn't go back very far,' says Steve. 'The disk needs replacing 'cause it keeps filling up so we have to delete the files to free up more space. Know what I mean? It's a pain.'

'A new computer might save you the bother,' says Quinn.

'Agree, but I don't hold the purse strings.'

Archer watches the screen as Steve opens a folder and finds the file from Saturday. He opens it. A black and white video begins to play.

'Could you fast forward to just before nine o'clock?'

The video speeds forward. After a few moments, Archer says, 'OK, stop. There she is entering the restaurant.'

Elena walks up to the counter, speaks to a smiling Pablo and orders. Pablo talks to her, but she seems distracted and responds in what seems like a polite manner. Sitting alone at another table is a punter fitting the description Pablo gave earlier. As Elena walks to her table, he watches her, licking greasy sauce from his fingers. Elena barely eats or drinks. She keeps checking her phone and tapping it on the table. The man is watching her. She gets up suddenly and leaves, turning left at the exit. The man wipes his fingers as he stands. He leaves, turns left at the exit and follows Elena.

'Rewind it, please,' Archer requests. 'Stop – there.'

He pauses the video at the point where the man is standing. Archer takes out her phone, opens the camera and takes a photo. Turning to Steve, 'Could you email this CCTV file to me, please?'

'I'm not sure. GDPR and all . . .'

'This is a murder investigation, Steve,' Quinn replies. 'Just do it.'

'Erm . . . OK.'

'Do you recognise this man by any chance?'

Steve leans in for a closer look. 'Yeah . . . he comes in now and again. I don't know his name. He's an Uber driver.'

Chapter 14

ARCHER MAKES A CALL TO Klara and asks her to work her tech magic and follow up on names for Uber drivers working in and around Paddington and the Praed Street area. Maybe she could discreetly hack the Uber employee database and get a face to match the man in the picture. It'll take some time, Klara responds, but she'll get onto it right away.

They arrive at the mortuary on Horseferry Road fifteen minutes early and explain the situation about DS Parry taking over the case.

'Does he know you'll be here waiting for him?' Doctor Kapur asks.

'Thought we'd surprise him,' says Quinn. 'He loves surprises.'

Kapur's thick bushy monobrow arches like giant centipede. 'I see. It's good you're here. I have some business to discuss regarding the victim from Pleshey Road. But that can wait.'

'Sure thing, doc,' says Quinn.

The pathologist leaves them. At 2 p.m., Archer and Quinn sit in the waiting area outside the lab as Kapur prepares Elena's remains. Fifteen minutes pass and there's no sign of Parry. Twenty minutes pass and still no show.

'Punctuality is not his thing,' Archer says.

Kapur emerges from the lab. 'Just the two of you,' he says, frowning.

'Looks like it,' Quinn replies.

'I have a busy day ahead.'

'We can start without him,' says Archer.

'Very well. Let's begin,' Kapur says, leading them into the lab.

Archer feels her muscles coiling at the sight of Elena lying on top of the stainless-steel table. She is covered up to the shoulders with a sheet. Her angelic face has been cleaned and is clear of dried blood. Her pale skin has a blue tinge and is almost translucent. Archer expels a breath she hadn't realised she was holding.

'OK?' Quinn whispers to her.

Archer nods.

Kapur stands at the other side of the table. 'The victim has suffered a blow to the face, the nose is broken.'

Archer hears the door swinging open behind her.

'Harry ... what's going on here?' comes the voice of DS Lee Parry.

'Lee, nice of you to join us,' says Quinn.

'Join you?' he replies, frowning.

'DS Parry, you're twenty-five minutes late,' says Kapur.

'I'm a busy man.'

'As am I. I have five more minutes to spare. Let's get on, shall we?'

'I think that would be a good idea,' says Archer.

'Wait just a minute,' Parry protests.

'No, DS Parry,' says Kapur gruffly. 'There's more to this case than meets the eye. DI Archer and DS Quinn have a vested interest in this case as it is connected to one of their own. So hold your tongue.'

'What does that mean, Doctor Kapur?' Archer asks.

'All in good time.'

Kapur pulls the sheet down revealing Elena's chest. There's a small round hole like a bullet wound to the heart.

'She's been shot, then,' says Parry.

'Not quite. There's no bullet or exit wound.'

Archer and Quinn exchange a glance.

'Stabbed?' Parry asks.

'After some consultation with my colleagues we came to the conclusion that this fatal wound was made with a gun. But not just any gun. We believe it's been made with a penetrating captive bolt gun. The type used to zombify cattle before they are slaughtered.'

They take a moment to let this set in.

Kapur is looking at Archer and Quinn. 'Ring any bells, detectives?'

'The wound from the Pleshey Road victim,' Archer says.

'What's going on?' asks Parry.

Archer catches Quinn's eye. His brow is furrowed. Everything about this case is about to change.

'Can someone please tell me what's going on?' Parry's voice is beginning to grate.

'I'll come to that in a moment,' says Kapur, as he covers Elena's remains, giving back her dignity.

On the adjacent table, he gently slides down the sheet covering the bones of the mystery victim from Pleshey Road. Kapur looks at Parry. 'This is the victim from Detectives Archer and Quinn's current investigation. If you examine the remains you may pick out similarities.'

Parry frowns and inches forward for a closer look. Archer can see exactly what Kapur is alluding to.

The pathologist takes out his chewed biro and begins pointing at the rib cage for Parry's benefit.

'What are you saying, Doctor Kapur?' Parry says.

Kapur glances at the old clock above the exit door. 'My time is just about done here.'

Quinn says, 'I think he's saying there is a pattern in the way Elena died and the way this unidentified victim died.'

'The same killer?'

'Possibly.'

Archer's mind is racing. Could this be a coincidence? No, she doesn't believe in them. But how is this possible?

'It's my case. You're not taking this away from me,' says Parry.

'You may not get a choice, mate,' replies Quinn.

Archer bites her tongue. The murders are almost thirty-five years apart. Could it be a copycat?

'Time is up,' Kapur adds, a hint of impatience in his voice.

Archer and Quinn thank the pathologist and exit the mortuary with DS Parry, who is like a bulldog unwilling to give an inch on Elena's case.

'You two look into your . . . bones . . . and I'll continue with Elena . . .' Parry pauses, his mind searching for Elena's surname.

'Zoric, DS Parry. Her name is Zoric,' Archer reminds him, sharply.

His eyes narrow and at the same time he smiles benignly. 'Was on the tip of my tongue.'

Quinn interjects, 'Whatever you discover, keep us in the loop.'

Parry squeezes Quinn's shoulder and winks, 'Course, mate,' he says, and strolls nonchalantly up Horseferry Road.

'Who the fuck does he think he is?' Archer says.

Quinn is watching his pal with a curious expression. 'He's ambitious. Never had much of a break.'

'Is that your way of apologising for him?'

Quinn turns to Archer. 'Not at all. He's desperate and sees an opportunity to lead a murder investigation that could advance his career.'

'He's not up to the task. You said it yourself.'

'I did. But we may have to work with him.'

Archer folds her arms. She's impatient and eager to move forward. 'As long as he doesn't get in my way.'

That afternoon, they gather all the data they can on both victims and set up an incident room. Archer briefs the team and gives them assignments. They are to meet at 10 a.m. the following morning.

At the end of the day, a call comes through. It's Doctor Kapur.

'The dental records have come back. She was sixteen years old and lived in Richmond Terrace, Bristol. Her name was Sally McGowan.'

Chapter 15

Sally

Stuart Mill House, Kings Cross, London. 1987

S
ALLY MCGOWAN STRIKES A SWAN match and lights up her third Silk Cut in one hour. Pressing rewind on her Walkman, she counts in seconds and inhales, taking comfort in the smoky hit. At the count of five, she stops the rewind and presses *play*. The tail end of the Smiths' 'Unloveable' is fading. Not her favourite song. She exhales and waits for the next track, a song that resonates so much with her, she thinks she might cry. 'Half a Person' begins. She closes her eyes and loses herself in Johnny Marr's hypnotic guitar and Morrissey's poetic words. Like the girl in the song, she's sixteen, clumsy (occasionally) and shy. She also came to London and died, but not that way. A tear slips from an eye heavy with mascara and rolls down her pale cheek. She died inside.

Sally opens her eyes and quickly wipes the tear away. *Pull yourself together!* She's in the tiny, rented room of her flatshare in Stuart Mill House. It's late evening, the room is lit by the glow from the city beyond her sanctuary. Sitting on the single mattress, she leans against the wall, hugs her knees and picks at a tiny hole in her black tights, tearing it and making it bigger. 'Such a rebel,' she says to herself as 'That Joke Isn't Funny Anymore' ripples through the small, orange earphones. A bright light disturbs the

85

calm of her room and a meaty cooking smell wafts in, making her stomach rumble. She looks up to see her live-in landlady, Maggie, framed in the doorway. Sally rolls her eyes. Why can't she ever knock? Maggie is talking, but Sally can't hear. She presses the *stop* button and pulls off her earphones.

'What?' she asks.

'I did knock,' Maggie responds, brushing her long dark curls.

'I was listening to my music.'

'I can see that.'

Sally folds her arms and sighs heavily to make a point.

Maggie chuckles. 'When I took you in, Sally, I didn't sign up for a hormonal teenager.'

'I'm not hormonal!'

'No . . . course not. Anyway, it stinks in here.' Maggie crosses the room and opens the window. Cool air sweeps inside. 'You should ease up on the fags. They'll stunt your growth, and kill you too.'

Sally ignores the comment. She's heard it a hundred times. She focuses her attention at the round pale flesh of her thigh revealed through a second hole she has just made.

'When was the last time you ate?' Maggie asks.

Sally shrugs and inhales the last of her cigarette.

'Wait there,' Maggie says and leaves the room.

Sally rolls her eyes again. God, doesn't she deserve a bit of privacy?

Maggie returns moments later and switches on the bedroom light. She's carrying a fork and a small plate containing what looks like a pasty. No pastry, though, it's covered in breadcrumbs.

'Eat this,' Maggie says.

Sally hesitates but it smells delicious and her mouth is watering. 'What is it?'

'It's a Findus Minced Beef Crispy Pancake. It's going free, so eat it.'

Sally takes it from her. 'Thank you.'

'It's piping hot inside, so blow on it before you eat.'

Sally sets the plate on her lap and tears open the pancake. Steaming mince covered in gravy spills onto the plate. She blows a cooling breath over the mixture and takes a forkful. It's still hot and she waves her hand over her mouth as if it will make a difference.

Maggie is watching her. Sally meets her gaze. It's then she notices the bruise above her eye. Sally tenses.

'What happened to your face?'

'Which one?' Maggie quips.

'Your eye.' Sally takes another delicious mouthful. 'Was it a client?'

'Never mind that.'

Sally had met Maggie earlier this year when she arrived in Paddington from Bristol, homeless and broke. She emerged from the station timid as a mouse. Scared too. It was evening, Maggie was outside the station with some other 'girls'. Sally needed help, directions to the YWCA at least. Maggie, who was dressed, let's be honest, like a slut, caught her eye. Maggie took pity on her and gave her a roof over her head. But Sally came to realise there was more to her kindness. Maggie was as enterprising as Oliver Twist's Fagin and saw in Sally a way of earning cash. On the streets, as it were.

'Sally . . . you're a month behind on rent.'

'I haven't got any money.'

Maggie folds her arms. 'That much is clear. So, what do we do in these situations?'

Sally's shoulders sag. 'I can't do it anymore, Maggie. Those men . . . some of them are disgusting.'

Maggie crouches down and perches on the mattress beside Sally. 'It's not easy. You got that right. But what else can we do? There are no jobs. The country's in a right mess. Times are hard, especially for women like us with no skills or training. This is our lot. It's how we survive. It's how we've survived for centuries, but remember it isn't for ever. Don't forget that.'

Sally looks at the bruise on Maggie's eye. 'That's going to be a proper shiner tomorrow. You wait.'

'No one is going to want a tart with a black eye. Which is why you need to go out to work. We need money to pay the bills.'

Sally sighs.

'And don't worry about me, or the eye. It was just some drunken idiot.' Maggie lifts her arm and gently strokes Sally's hair. 'Now, I need you to go down Soho. A few punters have been asking after you. You're a popular girl, you know.'

Despite feeling nauseous at the thought, Sally smiles. 'It's not for ever,' she says, repeating Maggie's words.

'Good girl. Deb is working tonight. I asked her to keep an eye on you.'

Sally pokes at the pancake with her fork.

Maggie pats her arm and stands. 'Finish your dinner.' As she leaves the room, she says, 'I'll get you some rubbers.'

It's almost forty minutes later when a dolled-up Sally, wearing a short black skirt, ripped black tights, and an oversized denim jacket she'd found in a vintage clothes shop, strolls into Soho's Cleveland Square, with the Smiths' 'Panic' blaring on her earphones. She spots a line of working girls on the other side of the square, amongst them is the bone-thin Deb pouting and positioning herself suggestively at potential punters as they cruise slowly by, assessing the 'talent' for sale. At the edge of the kerb, Sally checks for oncoming traffic and hurries across the road.

'Hey, Deb,' says Sally, who, wearing a glittery rainbow boob tube and leather mini skirt is criminally underdressed for the time of year. To complete her outfit is a small bag hanging from a gold chain over her shoulder.

'All right, girl,' Deb drawls in a thick Birkenhead accent. 'Clocking in, are ya?'

'Girl's gotta earn her keep.'

Up close, Sally is shocked to see Deb looking even more painfully thin than usual. Maggie had told her that AIDS was eating Deb from the inside out. 'Her time on this planet is limited,' she'd said. Sally checks her jacket pocket, relieved to feel the condoms Maggie had insisted she take with her.

'Maggie putting the thumbscrews on?' Deb asks with a knowing smile.

'You know Maggie.'

'Yes, I do.'

Sally takes out the packet of Silk Cut from her inside pocket and offers one to Deb.

'Cheers, girl,' she says, pinching a filter with her long nails and drawing it out. From her bag, she takes out a petrol lighter, flips it open and lights Sally's fag and then her own. 'Not much happening,' she comments as she inhales. 'Mind you, we're a little top heavy tonight.' Deb points her cigarette at the working girls dotted around the square.

Sally notices a woman with lank hair and a long coat carrying a plastic Marks & Spencer shopping bag crossing the square. Her face is tight, her eyes focused on Deb and Sally.

'Disgusting!' she hisses, as she hurries by.

'Fuck you, Mary Whitehouse!' Deb bellows.

The woman stops momentarily, her eyes wide in shock.

'Hey, I do girls, too, you know. You look like you might have a bit of lezz in ya.' Deb raises two fingers to her lips.

'Twenty quid, and I'll eat that pussy out until you scream your tits off.'

The woman flinches and looks for a moment as if she might pass out. From her pocket she fumbles for a set of keys and hurries off, disappearing into the shadows.

'That's a no, then,' says Deb.

'You're wild.' Sally chuckles.

They hear the screeching of brakes and look up to see a Capri turning into the square. Deb drops the remains of cigarette to the ground and waves at the car. 'One of my regulars, doll.'

The car speeds up and skids to halt beside them. Deb winks at Sally. 'Be careful tonight,' she says as she gets into the car. They're gone in minutes, Sally left alone in a cloud of bitter exhaust fumes. She waves them away, and across the square sees a man in a Ford Cortina looking her way. She hadn't noticed the car before. He nods at her. Sally hesitates – a moment of uncertainty that she can't explain. She shrugs it off and nods back at him. Before she can change her mind his engine starts up and the headlamps light up. He drives around the square, pulls up beside her and rolls down his window. 'Hello,' he says.

Sally folds her arms and looks away.

'I know a nice place we can go, if you like,' he says. 'We can go there for an hour and I'll drive you home again. How does that sound?'

Sally catches the eye of one of the other girls who is glaring at her. Sally knows she wants her out of there so the rest of them have a chance. She takes a breath, calms herself and puts on the fake smile Maggie had taught her.

'Sure. Where is this place?' she says climbing into the car.

'It's called Pleshey Road. Have you heard of it?' he asks, easing off the brakes.

'No.'

'It's nice, you'll like it there. You really will.'

'One hour, yeah?' Sally confirms.

'One hour.'

They drive out of the square. He glances her way. 'Seatbelt,' he says.

Sally rolls her eyes, pulls the belt across and clicks it into place.

Chapter 16

ARCHER IS HAPPY THAT QUINN'S mate, the joiner and decorator Liam Duffy, has done an efficient and speedy job of fitting the bathroom fixtures. He's even fixed the unfinished grouting and wiped down every surface. The space is unrecognisable. She runs the shower and adjusts the new Edwardian-style dial to get the correct temperature. The water pours like hot rain on her skin and hair. It's glorious.

As she dries herself, she hears music from the kitchen radio. For a moment she thinks of Grandad. Her stomach tightens, and a sadness sweeps through her like a winter breeze. Wrapping the towel around her, she steps out of the bathroom and onto the landing, creaking the floorboards as she goes. She sees Liam at the bottom of the stairs, crouched over his tool bag. He turns and looks up at her and smiles.

'I'm a bit early. Hope you don't mind.'

'It's fine.' Archer feels slightly self-conscious wrapped only in a wet towel. She tightens the grip on the cotton and turns to leave.

'D'you mind if I make some breakfast? I'm starving.'

'Be my guest.'

'Can I get you something?'

'A tea if you're making it.'

'Coming up.'

In the bedroom, Archer blow dries her hair and gets dressed, unsure how she feels about the friendly and super-attractive Dubliner that is currently in her house alone with her. She feels a mild fluttering in her stomach and wonders when was the last time she'd been with anyone. Her last boyfriend had been the cheating douche, Dominic, who she kicked to the kerb. After that, she'd come very close to getting together with Jamie Blackwell. The less said about him the better. She can certainly choose them. Switching off the hairdryer, she brushes her hair, and looks out the window. Clear blue skies and sunshine. It's going to be another hot day. From the wardrobe, she selects a thin cotton khaki shirt and black chinos. A little underdressed for the office but there was a good chance that she and Quinn would be going on a field trip so best to dress appropriately for the weather.

As she makes her way downstairs a waft of something delicious makes her mouth water.

In the kitchen, also spotlessly cleaned, Liam is cooking sausages in one pan and scrambled eggs in another.

'I know you're probably running out the door but there's plenty here.'

Archer eyes the food hungrily. 'I've got some time.'

He smiles at her. 'Take a seat. Breakfast is imminent.'

The table has a pot of tea, two plates laid out with knives and forks, and bowl of smashed avocado. Archer blinks, unsure what to make of it all. The toaster pings and two thick slices of toast pop up. She sits at the table. Liam places a slice of toast on her plate.

'It's sourdough. Freshly made.'

'You made sourdough while I was getting ready? Now I'm impressed.'

'I'm good but not that good. Picked it up at an artisan bakery on the way here.'

'Thanks.'

'Would you like butter?'

'I don't think there is any.'

'I bought some.'

'Oh . . .'

He places a block of Kerrygold on the table, peels back the wrapper and pours the teas. 'Sausages and scrambled eggs, OK?' he asks.

'Sure.'

He spoons a large portion of canary yellow eggs onto their plates and follows it up with two sausages each. Archer's not sure she can polish off both of them, but she'll give it a shot. Liam sits at the table and places the napkin on his lap. 'This is nice. I wasn't expecting a guest,' he says.

Archer looks at him with a bemused smile. Liam laughs. 'I'm only keep you going. It's nice to have a bit of company.'

Archer chuckles and sips her tea. 'Very good of you to have me for breakfast.'

'You're very welcome.'

Archer cuts into the eggs. They're soft and perfectly seasoned. The sausages are meaty and delicious. 'So you you're a builder and a cook.'

Liam is spreading avocado on his toast. 'Jack of all trades. Master of none. That sort of thing.'

They eat in silence for a few moments.

'Must be a tough gig. Being a detective and all,' Liam says.

Archer pauses to consider this. 'I suppose it can be.'

'Do you think you'll stick with it? I mean, is it your calling?'

Archer is unsure how to answer that. 'I don't know. I suppose it is.'

'Hope you don't mind me asking.'

'Not at all.'

Archer finishes her eggs and half a sausage before placing her knife and fork on the plate.

'What about you?' Archer asks. 'Do you have a calling?'

'Now you're asking. I don't think I do. Right now I'm just drifting through life. Picking up work here and there. I suppose I'm a bit nomadic. I have Gypsy in my blood going way back. I quite like the idea of that . . . of not being rooted to one place.'

'You're not planning to settle in London, then?'

'I don't think so. After being stuck in lockdown in Ireland for so long I'm itching to get back into the world. I have my campervan. I pick up jobs wherever I can. When I finish up here, unless there's another job, I may just take off.'

'Where do you think you'll go?'

'Well, as a citizen of the great European Union . . . by the way, sorry for your loss and all . . . I may head to France.'

'Can you speak French?'

'Since lockdown, I'm currently on day 436 of a Duolingo streak.'

'You must be fluent, then.'

Liam laughs. 'I can ask for a train ticket, order a baguette and a coffee, and point at various animals and tell the nearest French person what they are.'

Archer grins. 'You're all set, then.'

'We'll see.'

For a brief moment she loses herself in the fantasy of packing a case and leaving for another country with no cares or worries.

'So, what do you think of the bathroom?' Liam asks, interrupting her thoughts.

'Really happy with it. You did more than I was expecting in the time. Thank you.'

'Harry told me not to muck about.'

'Did he now?'

'He wanted to make sure you get the gold service.'

Archer is moved and does not know what to say to that.

'By the way, I saw the list of paints you want. Farrow and Ball, bold regency colours. Very stylish.'

'You like them?'

'I do. You've got a good eye.'

'I had a lot of time over the past two years to look at interior design magazines and create pinboards.'

'Do you want me to pick the paint up?'

'That would be helpful.'

He nods as he eats the last of a sausage.

Archer finishes the tea. 'Breakfast was very nice but I'm full.'

'No worries. I'll have the leftovers in a sandwich later.'

Archer laughs. 'Have a good day.'

'You too.'

In the incident room later that morning, Archer is having a stand-up meeting with her team. Present are Quinn, Klara, DC Marian Phillips, DS Joely Tozer and junior analyst, Os Pike. Klara has come up with a lead on the last known address of Sally McGowan's parents and the school she attended.

'That's all I have on Sally so far,' Klara says.

'Thanks, Klara.' Archer addresses the team. 'Any questions?' she asks.

Phillips raises a hand. 'Do we think it's a copycat killer?'

'I'm not writing it off. We'll need to sift through files and look for similar murders. Off the top of my head, I'm not aware of any, unless anyone else is,' she says but a collective shaking of heads quickly answers that.

Quinn says, 'If it's the same killer then we could be looking at someone in their sixties or older. Considering Elena was working as a prostitute, then it's fair to expect this killer is male.'

'Marian, what's the news on curtain twitcher Miles Davenport?'

'We paid him another visit, which he wasn't too pleased about. He was nervous and keen for us to be quick. There's something not quite right there. We don't have anything on our radar but we're keeping a close eye. I have some ideas up my sleeve and will keep you up to date.'

'Thanks, Marian. Klara, any update on the CCTV?'

'Still waiting on the Praed Street footage.'

'See if you can push that through.'

'Will do.'

Archer thinks about Parry conducting his own enquiries into Elena's murder and is about to instruct the team to do the same, without the backing of CI Fletcher, when a knock on the door interrupts the meeting. Her heart sinks when he steps inside. 'Excuse the intrusion. DI Archer – a word, please.'

Archer turns to the team, 'That's all for now. Keep in touch. Harry and I are heading to Bristol today. Call us if you hear or need anything.'

The team start to leave. Fletcher is scanning the murder wall, eyes focused on the picture of Elena. Quinn is last out. He gives her a quick nod before heading back to his desk. Fletcher closes the incident room door, slides his hands in his trouser pockets as he takes in the entire wall. He is silent. Tension crackles the air, for reasons Archer can't determine. Moments pass before he speaks. 'I read your report.'

'On Elena Zoric?'

'And the other girl.'

'Sally McGowan.'

Fletcher neither confirms nor denies.

'You're certain they are the same killer?'

Archer hesitates before answering. The truth is she cannot be certain. 'I'm working on that assumption.'

'It's an assumption,' he says, with an almost disappointed tone.

'Both women were murdered in the same way.'

He lets out a long sigh. 'The commissioner called me . . .' Fletcher leaves the sentence hanging.

Archer waits, wondering where he's going with this.

He turns to face her, levels his gaze, smiles benignly but insincerely. 'The commissioner would prefer it if you let her nephew lead with the Zoric murder.'

Archer bristles. 'Her nephew? Parry is her nephew?'

'It would seem so.'

'He lacks experience.'

'Nevertheless, that is her wish. And mine, too.'

'But—'

'No buts. You're doing a grand job.' And with that, Fletcher turns and exits the room.

Archer seethes as she watches him walk back to Pierce's office. She has no choice. Parry will lead Elena's murder case, but for her own sake, Archer will be keeping a close eye on him.

Chapter 17

QUINN IS DRIVING THEM OUT of London. It's news to him that DS Lee Parry is the commissioner's nephew.

'I'd heard he was related to someone senior in the Met but I was never much interested in gossip. Anyway, she wasn't commissioner then.'

'None of that changes anything for me. If there is a link between Sally's killer and Elena's then Parry needs to up his game.'

'Agreed.'

With Quinn's lead foot, it takes almost three and a half hours to drive to Richmond Terrace in Clifton, the last sixty minutes of that journey taking place at the end-of-day rush hour on the approach to the city. There's no free parking. Quinn stops on double yellows outside a row of garages. 'I suspect this won't take long,' he says.

It's a pleasant warm sunny evening, people are returning to their homes from a day's work. Above the garages at the top of a dozen or so steps is Richmond Terrace, a row of grand brightly coloured three-storey Georgian houses.

'Been years since I've been to Bristol,' Quinn says. 'Nice city, despite the dodgy accent.'

'Says the man with the dodgy accent.'

'Touché.'

They climb the stone steps. 'Nice spot, but I expect it's gone through some gentrification since the 1980s,' says Quinn. 'Also, I'd be surprised if anyone from that time still lives here.'

'It's worth a shot.'

They hit Sally's old house first. No longer a single home, the property is divided into flats. Pressing the buzzer on the first apartment, Quinn's speculation is confirmed. The longest anyone has lived here is ten years, and no one recognises Sally's name. They spend the next forty minutes doing a door-to-door with the same outcome.

'Well, that's that, then,' says Quinn. 'Fancy a bite?'

'Excuse me,' comes a man's croaky voice.

At the base of the steps is a man in his early to mid-seventies, with a blue PPE mask covering only his chin. He points behind them towards Quinn's car. 'Is that your motor?'

'We're just leaving,' says Quinn.

'You can't park there.'

'We'll be gone in a jiffy,' says Quinn.

'It's double yellows. People need access to their garages. Day and night.'

'We're really sorry,' says Archer. 'Do you live round here?' She smiles warmly at him as she descends the steps.

'I surely do,' he replies. 'Born and bred.'

'We're both vaccinated by the way,' she says.

His thick brows knit together.

'Your mask is down. Just in case . . .'

'Oh. Damn thing.' He pulls it up to cover just his mouth.

'You must know a lot of people here?' Archer asks.

'Not so much these days. It's all new faces.'

'Do you remember the McGowan family from number 42? They lived here in the eighties.'

He scratches his head. 'Now that's going back a bit.'

'Sally McGowan was sixteen years old. She went to Clifton High School. Parents were Paul and Michelle McGowan.'

He looks away, deep in thought and scratches his chin. 'McGowan, did you say?'

'That's right.'

'Ah ... I remember Michelle and her husband, now that you say. Of course. She passed. Cancer, I think.'

'You knew them?'

'As well as any of the neighbours. But my memory's not that good now.'

'Do you remember their daughter Sally?'

His brow creases as he thinks this over. 'Yes! Young Sally. Lovely girl.'

'Can you tell us about her.'

He taps his forehead. 'Oh ... My memory is not good. But I know someone who could help you. Sally and my daughter, Fiona, were friends.'

'Could we speak to her?'

'I don't see why not. Would you like me to call her?'

'Yes, please.'

A little late but Archer introduces herself and Quinn.

'You're police?' the old man says. 'Well, I never. Is Sally OK?'

'What's your name?' Quinn asks diverting the topic.

'I'm Gerald.'

'Could we speak to Fiona?' he asks, in an urgent but friendly tone.

'Yes, yes, of course.'

Gerald calls his daughter and gives the phone to Archer. She explains who they are and why they're in Bristol. Fiona is surprised but invites them to her home.

She greets Archer and Quinn at the door of her two up, two down in East Clifton and brings them into the kitchen where she is preparing dinner for her husband and two sons.

'The boys will be home soon,' Fiona says, furiously chopping carrots and tipping them into a pressure cooker.

'We appreciate you talking to us,' says Archer. 'We won't take up much of your time. So you knew Sally McGowan?'

'Is everything OK? She's not hurt, is she?'

'I'm afraid she's dead,' Archer replies.

Fiona lifts a tea towel, wipes her hands, her eyes blinking as she takes in the news. 'It doesn't surprise me, if I'm honest.'

'Why do you say that?'

'She moved to London. Very suddenly.' The woman's face pales, she swallows. 'Oh. I would often wonder what happened to her. We did lose touch. I just assumed she'd married and had kids like me.'

'She wasn't so lucky.'

Her eyes slide from Archer to Quinn and back again. 'If the police are here then something terrible must have happened.'

'How well did you know her?' Archer asks.

'We were mates. We lived close to each other and had a lot of fun together. Oh God, it's so awful. Especially after her mum and dad both dying from cancer. Some families just have no luck. How did she die? No, don't tell me. I don't want to know.'

'What was she like?'

'Funny. Gobby. Loved music, especially the Smiths. Lord knows why, they were so depressing.'

'What did she do after her parents died?'

'She was really cut up about it, as you would be. She had no one and they were going to put her into care because she was underage. She weren't having any of that. She was always fiercely independent.'

'So she ran away to London?' Archer asks.

'Thought the streets would be paved with gold. You know how people always think that. She sent me a letter once. Saying she'd found a room in London somewhere.'

'Did she say where?'

'If she did I don't remember.'

'Do you still have the letter?'

'I'm afraid not. All my teenage stuff was chucked a long time ago. In the letter, she seemed happy enough, but then she called me one night out of the blue, from a phone box. She was still upset about her mum. She was drunk, too. I asked her what she was doing for money. She said a friend was helping her out. A woman who had given her a place to live.'

'Did she tell you who this was?'

'No, but she was making money with the help of this woman.' Fiona wrings the towel in her hands and shakes her head. 'I begged her to come back. But she wouldn't.'

'How did she make money?'

'She was on the game.'

Archer and Quinn look at each other. She knows he's thinking what she is. Both Elena and Sally were sex workers. This is no coincidence. This is the work of the same person. Could there be others?

'I don't suppose you have a picture of her?' Archer asks.

'I doubt it. When I get a moment I could take a look in the attic. There's a lot of old photos from my school days in boxes up there.'

'That would be really helpful.' Archer takes out a business card from her pocket. 'If you find something here's my number and email.'

Chapter 18

MALLORY JONES FEELS LIKE SHE'S being hoiked unceremoniously from a cosy, warm womb. She groans as she wakes, her head pounding, her mouth dry as a barren wasteland. Something warm and stiff is pressing into her buttocks. *What the fuck?* Her eyes blink open and squint at the morning sunshine slicing through the half-open shutters of the bedroom. Memories from the night before come flooding in.

Fuck.

'Hey, sugar. Are you awake?' he asks, his fingers tracing the tattooed black foliage that runs from her shoulder and down her arm.

I am now.

'I'm horny. How about it?'

They'd met on a dating app, gone to a bar and drunk their body weight in cocktails. He's an American tourist, an archetypal jock with little upstairs and a disappointing downstairs. Still, he'd made her cum, and that's all she needed. Now she needs him to leave.

'Come on. One more time,' he replies, lying on his back, the sheet pulled away, his manscaped erection and balls on full display. His hand slides to the back of her head and he tries to guide her face down south. 'Take it in the mouth. Breakfast, baby.'

Mallory rolls her eyes. 'Got work to do,' she says. Taking a breath, she swings out of bed, ignoring the throbbing headache.

'That makes me sad,' he says, in a babyish voice that makes her want to smash his face.

'My boyfriend will be home soon,' she lies. 'He's going to flip if he sees you here.'

He flinches. 'What the fuck? Are you kidding me?' he says, tumbling out of bed and pulling on his clothes.

'Can I get you coffee?' She grabs a T-shirt from the top of her dresser, and pulls it on. 'Relax. You're twice his size.'

'No, I gotta go.'

Mallory shrugs, exits the bedroom and trudges into the loft apartment's vast bright combined living room and kitchen. The smooth concrete floor is cool beneath her bare feet. From a cupboard she grabs a tumbler and fills it with cold water. Searching through the drawers she finds a packet of Nurofen and swallows two. Yawning, she picks up the kettle and fills it. Her eyes slide across to Bruce's bedroom. The door is ajar, the only light is from the bank of monitors where she sees his silhouette. She pads across the living room, glancing at the photo of Bruce and her brother, Zach, his husband, laughing together on a snowy mountain top in Val d'Isère.

She feels an ache in her chest. They were happier times.

Mallory enters his room, wraps her arms around his shoulders and kisses the side of his head. 'Hey, Boo.'

Bruce had once told her that because his surname was Radley, his nickname as a kid had been Boo, after the character in *To Kill a Mockingbird*. She had laughed and henceforward, always called him by that name. Fortunately, he didn't mind.

'You stink,' he says.

'Yeah. Had a few too many.'

'Who's your friend?'

'Some dude from an app.'

'Classy.'

'Woman has needs, Boo.'

'And those needs must always be satisfied.'

'Did you get any sleep?'

'With all that screaming from the bedroom?'

She thumps his chest, 'I did not!'

He chuckles. 'To answer your question, I had a rough night.'

'I'm sorry.'

'I dreamed about him.'

A twist in Mallory's stomach. 'Zach?'

'No ... *him*.'

She closes her eyes and hugs him tighter. 'Oh, Boo. We'll find him. One day. I promise.'

'Yeah ... we will,' he replies, flatly.

He's in one of his malaises and she wants to bring him out of it. 'What are you looking at?' she asks brightly, steering the subject but also curious about the live police broadcast on his screen with a detective she doesn't recognise standing at a lectern.

'It's about to start,' says Boo, turning up the volume. 'Might be something we can use on a future show.'

With Bruce as her producer and researcher, they are the co-creators of the *Mallory Jones Investigates* true crime podcast. Mallory, a former reporter, fronts the show for which they both research and write. With her snappy delivery and sharp attention to detail, combined with Bruce's excellent production skills and extensive research, they are the brains behind the award-winning podcast that has won them followers from across the globe.

'Hey,' comes the jock's voice. 'I'll get going, then.'

Mallory uncurls herself from Boo and peeks through the doorway. She'd forgotten about him. 'OK. Bye. Nice to meet you,' she says politely with a fixed smile.

He hesitates, shifting awkwardly on his feet.

'Everything OK?' she asks.

'How do I get back to my hotel? I mean, where are we?'

'You can get an Uber. This is Hoxton. It's not far.'

'Oh, yeah. Good idea,' he says, fishing his phone from his jeans. With a curt nod goodbye, he turns and bolts through the front door, pulling it shut behind him.

She relaxes. *That was easier than I thought.* 'Coffee, Boo?' she says.

'Please,' he replies, the sound of the detective's voice chirping in the background.

In the kitchen she scoops two large spoonfuls of French blend, drops them into a cafetière and pours the steaming water over the top. Boo's dream, and the reference to 'him' has unsettled her. She rubs her arms and leans on the counter, waiting for the coffee to brew. Zach has been dead for five years, but grief never leaves you. It evolves and becomes something else. In both their lives Zach's ghost seems forever ever-present. They loved him. He loved them. And then, one day, he was gone. Just like that. Mallory rubs her arms. The coffee is ready, and she grabs two mugs from a cupboard and pours. As she carries them across the living space, Boo hobbles out, supported by his canes.

'Quick. Come see. We have a potential new show plus we might be able to help the police.'

She follows him back into the bedroom and places the coffee on the desk. On the monitor, the detective is answering questions from reporters. Superimposed on the screen is a photo of a woman in her mid to late twenties.

'That picture is of a woman called Elena Zoric,' Boo says. 'She was a sex worker murdered a few days back.'

The tablets are already easing her headache. Mallory takes a sip of bitter hot liquid and feels herself coming to life. The photo of the woman disappears from the screen and reveals DI Grace Archer and DS Harry Quinn lurking in the background.

Boo leans in for a closer look. 'Isn't that . . .?'

'Yes, that's her,' she says.

'Two women, both sex workers were shot through the heart with a penetrating captive bolt gun. The other woman is Sally McGowan. We have a third, Mal.'

'Hannah Daysy,' she says.

'The very one.'

Mallory looks at the monitor. The detective sergeant is answering questions. She has no idea who he is but she knows Archer. She needs to tell her. She owes her that at least.

Chapter 19

DS LEE PARRY, HOLDING SEVERAL sheets of paper, is leading a press conference with Archer and Quinn standing like extras in the background. Archer has no interest in the limelight and has accepted Parry as the face of Elena's investigation. That said, his lack of organisation, stuttering delivery, and inability to give solid answers makes her regret not stepping forward.

Too late now.

Archer leans towards Quinn. 'Is this his first time?'

'Aye. No question.'

'He's quaking.'

'Dying on stage, you might say.'

Shame, Archer thinks, selfishly wondering if this display will contribute to her taking the SIO position for Elena.

'So . . . erm . . . just a few more questions to wrap up, please.'

'The murders are more than thirty years apart,' says a female reporter from the *Daily Mail*. 'Are we looking at an older killer, perhaps someone in their sixties or seventies?'

'Erm . . . we could be looking at someone older, that's true . . . but we don't know his age yet . . . obviously. Initially, we thought it was a copycat killer, but we've struck the idea off the list.'

Wouldn't have shared that, Archer thinks.

'You're sure it's a man?' the reporter asks.

'It's looking that way.'

'One more question.'

Parry nods.

'What do you say to London's female sex workers? A killer is on the streets. Do they need to be more vigilant, and can they trust the police?'

'Well, of course they can trust the police. We're not . . . ha-ha . . . monsters . . . we're the . . . good guys.'

Snorts of derisive laughter from the audience. Parry tugs at his collar and clears his throat. 'OK. That's it for today. Thank you.'

'He's as good as six feet under,' Quinn whispers.

Parry turns and walks towards Archer and Quinn. His face is red, his brow glistening.

'How was that?' he asks.

'Smooth. You did all right, mate,' says Quinn.

Archer's phone rings. She doesn't recognise the number. She answers.

'DI Archer. It's Mallory Jones. Don't hang up. Please.'

Archer's jaw tightens. She ends the call. Mallory Jones has been a royal pain in Archer's backside since they first met eighteen months back during the @nonymous murders. Jones is a true crime podcaster and self-styled 'investigator' with too much time on her hands. One of her most popular shows is the 'The Girl Who Lived', a crass tabloid headline attributed to the twelve-year-old Grace Archer who had been abducted by child killer, Bernard Morrice. Jones's story, and subsequent successes with the @nonymous murders, the Aaron Cronin case and the Silent Man killings, had earned Archer a cult following. One that she did not want anything to do with.

Jones calls back but Archer rejects the call and blocks the number.

'Who was that?' Quinn asks.

'No one of any importance,' she replies.

Quinn's phone rings. He answers. ''Scuse me,' he says and steps away.

Parry is still hanging around. 'I was rubbish, wasn't I?'

Archer begins to feel a margin of pity for him. 'It was your first time, don't beat yourself up.'

'I need to do better for the next time.'

'Let's hope the next time is when we're closing this case.'

Parry considers this. His expression brightens. 'I suppose. Between us we should be able nip this in the bud sharpish.'

Archer's margin of pity narrows to nothing.

Quinn finishes on the call and rejoins them.

'I gotta shoot,' Parry says, turning his back. 'Later,' he adds with a wave.

'Fancy a coffee?' Quinn asks.

'Sure.'

They grab a table at Café Koha in St Martin's Court, sitting outside in the shade between the stage doors of the Wyndham's and Noël Coward theatres. Quinn orders a coffee, and Archer, a tea. Both also ask for cold water. Archer thinks Quinn is not himself. He said little on the walk to the café and is weirdly avoiding eye contact. She's about to ask him what's up when her phone rings. It's Clare Pierce.

'Clare, how are you, and how's Richard?'

'He's comfortable. Sleeping at the moment, thankfully.'

'How're you holding up?'

'It's fun. I really recommend it.' She begins to chuckle, which becomes a belly laugh, followed by a sob.

'Sorry, I shouldn't have asked.'

Pierce composes herself. 'Don't be. I should be sorry. This process has affected my head a little. I'm drained and feel a little wired.'

115

Archer can hear the exhaustion in the CI's voice. 'Poor man. Considering what I've put him through in the past ... he deserves better.'

By 'the past', Pierce is referencing her affair with DI Andy Rees, a corrupt Met detective that Archer had sent down almost two years back. Pierce knew nothing of Rees's extracurricular activities, yet when his arrest was made she was unfairly put under the spotlight.

'I saw the press conference this morning,' Pierce says.

'Not our finest moment,' Archer says, drily.

'Never mind about that. Listen, I may have a lead for you . . .'

Archer perks up, and gestures for Quinn to come closer and listen.

The coffee, tea and a bottle of water arrive. The waiter places them on the table, and pours the water into two clean glasses.

Archer mouths a thanks.

Clare continues, 'Years ago when I started at the Met, I was indirectly involved in a case to do with a missing girl. A sex worker. This morning when I heard the name, Sally, it triggered something, and I remembered. She was so young, you see. It moved us all. There was a Sally who worked in Soho who went missing at the same time your victim disappeared. It has to be her. It can't be a coincidence. I did some digging. She lived in Stuart Mill House in King's Cross. What an awful place that was. Full of drug addicts and dropouts. Sally was reported missing by a woman she lived with. I don't remember her name. That's it.' Pierce takes two tired breaths and scoffs. 'At the time the detectives were all male, and they didn't much care for women in general. Despite Sally's age, she was a sex worker, and as far as they were concerned, she was a low priority, or probably no priority. So I really doubt that anything

116

was recorded or properly followed up. But that's for you to find out.'

'Clare, this is really helpful.'

'Good luck with it. Let me know how you get on.'

'Will do. You take care, and best to Richard. If there's anything you need . . .'

Pierce thanks her and they say their goodbyes. Out of the corner of her eye, Archer sees someone approaching their table.

'Hey,' says Quinn.

Archer pockets her phone and looks up at the new arrival. Her stomach clenches. She turns to Quinn, eyes flaring. 'You have got to be kidding me,' she says.

'Hello, DI Archer. Nice to see you again,' says Mallory Jones.

Chapter 20

'WHAT'S GOING ON, HARRY?' ARCHER asks Quinn.

'Mal called me,' says Quinn. 'She has information.'

'Mal called you?' Archer repeats, wondering why she has his personal number.

Archer turns to Jones. 'Information, Miss Jones? That's terrific. I'm very happy for you. I'm sure your listeners will enjoy hearing whatever exaggerated horseshit you broadcast.'

Jones's jaw tightens. 'We only broadcast facts. We don't exaggerate anything.'

Archer looks at Quinn and recalls a conversation from some time back. '"Melodramatic" was the expression you used. Am I right?'

Jones turns to look at Quinn. 'Melodramatic?'

Quinn shrugs and shifts on his chair. 'I might have said that. But I enjoy your podcasts, Mal. You know that. Besides, don't they need a theatrical element to keep your listeners engaged?'

Archer blinks, eyes darting between Quinn and Jones, as it dawns on her there is more to this relationship than she is aware. 'Are you two . . . involved with each other?'

'No!' blurts Quinn.

'It was only one night,' says Jones.

'Two, actually.'

'You were drunk and fell asleep the second time,' Jones replies, tartly.

'This person has made a career out of exploiting people like me, and you literally get into bed with her,' Archer says.

'Who I sleep with is my business,' Quinn replies.

'I knew I was wasting my time,' says Jones.

'All right, look,' Quinn concedes. 'Let's just hear her out.'

Archer sighs and slides her gaze across the court at the mingling tourists and shoppers.

Jones stands. '"This person" is leaving. Good luck in whatever you do next. I'll contact DS Parry, as he seems to be in charge anyway.'

'Wait, Mal,' says Quinn. He turns to Archer. 'Grace. I think she's got something worth hearing.'

Archer thinks of the sixteen-year-old Sally McGowan and Elena, too. Who is she to discard any information just because of her dislike of the messenger? 'OK,' she sighs. 'Let's hear it.'

Jones hesitates. There's a defiant stiffness in her posture and for a moment it seems that she's going to leave, until she settles. Eyes down, mouth tight, she pulls back the chair and sits down. She removes several sheets of folded A4 paper from her bag and lays them out flat on the table. At the head of the first sheet is a name Archer doesn't recognise: Hannah Daysy.

'These are the research notes and transcript of a podcast my partner and I have put together,' says Jones.

'Who is Hannah Daysy?' Archer asks.

'Hannah was a down-on-her-luck mother. A woman of colour shunned by her family for getting pregnant at nineteen. She was a resilient and resourceful parent who thought working as a prostitute could help provide for her child. She was murdered with a single shot to the heart. Hannah Daysy was a victim ignored and forgotten by the police. One witness I interviewed recalls overhearing the detective investigating her case calling her "a black tart". Charming.'

Archer lifts the sheets from the table, and pages through them.

'What year was this?' Quinn asks.

'Nineteen ninety-one. And don't come at me with "the police have changed", Harry. We've had this discussion already.'

'I wasn't going to say anything.'

'Good, 'cause we both know it's bullshit.'

'Could you two please continue this "domestic" in your own time,' Archer says. 'Miss Jones, you have our attention.'

Jones levels her gaze with Archer. 'I'm not seventeen. If you insist on calling me "Miss Jones", then this meeting ends now.'

Besides being put in her place, Archer feels herself warming to the podcaster. 'Understood.'

'Bruce and I watched this morning's press conference. He immediately spotted the similarities with Hannah's murder. The bolt gun aside, all the victims have some sort of injury to the head.'

'He's disorientating his victims,' says Quinn.

'Makes them easier to kill,' says Archer.

'That was mine and Bruce's theory, too.'

Archer asks, 'So who's Bruce and what's his involvement in this?'

'He's my business partner. We set up the podcast together,' Jones replies and with her eyes cast down, adds, 'More importantly, he's family.'

Jones's phone rings. She glances at the screen. 'I have to take this. I'll be quick.' She gets up from the table. 'Hi, Tom. Thanks for calling back. Have you seen the news?'

121

When she's out of earshot, Quinn says, 'Mal had a brother, Zach. He and Bruce were married, until Zach was murdered by the Raincoat Killer.'

Archer recalls reading about the Raincoat Killer, who targeted drivers on remote, dark country roads. He would fake assistance to stranded drivers, and kill them, or he would run them off the road with his old, battered Jeep and finish them off if they survived the crash. To this day he remains at large.

'Zach and Bruce were travelling in stormy weather on a scenic route north through Yorkshire. Their car broke down. Zach stepped out and made an emergency call. Bruce slipped out of sight into the bushes for a wazz. Then a car approached. The driver got out. As Bruce finished up his business, he saw Zach fall to the ground. Standing over Zach was a figure in a long raincoat. Bruce ran to help him, but the killer climbed back into his vehicle. In the confusion Bruce didn't see the killer's car reversing at speed towards him. Broke his back and crushed his legs. He's lucky to be alive and can barely walk now.'

'Shit.'

'Say what you will about Mal, but the death of her brother broke her. She worshipped him. The reason she set up her podcast was to investigate his killer, to seek answers that the police seemed unwilling or incapable of finding. To date, our colleagues up North have still not apprehended him. It's been a year since his last kill and as far as I know the case is on ice for the time being.'

Jones is finishing up on her call and making her way back.

'It's all over the news. I'll call you later. Bye,' Jones says, ending the call.

Despite her misgivings, Archer finds herself warming to the podcaster and feels a pang of regret at how she has dismissed her without understanding her. She knows everyone has a story. She just didn't know the depth of Mallory's. Not a million miles from her own. But that doesn't excuse her exploitation of other true crimes, including the series she has done on Archer. Jones joins them at the table.

'I appreciate this, Mallory. I really do. Until we know more can you promise me you're not going to do a podcast on this case?' Archer says.

Jones considers Archer's request. 'One condition.'

'And what would that be?'

'When you crack it, I want exclusive access—'

'We can't give you access to files. Out of the question.'

'Not files. I want interviews with both of you, off the record.'

Archer looks at Quinn, who shrugs.

'Off the record and no mention of a contact in the police force.'

Jones grins. 'Deal.' She extends her hand.

Archer hesitates, but in the spirit of cooperation reaches across and shakes the podcaster's hand. On the walk back to the station, she unblocks Jones's number from her phone.

Chapter 21

East Ord, Berwick-Upon-Tweed

LILY MERCER DESPISES THE SUMMER and especially hates the heat, 'cause all she seems to do is sweat. Despite being fresh out of a lukewarm shower and wrapped only in a towel, she is still clammy and uncomfortable. She isn't a heavy girl by any means, although she has been described in school as 'curvy' and 'voluptuous' by one sixth former who was giving her the eye. She supposes she is but there's nothing wrong with that. Curvy is sexy according to the body positive hashtags on Insta and TikTok.

For the next hour she sits at the dressing table with the USB fan blowing cool air on her face that she painstakingly plasters with a pale foundation, decorates with two gloriously large eyelashes like the wings of a sparrow and completes by expertly painting her full lips a deep ruby red. She's an artist, if she says so herself. Sitting on the edge of her bed, she brushes and blow dries her thick auburn hair.

The dryer has raised the temperature in the room. Holding the fan close to her face, she opens the window and draws the curtains to keep out the sun, and the light. Across the hall she can hear Mum and Dad in their bedroom, Mum fussing over Dad (for a change) as he prepares for his big interview with the TV people. Holding her towel tight to her chest with one hand, she quietly turns the lock on her door. On her bedside table is a ring light. Lily switches it on and fixes it so that the soft white light bathes her pillow.

Lying back on her bed, she places the USB fan on her chest and enjoys the cool air on her hot face. Her phone is on the bedside table. She reaches for it, opens Instagram and flicks through her feed. Her friends are on holiday. God, when was the last time she was abroad? Five years ago, or more? When she was only eleven, perhaps? Shona is on a beach in Marbella wearing a flesh-coloured bikini. Lily scrunches her face. That is so not the right colour for her skin tone. 'Ugh, what on earth does she think she looks like?' she whispers. Pursing her lips, she scrolls up and sees Cassie swimming with dolphins in Florida. She feels a twist of envy and quickly flicks through other friends and influencers with their perfect lives. *Boring!* Swiping out of Insta, she selects the camera icon and taps the selfie button. Her face appears on the screen. She fixes her hair around her head so that it looks like a long wavy halo. *Très alluring.* She brings the lens closer and checks her make-up, her lashed-up eyes, her pale powdered skin and ruby red lips. She looks demurely into the camera and pouts. Holding the device a little further away she turns her head slightly to the left. She's about to tap the button but stops when she bursts into a fit of giggles. She waits for a moment to pass and composes herself. Peering up at the screen she resumes her sultry expression and takes several shots as she turns her head from left to right and back again. *And now for the money shot.* Lily undoes the towel and lets it fall open. With one arm pushing up her breasts and covering her nipples, she smiles with her eyes and bites her bottom lip like Marilyn Monroe. Using her thumb, she presses the camera button several times and with each click lowers her arm and reveals a little more of herself.

A pounding on her door startles her and makes her jump. 'Lily, are you ready yet?' Mum calls.

'Shit!' hisses Lily, suddenly remembering that she'd promised to go with them for Dad's big debut. 'Coming!' she calls, swinging off the bed and hurrying to the dresser.

'Well, hurry up, then!'

Lily tuts, rolls her eyes and pulls clean pants and a bra from her underwear drawer. Hanging on the wardrobe door is her floral fit and flare summer dress. As she gets dressed, she can hear her parents bickering and Dad's mobile phone pinging.

'They're ready for us!' Mum calls, as she hurries downstairs.

Lily slips into her white Adidas trainers, puts on her gold heart signet ring and checks the mirror one final time. Her phone pings with a message. It's him. John. She feels a fluttering in her tummy. In the hallway she hears Dad's heavy tread creaking on the floorboards as he exits the bedroom.

'I'm ready,' he calls, making his way down the stairs.

Lily opens John's message. The text says *Horny?*, and attached is a photo: a shirtless shot with chiselled pecs and steel abs. She smiles and bites her lip.

'For God's sake, Lily, will you hurry, please!' Mum calls.

Exiting the room she begins typing a message back to John.

It'll take more than a fit torso to set me on fire, babe. Let me go one better. You'll have to sing to see the rest . . .

Lily treads slowly down the stairs as she attaches one of her pics revealing a tiny bit of nipple.

The doorbell rings. She glances up from her device and sees Uncle Si, today's designated driver, through the mottled glass. 'Mum, it's Uncle Si,' she calls.

'Well, let him in, then!' Mum shouts from the kitchen at the rear of the house. Lily rolls her eyes and checks her texts. The coverage is rubbish here and picture is taking for ever to send. Hopping down the stairs, she holds the phone out of sight and opens the door. Mum's brother, Simon, smiles at her.

'Hi, Si.'

'How's my girl?' he asks, stepping inside.

'Forever oppressed by my "mommie dearest",' Lily replies, her eyebrows arched.

Si chuckles. 'As always, you have my sympathies,' he says conspiratorially.

She nods towards the kitchen. 'They're in there.'

Si winks and heads through. Lily checks her phone and tuts. The message is still sending. She shakes her head and joins her parents and Si in the kitchen. Dad is dressed in his best Marks & Spencer suit. Mum has brushed her grey hair and is wearing a buttoned-up white blouse, black skirt and tights (in this heat!). Also she looks like the help. 'Mum, why are you dressed like a waitress?' Lily asks.

Her mum opens her mouth to speak but instead just blinks, speechless and stung. A pang of guilt ripples through Lily. 'Wear your new Zara trousers. They're so nice on you. They'll look good with that blouse.'

'Do you think so?'

'I know so.'

'Isla, we don't have time,' says Dad.

Mum fidgets for a moment, uncertain.

'It'll only take a moment,' Lily says.

Dad sighs, lifts his phone from the kitchen worktop and checks it.

'Are they messaging again?' Mum asks.

'No,' he replies, placing the phone screen down on the worktop.

'Lily's right,' says Mum. 'I'll get changed in a jiffy.' She runs upstairs.

Dad and Si make small talk about cars and football. Lily retreats to the other side of the kitchen, where the signal is better, and checks her phone. To her dismay the message has failed to send. She presses the *retry* button and waits. Moments later Mum is back in the kitchen wearing the pale green slacks.

'Very nice, Isla,' says Si.

'You look great, Mum.'

Lily checks her phone delighted to see the message has at last gone.

'Shall we go?'

They make their way out of the kitchen, Dad leading the way. A phone pings back in the kitchen. 'Whose phone is that?' mum asks.

Dad is patting his pockets. 'Oh, it's mine,' he says, and returns to retrieve it.

'Are we ever going to leave this house?' Mum says.

Lily and Si laugh.

Dad returns, pocketing his phone in his jacket.

'Was that the producer wondering where we are?'

He shakes his head.

'Who was it, then?' Mum asks, following Dad out the door.

'Can we just go?' he replies, his face red and flustered.

Si leans towards Lily. 'They're a right pair, aren't they?'

Chapter 22

ARCHER AND QUINN HAVE READ through Mallory Jones's files on Hannah Daysy. She forwards them to Klara and when they are all in sync, they gather in the incident room.

'Before we start,' Klara says to Archer, 'how come Mallory Jones is on the scene? I mean, I'm surprised you guys are even talking, considering your history.'

'Harry engineered it,' Archer says.

'Did he now?' Klara gives Quinn a curious look. 'I didn't know you two were chums?'

'That's an understatement,' says Archer.

Klara's narrowed eyes dart between Archer and Quinn.

'He's been sleeping with her,' says Archer.

Quinn folds his arms and blows out a deep breath.

'Twice according to Harry. Once according to Mallory,' Archer teases.

Quinn looks at her with unimpressed hooded eyes.

'Mr Harry Quinn,' says Klara. 'You are such a dark horse.'

'Women find me attractive. What can I say? It's a burden I long ago learned to live with.'

'We all have crosses to bear,' says Archer. 'And some are heavier than others.'

'Amen to that,' Quinn replies.

Archer wipes clean the whiteboard with a cloth and grabs a black marker. 'OK. Let's get some thoughts down.' She draws four vertical lines creating three columns. At the top of each one she writes the name of the victims: Elena Zoric, Sally McGowan, Hannah Daysy. Underneath she writes their ages, where they lived and the date and location of their murder. 'All young women with the exception of Sally who was a teenager. Elena was twenty-nine; Hannah, twenty-six. The common thread is they're all sex workers. Young women trying to survive during difficult times in their lives.' Archer steps back and examines the board. 'Sally and Hannah are from broken homes. Alone in the world. Elena came to this country as a trafficked teenage sex worker . . . yet she's in a stable relationship with Marianne.'

Archer writes *Killer* on the board and underlines it. 'What do we know about the killer so far?'

'He's an older bloke, a client maybe, a regular one,' says Quinn.

Archer writes a list adding *Client* with a question mark, *male*, and in parentheses writes *60/70s*.

'He's a stalker. Maybe watching them for periods at a time,' says Klara.

Archer writes *Stalker* on the board. 'That would tie in with the suspect who was following Elena.'

Quinn says, 'I checked to see if Elena had made any complaints to the police about getting aggro but there was nothing.'

'Klara, would you be able to see if there are any historical reports of Sally or Hannah getting aggro from a client? Might be a needle in a haystack but could be worth a look.'

'On the list,' replies Klara, typing notes on her laptop.

'I'd hazard a guess and say he's probably white,' says Quinn.

'Why do you think that?'

'Just an instinct, I suppose. If he's been killing for years then it would be easier for a white man to fall under the radar than a black man.'

Archer folds her arms and considers this for a moment. 'I agree, but it's too early to determine. We'll leave it open for now. What else do we think?'

'I suppose the question is, why is he killing prostitutes?' says Quinn. 'Is it some sort of moral crusade?'

'Then why not kill pimps?' offers Klara.

'He hates women, sex workers especially,' says Quinn.

'Why?' Archer asks.

'Maybe he's religious. Maybe he thinks he's doing the world a favour.'

They're quiet for a moment, processing their thoughts.

'Why doesn't he have sex with them?'

'He's impotent. And angry as a result,' Quinn suggests.

Archer writes *Impotent* and *Angry* both with question marks under the killer's profile list.

Klara says, 'Why such a long break between killings?' She's paging through data on her laptop. 'From what I can see, there are no records of any similar murders between Hannah's death in 1991 and Elena's this year.'

'Assuming those murders have been recorded,' says Archer. 'People go missing all the time. Perhaps their bodies have not yet been discovered.'

'I'll need to do a proper analysis,' says Klara. 'Chilling thought to think there could be bodies of missing sex workers concealed around London,' she adds.

Archer ponders this momentarily. 'That's the world we live in. Could you look into instances of sex workers reported missing?'

'Already added to my to list,' Klara replies.

133

Archer's phone pings with a message. She can see Mallory Jones's number pop up on the screen. She opens the message.

Good to talk today. I hope we can bury the hatchet at last. Here's the links to the episode on Hannah Daysy. Any questions let me know.

Archer types back a thanks. 'I have the link to the podcast,' she says.

A knock on the door. DC Marian Phillips enters carrying an iPad. 'Two updates I thought you'd want to know about. We have ID on the man who followed Elena from the restaurant. His name is Hassan Bilal. He doesn't fit the early profile of an older white man but perhaps he's seen something. We have officers on their way to pick him up now.'

'Good work,' says Archer.

'Also, something important from CSI. They found flecks of green paint in the Persian rug that Sally McGowan was wrapped in.' Phillips shows a magnified picture to Archer. 'I recognised the tones. I painted my bedroom that very same colour. I asked CSI to do an analysis, and the report just came back with confirmation that it is Farrow and Ball's French Grey.'

'Right,' says Archer, who thinks maybe Phillips has lost the plot.

'Someone else has this paint on their living room wall. Someone I interviewed not two days ago . . .' Phillips leaves the sentence hanging, her eyes sliding to each of them like a party quizmasters waiting for one of them to scream out the answer.

'Are you going to tell us or what?' asks Quinn.

Archer takes the iPad and uses her finger to make the paint flecks bigger. She can see the colour in full and realises now where she has seen it. 'Miles Davenport's living room,' she says.

Phillips is smiling as if she's just won the bingo.

Archer hands the iPad back to Phillips. 'Good work, Marian. Let's get him in for questioning immediately.'

'Pleasure,' she replies, and leaves the room.

Archer presses *play* on the podcast app and turns up the volume.

Sombre music plays momentarily before Mallory Jones's voice speaks.

'The name Hannah Daysy probably means nothing to you today. Back in 1991, it meant something to a small group of people. Hannah's tiny circle of friends. Her estranged family. But most of all, it meant something to Anthony Daysy, the son she left behind. The devoted eight-year-old who adored his mummy, and she in turn, adored him . . .'

Chapter 23

Hannah

1991, London

*G*ET OUT, HANNAH. GET OUT ... *RUN!*
    The black cylindrical steel baton slams against her nose, crushing the cartilage. The shock stuns her.

His hands are on her. She is in a fugue, but adrenaline is kicking in.

She reaches for him, nails scratching his face. He swears, his grip loosening.

Arm twisted, she yanks the handle and pushes the car door open with all her strength. Hannah clambers from the car, legs kicking, arms flailing, his hands snatching at her T-shirt, trying to haul her back inside.

'Help me!' she cries into the desolate night.

Blood spills from her nostrils onto her lips and into her mouth. The coppery taste makes her gag. Her breath is short, wheezy, an asthma attack imminent. *Not now! Please not now. Inhaler! Where is it?* Her bag is on the floor of the car. *Fuck!* Her top rips, she falls onto her back on the gritty road. No light. Darkness everywhere. The sky is starless, the moon has abandoned her. She slides backwards, stones and glass cutting into her flesh. Twisting onto all fours, she scrambles away, widening the distance between herself and the Cortina, legs bare, one foot shoeless, knickers half on, half off. Short rasps of air puff from her shitty lungs, her head throbs from the knuckles that had slammed her temple moments before he broke her nose with the steel baton. Her heart is pounding, her throat hurts.

She manages to push herself up. Miracle of miracles.

'Help!' Her cry is hoarse, swallowed by the vast blackness. The narrow lane ahead seems to stretch into infinity. *Oh God!* No one around. No one to help her.

She hears the car door creak open and his boots crunching on the stony surface. The door slams shut, a match strikes. She tries to pick up her pace, but her tight, whistling airways are saying, *No, stop, girl, time to rest, give yourself a moment*, but she is charged, on fire, and desperate.

'Come back, I haven't paid you yet.'

She shakes her head. She doesn't want the money. She just wants to go home, to be safe, and warm, with her boy . . . *Oh God* . . . He's the reason she's here. She's doing this for him, her little Anthony. She wanted him to have a better life than she had, to never go without, like she had. What would he think if he saw the state she was in now? Battered, bloody and miles from home. She chokes back a tear. *Oh, Ant* . . . She promises herself this will be the last. No more. Starting tomorrow she'll look for a proper job. The money would be less, but they'd make do. Yes, they'd make do.

She stumbles on and shoots back a glance. He's leaning against the car smoking a cigarette. In one hand is the baton.

'I won't tell anyone,' she calls.

He chuckles. 'Yes, you will.'

His name is John. That's what he told her, but she didn't believe him. They were all called John, or Joe, or Jim. Always a name beginning with a J. Why was that? As punters go, he seemed OK, though. Friendly enough, clean. They'd agreed a price and she got into his car. As soon as they were out of the city, he changed. He went quiet and weird, like he was high or something.

Hannah lets out a sob and presses on, limping over tiny stones and bits of glass that cut into the soft pads of her bare feet. She tries to inhale through her nose, but the blood is clogging it. She sucks air in desperation and hurries away, her heart thudding weakly like a wounded rabbit's. Her toes slam on something hard, electric pain shoots through her foot and leg. She yelps, trips and falls to her knees. She'd hit a jagged rock the size of a fist.

She hears his footsteps approaching rapidly.

Her eyes widen. Her fingers grasp the rough cool surface of the rock. He is close. She braces herself. She hears the clatter of copper coins scatter around her.

'Told you I'd pay you,' he says.

His warm palm rests on her head. She shudders. Stinging tears fill her eyes. His fingers run over her scalp like spider legs. She whimpers and leans forward. 'I'll just go now,' she says, her chest wheezing like broken bagpipes. He yanks her by the hair and pulls her up. He presses against her and she feels his hardness, pushing against her hip. Her stomach turns, she pulls away from him, anger and disgust, flames searing her courage. She swings the rock at his head and connects with his ear. He stumbles sideways, clutching the side of his head, the baton dropping from his hand.

'You fucking bitch!' he cries.

She backs away but before she can escape he rounds on her, punching her hard in the stomach. She gasps, doubles over, her knees wobbling as she crumples to the ground, the rock falling from her grip.

He straddles her and rips her T-shirt, exposing her chest.

'No, please. My little Ant. He's waiting . . .'

His eyes are wild, hungry. He places the steel on her chest. It feels cool on her skin.

'Please, no,' she says, choking out a sob as she pushes desperately and weakly against his weight. The baton has some sort of lever at the top. He presses it and she hears a loud bang. She shudders, confusion clouding her mind at the icy cold sensation in her chest.

In her final moments as the world goes dark, she sees the smiling face of little Ant. *Don't forget me, baby. Please don't forget me . . .*

Chapter 24

MILES DAVENPORT IS SITTING AT the table in an interview room. Archer glances at him when she enters. His face is pale, his eyes wide and blinking. Despite that, there is a trickiness to his expression, which indicates he is going to fight his corner. Archer feels her pulse racing. *Bring it on.*

Neither Archer nor Quinn greets him, an agreement they had come to before making their entrance.

Davenport's brief is a man with a long face and a dour expression. Wearing round spectacles and an oversized pinstripe suit, he bears an unsettling resemblance to a younger Jacob Rees-Mogg. His name is Colin Bakewell. A suburban name in comparison to his older doppelgänger.

'Is my client being charged with a crime? If not, why exactly is he here?' asks Bakewell, in an accent that is pure South London. It wrongfoots Archer momentarily.

'We have questions regarding the remains of a young woman found in 48 Pleshey Road.'

'My client has no connection with that address.'

'Shall we begin?' Archer says, ignoring his assertion and turning to Davenport.

Davenport shoots a look at Bakewell who nods a confirmation at him.

'How old are you, Miles?' Archer asks.

'He's already answered those questions when he got here. You know how old he is,' replies Bakewell.

Archer waits for Davenport to answer.

'Fifty-two.'

'Have you always lived in London.'

'Mostly.'

'Where else have you lived?'

'I was born in Berkshire. Brought up in Caversham.'

'Nice part of the country. Posh . . . ish,' says Quinn.

Davenport shrugs.

'How long have you lived in Pleshey Road?'

'Twenty years or so.'

'And before that?'

'Various locations in North London.'

'You know the remains we found belong to a Sally McGowan?'

'I've read the papers and seen the news.'

'She was sixteen when she was murdered. If Sally was alive today, you and she would be the same age.'

Davenport frowns at Archer.

'Imagine if she was alive and well and happy, living her best life with a successful career, a mother, or both. Imagine.'

'I'm not sure what point you're making,' says Bakewell.

'Have you ever met Sally?' Quinn asks. 'Like, in the flesh?'

Davenport flinches at the suggestion, 'No, of course not!'

'But you've seen her. Been close to her.'

Davenport's face glistens, his breathing quickens like a rabbit's, caught in a trap. He turns to his brief. 'I've never met her. I don't know what they're talking about.'

Archer takes out the photo of the Persian rug that contained Sally's remains. 'Recognise this rug, Miles?'

'Why should I?'

'It's a similar style to the rugs in your home.'

'Lots of people have Persian rugs.'

Archer takes out a print depicting the magnified shot of the carpet with the flecks of green paint. 'This is a magnified picture of the rug. It contains residues of paint. Our analysis shows the paint is Farrow and Ball's French Grey.'

Davenport blinks three times, his face blank, the colour draining rapidly from it.

'Miles, this is your rug, isn't it?' Archer asks.

He swallows and seems to shrink into himself. Tears fill his eyes and he begins to cry.

'Speak to us, Miles,' Archer says gently.

He drops his face into his hands and weeps some more.

Archer catches Bakewell rolling his eyes. 'Can I have a few moments with my client, please?'

Archer nods.

'Taking a break in the interview,' she says, pressing the *pause* button.

'Miles, can we get you a drink of something?' Archer asks.

'Tea, please. Milk, two sugars.'

Archer exits the interview room with Quinn. At the vending machine in the corridor outside, Archer punches the code for Davenport's tea. 'Drink?' she asks Quinn.

'Not for me, thanks. So, what're your thoughts?'

'He's guilty of something. What that is, I'm not entirely sure.'

'Do you think he killed Sally?'

'It's possible. Do you?'

The styrofoam cup drops into its slot and begins to fill with hot liquid.

'Same. I'm thinking he started young, killing her at sixteen. Got a taste for it, and went on a spree over the coming years.'

'Why move the body to the attic room of Bob Innes's house?'

'He lives in a big house. Maybe he was storing her as a souvenir.'

'Charming thought. I'm not so sure, though. Something's not adding up. Moving the body to the house opposite to where you live is just so . . . amateurish.' Archer takes the tea from the machine.

The interview room door opens and the pound-shop Rees-Mogg steps out. 'He's ready.'

Archer hands across the tea and presses the recording. 'Resuming the recording with Miles Davenport. Present are Detective Inspector Grace Archer, Detective Sergeant Harry Quinn, Miles Davenport and his solicitor, Colin Bakewell.'

'I didn't kill her,' Davenport begins, 'I swear. This is all a big mistake, and I'm sorry. Truly sorry.'

'Start from the beginning, please, Miles,' says Archer.

The suspect sips his tea and takes a moment to compose himself. 'It was two weeks ago. I was doing some renovations in my own attic. I want to sell up, you see. House prices are so good at the moment. My mortgage is paid off and with further work I could easily make over 1.6 million, according to the estate agent. I could retire on that.' Davenport trembles and wraps his podgy hands around the cup. 'I decided to get my loft converted to a fourth bedroom with an en-suite. I'd never really been up there. The only access is with a ladder. There's no electrics and no floorboards, so it's never really been useful for anything. When I moved in all those years ago, I looked in and saw a massive roll of loft insulation. I remember being perched on the ladder, pointing my torch and seeing it for the first time. It seemed to glow in the darkness and I recall feeling an odd shiver down my spine, which I could not explain. Anyway, the loft was a project for a later time so I climbed back down and set about doing up my home, living my life, all those years not realising that she was there.'

'Do you mean Sally McGowan?'

He nods his head and says, 'She was inside the loft insulation.'

'When did you discover her?'

'As I mentioned, two weeks back. I started clearing out the loft. I rolled the insulation across to the hatch and begin to cut at it so that I could squeeze it through. I trimmed enough off and pushed the remains through the hole. It unfurled like a coiled snake and from its clutches, she fell to the landing floor. I peered down from the hatch wondering what the hell I was looking at. It looked like some old, stained clothes at first, but then I saw the bones. I climbed down in a state of disbelief, praying that this was in my imagination, but it wasn't. There was a dead body on my landing floor.' Davenport drops his head and runs a hand through his thinning dark hair.

'Why didn't you call the police?'

'I panicked. So much went through my head. My house, my retirement. No one would buy this house if they knew a dead body had been found hidden here.'

'So you moved her?' Archer asks.

'I know it was the wrong thing to do but I had no choice. I thought I'd move it to Bob's house and let the body be discovered there. As long as she was found what did it matter?'

From the corner of her eye, Archer can see Quinn shaking his head. 'It matters because she was murdered and a crime scene with vital evidence has been tampered with.'

'I'm sorry, I wasn't thinking.'

Quinn chips in, 'On the contrary. You were thinking. You were thinking of your money and your retirement. That's where your priorities lay.'

'I can't explain it!' Davenport protests. 'I wasn't thinking logically. Besides, I hadn't been well.'

'Being unwell doesn't cut it, Miles,' snaps Quinn.

'What did you do with cut-offs from the insulation?' Archer asks.

'I bagged them and put them in the rubbish. They were taken by the bin men the morning after.'

'When did you move the body to Mr Innes's property?'

'The following evening. I rolled her up in an old rug and stored her in the spare bedroom. It was terrible. I couldn't sleep. I wracked my brains trying to figure out what to do. I had to get her out of my house. There was no way I could drive her and dump her where I'd get seen on CCTV or something. Bob's place had been empty for a few years, and it seemed to be the ideal spot. So that night I carried her inside the rug – she was surprisingly light – into the back of my car and parked outside Bob's place. I hurried back to my house, waited and watched the street from behind the curtains. When all the lights were off, and I was sure no one was watching I carried her from the car. Using Mrs Dunmore's spare key, I entered the house and took her upstairs.'

'Why did you contact Dixy, the content creator?' Archer asks.

Davenport rubs his arms and rocks on his chair. 'Oh God! I've really screwed up.' He pauses before answering. 'The weeks passed, and I couldn't sleep knowing what I'd done, knowing also that she was there in the attic watching me. I wanted her gone. I wanted someone else to take the blame and I had to figure out how I could do that. I'd seen a social media post about Dixy's Night Terrors videos. I thought he was an utter idiot and could take the fall.'

'Did you offer him money to burn the house?'

Davenport shifts in his chair and hesitates before answering. 'Not to begin with. I was expecting him to film the body, post it on his social media and for the police to arrest him. It seems to have taken weeks for the police to take any notice.'

'How much did you offer to pay Dixy?'

'Fifteen hundred pounds.'

'Did you pay it?'

'No.'

'Why?'

'Because he became obsessed with her. She became his muse.'

He scoffs at this. 'What the hell is wrong with people today?'

I might ask the same of you, Archer thinks.

'And then we came knocking,' Quinn says.

Davenport sighs.

'Who did you buy your house from?' Archer asks.

'It was so long ago; I don't recall their names. It was Foxtons agency, though. It was a shell of a place when I moved in. It was disgusting inside as if it had been a doss house for years.'

Archer sighs and looks at Quinn. He understands they're done here for the time being. He nods and Archer ends the interview and the recording.

'It's far from over yet, but for now, you're free to go, Mr Davenport.'

Chapter 25

LILY MERCER'S DAD, BARRY, IS taking part in a crime documentary for a TV production company called Big Stories, who, in her humble opinion, create tacky true crime TV shows for some satellite channel that no one ever watches. For as long as she can remember, Dad has been the local butcher, yet prior to that, and prior to Lily being born, he had been a constable here in Berwick-Upon-Tweed before moving around the country working as an officer in different towns and cities. Lily never knew why he left the police force. It was a subject that was never up for discussion at home. She'd overheard Mum and Si talking about him being burned out. That's all she knew. He'd been involved in a murder case here in the town that had become the stuff of legend over the years. A local woman, Julia Morris, the landlady of a pub, had gone missing. They'd spent a week looking for her with no luck until one day Dad saw the woman's cousin, Jennifer Morris, drag a heavy suitcase on wheels across town and up to the station. To most people it must have seemed like she was going on a trip, but Dad had tried to make small talk with her and when she didn't respond he thought her behaviour a little strange. So, he followed her into the station where she stood at the edge of the platform. It was then he noticed the blood dripping from the bottom of the case.

They are filming on Platform 2 of Berwick-Upon-Tweed station, in a spot sectioned off from the rest of the platform. There are rail travellers at the other end, watching with interest as they wait for the next train. Likewise, people watch from the platform opposite. Enlisted as extras, Lily is sitting in between her mum and Uncle Si on a grey metal bench, thankfully shaded from the hot afternoon sun. Dad is having his clammy face powdered while being briefed by some skinny dude called Felix dressed in black jeans, a black T-shirt and an earpiece hanging out of his ear. Close by, with his face buried in sheets of A4 paper, is the presenter, a middle-aged man with a dour expression, thinning salt and pepper hair and a jutting square jaw. Mum leans across and whispers into Lily's ear.

'Didn't he used to play that detective in that BBC programme?'

'What detective in what TV show?'

'You know the one.'

Lily purses her lips. 'I don't, Mum. He's more your generation than mine.'

'Wait!' Mum says excitedly. 'I'm sure he's done *Strictly* too.'

Lily watches *Strictly* religiously but still doesn't recognise him.

'Ooh, I think I might ask him,' Mum says, standing.

Mortified, Lily grabs Mum's elbow and pulls her down. 'Don't, Mum! You're so embarrassing.'

Mum sits back down and says, 'Now that I think about it, I'm sure he was from the early days when Bruce was still doing it.'

Lily scrunches her face as she tries to imagine the dour-looking man dressed in sequins and spinning around the *Strictly* dance floor. Somehow, she just can't picture it.

Mum turns to Si. 'Si, isn't that thingy from the detective show and *Strictly*?'

Uncle Si narrows his eyes at the celeb. 'I think you're right, Isla. He's definitely Thingy from *Thingy*.'

Lily giggles. Si loves to tease her mum.

Mum tuts. 'Anyway, he looks much older in real life. Greyer than I expected. His hair, I mean.'

The dude called Felix, who seems to be in charge, begins to herd people around Dad. He turns to the presenter and says, 'All good, Lawrence?'

The *Thingy* detective cum former *Strictly* contestant called Lawrence looks up from his papers and nods.

'Now that I think about it,' says Mum. 'I'm sure he went out in an early round. Like week two or three.'

Lily is confused. 'What're you talking about?'

She nods at the celeb. 'Him, Lawrence Whatshisname. He wasn't a very good dancer. A bit stiff and robotic.'

Lily rolls her eyes.

'Quiet, everyone,' says Felix as Lawrence stands opposite Dad, nodding a hello.

Lily's phone pings loudly.

Felix turns to glare at her. 'Everyone's phones off, please.'

'Sorry,' says Lily, turning her phone to silent. She glances at the message. It's from Gemma.

Still on for tonight?

Lily feels an excited tingling in her tummy. She types a message in return: *Can't wait!*

Mum leans across. 'Put your phone away. They're filming,' she says.

Lily tuts and catches Uncle Si looking her way. He smiles and winks. She smiles back at him.

They had been instructed to not watch the interview and to just act like regular people waiting for a train. Lily, Mum and Si are staring across the platform listening to Lawrence

Whatshisname begin. She side-eyes her mum, who is sitting unnaturally bolt upright stiff as a poker. Lily snorts, suppressing the giggles.

'The year is 1995, the date is the fourteenth of August,' says Lawrence in a solemn voice. 'The location is Berwick-Upon-Tweed, a pretty Northumbrian town, south of the Scottish Borderlands. Thirty-eight-year-old Julia Morris has been missing for one week. Her husband and kids are frantic with worry. The police are baffled. Gossip and suspicion rumble throughout the townsfolk. No one knows where Julia could be. She was a loving mother, a caring wife and the landlady of a popular local pub. She was close to her extended family, including her aunts, uncles and cousins. One, in particular, Jennifer Kyle. Barry Mercer was a constable, here at Berwick-Upon-Tweed, at the time and knew both women. Barry, tell us about Julia and Jennifer.'

'I know what you did, Barry Mercer!' a man's voice bellows.

A deafening silence follows. All heads turn to look at a man standing on the platform, fists bunched, face like thunder, eyes wild and staring directly at Dad. Lily has never seen him before. He's a black man, in his fifties or older.

'Tell them what you did!' the stranger shouts.

Whispers spread across the platform.

'I'm sorry, do I know you?' Dad asks.

'We've met,' the man spits.

Lily notices Felix directing the cameraman to focus on the stranger.

'I've never met you,' says Dad.

'People are dead because of you!'

A collective gasp ripples through the crowd. Dad's face reddens.

'What's he talking about, Mum?' Lily asks, her stomach clenching.

'Pay him no heed. He's just some madman.'

The stranger points his finger at Dad. 'I see you, Barry Mercer. I know what you did.'

'Get out of here or I'll call the police!' Dad shouts.

The cameras are filming the entire exchange. Felix is watching it unfold as if he has just landed an incredible scoop. 'What's your name?' Felix asks.

The stranger ignores him, his eyes full of hatred, never leaving Dad's. Mum stands up quickly and hurries towards the stranger. 'You get away from here now or I will call the police.'

'And what will they do?' the stranger says. He turns his eyes back to Dad. 'What have they ever done?'

Lily tenses but feels Uncle Si's arm around her shoulder. 'Forget him. It's just some crazy,' he says.

The stranger retreats slowly. 'I see you, Barry Mercer. I see you!' he says. His eyes fall on Lily and linger momentarily, a frown creasing his face. She shudders and feels Si's comforting arm squeeze her gently. And then the stranger turns, disappears into the crowd, exiting the station.

'Who was that?' Lawrence asks Dad. 'Is he connected to Julia Morris or Jennifer Kyle?'

Dad tugs at his shirt collar. He's shocked by the stranger's outburst and accusation. 'I have no idea who he is.'

'Maybe we can take a break before continuing,' Felix suggests.

'Please,' says Dad.

The remainder of the afternoon is awkward. Dad struggles through the interview, tripping over his answers and losing the thread on multiple occasions. Felix and Lawrence's patience wears thin. At one point, they huddle together, leaving Dad alone and wringing his hands. Lily overhears Felix telling

153

Lawrence that this isn't working, just to wrap it up. Lily feels so sorry for her dad. The stranger, whoever he was, and his outburst, had clearly shaken him. When it is over, they shuffle to Uncle Si's car, a silence so palpable you could slice it with a knife. Her parents, and Uncle Si for that matter, are not the type of people who discuss awkward, embarrassing subjects, especially in front of Lily.

'Where to now?' Si asks, as they strap themselves in.

Lily feels her hackles rising. She wants to talk about what happened. She needs answers. 'Who was that man?' she demands.

Her father sits quietly, looking out the window in the front passenger seat and does not reply.

'Let's go to the restaurant as planned,' says Mum, ignoring Lily's question. 'The table's booked. It'll do us good. What do you think, Barry?'

'I just asked a question!' cries Lily.

Mum glares at her. Dad's silence lingers. 'Take us to the restaurant, please, Simon.'

Lily expels an exasperated breath and swears quietly.

Mum leans across. 'You mind your language, young lady!'

Chapter 26

IN HER SECOND INTERVIEW OF the day, Archer sits in the same room where she and Quinn had interviewed Miles Davenport only two hours earlier. She has brought a laptop, which she opens and connects to the network as Quinn makes small talk, putting the suspect, Hassan Bilal, at ease for the time being. Bilal fidgets nervously opposite them. He's a round man, with an anxious expression.

Archer takes out her phone and checks her messages. She had texted and called DS Parry earlier to say that Bilal was being brought in for questioning. She'd suggested he led the interview considering Elena was officially his investigation. Parry had not responded to either request. She had eventually tracked him down at home. The conversation had not gone well.

'I've been trying to get hold of you,' she said.

'It's my day off today. I've been on the golf course. No signal. You know how it is.'

'No, I don't know how it is,' she replied tersely.

He chuckled. 'It's a bloke thing.'

Archer had to bite her tongue. 'I need two things from you.'

'Only two?' Archer notes the sarcasm in his tone but ignores it, for now.

'Did you talk to Elena's former pimps, the Kowalskis?'

'Yeah. I met with them. They know nothing but seemed pleased to hear about Elena's murder.'

Archer feels her muscles coiling.

'You said two things.'

'Can you come in? We've found the man who followed Elena Zoric from the Southern Fried Chicken Shop. We've brought him in for questioning. Maybe you'd like to lead the interview.'

'No can do. Got stuff on.'

'What "stuff" is more important than finding Elena's murderer, DS Parry?'

'Can you reschedule for tomorrow or the day after?'

'No I can't. He's in the building. If we let him walk, he might just do a runner and we don't want that, do we?'

'I can't say that we do.'

'Harry and I will do the interview. The report will be waiting for you when you return tomorrow.' She'd ended the call without saying goodbye. 'Dickhead,' she said.

Quinn introduces himself and Archer. 'Mr Bilal – mind if I call you Hassan?' he asks.

'Is OK.'

'Hassan, are you sure you don't want a brief present? It may help you in the long term.'

'Help me why? I have done nothing wrong.'

'As you wish.'

Archer brings up the CCTV recording from the restaurant. She shoots a glance at Quinn and nods. Quinn presses *record* and states the time, date and the names of the people present.

'What's your date of birth, Hassan?' Quinn asks.

'Twenty-fourth of December, 1975.'

'Are you married?'

'Yes.'

'Children?'

'Two. Daughters.'

'Nice. What ages?'

'Seventeen and fourteen.'

'Teenagers can be a handful, no?'

'They are good girls.'

'I'm sure they are.'

Quinn's tone and its implication pulls Archer from the preparation of the CCTV footage for viewing. Quinn is an old hand at psyching out and unsettling suspects. The air crackles between Quinn and Bilal. A beat of silence dies like the last ember of a fire.

'What do you do for a living?' Quinn asks.

'Taxi driver. Uber.'

'How long have you been doing that?'

'Four years.'

'Enjoy it?'

'It's a job.'

'You must meet a lot of people.'

'Of course.'

'A lot of women.'

'Women take cabs as much as men. More so sometimes.'

'Yeah, the streets are not safe these days, are they?'

'I wouldn't know.'

A second beat. Longer this time.

Archer is watching as Klara's CCTV footage depicts Bilal following Elena up Praed Street. Elena stops at the corner of Bouverie Place and is typing into her phone. Bilal hesitates and watches her momentarily. He then rests his hand on her shoulder and stands inches in front of her. She jumps and steps backwards. They talk for a few moments. Bilal keeps reaching out to touch her, but Elena keeps pushing his arm away. Moments pass and things escalate into a heated exchange before she backs away, turns and hurries down Bouverie Place. Bilal follows her and grabs her arm but she slaps it away and rushes into St Michael's Street. He pursues her, which is the last they see of both of them. There is no CCTV in that quiet street.

'Do you ever eat at the Southern Fried Chicken Shop on Praed Street?' Quinn asks.

'Sometimes.'

'I hear the chilli Korean wings are pretty good.'

Bilal says nothing to this.

Archer looks up. 'Mr Bilal, we want to talk to you in connection with the murder of Elena Zoric.'

Bilal's face drops. 'Murder? What're you talking about?'

'Does the name mean anything to you?'

He frowns. 'No! Why should it?'

Quinn shows him a photo of Elena. 'Do you recognise this woman?'

He stares at the photo and shifts awkwardly on his chair. Shaking his head dramatically, he replies, 'I . . . I don't know her.'

'Her name is Elena Zoric. She was in the Chicken House on the twenty-third of July, the same evening you were eating there,' says Archer.

Bilal's face is a mask of confusion.

'You were watching her and you followed her up Praed Street and down Bouverie Place.'

'No, no, you're mistaken.'

Archer turns the laptop to face him and plays the CCTV footage from the restaurant.

Bilal swallows as he watches, his face an expression of disbelief. 'It's not what you think.'

'What do we think?' Archer asks, bringing up the footage of the heated exchange.

'You think I followed her and hurt her. You think I killed her. I didn't! I would never do that.'

'You followed her from the restaurant. You hassled her on the street, moving in on her personal space and grabbing her arm when she tried to get away from you. And then you disappear up St Michael's Street with Elena and she's never seen again. Do you see how this looks?'

Bilal wrings his hands together. His breathing begins to increase rapidly in short wheezing bursts. His face goes grey.

Archer and Quinn exchange a concerned glance.

'Hassan, are you OK?' Quinn asks.

He's trembling now. From his jacket pocket he takes out a blue inhaler and puts it into his mouth, inhaling a puff of the healing spray. A moment passes and he raises his hand to indicate he's OK.

'I'll get some water,' Quinn says, rising from the table and exiting the room.

Bilal has calmed and is taking in slow deep breaths. Quinn returns with the water, from which Bilal takes a sip. 'Thank you.'

'Talk to us, Hassan,' says Archer. 'Tell us what happened.'

He's still clutching the blue inhaler as if it is some lucky charm. He nods his head and meets her gaze, 'I had seen her around. I knew her from the Chicken House. It's what they call the brothel above the restaurant. I would see her sometimes. I liked her. A lot. One time I drove her home. I would talk to her, say nice things to her, tell her she was very beautiful. I even gave her my number, asked her to call me personally if ever she wanted a lift. "Special price just for you," I told her.'

'Did she ever call you?'

He shakes his head. 'No.'

'And then she was gone. I'd watch the Chicken House from the street sometimes, the windows upstairs, looking for her but

159

I never saw her. I wondered if she'd moved away or gone to another whore house. And then that night I saw her again. I couldn't believe it. There she was, sitting alone in the restaurant. She left suddenly. I didn't know what to do so I followed her. I just wanted to say hello and maybe get to know her.' He drops his head into his hands.

'From the CCTV it looks like you had some sort of argument,' Quinn says.

'It wasn't like that. I was . . . I asked her . . .'

'You wanted to have sex with her?' Quinn says.

Bilal nods.

'Could you answer yes for the recording?' Quinn says.

'Yes, yes . . . I asked for sex. But I didn't have the money and she got angry. She insulted me, spat at my feet, and walked off. I didn't like that. I became angry, too, and grabbed her.'

'What happened after that?' Archer asks.

Bilal sighs. 'Nothing. I didn't kill her. I know you think I did but I didn't. I wouldn't do that to a woman. I have two daughters.'

'You have a wife, yet you asked Elena for sex,' Archer says.

'It's not what you think. I am a man. I have needs.'

'And what did you think Elena's needs were?' Archer says.

He considers this for a moment before answering. 'Money. Whores want money.'

Archer's jaw tightens.

'Where did you take Elena?' Quinn asks.

'I took her nowhere. I swear! She walked up St Michael's Street. I called after her apologising, but she wouldn't listen. It was then she stopped and talked to someone.'

'Who?' Archer asks, leaning forward.

'I don't know.'

'Male, female?'

'I don't know. She was talking to someone in a car.'

'What type of car?'

'Like an Astra. Old.'

'Do you recall the colour or registration?' Quinn asks.

'I think it was dark, like a blue or a black.' He frowns. 'How would I remember the registration? I didn't even look. Whoever looks at registrations?'

'It was worth a punt.'

As a suspect, Archer knows he might be slipping away, yet given his unashamed male entitlement, she can't help but feel the urge to lock him up and lose the key. 'What did you do after that?' she asks.

'I went back to work.'

'How soon did you go back to work?'

'I don't know. Fifteen minutes. Twenty. I picked up my car and logged back into the Uber system.'

'Do you have your work phone with you?' Quinn asks.

'Yes.'

'Then you won't mind if we look back on your records for that evening?'

'But—'

'No buts. We're not done yet. For now, we'll need to do more investigating. As Detective Sergeant Quinn has indicated, that will include a digital forensic search of your phone and a search of your car. Do you understand?'

To Archer's vexation, he rolls his eyes and shakes his head. 'Yes, I understand.'

Archer holds him firmly in her gaze, 'A young woman has been murdered, Mr Bilal. You remain a suspect. You'd do well to keep your attitude in check.'

Bilal casts his eyes downwards but says nothing in response.

Chapter 27

T OM ELSTON HAS PARKED HIS old blue Land Rover in a bay of Berwick-Upon-Tweed station car park, face concealed under the visor of a baseball cap and a PPE mask. He is watching the Mercers emerge from the station and cross the road. With his family in tow, Barry Mercer had walked by only moments back. Tom's hands had tightened on the steering wheel. Mercer had not clocked he was being watched. He seemed in a daze, his face sombre, pale and riddled with guilt.

Good!

They climb into the silver Škoda people carrier and drive slowly across the station car park towards the exit. The car pulls up at the stop line near to where Tom is parked. He turns his head to the left with his phone to his ear under the pretence of taking a call, his arm covering his face. With his free hand he starts up the engine. The Škoda exits the car park, turning left onto Railway Street and driving up the hill and past the Castle Hotel. The car is indicating right. They are going into town. Tom allows a Ford Focus to drive in front of him and follows the Škoda, shielded by the Ford.

His phones rings from its dashboard mount. Mallory Jones's name appears on the screen. He considers ignoring it but decides he could use someone to talk to. He answers on speaker.

'Hey,' he says.

'I left you a message, did you get it?'

'I've been busy,' he replies; suddenly, his voice is dry and croaky.

'You sound tired. Have you been sleeping?'

She never misses a trick. 'Usual.'

'Oh. I'm sorry.'

The Mercers' car is heading down to Marygate.

'Are you driving?' Mallory asks.

'Yes, and . . .?' he says tersely, but instantly regrets his tone. 'Sorry . . .'

'No, I'm sorry. I'm just tired,' Tom replies.

'Are you still in Berwick?'

'Yes.'

'Why there of all places?'

'Have you ever been?'

'No.'

'Then don't judge. It's a nice place.'

'It's just so far from everything you know.'

Tom says nothing to that. The Škoda is turning right onto Hide Hill.

'Anyway, I'm sure it's lovely. Listen, Tom, I wanted to talk to you. Did you see the news report I mentioned?'

'I haven't seen any news,' he lies.

'There's been a recent murder, Tom, and an investigation into another dating back to 1987. It's the same man. I'm sure of it. Tom, this is big. I met with Detective Inspector Grace Archer of the Met. She's going to reopen Hannah's case.'

The Škoda is indicating right and pulling into a parking space outside a restaurant and wine bar. He drives slowly by, watching them emerge from the car. Mercer still looks miserable. Tom feels a small measure of satisfaction. His daughter,

Lily, looks furious. He notices a free parking space further up the road.

'Hello . . . are you there?' Mallory asks.

'I have to go,' he says.

'Call me anytime. You know that, right?'

'Yeah. I know that,' he replies and ends the call.

Tom parks the car and makes his way down Hide Hill, stopping outside the restaurant. Two different couples occupy two tables outside. One couple is paying their bill to a waitress holding a card machine. Inside, he sees the Mercers and the Škoda driver, whoever he is, sitting around a table, quietly perusing their menus. Tom holds his phone, dips his head as if looking at it, and watches them from under his visor. They seem like a normal, boring suburban family, yet scratch Barry Mercer's surface, and you'll find dirt and lies. The couple are leaving, the waitress is clearing their table. Tom approaches her. 'May I take this table?' he asks.

'Sure,' she replies.

Tom sits at the table facing inwards and watches.

Lily is getting bored with her mum's chittering and banal small talk. It's as if nothing has happened. I mean, it's not every day someone gatecrashes your dad's big TV interview and accuses him of being responsible for the death of some people. What on earth was that man talking about? The food arrives. They had all ordered fish and chips with the exception of Uncle Si, who ordered the vegan burger, which looks gross. Dad pushes his chair from the table, the legs scraping harshly across the wooden floor.

'I'm just going to spend a penny,' he says.

'We'll wait for you,' Mum says.

'No . . . start without me.'

They watch him make his way to the Gents'. Mum and Si look at each other.

'Do you know who that man was?' she asks.

'Oh, now we can talk about it,' Lily snaps.

'Hush, Lily,' Mum replies. 'Your father is mortified.'

'We're all mortified, Mum. All the town gossips will be whispering on the grapevine.'

'I didn't recognise him,' says Si.

'Did you see those hollow rings under his eyes?' Mum says. 'Drugs, I reckon.'

Lily forks a chip into her mouth and shakes her head.

'I'll ask around. See if anyone knows him,' says Si.

'He practically accused Dad of being a murderer! Why would he do that?' Lily asks.

'When you're a police officer, like your father and I were, you encounter all sorts,' says Mum. 'He's on drugs. Trust me. I know the signs.'

Lily cuts into the crispy coating of her cod, unsure if she can, or even wants to take her mum seriously. It's been decades since she was in the police, so what could she possibly know?

'Your mum's right,' say Si. 'Police officers do come face to face with oddballs. I shouldn't worry about him.'

Lily chews on the delicious fish. Maybe he was just some crazy person.

'Hush, now. Your father's coming back. This topic is not up for discussion any longer,' says Mum.

Dad pulls out his chair. She notices his hair is slightly damp, his forehead too. Has he just splashed water on his face? He winks at Lily. 'How's lunch?' he asks.

Lily has a mouth full of chips. She nods her head and gives him the thumbs-up.

166

'Good. I've been looking forward to this.'

For the rest of the meal the subject is not brought up. The talk centres around local affairs, the pandemic, and the impact to food prices and food supplies. Lily extracts herself by scrolling through Instagram. Her phone pings with a message. It's Gemma.

'Who's Gemma?' Uncle Si asks.

Lily feels a surge of irritation that he was watching her phone.

'Sorry, love, I wasn't spying. When your phone pinged my eyes followed the noise.'

'She's just a friend.'

'She's a bit older than you, though,' Mum interrupts. 'Should you really be hanging out together?'

Lily gives Mum a withering look.

'I'm just saying. That's all.'

'She's two years older than me. That's hardly much older!'

Lily's tone is sharp. Mum purses her lips, drops her eyes and pokes at her chips.

'She's nearly seventeen, Isla,' Dad says, coming to her defence. 'She's old enough to make her own decisions.'

Lily smiles at Dad and turns her attention to the message.

Babes. We're on. Kitten Club broadcasting tonight at 10 o'clock. Can you be there? Cash in hand.

Gemma adds two smiley face emojis and two dollar sign emojis. Lily types a message back.

I'll be there, babes. As per our agreement, right?

Gemma is typing back.

The mask is yours, bitch! LOL XX

Lily feels a frisson of excitement. She turns her phone over, looks up and smiles insincerely at her mother.

'Back with us, are you?'

The waitress arrives. 'All done?'

'Yes, that was delicious, thank you. Our compliments to the chef,' says Mum.

The waitress gives Mum an odd look and Lily feels herself cringe to the point of death.

'Dessert?' the waitress asks.

'Not for me,' says Dad.

Mum and Si also decline.

'I'll have the brownies with ice cream,' says Lily.

Mum arches her brows and gives her that irritating fat-shaming look. Lily sets her mouth and holds her gaze defiantly.

Chapter 28

TOWARDS THE END OF THE working day, Archer receives a text from Liam asking if it is OK if he works a little later to finish painting the living room. She replies with a yes and tells him she is working a few extra hours, and that taking whatever time he needs is OK. He replies with a smiley emoji. Moments later, he texts back and asks if she fancies a drink at the Kings Arms after work. She blinks at the invite, unsure how to interpret it.

Biting her lip, she glances across at Quinn, Liam's mate. His head is buried in paperwork. She takes a moment to consider and replies: *Sure. Why not. I'm putting in a bit of overtime. I'll let you know.*

She hesitates before pressing 'send' and feels a pang of doubt, regretting her wishy-washy vagueness.

Liam is replying.

No worries. I'll get back to it. Cheers. L.

Archer glances back at Quinn, sets her phone screen side down, and feels a tremor of confusion mixed with excitement. Did Liam just ask her out on a date? Does he like her? How has she not spotted the signs? Does she like him? He's certainly easy on the eye. Another message pings. A small smile parts her lips as she picks up the phone.

'Someone's popular,' says Quinn. He watches her with a curious expression.

'It's no one,' she replies, dropping her gaze.

The number on the screen is one she doesn't recognise. She feels a twinge of disappointment before shaking herself out it. Composing herself she opens the message.

'What's his name?' Quinn asks.

Archer gives Quinn a look and ignores the question. She reads the message.

Dear DI Archer, you asked me for a photo of Sally. I went into the loft, after your visit the other day, and found this photobooth shot of Sally and me. It was taken about a year before she left Bristol. She looks really happy. I suppose we both do. Anyway, I found some others but they're not so great. This is the best shot I have. Let me know if it's good enough. All my best. Fiona.

'It's from Fiona Brooks.'

Archer opens the attachment. It's a black and white photo of two smiling teenagers inside a photo booth. Fiona has short dark hair combed into a side parting. Sally, on the other hand, has thick blonde hair teased into a curly shag style. A heavy fringe half conceals her eyes lined thick with eyeliner. She has a strong jawline and a sweet smile. Archer feels an anger burn inside. Quinn is beside her, standing so close she can smell the soap on his skin. He sighs. 'It's one thing knowing she was just a teenager but seeing her like this . . .'

'We have to find this motherfucker. Make him pay for what's he done,' says Archer.

'We will.'

DC Phillips's voice interrupts the sombre moment. She's sitting at her desk. Her computer screen contains CCTV footage. 'Sorry to interrupt. You might want to see this. I've gone through the CCTV from the night Elena was murdered and found the car Hassan Bilal was referring to. It's a Vauxhall Astra. It belongs to a widow, a Mrs Eileen McKenna, who reported it missing the morning after Elena was murdered.'

Archer looks at the grainy footage of Elena stepping into the car. The driver is hidden from view.

'I'll fast forward a bit,' says Phillips. 'There's no clear shot of the driver, as you can see.'

Phillips pages through the shots. She can just about make out Elena, but the driver has his visor down and he's wearing a PPE mask.

'Crafty fucker,' says Quinn.

'We lose the car in Edgware near the Silk Stream.'

'Has it been found?' Archer asks.

'Not yet. That's my next task.'

'Good work. Thanks, Marian.'

'Grace, Harry, I've found something,' comes Klara's voice. She's approaching them with an open laptop, which she sets down on Archer's desk. 'I was searching through the records of Sally McGowan's last known address at Stuart Mill House. She wasn't registered there but obviously other people were. Onscreen is a report from a council database with a list of people registered at that address over the years. Recognise a name on that list in 1987?'

Archer and Quinn lean in for a closer look. Scanning the names, Archer's eyes fall on one in particular.

'I'm surprised, but not,' Quinn says.

'Are you in any rush to get home?' Archer asks.

'Nope. Shall we pop in?'

171

'Let's do it. Great work, Klara.'

'You're welcome.'

Twenty minutes later they are once more climbing the stairs of the Chicken House. Margaret Jackson watches them approach with a less than impressed expression.

'We're quite busy at the moment, so can we make this quick?' she says.

'Let's go to your office.'

'We can talk here.'

Archer is no mood for Margaret Jackson's sass. 'Recognise this ... child?' Archer asks, showing her Fiona's photobooth shot which has since been cropped to depict only Sally.

Jackson's eyes linger on the picture.

'Sally's last known address is Stuart Mill House. According to records you lived there, too.'

She closes her eyes for a moment and nods.

'Have you seen any of the news coverage over the past few days?' Quinn asks. 'We announced Sally McGowan's name.'

'Come inside ... please.'

They follow her down the narrow corridor and into her office. She closes the door shut behind them.

'Can I get you anything – tea, coffee, something stronger?'

'Let's start with some answers.'

Jackson wrings her hands and nods. The woman is visibly shaken. 'If you don't mind, I'll just pour myself something.' She sits behind her desk, takes out a bottle of Grey Goose vodka and a shot glass. She pours herself one and downs it, before pouring a second. 'Yes, I knew Sally, back then.'

'How did you meet?'

'I was working at Paddington and she arrived, alone and lost.'

'Were you in the same line of business back then?' Quinn asks.

'Yes.'

'So you saw a child that you could exploit and earn money from?' Archer asks.

'No! It wasn't like that.'

'She was living with you. You were on the game and so was she.'

'You don't understand.'

'Make me understand,' Archer snaps.

Jackson flinches and pours herself another vodka. 'I'd arrived in London just like her, some years before, abandoned and lost with no one to support me. I had escaped an abusive marriage that I was too young for. Disowned and rejected by my parents for embarrassing the family for leaving my husband, I used the last of my money to get as far away from them as I could. I came to London to follow the same mythical dream of finding a career and reinventing myself. Both came true all right, just not how I anticipated. But I soldiered on. Women like me have to survive and we do whatever we can to earn a living. It was the early eighties. There was a recession. It was impossible to find work. We had our benefits but that wasn't enough. Like thousands of women before me, I did what I had to do and became a sex worker, walking the streets at night. It was truly awful but the money was OK as long as you avoided certain pimps.'

'If it was so awful why bring Sally into it?' Archer asks.

'When I saw her emerge from the station it was like watching myself arrive in London for the first time. I saw a lost and frightened young person who knew nothing of the city she'd just arrived in. She hung around for an hour alone looking at passers-by as if they might suddenly reach out and help. Occasionally, our eyes would meet but she was shy and would look away. In the beginning, that is. She was such a lovely girl.'

173

Her eyes blink. Tears gather. 'It had been quiet. Thin on the ground with punters. I decided to take the rest of the evening off. I crossed the road, said hello, and offered her a cigarette. She hesitated before taking it. I was dressed provocatively and don't think she knew what to make of me. Although she told me later, she knew exactly what I was.' She laughs at the memory and dabs her eyes. 'I suspected she didn't smoke but I lit us both up anyway. She choked out a horrendous cough. I smiled at her and took the cigarette from her, pinched the embers and put it back in the box. It was an ice breaker, I suppose. I asked her what she was doing here. She told me some cock-and-bull story about having a job and family. I didn't believe her. She continued on as if she believed it herself. She was good at that. Fantasising about another life. After half an hour of this, I'd had enough and wished her luck. As I turned to leave, she let out a little sob. I said to her, "None of what you told me is true, is it?" and she shook her head. I told her to come with me. She could sleep on my sofa for a few nights until she got her bene-fits and got on the housing list. So she came but she stayed.'

'How did she get into sex working?' Archer asks.

'A month had passed, and she was still on the sofa. I didn't mind and neither did Dora, my flatmate. She was a sweet kid and we both liked her. Mothered her, I suppose. Anyway, Dora decided to leave London. That left her room free. Sally begged to have it. But the rent was high and her benefits would barely cover it. Dora and I were both on the game. Sally knew that and what she saw in us were two strong women, seemingly in control, despite the bruises and split lips that we sometimes came home with. She wanted to do it. It was her decision.'

'How could you let a sixteen-year-old, someone who's not allowed to vote or drink alcohol, make the decision to become a sex worker?'

'I had made it clear to Sally there was no way that I would let her do that. We argued. She screamed at me that I wasn't her effing mother. I wasn't trying to be. She brought out something in me. My maternal side, I suppose. The weeks and months passed, and everything seemed OK. And then I'd noticed she had some extra cash. She told me she was doing the double, getting benefits and working part time in a bar. Good for her, I thought until I found out the truth. Sally had met with an ex-pimp of mine, a shady character called Lox.'

'Is he still around?' Quinn asks.

'He took a bullet in the head from a rival the same year. He's long gone, thankfully.'

Jackson seems deep in concentration for a moment. 'Where was I?'

'Sally had met with Lox,' Archer replies.

Jackson frowns. 'Yeah. He'd put her to work.'

'How did you find out?'

'A friend told me. I confronted Sally, warned her about Lox but she said she could handle him. I'm sure he'd had her. He liked them young. Bastard. When he was shot it was a relief, although we were all horrified. Many girls were free, Sally included, but she insisted on going back on the streets. I couldn't stop her. She'd become wilful. The only way I could win was to look after her myself.'

'You became her pimp?'

'Not exactly. I had an agreement with my pimp, Johnny Rubbers—'

'Johnny Rubbers?' Quinn says.

'It was his nickname. He always made sure his girls had rubbers because of AIDS. He was a good sort in his own way.'

'Where's Mr Rubbers now?' Quinn asks.

'Died from an AIDS-related illness back in the nineties.'

175

'Ironic,' Quinn says.

'Not really. He'd been diagnosed in the eighties.'

'The pimps in this tale have pretty short lives so far,' says Quinn.

Jackson continues. 'Anyway, I looked after Sally, took a cut of her earnings which paid for her rent, bills and food. It was a cushy number that worked for all of us.' Jackson eyes the bottle of Grey Goose and the empty glass, clearly pondering another shot. 'And then she went missing.'

'Why did you not call us when her name was announced on the news?' Archer asks.

'What's the point? The police have never been interested before.'

'There are no records of Sally being missing. Did you not think to report this to the police?' Archer asks.

Jackson turns on her, jaw tight, eyes flaring. 'I reported it all right. Several trips to the police and here's the thing – they did not give two shits. She was just another whore who wasn't worth their spit. No matter how hard I pressed them, no matter how much I pushed, they weren't interested. The weeks passed and I returned. There was nothing they could do, they said. In their eyes she had run away again, probably back to Bristol or to some other city.'

'Do you remember the name of any of the officers you spoke to?'

'I remember one officer. He wasn't in charge, he was a constable at the time. Young, but what a son of a bitch he was.'

'In what way?' Archer asks.

'The way he spoke to me. The way he spoke about Sally too. We were "low life whores". I'll never forget that. I'll take it to the grave with me.'

'Do you remember his name?'

'His bitter, horrible face, and his name feel carved into my soul, unfortunately. He sounded like he was from Yorkshire. Had a strong accent. His name was Fletcher.'

'Les Fletcher?'

'Yes, that's him. Pig!'

Chapter 29

I
T'S ALMOST 10 P.M., THE evening is balmy, quiet, and mellow. Tom is driving into town, his window is open, a cool breeze soothes his hot face. He has always preferred the night-time. It brings with it a comforting solitude that he can lose himself in. Yet not tonight. His mood is all over the place. His outburst today has discombobulated him. It was impetuous and stupid and could ruin everything. His stomach is in knots, his chest tight, his breathing shallow. He wonders if he's taken his Warfarin but can't recall. *One day won't matter.* He needs a drink. Parking the car in the town centre he takes a short walk to the Brewers Arms. The crowd is thinning inside. He orders a double Jameson and takes a seat at a small round table near a boisterous bunch of older people having a night out. They look to be in their sixties and are celebrating someone hitting the big 7-0. He feels an ache inside listening to their banter. An ache that comes from loneliness and bitterness at the wrong choices made. He closes his eyes and thinks of her. If only . . .

'You all right, love?'

A woman from the next table has taken the empty seat next to his. She's short and round wearing a plastic gold crown, a bright green feather boa and a T-shirt with an *I am 70* badge printed on it in large pink letters.

'I'm fine, thank you . . . Happy birthday.'

She smiles. 'Thank you. I need a break. Mind if I sit away from the rabble for a mo?' She has a strong Scottish accent.

He wants to say 'yes' but can't bring himself to be rude. 'Having a nice time?' he asks.

'Aye. I'm seventy, in case you hadn't guessed.'

'I saw your T-shirt and did wonder.'

She chuckles. 'I was just on my way to the loo and saw you sitting here. You looked sad. Do you want to join us?'

He glances across at her friends who seem perfectly pleasant. Shaking his head, he says, 'Thank you but I'm not staying long.'

She meets his gaze without judgement. 'I hope you're OK.'

A man calls across from the other table. 'Theresa, we need to get going.' He smiles and nods at Tom, who raises his glass in return.

'Aye, I know,' Theresa shouts back. She turns back to Tom. 'We should have been halfway to Edinburgh already,' she says laughing. She regards him for a moment before reaching forward and squeezing his hand. 'I know loss when I see it.'

Tom feels a tightness in his throat.

She points to her chest. 'The people we lose. We carry them here always.' She squeezes his hand once more and pushes herself up with some effort. 'Nice to meet you.'

Tom feels water rushing to the back of his eyes, but he holds back the flood as he has done many, many times.

'Thank you, Theresa.'

'You're very welcome. Have a good night.'

'Safe trip home.'

Tom downs his whiskey and gets up, feeling buoyed by her kindness and for a moment wishes he was more like her. Less . . . angry.

Outside, he crosses to the Land Rover and climbs inside. He hears laughing voices and sees Theresa and the man holding each other steady as they shuffle from the pub and into a waiting taxi. He wonders if things had been different, had he been more forgiving, would his wife and daughter still be with him today? He feels suddenly alone, more alone than he normally feels. He shudders and wishes the night could calm him, but it doesn't. The reason he's here and his confrontation with Mercer earlier that day come flooding back to him. His mood darkens, not helped by the double shot of whiskey. He feels his bitterness clawing its way back. Vengeance. Vengeance at whatever cost. He has made up his mind.

East Ord is a small, picturesque village two miles south-west of Berwick-Upon-Tweed. Tom pulls up near the Mercer home, a detached period house made from stone, situated opposite the green. He watches the house. The downstairs windows are warmly lit. It looks cosy and comfortable and conjures memories of better times. His hands grip the steering wheel tightly. The front door opens, and the daughter's silhouette appears, her face lit by the glow of a phone. A car pulls up outside the house. An Uber. Lily looks across at it, waves, pulls the door shut behind her and hurries into the car.

The car pulls away.

Tom's mind races. What should he do? Stay here or . . .? Without thinking, he starts up the engine and follows the taxi. Ten minutes later, they are approaching the Roundhouse in Spittal, a development site of approximately two acres. The Uber slows to a stop. Tom hangs back, pulls over to the side of the road and kills the lights. Lily gets out and the Uber drives off. There's nothing here but tree copses, weeds and wild foliage. *Why on earth would she come here at this time of the evening?*

He watches with interest as she crosses into the field. His curiosity is piqued. From the back of the car, he takes a hoody from a holdall and puts it on. He tosses the baseball cap into the bag and pulls the hood up over his head. Hurrying down the road, he feels a dull throb in his chest and slows his pace. He stops and takes several breaths, glancing around to make sure no one is watching. He can't see much of anything and crosses into the field to the same spot Lily had passed only minutes back. In the short distance, he sees the small beam of a phone torch light jittering in the darkness. Keeping his distance he follows in its wake. Tom reaches a small copse and from behind a tree sees an old cottage on the perimeter of the field. The front door opens and white light spills onto the passageway. There's a row of empty beer and wine bottles outside the door. A young woman with curly dark hair, dressed only in her underwear, emerges and embraces Lily. A second person appears, a tall shirtless man with shoulder-length blond hair. He is smoking and the unmistakable bitter smell of weed wafts across the field and into the trees. They chat for a moment and laugh before the man beckons them inside.

Tom is uncertain about what to do. Part of him thinks this may just be some friends having a party, but part of him thinks it might be something else. He waits until he is certain no one else is around and then approaches the cottage, slowly and cautiously, then stands close to the front door. He can hear their voices, just the three of them. The man is called Chris. He is directing them tonight for the Kitten Club, whatever that is, and working the cameras. He tells them he may join in if the mood takes him. Gemma laughs at this. Lily doesn't. Tom hears them move to the living room. Pop music begins to play. The window is slightly ajar, but the curtains are closed and the thinnest of gaps shows a shard of bright white light.

'All right, Gemma, get into position, please,' Chris says.

Tom inches closer and peers through the gap. The room is painted white with erotic photos of naked women on the walls. There's a bed dressed in lurid red and pink colours. The young woman called Gemma is perched on top of it wearing large horn-rimmed spectacles and what looks like an old teacher's cloak over her underwear. She's holding a cane. In front of the bed is a camera and a large ring light.

'We're going live soon, Lily,' the man shouts, toking on the weed.

'Come on, Lils,' Gemma shouts as she gathers her cape.

'Coming!' Lily cries.

Lily walks into the room dressed as a schoolgirl, wearing a blonde wig with pigtails and a domino mask covering her eyes. Painted freckles dot her cheeks, her lips are coloured a pillar box red. She is squeezed tightly into a crisp white shirt that is too small and is wearing a short tartan skirt. She sits on the bed next to Gemma, her hands resting on her knees like a proper lady.

'OK,' says Chris. 'Three, two ... Lily, open your legs a bit ... that's it ... one. GO!'

Gemma begins talking into the camera in a seductive manner but the sound of a car in the distance causes Tom to pull back. His foot collides with a bottle. Like dominoes, it topples against the others making a loud crashing sound.

'Someone's outside,' Gemma says.

'Probably just a fox,' Chris replies.

'Go look!'

His heart pounding, Tom hurries away, ducking through the overgrown bushes and hiding in the copse. Looking back, he sees Chris outside the cottage looking around for signs of an intruder. 'There's no one here!' Chris says. He returns inside, closing the door behind him. Tom waits for his breath to return before skirting the field's perimeter. Turning back, he sees the narrow gap in the curtains darken suddenly. Someone is standing at the same spot he'd been standing in only moments back. His mouth dries. He turns and leaves.

Chapter 30

WHEN MALLORY HAD MET WITH Detective Inspector Archer and told her about Hannah Daysy and her belief that Hannah's murder was connected to Elena Zoric's and Sally McGowan's, the detective had requested that she not release a podcast on the current investigation. Mallory had, of course, agreed with one condition: that she gets an exclusive from Archer once the investigation was over. To Mallory's surprise, Archer had agreed. However, what Mallory had neglected to mention was that she and Bruce had later repurposed Hannah's original podcast with a new intro from Mallory about the case being reopened. She had not mentioned any other names or who was leading the investigating. This was Mallory's scoop. A major one that could dramatically increase her four thousand listeners. It was also a gamble. Archer might take exception and pull back on their agreement, but Mallory thought it worth the risk. After all, even without DI Archer's help, when the investigation was over, she could still write and broadcast the women's stories, giving them a voice, keeping them alive in people's minds. Bruce was already looking into the victims' family and friends. They were racing ahead. The repurposed show had gone out as a special at dinner time yesterday. They had gone full steam on marketing on the socials with the show available on all the platforms.

In bed the following morning, Mallory sups a coffee and opens her laptop. She logs into the podcast site and can't quite believe what she's seeing. Overnight the listening figures have surpassed the two thousand mark.

'Bloody hell!'

She springs from bed and hurries across the apartment. Bruce's bedroom door is ajar. 'Boo, are you up?'

He doesn't answer. She pushes open the door. The room is gloomy. The only light is the glow from the bank of monitors on his desk. She steps inside. 'Boo?' Her eyes scan the room, the bed is unmade, the desk untidy. This is not like him. She notices his walking sticks lying on the floor below his ergonomic office chair. She sees his feet. They're trembling. Her heart sinks. He's lying in a foetal position on the floor, his face grimacing in pain. She rushes to him, kneeling by his side. 'Oh, Boo, are you OK?' He's had another attack. The third one this week. He's rigid, his muscles and bones bound in a synthesis of unfettered agony. She doesn't touch him because she knows even the slightest movement can cause severe pain.

'I'll live,' he replies, his voice a croaky dry, empty whisper.

Mallory's heart is pounding but she knows the drill. 'How long have you been lying here?'

He hesitates before answering, 'It doesn't matter.'

'How long?' she persists.

'Just a few hours.'

'A few hours! Why didn't you call me?'

'I needed to lie down.'

Mallory feels her throat constricting. She blinks away tears.

'Morphine,' he says. 'Bedside table.'

Scrambling across the room, Mallory opens the shutters. Morning sunshine fills the room. She sees the brown bottle of tablets on Bruce's bedside table and grabs them. Dropping to his side, she empties two into her palm. He opens his mouth. She slides them inside. 'I'll get water.'

She hears him crunch down on the pills and hurries to kitchen where she fills a glass with water. Back in the bedroom she crouches by his side.

'I'm just going to tilt your head a little, OK?'

'. . . k . . .' he replies.

With the delicacy of a nurse holding a newborn, Mallory slides her hand under his temple and gently lifts his head, tipping a small measure of water into his mouth. He swirls it around, swallows and lays his head back down. 'Thank you.' She watches him, her stomach in knots. He's been working late again. She wishes he wouldn't, but he's plagued with insomnia and his commitment to track down his husband's killer – and every other murdering son of a bitch – is what gives him purpose. It's what keeps him alive. His body trembles and he groans. She wants to stroke his hair, tell him everything will be all right, but how can she? Never mind the physical pain it might trigger, but who is she to say everything will be fine after what he's been through? What she's been through. What they've both been left with. Like a snuff movie in her head, the scene of her brother Zach bleeding to death at the roadside, as a truck reverses at speed over Bruce, plays in her mind. She swallows and pushes it from her head.

'Tell me something beautiful . . . doesn't have to be true,' Bruce says.

Mallory lies on her side facing him and smiles.

He smiles back.

'We had 2,103 downloads of the new Hannah Daysy podcast.'

His brow creases as he studies her face for a moment. 'Truth or lie?'

'Truth.'

Bruce's face lights up. 'You're shitting me!'

'I shit you not.'

'That's an all-time record.'

'I know!'

'That's fucking awesome!'

'We should celebrate.'

'I think we're out of champagne.'

'I can remedy that.'

Bruce shifts on his side; his body is slowly relaxing as the drugs take effect. 'Hey, I found something for you last night.'

She wonders if that is why he's lying on the floor crippled with pain. 'I hope it was worth it,' she says, trying not to sound like she's chastising him.

Bruce ignores the comment.

'I have an assignment for you. I might have found us another murder.'

'A new case?'

'Yes, and no. I think it could be related to Hannah and the others.'

'Same killer?'

'That's for you to investigate, Nancy Drew.'

Mallory hears a key rattling in the front door. 'Nurse Ratched's arrived,' she says.

Bruce laughs and at the same time stiffens, 'Ow, ow, ow,' he says, unable to contain his giggling.

A Spanish voice trills across the apartment. 'Hello, darling, is me, Pedro! How are'd you?' Mallory's 'Nurse Ratched' is Pedro Rodriguez, a private carer who visits Bruce every second day.

'In here,' Mallory calls.

'Oh my God, what happen? Did you fall?' Pedro rushes to Bruce's side, dropping to his knees, edging Mallory away. Pedro is in his late twenties, a five foot five force of nature who has been a godsend for Bruce during his recovery. They have become friends, often bickering like an old married couple. He is good for Bruce, not just because he goes above and beyond as a carer, but because he provides friendship that Bruce has lost since that night. Bruce's agoraphobia has seen him gradually lose contact with many friends over the years. Pedro had filled a void. Mallory has been happy to see that. She likes Pedro. He's a good person. Bruce once described him as 'as gay as Christmas but also a wise old soul inhabiting a young body'.

'Just the usual.'

'Why you not call me?'

'Because it was five in the morning.'

'Yes. That's too early.'

'He didn't even call for me,' says Mallory.

Pedro purses his lips and arches a delicately plucked brow at her. 'Maybe you were entertaining one, or more, of your gentlemen friends and he didn't want to disturb you.'

Mallory looks at him with narrowed eyes and silently mouths, 'Bitch.'

'The drugs have kicked in,' says Bruce. 'Can you two help me up, please.'

Mallory and Pedro take an arm each and gently hoist him by the armpits.

'Put me on the edge of the bed.'

Gently, they lower him so that he's sitting with his feet on the floor.

'Do you want to sleep, sweetie?' Pedro asks.

'No. I need a shower.'

'Let's sort that out,' replies Pedro. He turns to Mallory. 'Maybe we can have some coffee, no?'

189

Pedro has the uncanny knack of making Mallory feel like she is the help.

'Black. Strong.'

'Like those old men you offer yourself too,' she replies.

Pedro purses his lips. 'We'll have it in twenty mins, once he is fresh.'

Mallory raises her hand in a mock military salute. 'Yes, ma'am.'

She catches Bruce's eyes. He's biting his lip trying not to laugh.

As Pedro ushers her out, Bruce says, 'Check your inbox. There's an email from someone called Gwen Baker about a Star Royale in Somerset back in 1988. Might be worth a look.'

Mallory opens her email and makes a quick scan of the unread messages. She sees Gwen Baker's name, opens the mail and reads it.

Dear Mallory,

I really hope you don't mind me emailing you like this. You probably won't (I hope) 'cause I saw on your website asking for new unsolved crime stories. I was listening to your podcast on Hannah Daysy only last night and was utterly gripped. It reminded me of someone I once knew, almost thirty years ago. Her name was Star Royale. Star was on the game, like Hannah, and was killed just like Hannah, too. Please email me if you want to know more.

Loving the show.

Gwen xx

Chapter 31

ARCHER WAKES TO THE SOUND of the key turning in the front door and Liam's voice bellowing up the stairs. 'Only me,' he calls.

Her eyes blink open and she recalls their text exchange from early yesterday evening. He'd invited her for a drink. She'd agreed and told him she was working a few extra hours. She had worked later than anticipated and had forgotten to text him to say she couldn't make it. 'Shit!' she says.

She swings out of bed, pulls on her robe and opens the curtains. The morning sun is fierce. She squints and turns from the glare. She quickly checks herself in the mirror, combing her hair with her fingers, and steps onto the landing. Liam is at the bottom of the stairs. He's wearing cargo trousers with pockets at the sides and a fitted white T-shirt.

'Morning,' she says.

He looks up and smiles warmly. 'Sleep well?'

'Not bad, thanks. Listen, I'm sorry about last night. Something came up, and I worked later than expected.'

'No problem. I understand.'

'I should have texted you.'

'Honestly, it's no bother.'

Her gaze lingers for a moment. 'I'm just going to get ready,' she says, nodding at the bathroom.

'Would you like a tea or coffee?' he asks.

'Tea would be nice.'

'I brought some fresh baked croissants from that artisan bakery, if you fancy one.'

'Perfect.'

He smiles. 'I'll get everything ready.'

Archer enters the bathroom, closing the door behind her. She's still not used to the new design and feels a surge of pleasure at how classy, fresh and modern it now looks. She runs the shower and hangs her robe on the door. Stepping under the hot water, the events of last evening play on her mind. Klara had discovered Margaret Jackson and Sally McGowan had shared a flat. Margaret had become her landlady, her friend and later her pimp-cum-mentor. And then Sally was murdered. Jackson had told a good story with a twist that she could not have anticipated. Archer's new boss, Chief Inspector Les Fletcher, had been a PC that been involved with the investigation. Archer soaps her body as she mulls over this revelation and recalls her conversation with Quinn afterwards.

'We need to tread carefully with this news about Fletcher,' Quinn had said.

Archer had bristled at Quinn's suggestion. 'What we need to do is question him.'

'If Margaret Jackson is right, and I'm not suggesting she isn't, then interviewing him might scupper any further work on the investigation.'

'He needs to answer for his attitude, which frankly seems unchanged in thirty years. That aside, it's possible his behaviour impacted the investigation and prevented them finding the killer.'

'You're right. I agree one hundred per cent, but let's hold back for now. Fletcher is a motherfucking gammon son of a bitch who cares only about himself. If we get him on the ropes he'll push back on us and the investigation. Look what he did with Elena's case, bending over to the commissioner and handing it to Parry who has no experience leading murder cases. He didn't do that because he thought Parry was the best person for the job. He did it for himself, for his career.'

Archer had listened and silently fumed at being denied the satisfaction of holding Fletcher to account. But the more she thought about it the more she knew Quinn was right. She hadn't been thinking straight. She was letting her emotions on this case get to her and that was so unlike her. She needed to step back, distance herself, and focus. Besides, perhaps they'd uncover more of Fletcher's past. And if they did, when the time was right, she would hold him accountable.

She towel dries her body and hair and hurries back to the bedroom, mindful of the time. She can hear the kettle boiling and the music playing on the radio downstairs, which feels weird because it's been just her living alone since Grandad died and this bloke, her (hot) joiner-cum-decorator who flirts with her, is preparing her breakfast for the second time. Archer quickly blow dries her hair. Standing in front of the mirror, she brushes it back it into a ponytail. She pulls on a pair of fitted Levi jeans, her brogue boots and selects a navy cotton shirt from her wardrobe.

Liam is leaning against the worktop, supping a coffee and scrolling through his phone when she walks in. He pockets his phone, lifts the teapot from worktop, and pours it into a mug. 'Tea coming right up. Croissants on the table.' He hands her the drink.

'Thanks.'

The kitchen table contains an arrangement of different croissants: plain, almond, pain au chocolat. Archer takes a plain croissant. 'You didn't have to prepare breakfast again.' Archer takes a bite of the delicious buttery pastry.

'I wanted to. Besides, I have to eat too. Busy day ahead. Need to keep my strength up. How'd you like the living room?'

She stops chewing, her eyes widen. With so much turning over in her head about the case and Fletcher, last night she had got home and gone straight to bed, forgetting to check in on the living room.

'You haven't seen it, have you?'

'I'm sorry. My head was full last night.'

That smile again and the lingering gaze. 'Shall we take a look?'

'Yes ... great.'

She doesn't recognise the space. It seems bigger, longer – in fact, brighter, too. The walls have been covered in Georgian-style wood panelling.

'The panels are made from MDF. I had some help from a pal, which is why they're up a day earlier.'

'Wow,' Archer says, pleasantly shocked.

'They'll look even better once they're painted. In fact, they'll look incredible.'

'Yes, they will.'

'The parquet floor arrives today. We'll get that done after painting.'

'Of course. Makes sense.'

He holds her gaze for a moment. 'I'm glad you like it.'

'I do. I really do.'

'Good. I'll get back to it.'

Archer grabs her backpack from the hallway floor.

'Have a good day,' Liam says.

'You too.' She opens the front door and steps outside. 'Let's go for that drink sometime,' she says.

'Just let me know when,' Liam replies.

Chapter 32

LILY STIRS IN HER SLEEP to the sound of the house phone ringing. She's in another world, a dreamworld where she is a model on a runway dressed in a stunning black and gold bodice and heels as high as stilts. She is loved, admired and applauded by all watching her. But the shrill digital tone yanks her from the fantasy. She feels a surge of vexation. She's not ready for the real world yet. Just one more hour is all she needs. Taking a breath, she empties her mind and tries to return to that place, but Mum's irritating voice calls up the stairs.

'Lily, are you up? It's gone ten o clock!'

'Fuck off,' Lily hisses, curling into herself and disappearing under the summer duvet.

'Lily!' Mum calls, her voice high and determined.

Lily hears the thud of footfalls on the stairs and tuts. Her bedroom door flies open.

'Do you know how late it is? The day is almost over.' Mum pulls open the curtains. 'It's beautiful outside. You shouldn't be wasting it in bed.'

'I'm trying to sleep,' Lily protests.

Mum snorts. 'Well, if you will stay out all night!'

'I was back at midnight!'

'I know! You woke us both up. And the neighbours.'

Lily bites her tongue. The last thing she wants is to get into an argument about last night. She knows her mum will see through the lies. She takes a breath and wills her to leave.

'That was Gemma's mum on the phone.'

Lily frowns. Why would Gemma's mum be phoning? She pulls the duvet away from her face. The glare is fierce, she squints and blinks as her eyes adjust to the light. 'What did she want?' Lily asks.

'To know where her daughter is. Gemma's not answering her phone, apparently. She's worried because it's not like her.'

Lily shrugs. 'She's probably with her boyfriend or something.'

'Well, here's the thing, Lily. According to her mum, Gemma was staying here for a sleepover last night.' Mum stands at the foot of her bed, arms folded, brow furrowed. 'Which is news to me.'

Lily's mouth dries but keeps a defiant expression. 'I don't know why she would say that.'

'Where were you last night?'

Shit!

'I told you, I was at a party.'

'With Gemma?'

'Yes.'

'Where was this party?'

'At a friend's house.'

Mum rolls her eyes. 'Does this friend have a name?'

Lily tries to think of a name. After a moment she says, 'Lauren. We all went to Lauren's.'

'This is the first time I've ever heard Lauren's name mentioned.'

'She's new. We don't normally hang around with her.'

'Why would Gemma tell her mum that she was staying here?'

196

'I don't know! Maybe her mum got confused. It does happen to older people! You couldn't even remember that actor's name.'

'What actor?'

'Exactly my point!'

Mum narrows her eyes. Lily's mouth tightens as she holds her gaze, a guilty heart pounding inside her chest.

'I don't know what you two are up to, but you'd better get hold of Gemma and tell her to call her mum.'

'OK!'

'And let me know when you talk to her.'

Mum begins picking up Lily's discarded clothes from the floor.

'I need to get up now,' says Lily.

'I should think so. The day's nearly over.'

'You don't have to keep saying that!'

Lily's watches her mum leave, eyes glaring. Climbing out of bed, she closes the door and takes the phone from her bedside table. She calls Gemma. The phone rings five times before going to voicemail.

'Hey, babes. Call me. Your mum's looking for you, and mine is asking all kinds of annoying questions. Love ya.'

Lily twists the signet ring round and round on her pinkie and wonders what's going on with Gemma. She must have had a late night with Chris. She's mad for him and he had been all over her last night, touching her inappropriately at every opportunity. Gemma loved it, which was gross. Despite being fully aware of what they were getting into, there was a line that was not to be crossed – in Lily's mind, anyway. That was what they had agreed. She had seen the videos of Gemma doing solos for the Kitten Club webcam. The money was good and she had no problems doing it alone or girl on girl, but she didn't sign up for some grungy bloke that stank of weed.

Anyway, she'd done her two hours and a photoshoot before getting dressed and out of there. Chris had agreed to drive her home. He dropped her a short distance from the house and handed her a nice wad of cash.

Lily showers, gets dressed and tries calling Gemma a second time. No answer. She types a message instead.

Gem, I'm heading into town. Text me back. X

She makes her way down to the kitchen, pocketing her phone in her bag. Through the window she sees Mum and Dad sitting in the garden. Dad is reading the paper; Mum is talking but he doesn't seem to be listening. Lily doesn't want another third degree and backs out of the kitchen, pulling her bag over her shoulder.

'Morning, Lils,' comes a voice.

Lily jumps and gasps, her hand flying to her chest. Uncle Si appears at the kitchen door.

'I'm just coming to make some coffee. Can I get you anything?'

'You gave me a fright.'

Si chuckles and lunges towards her. 'Boo!' he cries.

Lily lets out a small squeal and laughs.

'Lily, is that you?' her mother calls.

Lily purses her lips. 'I was hoping to sneak out before she got her hooks in.'

Si smiles. 'She's worried about you. That's all.'

'She's overbearing.'

Mum is looking their way. 'Come into the garden. At least you could say good morning to your father.'

'See what I mean.'

'I see it now,' laughs Si. He fills the kettle. 'Tea or coffee?'

'No thanks. I'm heading out.'

'Lily!' Mum calls.

She rolls her eyes for Simon, exits the kitchen and walks into the garden. 'I'm here. Don't panic,' she says. Dad doesn't look up from the paper. He's frowning and seems tense.

'Are you going out?' Mum asks, clocking her shoulder bag.

'I'm going into town.'

'Into town?'

'That's what I said.'

Mum's shoulders sag. 'Don't be like that. I'm sorry about this morning. Come and sit with us for a little bit.'

'I can't. I'm in a hurry.'

'Do you want a lift?' Mum asks.

'No, I'll take my bike.'

Lily turns her attention to Dad, who has still not acknowledged her presence. 'Morning,' she says but he ignores her. She looks at Mum, frowning. She shrugs an apology on his behalf and makes a face indicating that she has no idea what's up with him.

'Two coffees,' says Si, emerging from the kitchen. He sets a mug down in front of Mum and the other with Dad. 'Sure I can't get you anything?' he asks.

Her eyes are on Dad, unsure what to make of his attitude. 'No, I'll go where I'm wanted,' she replies tartly.

Lily is cycling across the Royal Tweed Bridge. Below, the River Tweed, still as a mill pond, glitters in the late morning sunshine. It's a glorious day, the sky is aqua blue. Half a mile down the river is the ancient sandstone Berwick Bridge. Above it, a scattering of clouds hovers like raw cotton. The wind blows through her hair, ruffling the curls. She breathes in the cool, fresh air and pedals faster, her back moistening with a thin film of sweat. She arrives in Berwick minutes later, pedalling through the narrow roads and stopping at Main Street where she chains her bike to a signpost outside the Co-op. Inside she queues at the shop counter, holding firmly onto her bag. The server is a thin woman with a smoker's cough called Agnes Coates, a notorious local gossip. Lily inches backwards and considers leaving to find another pay point to deposit her cash. She thinks there's one on the other side of town.

'Are you in the queue?' comes a man's voice.

Shit! Just do this. Lily doesn't look at him. 'Yes.' She inches forward back into line.

Minutes later she is at the counter.

'Hi, Lily. How are you. It's been a long time.'

Lily offers a wan smile and says hi. She pushes across the cash with her Monzo card. 'Can I top up my card, please?'

Agnes's eyebrows arch at the thick roll of cash. She looks at Lily with a curious expression. 'That's a lot of money, Lily. Have you robbed a bank?'

'It's savings. Birthday money. Odd jobs money. That's all.'

Agnes is counting the cash. 'Three hundred pounds. Not bad. I want your life, Lily,' she trills, registering the money and updating the card. She hands it back with a receipt. 'Here you go. It should appear in your account in ten minutes.'

Lily smiles an insincere thanks, takes them, and makes a hasty exit.

'Bye, and say hello to your mum for me.'

Lily swallows and hopes to God Agnes keeps her mouth shut. She unlocks the bike and cycles to Silver Street, and her favourite coffee shop where she orders a latte and a brownie and takes a seat under the shade of a tree in the garden area. She checks her phone. Still nothing from Gemma. She nibbles on the brownie and wonders why she's not responding. She dials her number but once again, it rings into voicemail. Maybe she got so off her tits last night and left her phone at the cottage. She thinks about Chris. If Gemma's not at home, maybe she's with him. She calls his number, but he doesn't answer. She sips her latte and munches on the cake which is chewy and delicious. Her phone rings, startling her. It's Chris's number. At last. She answers.

'Hi. Is Gemma with you?'

He doesn't answer at first. All she hears is heavy, erratic breathing. 'Lily . . . is that you?' he asks, his voice quivering.

'Course it is. You called me back.'

'I didn't do it!' he cries, his voice breaking. 'I didn't do it!'

Lily's confused. 'Didn't do what?'

'Oh God!'

'Chris, where's Gemma? Is she with you?'

'Oh God . . . Gemma!' His voice is rising in pitch and begins to sob. 'Fuck! Fuck! Fuck! I didn't do it, I swear I didn't.'

Lily begins to fear the worst. Have the police or someone got hold of their videos? 'Take a breath, Chris, and tell me what's going on? Or put Gemma on.'

'I didn't hurt her. I promise, I didn't touch her.'

Lily catches her breath. 'What do you mean by "hurt her"?'

'You have to help her, Lily. I can't go back there. Maybe I got it wrong. Maybe she's OK.'

'What are you talking about?'

He takes a moment to respond. 'I don't know . . . last night when I dropped you, I went back to the cottage, and she was there. She was . . . she was . . .' He starts sobbing again.

'Where's Gemma, Chris?'

'She's at the cottage, where I left her.'

'What happened?'

'Tell them it wasn't me,' he says, ending the call.

'Shit!' Lily drops the phone in her bag, flies out of the coffee shop and unchains her bike. Pedalling as fast as she can, she reaches the cottage in just under fifteen minutes. There's no sign of Chris's car or any other car for that matter. Lily hops off her bike, lets it fall to the ground and runs into the cottage. 'Gemma!' she calls. The front door is ajar. She pushes it open and hurries inside. Other than the buzzing of flies, it's quiet. 'Gemma, it's Lils.' There's no response. A strange foreboding sensation that she can't explain takes hold of her. She swallows but makes her way towards the living room where they had performed live on camera. Pushing the door open, she notices the equipment, the camera, the ring lights, lying smashed up on the floor. She holds her breath. Peering round the door she sees a bare foot on the bed. She recognises Gemma's orange nail polish on her toes. 'Gemma,' she says, stepping into the room.

Confusion and horror sweep through Lily. Gemma is lying on the bed, naked, eyes wide, staring blankly at the ceiling. There's a gash on her forehead, and her chest is covered in blood. Lily stumbles backwards, her mouth open, speechless. She wants to scream but all that comes out is a pitiful weak cry. Shaking, she hurries from the room, slamming her shoulder on the door frame. Ignoring the pain, she stumbles from the house and runs from the cottage and onto the green. She keeps running until she trips and falls on her face on the grass. Gasping for breath she pushes herself up and then, finally, screams.

Chapter 33

ARCHER'S TEAM ARE GATHERED IN the incident room. Klara, Marian, Joely, Os and Quinn are all present. She brings them up to date with Klara's scoop on Chicken House madam, Margaret Jackson, and her connection with Sally McGowan. She does not mention the involvement of Fletcher on the investigation. Until they know more that info is being kept under wraps. The team give their updates. Across the office, Archer half listens; the chief inspector is watching them or is he watching her? She can't be sure.

'I have an update on Miles Davenport's house,' says Joely. 'The owner prior to him died a long time ago. I spoke to the agency Mr Davenport bought it from and can confirm he was correct in characterising it as a squat. There were squatters in and out of that place back in the eighties and early nineties. It may come as no surprise that we don't have any names.'

'Good work.'

'Grace, Os and I found a possible new lead that might be worth looking into,' says Klara.

Archer pulls her gaze away from Fletcher.

'It may not be related but it's worth checking up on. It's a case dating back to 1989. The victim was a thirty-five-year-old woman called Angela Bailey. She lived by herself in Warfield. According to the police report, she was a well-known alcoholic with a few minor convictions for stealing. There's nothing about her being a sex worker; however, the way she died matches Elena, Sally and Hannah.' Klara hands out a set of photocopied sheets to the team. 'Inside you'll find the police report and a few articles from the local papers.'

'Do we know who the investigating officers were?'

'As you can see on the report there is little mention of anyone other than the SIO and a detective constable whose name is John Reilly.'

'Have you been in touch?'

'I heard back this morning from his daughter, Samantha. He's in hospital. He has a weak heart and Covid to boot. There's no visiting, obviously, but as long as he agrees, we could possibly do a FaceTime later this morning around eleven. She says he's on the mend but there may be an issue. Covid has left him with brain fog, which has also impacted his memory.'

Any glimmer of hope vanishes suddenly.

'She's been helping him with puzzles and other stimuli to keep his mind active. She added that he loved his job and would probably jump at the chance to help out with an investigation.'

'Sounds promising,' says Quinn.

'Fingers crossed his memory is not as bad as Samatha made out,' Klara says.

The meeting ends. Archer heads for her desk and notices Fletcher standing in his doorway, hands in pockets, looking her way.

'A moment of your time, Grace, please.'

'Good luck,' Quinn whispers.

In his office Fletcher turns, nods at the small meeting table and says, 'Take a seat.' He stands over his desk momentarily and idly flips through a file.

'How can I help you, boss?' Archer asks.

Fletcher sighs heavily through his nose. After a moment he says, 'You were in therapy, I understand.'

'A while back.'

'How did that go?'

Archer feels herself bristling. Where is he going with this? 'It went as well as can be expected.'

His gaze is focused on the file, his fingers tapping it like a seagull hunting for worms. Has he compiled a file on her? A silence hangs in the air.

After two long minutes her patience is already thinning. 'Excuse me, but—'

He raises a finger. Archer sets her jaw, a cold fury igniting inside her.

'I understand you're still involved in the Elena Zoric investigation.'

'That's Lee Parry's case, sir.'

'Indeed it is, but you are still interfering.'

'DS Lee Parry would prefer to play golf with his pals than lead an investigation, sir.'

He turns to look at her, his neck and face flushing. 'His pals? You watch who you're talking to, DI Archer.'

Archer is stunned at the chief inspector's overreaction. But then it becomes clear. 'Apologies, boss. I hadn't realised DS Parry and you were golf buddies.'

Fletcher's jaw tightens but after a moment he relaxes, regaining his composure and control. He taps the file once more. 'Therapy. You knew Elena Zoric, personally. I'm thinking of you here. Perhaps some time out and therapy might help you adjust.'

Archer tries to quell the fire that is burning inside her. 'Boss, I'm a grown woman. A detective inspector who has seen worse than the murder of Elena Zoric, may she rest in peace. Forgive me for my bluntness, it's not clear to me what you're implying—'

'I'm not implying anything.'

Archer stands and meets his gaze.

'I am not a fragile female incapable of doing her job because someone she knew has been murdered.'

The air crackles between them. Fletcher closes the file.

'Was there anything else?' Archer asks.

'Keep me up to date. That's all I ask.'

'We update our reports on the system every day. Also, you're invited to every team meeting but you never come.'

'I prefer a personal update. Might be good for you and I to . . . bond.'

Archer feels her skin crawling. She has the sudden urge to throw Margaret Jackson's accusation at him but holds back. Now is not the time.

'That'll be all,' he says.

It's around 11.30 by the time they hear from Samantha Reilly giving them the green light to phone and FaceTime her father. Archer makes the call from the incident room using her iPad. Quinn sits out of sight listening in. She dials the number and waits for the video to connect. Within a few dials the call is answered by a woman in her thirties wearing a PPE mask. She is sitting beside a hospital bed. A thin, grey man wearing green pyjamas and a blue PPE mask is propped up with pillows. He's looking into the screen.

'Hello,' says the woman. 'Is that Detective Inspector Archer?'

'Yes. Hello.'

'I'm Samantha but everyone calls me Sam, and this is my dad, John.'

'Thank you so much for agreeing to talk to us.'

'You're very welcome,' she replies. 'I'll just hand you over to Dad. His voice is a bit gravelly and low, and the mask won't help. If you can't make out what he's saying let me know and I'll relay it.'

'OK. Perfect.'

Samantha hands her device to her father who holds it too close to his face.

'Hello, John,' Archer says. 'Can you hear me?'

He nods his head and gives the thumbs-up.

'John, we heard about a woman called Angela Bailey murdered back in 1989. Can you tell us a little bit about her, please?'

He nods his head and begins to speak but as Samantha had implied, his voice is low and hindered even more by the mask. 'I'm sorry, I can't hear you, John.' He beckons to his daughter. She leans in and he speaks into her ear. 'Dad says, if you ask the questions, I will relay,' she says, pulling her mask down. 'Don't need this. I've had my vaccine and boosters. As long as Dad is protected, we're OK.' She leans in again and listens to her father. After a moment, Sam answers the question. 'About Angela Bailey, he knew her by reputation, he says.' John is making a drinking sign with his hand. 'She liked to drink . . . do you mean she was an alcoholic, Dad?' He nods a yes. John is talking once more. Samantha is nodding as she listens. 'She was unemployed, he thinks, and was often in trouble for shoplifting. She had no family and few friends, he thinks. Although she wasn't homeless, she did spend a lot of time with homeless people. They would stay at her house, a mobile home, somewhere in Warfield, on a site which he thinks is no longer there.'

'What does he remember about the murder?'

'She had been badly beaten, he says. There was obviously a struggle. She had died with a puncture wound to the heart. They thought she'd been shot but no bullet was found at the scene. He'd never seen anything like it. She wasn't found for a week or so, when people began to notice the smell.'

'John, do you recall if there were any similar murders at the time?'

John shakes his head.

There's nothing in the report about witnesses but Archer decides to ask anyway.

Samantha is listening to his response.

'They interviewed quite a few homeless people, but nothing came of it. They all had some sort of alibi and there was no evidence or motive.'

John leans across and whispers.

'He remembers something else,' Samantha says.

After a moment she speaks. 'Something he found unusual. There was a ring missing from her finger. The indentation was still there on her corpse, but the ring was gone. Someone had gone to great lengths to take it. He says it seemed her finger had been broken in three places. He says it might have been a robbery.'

Chapter 34

Ange

Warfield, Berkshire. 1989

THE CLINK OF TUMBLING EMPTY bottles wakes Ange Bailey from a Buckfast-induced coma. She blinks open heavy eyes and turns her head, scanning the blurred gloom of the living room. The lights are off, all she can make out are shadows, motionless and quiet like a graveyard at midnight. Her head is mushy as she lies on the sofa, listless and weak as if the bones in her body have dissolved to dust. As her eyes adjust, she peers across at the window. The world outside is black and white, the small community of mobile homes, many of which are holiday rentals, is out-of-season dead. She hears the clinking once more. This time it sounds as if the bottles are being placed upright. Someone is outside.

She takes a breath, tries to ease herself forward but fails. She realises she's cradling a bottle. The sickly sweet smell is unmistakable. *Buckfast.* Had she polished off the entire contents? Of course she had. Nothing new in that. Her fingers ease off the bottle, it rolls and drops to the floor where it clatters amongst a litter of empty beer cans. *Shit! How much did I drink?* She feels her strength slowly returning and is able to roll onto her side and push herself up. Her head spins with disorientation momentarily as she straightens her back, rests her hands on the knees of her patched-up jeans. Two more breaths. She's feeling better, although she's parched, her tongue as thick and as dry as a rug.

Standing, she hobbles towards the window and peers outside. In the darkness, it's difficult to make anything out but a small flame appears, a matchstick glowing in the face of a stranger sitting at the white plastic garden table outside her home. He lights the tip of a cigarette and takes a swig from a can of something. He does not acknowledge her or show any indication that he knows she is watching; he just looks off into the distance as if deep in thought. She sniffs, wipes her mouth with her sleeve and combs her greasy hair back with her fingers. She opens the doors and steps outside onto her porch.

'This is private property,' she says.

He turns to look her way, exhales and takes a deep swig from his can. He swallows, bends down and lifts three cans of Special Brew hanging from a plastic connector ring. 'I'm just having a drink. Join me, if you want.'

Ange rolls her dry tongue over chapped lips, eyes sliding from the stranger to the beer and back again.

'Just one and I'll be on my way,' he says.

One can do no harm. Her head is still light as she makes her way down the steps to the table where she pulls out a chair and sits. With the fag between his teeth, the man pulls a can free from the ring and tosses it across. She catches it, snaps it open and takes three long gulps. The beer is smooth and sweet and deeply satisfying.

'Thirsty?'

She can make out his face now and realises she's seen him before. 'I've seen you. In the village.'

'Which one?'

'Warfield.'

'Possibly.'

'You sleeping rough?'

He does not answer.

'Can I have a fag?'

He slides across a packet of twenty Embassy Regal with the matches.

Ange takes out three, slips one into her mouth and two into the pocket of her denim shirt. She lights up, inhales the glorious smoke and slides the fags and matches back across. The booze and nicotine are kicking in and she's feeling better already. 'So what brings you all the way out here?'

'I was passing.'

She snorts a laugh. 'Passing? It's miles from anywhere and the buses stopped running hours ago.'

He holds her gaze with a flicker of a smile. 'I like walking in the countryside at night. I was going to drink these and find a field to sleep in for the night and then I came across this place.'

'Just like that?'

'Just like that.'

'You can't stay here.'

'I wouldn't intrude.'

They sit in silence for a moment, their smoke trails merging into one cloud.

'What's your name?' he asks.

'Angela. Most people call me Ange.'

'This your place?'

She nods.

'Nice.'

'It's a bit of a mess.'

'What do you do?'

'I'm in between jobs. Did a bit of cleaning and whatnot. On the dole but will be back to work soon enough.'

He says nothing.

'What's your name?'

'John.'

'What's your story?'

He sighs and looks down at his beer. She notices his knuckles are blistered. 'Been in a fight?'

He shrugs.

Ange swallows the last of the can, squeezes it and looks at the remaining two. John pulls a second off for her and sets it on the centre of the table.

'Thanks,' says Ange. 'I needed that.'

He opens the last can and drinks. 'Quiet here.'

'Most of these is second homes. Only a few of us live here.'

'How're your neighbours?'

'Don't have much to do with them. They're a bit stuck-up. Think they're better than me.'

'People can be like that,' he says, pinging his index finger off the can, his eyes never leaving hers.

She looks to the side and starts to bite her nails. How long has it been since anyone has shown interest in her? They sit quietly for what seems a long awkward five minutes before he shifts in the chair and says, 'I should get going.'

Ange bites her lip.

John stands. 'Nice to meet you.'

'No point in sleeping in a field. You can stay here if you like. Just for the night, mind.'

He smiles at her. 'You're a Good Samaritan.'

She smiles back, stands and leads the way, holding the door to her home open for him. He follows her inside.

'I'll just go to the toilet. Make yourself comfortable,' she says, scooping up the empty cans and throwing them into the sink which is already full of unclean dishes.

She makes her way down the narrow hallway and enters the small bathroom. Her nose wrinkles at the smell of dried shit and vomit on the toilet bowl. Pulling down her jeans, she squats down and pees. When she's done she takes the toilet brush and begins scrubbing the bowl. As it flushes, she runs cold water, rinses her mouth and fixes her hair in the mirror. She looks rough. He isn't much to look at, though, so beggars can't be choosers for either of them. With a final check in the mirror she steps into the hallway and jumps at the sight of his frame filling the small space. He has a vacant expression on his face. He's holding the empty Buckfast bottle by the neck above his head. She frowns. He slams the base of the bottle into her face. She stumbles backwards in shock and falls to floor, eyes wide as he straddles her. He presses something hard into her chest.

'Stop!' she cries but her voice is drowned by a loud cracking sound. A sharp icy pain explodes in her chest before the world fades to darkness.

Chapter 35

'COULD HAVE BEEN A ROBBERY?' Quinn says. 'Not the same killer, then.'

The FaceTime call had ended five minutes back. Archer is thinking, her index finger gently tapping the glass surface of her iPhone.

Quinn continues: 'Angela Bailey hung out with rough sleepers and drunks. Perhaps one of them saw an opportunity to take from her. She put up a struggle and got done for her trouble.'

'Do you really believe that?'

Quinn shakes his head. 'Nope.'

'Could be we have just learned something about the killer.'

'What're you thinking?' Quinn asks.

'I'm thinking we should talk to Marianne.'

'OK . . .'

Archer presses a key on the laptop and brings the screen back to life. She clicks on the HOLMES2 icon, logs in with her credentials, and searches for the files listed under Elena Zoric's murder. Scrolling through the windows, she finds what she's looking for: the Exhibits document containing all the items, including Elena's belongings, seized from the scene.

'I see where you're going with this,' Quinn says.

'I knew you'd catch up.'

Archer grabs her phone and types a text to Elena's girlfriend:

Marianne, can we meet? I need to ask some questions. Hope you're OK. Grace

Moments later her phone pings.

I'd rather not.

Archer texts back.

There are more murders by the same man. Please.

Moments pass with no answer. And then: *I'm in Blarneys Pub in Edgware.*

Archer texts back saying they're on their way.

'We're off to Blarneys,' Archer says.

'Don't want to rain on your parade but what about Parry? According to him and Fletcher, Elena's murder is his case.'

Archer runs a hand through her hair and takes a moment to think this over. Quinn is right. Excluding Parry could trigger a Fletcher shitstorm that might result in her having zero involvement in Elena's case. Any excuse to drop her. She calls him on her mobile. After five rings the call goes to voicemail. *Typical.* She leaves a message: 'DS Parry, it's Grace Archer. Call me as soon as you get this.' She hangs up and turns to Quinn. 'Does he ever answer his phone?'

Before Quinn can respond, Archer's phone rings. 'It's him.' She swipes to answer and turns on the speaker option. 'DS Parry, it's Grace Archer. I'm with Harry and you're on speaker.'

'Sorry I missed your call. I was driving and just pulled over.'

'Appreciate you calling back . . .' Archer updates him on the murder of Angela Bailey.

'How sure are you it's related to Elena and the others?'

'I'm certain they're related—'

'Is this a hunch or a fact?'

'Marianne could help confirm it's a fact.'

She hears him sigh. 'OK, I'll call her when I get into the office.'

Quinn interjects and winks at Archer. 'Lee, mate, don't come at us but we've already been in touch with her. She's in a boozer called Blarneys in Edgware. Can you meet us there?'

'Um . . . is she? OK, sure. Um . . . I'm not far. I can be there in twenty minutes.'

'Great,' says Archer. 'See you there.'

With the call ended, Archer says, 'Funny how he responds better to you.'

'He's a dick.'

'A misogynist dick.'

On the drive there, Archer's Google Maps search reveals Blarneys is ten minutes from the Silk Stream. Archer wonders if Marianne has been visiting the spot where Elena was murdered and is seeking solace in the first bar she passes by. They're driving through Edgware, approaching a row of shops and businesses. Painted an eye-watering lurid green, Blarneys, a shabby traditional pub, is squeezed between a cheap holiday and tours agency and a news and wine shop (a winning combination, obviously). Archer is searching for parking spots on Google GPS. 'We should find something next left. Watling Avenue.'

Quinn indicates, turns left and drives down Watling Avenue, a wide, long and busy thoroughfare with multicoloured shops, catering for all ethnicities from the local neighbourhood. There's a lane of parking spaces lining the pavement, but they are all occupied. Quinn plumps for a loading bay, which is being vacated by a white van.

Marianne is waiting for them inside Blarneys, sitting alone with no sign of Parry. Her head is down, her hands wrapped tightly around the frothy remains of a pint of Guinness. She looks up as they approach, her expression grim, distant, her eyes puffy and red. Archer takes the seat opposite. It would be glib to ask how she is so she gets straight down to business.

'Thanks for seeing us at such short notice.'

Marianne gives her a blank expression and finishes the remains of her pint.

'Can I get you another one of those?' Quinn asks.

She pushes the glass across the table.

'Coming up.' Quinn heads to the bar.

The pub door opens. Archer looks back, expecting to see Parry but it's not him, just a customer, a man with walking sticks shuffling inside.

'It's good to see you,' Archer says.

Marianne's eyes are fixed on the tabletop.

'I have a list of items recovered from Elena,' Archer says.

Marianne frowns, lets out a heavy sigh and drops her head.

'I need you to look at it.'

She shrugs, shakes her head and asks, 'Why?' There's the slightest of slurs in her voice.

Archer slides the sheet across the table. 'Tell me if anything is missing.'

Marianne narrows her gaze at Archer. 'What's the point? She's gone!'

Quinn returns, takes the seat next to Archer and sets the pint in front of Marianne. 'Here you go,' he says.

Marianne necks half of it.

'Did you get Parry's text?' Quinn asks Archer.

She taps the phone on her screen. No new messages. 'Doesn't look like it.'

'He can't make it,' says Quinn.

Archer feels a stab of irritation. 'No surprises there.'

'Says Fletcher called him in. Didn't say why.'

A knot in her stomach. Archer has the sense this case may be slipping from her fingers. She tries not to think about it and focuses back on Marianne. 'The man who killed Elena is still out there. He will kill again.'

For a moment, it had seemed that Marianne is not listening, but she takes a sharp intake of breath and closes her eyes. Trembling, she blinks, eyes watering. Tears roll down her cheeks. She lifts the pint, arm shaking, and swallows a mouthful.

Archer and Quinn exchange a concerned look.

Archer's phone rings. Fletcher. What does he want? He'll have to wait. She turns the phone to silent.

Marianne sets the glass down and wipes her eyes with the back of her hand. She looks down at the exhibit sheet from Elena's file. Tentatively, she takes it in her hands and reads through the list of items. Her face contorts with a pained expression as she reads through the list of clothes and personal items that were scooped from the scene where the love of her life was brutally murdered. She frowns and touches her chest. Archer can see the imprint of a necklace underneath her T-shirt. Marianne places the sheet on the table and leans in for a closer look, running her finger down each item one at a time.

'What is it?' Archer asks.

Archer's phone rings once more. Fletcher, again. She lets the call go to voicemail.

After a moment, Marianne meets her gaze. She reaches under the neckline of her T-shirt and pulls out the necklace. It's a fine gold chain containing a gold pendant, half a heart which is also part jigsaw puzzle.

'Elena has the other half of this heart. We bought them before the pandemic. We've never taken them off.' Marianne's face tightens, her finger stabs at the paper. 'Hers is not on the list.'

Archer lifts the sheet from table and folds it. 'No more questions, Marianne. Thank you.' She stands. 'If you need anything, please call me at any time of the day or night.'

'Just find whoever did this. Find him and lock him up. Forever.' Marianne's expression is fused with both rage and sorrow.

Archer feels Marianne's emotions ripple through her. She had been so fond of Elena. She was a bright light, a ball of energy and optimism that drew you to her. They had much in common with childhood traumas. Elena had been the victim of human trafficking. With Archer's help she had escaped and put her captors in jail. She had rebuilt her life with her lover and best friend, Marianne. For some, Elena's life choices would not have added up to much of a life. Yet for these two women it was theirs and they were happy. Archer feels a tightness in her throat. 'I promise you, I will find him.'

Chapter 36

CHIEF INSPECTOR FLETCHER HAD LEFT a voicemail for Archer instructing her and Quinn to return to Charing Cross Police Station 'pronto'.

'Pronto?' Quinn had said on the drive back. 'Who says "pronto", for Christ's sake!'

'He once said "capiche" to me at the end of a sentence.'

'And suddenly he's Tony Soprano,' Quinn laughs.

Reaching the third floor, Archer is surprised to see Parry sitting at the table in the incident room with Fletcher at the head. Klara, DC Phillips, and DS Tozer are there too. Parry and the team are all smiles, lapping up whatever anecdote of 'wisdom' is spewing out of Fletcher's ego, despite the grim stories depicted on the murder wall. Over the years, Archer has come to view the hub of a multiple murder investigation with an ecclesiastical degree of respect, and she expects the same from her team. She knocks on the office door. Fletcher summons them inside.

'Are you in the habit of ignoring the boss's calls?' Fletcher says by way of a greeting. He chuckles as if he didn't really mean it.

'Apologies, boss, we were interviewing Elena Zoric's girl-friend.' She looks at Parry. 'Shame you couldn't be there,' she says tersely.

'Don't blame Lee. I called him.'

Archer turns to Fletcher. 'You're the "boss".'

'Yes, I am.'

Archer remains tight-lipped and takes a seat.

'What have we missed?' asks Quinn.

'There's been another murder, it seems,' Fletcher replies.

Archer feels her stomach clench. 'Where, when?'

'In Northumbria. Berwick-Upon-Tweed, to be precise, yesterday. A young woman was killed in a cottage that was the location for some sort of photography studio that records porn and live sex performances. I'd like you and Lee to go up there and see if it is linked to the current case. Harry can stay behind and look after things down here.'

Archer is confused. Why is Fletcher suddenly supporting her involvement in the case? As if reading her mind he says, 'Perhaps we've had our ups and downs on this investigation, but Lee persuaded me that it was best to keep you onside.'

'Onside, boss? That implies I'm the enemy.'

Fletcher lifts his arms in a placating manner, 'That's not what I meant. It just seems that you two were not . . .' Fletcher is searching for the words, '. . . gelling.'

'Gelling,' Archer says.

'That's correct.'

'We're making headway now, sir,' Parry interjects, his fist almost punching the air. 'As I said, Grace and Harry have made good progress and we're coming together as a team.'

Quinn coughs in the background.

Archer blinks. Is Parry asserting himself as SIO? She catches a look from Quinn. His eyebrows are arched to the point of crashing through the ceiling.

'Any questions?'

Tension crackles in the air. Archer's narrowed eyes dart from Fletcher to Parry and back to Fletcher, like the final showdown of a spaghetti western.

'Right then. I'll leave you to it.'

Fletcher stands and rolls his shoulders. 'Keep me abreast of everything.' He leaves, and strides towards his office.

Parry is about to speak but Archer raises her hand. 'Hold that thought, DS Parry.' She marches out of the incident room, across the third floor, and follows Fletcher into his office. 'A moment of your time, boss.'

Fletcher holds her gaze for a moment with an unamused expression. 'I thought we were done.'

'What's going on?' she asks.

'I'm not sure I understand the question.'

'Have you put Parry in charge?'

'What makes you ask that?'

'I get the impression you are sidelining me from the invest- igation.'

'Sidelining you?'

'Parry does not have the experience to manage a case of this size and complexity.'

Fletcher sits behind his desk and leans back. He hesitates before saying, 'Go on.'

'Parry has been a DS for just under a year. I have no doubt he will get to where he should be, but he needs more experience. Right now he doesn't . . .' Archer hesitates. Should she come out and say it? *Fuck it* . . . 'He has no sense of responsibility or urgency. If he were on my team I would have had him on report by now.'

Fletcher nods his head, slowly. 'Is that so?'

Archer wants to say more. She wants to question Fletcher's bias because of his connection with Parry and his family but decides it's best to say no more.

'Grace, I agree,' says Fletcher.

'You agree?'

223

Fletcher leans forward, elbows on the desk, sausage fingers entwined. 'He needs coaching. I can help. And so can you.'

'You want me to coach Parry.'

'As you stated, you are the SIO. From today I'd like you take over Elena Zoric's case, too.'

Archer is confused. 'But you didn't mention that in the incident room just now.'

'I did. You just weren't there to hear it. I've had a quiet word with Lee, and he recognises your experience and track record. With the latest murder in mind, he is happy to work alongside you as a senior member of the team.'

'A senior member ... is there some hidden meaning in there?'

'For this investigation, Parry will be your second. He's your new DS.'

Archer folds her arms. Through the glass walls and across the office, she sees Quinn looking back. 'Respectfully, boss, I already have a DS.'

'Respectfully, Grace, Parry will take over from Quinn.'

Archer feels her shoulders tightening.

'Get the train to Berwick first thing tomorrow morning. Make sure you both travel together. Mentor him, Grace. Make him a better detective. It can only help the investigation. And it will look good on you. The commissioner will be pleased.'

Archer holds Fletcher's gaze and briefly pictures herself smashing his red face in. She knows that he understands she is the only chance he has of finding the killer and closing the case. The truth is she has no choice in the matter and will go to Berwick with Parry, holding his hand, as Fletcher has implied. Besides, she is done talking. 'If that's what you want.'

'It is.'

Fletcher nods in a sage-like fashion, an unconvincing gesture for a man of his limited intelligence. 'Remember to keep me up to date at every opportunity.'

'Yes, sir.' Archer turns and exits the office with a dark cloud following overhead.

Chapter 37

TWENTY-FOUR HOURS HAVE PASSED SINCE Lily found Gemma's body at the cottage, in the same room where she and Gemma had performed live sex acts on camera for money. Money given to her by that seedy swine, Chris Townsend, the man wanted for Gemma's murder. Shock had set in, followed by a stage of disbelief and then came the horror, grief and tears. They had fallen from her until it seemed she had dried up and shrivelled like a raisin. She feels numb but also terrified that the police and everyone else will find out what she was doing that night at the cottage. Oh God, she wants to die! Her mind is racing. Not just with the implications for her but what could have happened. Had she stayed longer that evening, would Chris have murdered her, too? He is certainly strong enough to overcome both of them. The thought is just unbearable. But if that was his plan, why didn't he do it when he got her away from Gemma and into his car? She wonders if Gemma and Chris had had an argument after she'd gone. Gemma had mentioned how he'd sometimes fly off the handle and lose his shit. Maybe he was high on something more than weed. Lily shudders at the thought. When she spoke to him yesterday on the phone, he seemed desperate, frantic in his denial of hurting Gemma. For a moment she had believed him until she remembered Gemma's concerns about his temper.

She had told this to the police at the scene. They had taken their notes, thanked her and told her detectives would come to see her soon. She thinks of Chris. In her head he's guilty, despite his cries of innocence on the phone. The truth is she has never much cared for him anyway. He is scruffy, cocky, full of himself and seven years older than Gemma. Lily could honestly never see what Gemma saw in him. She could have done so much better. Poor Gemma. She'll never do better now. Lily scratches the skin on her arms, a terrible habit she has had since she was young.

She hasn't slept a wink and is utterly wiped out. Every time she had closed her eyes during the night the image of Gemma's bruised and bloody body flashed in her mind. She had lain awake with the lights on, reading with despair the awful rumours and speculation spreading across social media with the ferocity of another bloody pandemic. Mum had popped her head around the door, but Lily shut her eyes and pretended to sleep. She couldn't face her, not with the sordid memories of what she and Gemma had been doing that night. On local chat groups, people were listing names, speculating who the dead girl at the cottage could be. Over a dozen names were mentioned, Lily's included, but each of them was accounted for by neighbours, relatives or friends who had seen the named individuals after the mysterious murder. As for Lily, she had allegedly been spotted on her bicycle cycling into town, after the event. Apparently, she'd deposited a large amount of money, someone mentioned. Lily had gasped when she'd read that, cursing shopkeeper Agnes Coates and her blabbering loose lips. Cow! That aside, the weird thing about all this conjecture was that Gemma's name was not even mentioned. Gemma was well known, popular and pretty, and seemingly forgotten. It's as if, without knowing that Gemma is the actual "dead girl", they have already erased her from their consciousness. Lily shivers at the thought.

The doorbell rings, shaking her from her reverie. She hears talking. Men's voices that she doesn't recognise. Footsteps on the stairs follow and a gentle knock on the bedroom door.

'Lily, can I come in?' Mum says.

More than anything Lily wants her mum right now, but guilt is clawing at her with jagged nails. The thought that Mum, and everyone else for that matter, will find out what she's been up to is making her nauseous.

'One minute,' Lily replies.

Mum enters, sits on the edge of the bed and takes Lily's hand. 'How are you feeling?'

Lily takes a moment to answer. 'Confused, scared . . .'

Mum is pale and drawn. Lily knows she has also not slept.

'Oh, my girl,' she says, kissing her forehead. She sits back up and strokes her hair. 'Can you come downstairs?'

Lily shakes her head.

'The police are here.'

Lily's stomach churns. 'I can't talk to them again, Mum. I told them all I know.'

'I understand that, love, but I need you to be brave. This is a murder investigation, and the men downstairs are detectives. One of them is the son of your dad's friend, Stuart Vickers.'

'But—'

'No buts. We must do what's right for Gemma. We need to find this Chris.'

'But I don't know where he is.'

'You may know more than you realise. Let them do the talking. Dad and I will be with you.' Mum stands. 'Come with me. I'll take you down.'

Lily sighs heavily and hauls herself out of bed.

Dad is standing at the fireplace, arms folded, a grim expression on his face. The detectives are sitting next to each other on the sofa. Lily doesn't meet their gaze as her mum nudges her into the living room. They introduce themselves. One is red-haired and pale and goes by the name of DC Andy Ball. The second, DC Stuart Vickers, is bald with a beard.

'The kettle's just boiled,' Mum says to the men. 'Can I get you anything to drink?'

'Tea, two sugars, please, Isla,' says DC Vickers. The one called Ball asks for the same without the sugar.

'Lily, how about you?'

Lily shakes her head.

'Sit down, then,' Lily's mum says, gesturing at the armchair.

Lily sits down and scratches her arms. Red welts appear.

'Lily, don't scratch your arms,' Dad says.

Lily flushes and folds her arms.

'Stu mentioned you were a copper once,' Ball says to Dad.

Lily's dad puffs his chest out. 'I was. Fifteen years on the force. Worked all over. London, Bristol, other parts of the West Country.'

'He worked here in Berwick. With my old man,' says DC Vickers.

Arriving with the drinks, Lily's mum hands them across.

Dad laughs. 'Yes, we were young constables together. That was an age ago.' 'How's he doing?'

'Just become a grandad so he's happy.'

'Say hello from me. Funny, I was being interviewed for the telly recently about an investigation I was involved with back then.'

'We heard,' says Ball.

230

Lily can detect an edge to his tone and watches him furtively, wondering what he's thinking.

'You know the case?' Lily's dad asks.

'Not much. We heard there was an altercation.'

Lily's dad shifts on his feet. 'It was nothing.'

Lily feels DC Vickers watching her. She stares down at her feet, pretending she's not there.

'Shall we begin?' Ball asks, who seems to be taking the lead.

'Please,' replies Mum. 'Obviously, Lily's not feeling her best, so let's make this as quick as we can.'

'We'll do our best,' says Ball. 'So, to give you an update, we have had two sightings of Chris Townsend in the Highlands. He has family and friends there. Thinks he can hide out, I suppose, but we're on his trail and are pretty close to finding him.'

'How close?' Mum asks.

'It's hard to say,' says Vickers.

'We'll keep you up to date,' adds Ball. He turns to Lily. 'How well do know Mr Townsend, Lily?'

Lily shrugs. 'Not every well. Gemma liked him. They were close.'

'Boyfriend, girlfriend close?'

'I don't know if they were official, but they were seeing each other.'

'Did you ever see him be violent towards her?'

She shakes her head.

'Would you say he has a temper?'

She nods.

'Did you ever see him lose it?'

'No.'

'How did you know he had a temper?'

'Something Gemma would say.'

'Like what?'

She takes a moment to think. 'Um . . . if she was late, he'd flip . . . if she talked to another bloke, he'd lose his rag. He's jealous. Gemma always said he was insecure.'

'Did Gemma mention him being violent?'

'No.'

The detective narrows his gaze as if disappointed by her answer. 'Had you been to the cottage before yesterday?'

'Once or twice.'

'What was Chris doing there?'

Lily picks at the polish on her nails. 'What do you mean?'

'Clearly, it wasn't Mr Townsend's residence. It's a long-time empty property. All the rooms have no furniture.'

Lily shrugs. 'I dunno.'

'I say they had no furniture – the living room was the exception.'

Both policemen are watching her curiously.

'Did you know what he used it for?'

Lily feels herself closing in. She wants to leave, to run for the door.

'Lily, if you know something, please tell us,' says her mum.

Lily shakes her head, eyes fixed on the beige carpet.

'It looks like it was set up as some sort of photography studio. Do you know anything about that, Lily?' Ball asks.

Lily's heart is pounding. She feels herself flushing. 'I don't feel very well,' she says.

'I'll get you some water,' her mum says.

Lily's stomach is roiling. She can taste the bitter bile in her throat and bolts from the living room to the downstairs toilet. Falling to her knees, she retches and vomits.

Her mum appears and holds back her hair. 'Oh dear. This is all too much for you.'

To her relief, she hears the detectives leaving. Mum strokes her back. Lily leans into her mum's arms, sinking into her warm embrace. Tears fill Lily's eyes, and she begins to sob.

'Oh, my darling.'

She hears Dad approaching. His shadow fills the doorway.

'They're gone,' he says. 'But they'll need to talk to you again.'

Lily presses herself into her mum. 'I can't, Mum. I can't.'

'Let's see how we get on,' she replies.

Chapter 38

GEMMA MCFADDEN'S MURDER HAS MADE the front pages. Her young, smiling face is plastered across the newsstands of a bustling King's Cross Station, with lurid headlines and wild speculation about sex, pornography, drugs and murder. Archer picks up the *Guardian*, hoping for a more balanced report on Miss McFadden's death. It's ten minutes away from 7 a.m. and there is no sign of Parry. In truth, she's expecting another cancellation. Perhaps he'll cry off sick and follow her up in a day or two when it's all over. The train leaves at seven. She isn't waiting any longer and is actually relieved he isn't coming. At the self-checkout, she scans the paper, pays with her card and makes her way quickly across the concourse to the platform.

'Grace! Wait up,' comes a voice. It's Parry.

Archer grits her teeth and turns to see him threading his way through the crowd.

'Morning. Sorry. I was hoping to get here earlier but . . . London, y'know.'

'Our train is leaving in minutes. We should hurry,' Archer says, quickening her pace.

'Yes, yes. Of course. Berwick-Upon-Tweed. Here we come!' He chuckles.

Archer frowns to herself. *Does he think we're going on some sort of jolly?*

They're twenty minutes outside of London. Next stop is Peterborough. Archer is burying her irritation at Parry in the pages of the *Guardian*, rereading the article for the third time and taking in everything she can about the twenty-year-old, Gemma McFadden. According to friends and neighbours, she was the kindest, sweetest, and gentlest girl who cared and made time for everyone no matter who they were. According to an anonymous source: 'The horror and devastation was palpable among the local community.' Someone else commented: 'You read about this kind of thing in the papers. You see it on the telly but you never expect it to arrive here in Berwick-Upon-Tweed, of all places.' Agnes Coates, forty-eight, widow and shopkeeper says she had warned Gemma to stay away from that Chris Townsend. 'He's a bad egg, that one. She didn't listen and now look. It'll happen again. You mark my words! Could be me next. I'm afraid to go out.'

Parry is sitting opposite, his fingers drumming the tabletop. The drumming stops suddenly. She hears him shuffling around. Over the top of the paper, she sees him with his phone. He presses the screen and puts the phone to his ear. She catches his eyes.

'Just calling the big man,' he says.

The big man.

She raises the paper and puffs out a breath.

'Morning, Les. Hope you're well. Just phoning with an update. Grace and I just about made the train this morning ...'

Archer shakes her head. This is going to be a long journey.

'We're on our way to Berwick-Upon-Tweed. We'll be there for 10.30, I think. I'll let you know when we arrive. Anyhoo, more importantly, did you see the match last night? It was a blinder! That goal in the last thirty seconds. How jammy was that ... you have to go ... OK ... have a good one and talk later . . . bye.' Parry ends the call and places his phone on the table. Folding his arms, he turns his gaze to the countryside beyond the window and smiles.

'Four women have been murdered,' Archer says lowering the paper.

Parry meets her gaze and blinks. 'I know,' he says quietly.

'But last night's football match is more important?'

'I didn't . . . that's not . . . no it's not.' His face pinches. 'I was giving him an update that we were on the train.'

They sit in silence for a moment. Archer takes a breath and tries to rein in her vexation, knowing she is going to have to work closely with Parry regardless of what she thinks of him. That aside, she's beginning to wonder if there is more to this pairing than she imagined. Does Fletcher expect Parry to report back on what she's up to? Maybe she's being paranoid, but it wouldn't surprise her if Fletcher was looking to discredit her at the first opportunity. He knows she doesn't always play by the rules. That's reason enough for a patriarchal dinosaur.

'Um . . . Grace, sorry if we got off on the wrong foot today. I apologise. I didn't mean to . . . I know my mouth can get ahead of my mind sometimes.'

Archer sighs. She really doesn't want this investigation to be any more difficult than it already is. 'Apology accepted.'

Parry smiles and shuffles out of his seat. 'Excellent! Thank you. I fancy a tea. Can I get you anything?'

'I'll have a tea also. Just milk.'

'Can I get you biscuits or a sandwich?' Parry doesn't give her time to answer. 'I'll just get you a mixture,' he says, disappearing towards the buffet carriage.

Her phone rings. She smiles and swipes to answer. 'Good morning.'

'Good morning to you,' says Liam Duffy.

A voice comes over the tannoy announcing the imminent arrival in Peterborough.

'Are you on a train?' he asks.

'I am.'

'Well, that might explain why you're not here.'

'I had to leave early this morning. Urgent trip.'

'I see. That's a shame. I have fresh croissants and bagels. The coffee's brewing.'

Archer feels oddly warm at the thought of sitting with Liam at the breakfast table eating croissants and bagels and drinking freshly brewed nutty coffee. 'I could do with that now.' She notices Parry wobbling down the carriage, arms full with packaged sandwiches, crisps, biscuits, and a cardboard tray containing hot drinks. 'My breakfast looks fit for the economy ticket holder.'

'No first class for you, then? That's a travesty.'

'The police have no idea how to treat a girl,' Archer says.

'It would seem so.' Liam chuckles.

Parry bends over the table, slides the drinks across and gently lets the food tumble to the surface. She catches him giving her a fleeting frown. Liam is talking but Archer realises that Parry had heard her statement about the police not knowing how to treat a girl and has probably, in the context of the investigation, misinterpreted her words.

'So what do you think?' Liam asks.

Archer is caught off guard. 'I'm sorry, I didn't catch that?'

'I was saying that the painting will be finished by the weekend, and then we can think about laying the parquet flooring.'

'Sounds good.'

'Grand. Listen, when are you back?'

'It's hard to know at this stage.'

238

'No problem. If you're not going to be home, then what do you think about me working into the evenings? I could finish the painting sooner, obviously.'

'That sounds like a great idea.'

'OK. Listen, I'd say have a good trip, but that's probably inappropriate.'

'I appreciate the sentiment. Thanks. Have a good day.'

'You too.'

Chapter 39

TWO DAYS EARLIER, AFTER THE successful release of the Hannah Daysy podcast, Bruce had picked up an email from a Somerset listener called Gwen Baker. She had indicated that she believed there was another murder, similar to Hannah's, of a woman called Star Royale. Mallory had emailed her back straight away. She waited, excited about a new story but Gwen's response arrived later that evening just before Mallory was turning in. Gwen had apologised, saying there was a family crisis that she had to deal with, but it was all fine now. She had left her number. Mallory called immediately but no one answered. She rang again and again but each time it went to voicemail. She left a brief message on the third attempt and went to sleep, disappointed.

Mallory dreamed of Hannah at night on a remote road, breathless as she tried to run from the man who had picked her up in his car. She had felt Hannah's terror and gasped as the figure of the killer emerged from the darkness. Her heart pounded. Something was not quite right. It wasn't Hannah's killer. It was her brother's, the Raincoat Killer, dressed in his long wax coat and hat. He approached with his knife dripping blood. Zach's blood. She didn't know how she knew it was his, she just did.

His face is concealed in the darkness, but his mouth is open and a long red tongue slides out and licks the blood from the blade. Terror turns to fury and she screams at him. He laughs, runs at her and plunges the blade into her chest—

Mallory's eyes shoot open as she wakes to the sound of her own screaming. Her bedside lamp is on.

She feels a warm hand resting on her arm and flinches.

'Hey. It's only me,' says Bruce.

Her heart is pounding, a layer of sweat coats her skin. As her vision adjusts, she sees Bruce in his wheelchair, dressed in boxers and a T-shirt, looking at her with a worried expression.

'Sorry . . .' Mallory shudders at the memory of the dream and rubs her chest, half expecting to feel warm blood.

'I heard you from my room. Must have been a bad one,' Bruce says.

'A humdinger.'

'Room for one more?'

Mallory pulls the covers down and makes room for him. He slides from the wheelchair, drags his legs onto the bed and curls up beside her. Mallory pulls the covers over him and leans into his side. Zach's murder is still painful and raw like an untreated wound. It has become an unspoken rule that they will be there for each other to provide comfort and support as and when needed.

'Sorry if I woke you,' she says.

'I was awake already.'

She doesn't press him on this. She understands her nightmares are nothing compared to the terrors he relives when he closes his eyes.

'Do you think we'll ever get through this?' he asks.

Three years have passed since that night. That fucking, fateful, horrible night when their lives changed for ever.

She feels the tears building behind her eyes and closes them. 'It's going to take more time, Boo.'

'Yeah . . . I know,' he whispers.

They lie together until Mallory's 7 a.m. Alexa alarm shakes them from their dozing.

'Alexa, stop!' Mallory says, her voice dry. She slides across the bed and stretches. Bruce swings himself around and sits on the edge of the bed, rubbing his arms.

'OK, Boo?'

He yawns. 'I need to sleep more,' he replies and shifts across to his chair. 'I'll make some coffee. Do you fancy eggs?'

'And a side of pancakes, sausage and bacon, please.'

They rarely have food in the apartment. He raises an eyebrow at her.

'Deliveroo it,' she says.

Mallory showers, dresses and, after picking at her breakfast, eventually gets a call from Gwen Baker.

'I'm sorry I missed your calls,' Gwen says in a sweet, soft West Country accent. 'It had been a long day, and I was knackered, so I took myself off to bed.'

'No worries.'

Mallory hears the sound of young people arguing in the background.

'Listen, I'm just running to work and have to drop the kids at school. Can I call you later?'

Mallory is beginning to wonder if Gwen is serious or not. 'Sure, listen, I tried to look Star up online and couldn't find anything about her.'

'That doesn't surprise me. That's not her real name.'

'Mum, hurry up!' comes the voice of what sounds like an impatient teenager.

'That would explain why.'

'I'm on the phone, Lizzie, can you please wait?' Gwen says to the teenager. 'I'm sorry, I have to go. The police have a lot to answer for.'

'Why do you say that?'

'They weren't interested in her. Some police believed she got what was coming to her.'

Mallory has heard all she needs to hear. This was the same police reaction to Hannah. 'Do you get a lunch break?' she asks.

'Erm . . . yes.'

'Can you meet me? I'll buy lunch. Wherever you like.'

'But you're in London.'

'Yes, but later I will be in Somerset.'

'Oh!'

With the lunchtime meeting agreed, Mallory grabs her purse, phone, laptop and all the chargers she needs before checking in with Bruce. She pops her head around his bedroom door. The shutters are closed, and it's gloomy. It's always gloomy. Bruce is lying on the bed, snoring quietly. She notices a bottle of sleeping tablets on his bedside table. She prays he's not reliving that night. 'Sweet dreams, Boo.' She slips quietly away and makes a mental note to call him later.

At Paddington station, she hurries across the concourse, scans her ticket and, with a minute to spare, hops onto the last carriage of the 9.37 to Taunton as the whistle blows and the doors close. She makes her way to the middle of the train, excited at the possibility of a new story that could be related to Hannah Daysy, and the other victims currently being invest-igated by DI Grace Archer. She has considered calling Archer to update her but decides against it. She's already handed over everything on Hannah, and decides she will do so again once she's got the scoop on Star Royale.

Mallory scrolls through the news on her phone and holds her breath at a headline.

Sex trade woman murdered in Northumbrian porn cottage

A crass title that somehow strikes a chord. She speed reads the article, her heart racing. Gemma McFadden. Eighteen years old. Possibly involved in pornography or the sex trade, the article speculates. The grisly details of her murder match those of Elena, Hannah and Sally. Mallory bites her thumb. Scrolling through other newspapers she finds similar articles. Is Archer aware, and working on the case? At the least, she must know about it considering the murder is all over the media.

Mallory changes for the Bridgwater train at Taunton almost two hours later and, despite the train running behind schedule, arrives with enough time to make it to the café. Navigating with Google Maps, Mallory makes her way across town, uncertain what she feels about the place, which seems to be made up of bland modern cottages, many with England flags in the windows. The pavements are narrow, the road gridlocked with cars and trucks, and the bitter taste of diesel is in the air. She arrives at Eastover, a small bridge spanning the River Parrett. On the side is the West Quay where there is a row of shops, pubs and cafés. The Fountain Inn is an ornate Victorian building painted black and grey. She is fifteen minutes early, and there are some tables available outside overlooking the river. She grabs one and waits.

There are several people walking across the bridge towards the pub. Mallory is certain the middle-aged woman with the dyed auburn hair and sleeveless white blouse is Gwen Baker. It's not a hard call. Besides, she's looking across at Mallory with a warm smile on her face. Mallory stands and returns the smile. 'Gwen?'

'Yes, I recognised you right away.'

'The tattoos, I suppose.'

Gwen looks at Mallory's arms, which are painted with a rich tapestry of black foliage. The only colour is the large butterfly, inked in reds, greens and blues in the crook of her elbow.

'You got that after your brother died,' Gwen says.

'He loved nature. Butterflies, especially. It's actually a painting of his.'

'Yes, I heard you talk about it on your show. It's very beautiful.'

'Thank you. Can I get you a drink?'

'A Diet Coke would be nice.'

Mallory returns five minutes later with a Diet Coke each. 'Thank you for seeing me at such short notice.'

'Not at all. It's so sad that there's been no justice for Star all these years later. Her life ended so horribly. Her story should be told.'

'Gwen, do you mind if I record this conversation? Perhaps I can use some of it on the podcast.'

'No, that's fine,' she replies, taking a sip of her drink.

Mallory presses the *record* button and pushes the phone across the table closer to Gwen.

'Tell me about Star. What was she like?'

'I always think of Star as a girl. But she wasn't really.'

'What do you mean?'

'Star was a boy. I don't know what he was back then. Not sure he did, either. He'd say he was a transvestite 'cause he liked to dress in women's clothes now and again. But you never hear that term now, do you?'

'No, I suppose you don't. What was his real name?'

'Kelvin Glover. I knew him from school. He was quite flamboyant even back then, when it was not really accepted like it is these days. He loved to dress up. At the time, Boy George and all those types were popular. It was becoming common, although not so much in Bridgwater, but that didn't deter him. Kelvin and I left school at sixteen. We lost contact, but I'd see him occasionally in the supermarket or the streets but never

246

as his alter ego. She appeared a few years later with a notorious reputation that'd make your toes curl. Star loved that people talked about him. Anyway, time passed quickly, as it does. I'd heard he'd was involved with the wrong people and was doing drugs. Heroin, mostly. I bumped into him one night when I was coming home from the pub. He was dressed to kill and looked fabulous. That's when he revealed to me he was Star Royale, and Kelvin Glover was no more. We were both pissed. He also told me he was a "working girl" – was quite proud of the fact, too. He became one to fund his addiction. The punters were fond of him.' She leans across the table. 'Gave the best blow jobs, apparently. And swallowed, too.' Gwen giggles and grimaces at the same time.

'Each to their own,' Mallory says with a smile.

'His clients all knew he was a boy, but he did as much business as the real girls, if not more. He used to come into the Ship Afloat pub where I worked. That was the last place I saw him.'

'Still in Bridgwater?'

'Yes, about ten minutes away on Market Street. It's called the Star on the Harbour now, ironically. It was a rough place, and you'd often find the odd sex worker who'd offer a knee trembler in the toilets for a fiver. Anyway, she swanned into the pub like some movie star . . . I think that's why she chose that name . . . and insisted on a getting a drink. She had been banned by the landlord, Bob the Bastard. That was our nickname for him. But that didn't stop her. Besides, Bob was upstairs. One punter, a stranger, took an interest in her. I overheard a bit of their conversation. Small talk, really, but he called himself John. They spent a little bit of time together before Bob showed up and kicked off. Star and the stranger left the pub, and a few days later, her body was found.' Gwen looks across at the River Parrett. 'Just down there, hidden in the reeds.'

'Is that why you wanted to meet here?'

Gwen nods. 'It's not morbid, is it?'

'Not at all. It's respectful.' Mallory stands and peers down at the riverbank, the water is shallow, the reeds thin but high.

Gwen continues, 'No one noticed her. She was wrapped in a tarpaulin, among the rubbish people used to leave there. It was so awful.'

Mallory shudders at the thought of Star's murdered body being dumped at the riverside with people strolling by for days, unaware that her body is lying waiting to be discovered. 'You said you were working in the bar the night that Star met the stranger.'

'That's right.'

'Do you remember what he looked like?'

Gwen thinks for a moment. 'It was so long ago. That said, he just seemed like a typical pub punter. Nondescript.'

'Was he white or black? Young or old?'

'White, I think, but I didn't pay him that much attention. I couldn't say his age. He was older than me. I remember that much but then everyone in the pub was. I'd say he wasn't that tall, about five foot eight.'

'What about hair colour?'

'Don't remember. The pub was quite dimly lit. He wasn't from around here, I knew that much.'

'Did he tell you that?'

'No, I overheard him talking with Star. He said his name was John, and he was passing through.'

'Did he have an accent?'

'He spoke quietly, but there was definitely a hint of something.'

'West Country?'

'No. Northern. I'm sure of it.'

Gwen checks her wristwatch. Her eyes widen. 'I better get back to work.' She finishes her drink and stands. 'So nice to meet you.'

'You too. Is there anything else you can think of?'

'I've said all I remember. If I missed anything, it may be in the police report, if they bothered to write one, that is. They weren't interested in Star. They believed she had it coming.'

'Did they say that?'

'No. Eve told me.'

'Who's Eve?'

'Eve Brunet. She used to live around Bridgwater. She was another sex worker. She was attacked by a punter four weeks before Star and believed the same person who attacked her was the one responsible for Star's murder.'

'Why did she think that?'

'I'd heard what happened and went to see her. I told Eve about the stranger called John. I described what little I knew of him, and she went white as a sheet. It's the same man, she said. We went to the police, but they didn't take us seriously. Said they'd look into it. That was more than thirty years ago.'

'Where is Eve now?'

'We lost touch a long time ago. She moved to Taunton after Star's murder. I had heard a rumour she was working in a flower shop.'

Chapter 40

MALLORY IS ON THE TRAIN back to Taunton, her mind racing about the fact that a victim of the killer who murdered Star, Hannah, Elena and Sally is still alive. Gwen's description of the man had been helpful, but could Eve's be better? She must have spoken to him, looked him in the eye, been close to him, smelled him and heard his accent, tone, seen his hair and eye colour. DI Archer enters her thoughts suddenly. Mallory's gut pinches with guilt. She should report this to her right away. Mallory bites her lip. Maybe not just yet. Not until she gets the scoop from Eve. After that, she'll call Archer.

The train is travelling at a snail's pace. Mallory sighs, opens Facebook on her phone and does a search for Eve Brunet. Dozens of names appear. A quick scan reveals they are mostly French or Canadian. Brunet sounds like a French name, so it is no surprise. There are some women that could be in their mid-fifties, but not one of them lives in Taunton. Could she have emigrated or married? It's possible. She decides to message the women in the age range directly and begins composing the message on the Notes app on her phone.

Dear Eve, hello, you don't know me. I'm a journalist and true crime podcaster who is searching for an Eve

Brunet who use to live in Bridgwater, Somerset, and was once attacked by a maniac serial killer who murdered defenceless sex workers. Did you encounter him? Are you the one that got away? If you are . . .

Mallory rereads what she's written, swears under her breath and deletes the lot. That's enough to freak anyone out. Besides, cold contacting people by Facebook should be the last resort. There are other ways of tracking people down.

At last, the train pulls into Taunton station. Mallory exits, hurries up the platform to the concourse and outside where she jumps into a waiting cab.

'Town centre, please.'

'Anywhere in particular?'

'A café with really good WiFi, if you know one.'

'They've all got WiFi. I don't know how good they are, but I can drop you somewhere with a range of cafés and you can choose for yourself.'

'Sounds good to me.'

Fifteen minutes later, she is ordering a latte and a glass of tap water in a rustic coffee shop in the town centre. As the coffee is being prepared, she sits at a table, opens her laptop and connects to the WiFi. She opens the Newspapers archive website and logs in using her account.

Her latte arrives and she thanks the barista.

'Sugar?' he asks.

She looks up at him. Slim, thick, wavy hair. Lots of white teeth. She hadn't noticed him earlier. He gives her a flirty smile and a wink. She cocks an eyebrow. Cheeky bugger. He can't be much older than eighteen. 'No, thank you,' she replies, with an amused gaze.

'Nice tattoos,' he says.

'Thanks . . .' She waits for him to leave.

'Let me know if you need anything else. The name's Hugo, by the way.'

'I'll keep that in mind, Hugo by the way,' she says, smiling and focusing back on her laptop. She enters Eve Brunet's name, the year she was attacked and the location, but nothing appears. Could she have used another name? Maybe she asked them not to use her name. She removes Eve's name and enters 'sex worker attacked'. Nothing comes back. This is 1988. Maybe the politically correct term 'sex worker' hadn't made it to the wilds of the West Country. She tries again this time she types 'prostitute attacked'.

It works!

A single periodical appears: the *Somerset County Gazette*. She begins to read through it until she finds a tiny article with the title: PROSTITUTE IN ALLEGED ATTACK.

Alleged?

Mallory reads the article:

A prostitute working the streets in Bridgwater claims she was attacked by a punter who drove her out of town for a 'good time'. She claims he hit her on the temple with a metal object as she tried to leave his car. She fled from him and says that the sound of voices must have scared him off. Police are looking into it. The details of the incident are still emerging, and it is crucial to await a thorough investigation before drawing any conclusions. However, initial accounts suggest that the alleged attack occurred during a transaction between the woman and her client, emphasising the vulnerability of individuals in this line of work.

No one believed her. Not the police, not even the press. She notes the piece was written by a bloke. Mallory feels a surge of anger burn through her. *Fuckers!* She can find nothing else on the incident, which indicates the story was dead in the water. She finds the articles on Star Royale, 'the tranny hooker', who was found dead by the River Parrett. There is nothing in those thin, judgemental articles that she hadn't already learned from Gwen Baker. She finishes her coffee. It was bitter and has left an aftertaste. Maybe she should have had some of Hugo's sugar. She takes a sip of the water and thinks. Gwen had mentioned Eve worked in a flower shop. And so she begins a new search. It takes almost five minutes and the correct terms and dates before she finds what she is looking for.

'Bingo!'

'Can I get you another?' comes a voice. It's Hugo, the toothy barista.

'No, thank you,' she replies and opens the article.

The title reads: FLOWER SHOP EMPLOYEE BECOMES ITS NEW OWNER

Local woman, Eve Sommers, an employee of the popular Somerset Bouquets, has bought the profitable and popular shop from Dorothy Bennett, who retires later this month. Eve, 44, wife of local businessman, Craig Sommers, is excited to be starting a new chapter in her life. The store will be modernised and will focus on a broader market, she says.

The rest of the article is all fluff with nothing else. A further search reveals another article published three months after the announcement. The headline reads: THE WILTED ROSE OPENS. There's a colour photograph included. A statuesque, smiling blonde woman. It's her. Eve Sommers, according to the caption, is cutting a ribbon draped across the entrance of the flower shop. Mallory feels a surge of excitement. She's getting closer. She googles the shop, finds the contact number and dials it. A woman answers.

'The Wilted Rose, how can I help you?'

'Could I speak to Eve, please?'

'You're speaking to her.'

'Oh great,' Mallory replies breezily. 'Hi. My name is Mallory Jones. I'm a reporter and a podcaster. I'm following up on a story and was wondering if you would be interested in talking to me about the man who attacked you back in 1988?'

She hears a sharp intake of breath. 'No, I would not. Don't ever call back here again.' The call disconnects.

'Shit!' says Mallory. Cold calling is even less productive than reaching out cold on social media. She should know better. She chews on her thumb for a moment before making a decision on what to do next. Opening Google Maps on her browser Mallory searches for the shop. It's a fifteen-minute drive from her current location. What does she have to lose? Packing up her laptop, she opens Uber on her phone and orders a cab.

Chapter 41

ARCHER AND PARRY ARE MET at Berwick-Upon-Tweed station by one of the detectives leading the investigation into Gemma McFadden's murder. He's a stocky man, built like a rugby prop, bald with a bushy beard.

'DC Stuart Vickers. Call me Stu,' he says, extending his hand.

Archer shakes it and introduces herself and Parry.

'You mentioned you'd like to see the body first?' says Stu.

Archer has no memory of making that request.

'Sorry, I should have mentioned . . .' says Parry.

'Yes, you should.'

'Um . . . we could do something else.'

An awkward silence hangs in the air and is finally broken by Vickers. 'I've made the appointment. Might have to wait to get another one.'

'Let's go straight there,' Archer instructs Vickers.

'Sure. After that, I'll take us to the station. My colleague, DC Andy Ball, has some new digital evidence acquired late last night.'

A sheet covers Gemma McFadden's body in the town mortuary. The pathologist, a sixty-something woman called Joan McBride, with a strong Glaswegian accent, pulls the sheet respectfully away. Gemma's skin is porcelain pale. It's almost blue under the harsh light of the cold, barren space. Archer gets a flash of Elena's body and swallows. There's a large scar at the side of her forehead and a hole in her chest where the heart is.

'Something penetrated her heart. That's what killed her,' Parry observes.

McBride looks at him curiously, 'No shit, Sherlock.'

Parry shifts on his feet. 'I just meant it was obvious.'

'Doctor McBride,' Archer says, grabbing the woman's attention, 'is there any indication of sexual activity?'

The pathologist shakes her head. 'There's no indication of forced penetration in either the front or back orifices, or the mouth, for that matter. Also, there's no evidence of semen or any other fluids.'

'Do you know what kind of object made this cut to the victim's temple?'

'It was a blunt instrument. Stu might have more insight there.'

'We recovered a frying pan at the scene, with blood and hair. We believe the killer struck her with it before punching a hole in her heart.'

'Elena Zoric's heart was pierced by a penetrating bolt gun. In your opinion, do you think this chest wound was made by a weapon like that?'

The pathologist considers this before answering. 'I would put money on it.'

They stand in silence for a moment.

'Are we done?' McBride asks.

'I have no more questions,' Archer says.

The pathologist pulls the sheet back over Gemma McFadden, leaving a haunting ghost-like imprint of her body. Another innocent young life taken. She needs to move, to work faster and harder to prevent the next murder, whoever and whenever that will be.

At Berwick Police Station, Archer is introduced to Stu's colleague, Andy Ball, a slim, red-haired man with a serious face. He's carrying a laptop and joins in the meeting room where Archer, Parry and Stu have spent the last half hour reviewing the investigation reports.

'Has Stu brought you up to date with everything?'

'We're almost done,' Stu replies.

'Good.' From his pocket, her removes a memory card and holds it between his finger and thumb. 'Amongst the debris at the crime scene we found this. It contains a catalogue of photos and a dozen taken the night of the murder.'

'Townsend is a photographer, isn't he?' Archer asks.

'Local wedding photographer who has a secret portfolio, it seems.'

DC Ball inserts the card into a laptop and opens up the photos. A hundred thumbnails of well heeled, merry people from different weddings appears on the screen. Ball pages through them until he finds a different subject matter. The first six shots depict a masked Gemma, sitting on the edge of a bed, undressed down to her red silk underwear. She is not looking into the lens. If anything, it seems she might be looking into another camera. From the seventh picture onwards a second masked female in a blonde wig and a school uniform enters the shot and begins to undress with help from Gemma.

Archer notices something on the little finger of the second woman's hand. She leans in for a closer look. A heart signet ring perhaps? 'Do we have an ID on this person?' Archer asks.

Ball and Stu exchange a grim look.

'I'm pretty sure we do,' Ball replies.

He closes up on the second woman's face. She looks young.

'Stu and I are certain this is a local girl. A teenager. Her name is Lily Mercer. She's the daughter of an ex-cop.'

'She was also best friends with Gemma,' Stu adds.

'The teenage daughter of an ex-policeman. This is going to be tricky.'

'Something worth noting,' says Ball. 'Two days ago, Lily's father, Barry, was interviewed at the train station. A TV production company was interested in his involvement with a case when he was a young copper. During the interview he was heckled by a stranger accusing him of being responsible for the death of some people.'

'Which people?'

'No one knows. They reckon he was just some crackpot.'

'Interesting. Who was this stranger?'

'We don't know yet. We're still trying to figure that out.'

'Keep looking for him. There might be something in this.'

Ball nods a confirmation.

Archer looks back at the laptop screen and pages through the photos once more. Both Gemma and her friend are looking away from the person taking the shot.

Archer flicks through the shots once more.

'It's like someone else is photographing them,' Parry says.

'Or they are performing live,' Archer says.

'The camera is missing,' Ball says.

'Townsend could have taken it when he bolted,' Stu says.

'Possibly,' Archer says. 'If they did broadcast live then they must have gone through a platform, which means it might have been recorded.'

'We'll look into that.'

'Thank you. Who else knows about these photos?'

'Just us.'

'Let's keep it that way for now. So, tell me about Townsend.'

'He's from a middle-class Edinburgh family. They gave him money to set up his photography business. Does shoots for weddings, portraits, products and porn, it seems. Townsend's well known as someone to keep your daughters away from. He has a small office-cum-studio in town. We got the green light to search his flat and office, which only came through this afternoon. The team are sifting through his stuff now.'

'Has he been in trouble before?'

'He got his lothario reputation after getting a client's daughter pregnant. Killed his business, apparently. That's possibly why he went into porn. He's been cautioned for carrying class As and smoking weed in public. Other than that, we've had no reason to suspect he's a killer, until now, obviously.'

'What did you get from Gemma's parents?' Archer asks.

'It's just her mum. Gemma's dad died two years back. As you can imagine, she's utterly destroyed. We went in as gently as we could, but she couldn't quite hold it together.'

Archer nods. 'Understood. And Lily Mercer?'

'We spoke to her but she's distraught and a little highly strung.'

'Let's go talk to her again.'

'I'll call ahead and make sure that's OK.'

'Don't do that. This is a murder investigation. Call her parents. Find out where she is and tell them we are coming immediately.'

'Of course.'

'Just two of us need to go. We don't want to intimidate.'

'I've known the Mercer family for a few years. I can come with you,' says Stu.

'Thanks.' She turns to Parry. 'Could you catch up with Andy, review the reports and find any possible leads?'

'Yes . . . I can do that.'

'Thank you.'

Chapter 42

THE MERCERS' HOME IS AN attractive brownstone house facing a green in the quiet pretty village of East Ord. Isla Mercer, a brusque, thin woman with grey hair opens the door with an intense, unimpressed look on her face. Her eyes dart from Stu to Archer and back again.

'This is really not acceptable, Stuart. You saw what she was like.'

'Isla, this Detective Inspector Archer. She's from the Met Police and is leading the investigation.'

'The Met Police? What has this got to do with them?'

'Mrs Mercer, may we come in?' Archer says.

Isla Mercer stiffens and for a moment it seems like she is going to say no and shut the door, but she stands aside and lets them in.

'I don't like doing this without my husband being present.'

'Will he be back soon?'

'He's gone fishing. I can't get hold of him. It's a dead zone where he is. I've left messages. Hopefully, he'll get a signal and come back soon.'

Closing the door, she leads them into an expansive living room painted canary yellow. A large family portrait hangs over the fireplace. Archer wonders if Chris Townsend took the photo. A young woman sits nervously on the sofa, watching them enter, her hands perched firmly on her lap. From her build and round chin, Archer can see it's the girl in the photos, Lily Mercer.

Archer meets her gaze and smiles warmly. 'Hello.'

A flicker of acknowledgement appears on her pretty doll-like face.

'Hello again, Lily,' says Stu.

Lily's gaze drops and she begins to scratch at her arms. Archer notices the gold signet ring on the little finger of her left hand.

'Lily, don't do that,' Isla chides.

Lily sighs heavily and folds her arms.

'That's a pretty ring,' Archer says.

Lily twists it around her finger.

'Please, sit down,' Isla says to Archer and Stu.

Archer gestures to the space next to Lily. 'May I?'

Lily gives a polite nod.

'Can I get you something to drink?' Isla asks.

'Not for me,' says Archer.

'No, ta,' says Stu.

Isla sits opposite Lily, worried eyes fixed on her daughter.

'Thank you for seeing us at such short notice,' Stu says.

'I'd rather wait until Barry gets back.'

'Time's not on our side,' Stu says.

'I understand you and your husband once worked for the police,' Archer says.

'That's right. We both worked for Thames Valley Police back in the late 80s – him on the beat, me in the office.'

Archer smiles. 'Then you'll have an idea of how this goes.'

Isla shrugs.

Archer turns her attention to the daughter. 'My name is Detective Inspector Grace Archer but please feel free to call me Grace.'

Lily stares at the floor and chews her bottom lip.

'I'd like to ask you some questions that you may have been asked already. I'm sorry to do this to you, Lily. It's just routine and I'd like to get my own perspective.'

Another quiet nod. Archer has the sense she's making inroads with gaining her trust.

'First up, I'm sorry for your loss. I understand you and Gemma were very close.'

Lily sniffs and rubs her forearms. 'Best friends. We'd do anything for each other.'

'I'm sure. The night in question, you were not home. Is that correct?'

A twitch in her eye. 'There was a party.'

Archer nods. 'Can I ask whose party it was?'

'A girl called Mathilda from school.'

'You said it was Lauren's party!' her mother says.

Lily flushes. 'No, I said it was Mathilda!'

'I might be old, but my memory is not that bad. You said Lauren. This is the first time I've ever heard Mathilda's name mentioned.'

Lily puffs and waves her arms. 'Whatever.'

'Where does Mathilda live, Lily?' Archer asks.

'Braeside. Number 13.'

'And Gemma was there?'

Lily hesitates before shaking her head.

'But you were there?'

Lily swallows. 'Briefly.'

'Where were you until midnight, then?' her mum interjects.

Lily glares at her mother and seems at the point of exploding.

'Mrs Mercer, maybe I could do with a cup of tea, if you don't mind,' says Archer.

She's flustered and clearly knows her daughter is hiding something. With some reluctance she makes her way to the

265

kitchen. Archer meets Stu's gaze and nods for him to go with her. He winks and follows her.

Archer turns her attention back to Lily. 'Did you know where Gemma was that night?'

'She was with Chris.'

'At the cottage?'

'Yes.'

Archer looks across at the doorway leading to the kitchen and with a conspiratorial edge, asks: 'Do you know what went on there?'

Lily shifts uncomfortably on the chair. From the kitchen down the hallway, they hear the kettle boiling, the clink of china and Mrs Mercer and Stu deep in conversation.

'Lily, I'm going to tell you something that no one else knows.'

The girl meets her gaze and blinks.

'I have seen photographs taken in the cottage, I presume by Chris Townsend, from the night Gemma was murdered.'

Archer leaves that thought to hang for a moment.

A second glance at towards the door leading to the hallway. 'What kind of photographs?' Lily asks, timidly.

'Two young women dressed provocatively, wearing masks and wigs . . .'

The colour drains from Lily's face.

'I don't want to circulate them to the local police or the public.'

'Why would you do that?'

'We need to confirm the identity of the women. Maybe someone will recognise them under the drag.'

Lily begins to rub and scratch her arms. 'But one of them is Gemma, surely.'

'What do you think?'

Lily trembles, tears fill her eyes.

'Do you know who the other person is?'

The tears roll down her face. She twists the signet ring on her finger.

'In the photos she's wearing a ring just like that.'

Lily gasps, her neck and face flushes. She looks as if she might spring from the sofa and run from the house.

'It's OK,' Archer says gently. 'You just wanted to make some money, right? Chris Townsend offered you and Gemma an opportunity to make some hard cash. Who wouldn't jump at that?'

'It was Gemma.'

'Gemma asked you to do it.'

'Chris asked her. She was up for it. I didn't want to do it—'

They hear the sound of voices leaving the kitchen and approaching from the hallway.

'Shit! Shit! Shit!'

Archer places her hand gently on Lily's. 'Take a deep breath, Lily. We only have a few moments. I don't intend to bring this up with your mum, but at some stage she will find out. You could tell her when we leave.'

The girl bites her lip.

'We must make sure other people do not see these pictures.' Archer is taking a punt here. Gemma is a minor but still old enough to understand the gravity of the situation.

'But why will other people see them?'

'Because this is a murder investigation. It's national news and people will be hungry for every detail.'

Lily scratches her arms.

'Tell your mum the truth, and we can talk again later.'

Mrs Mercer and Stu arrive with a tray of mugs, a teapot and biscuits. She shoots a concerned look at her daughter. 'Lily, is everything OK?'

Archer stands. 'I'm sorry, Mrs Mercer, I've just had a call and we have to leave.'

'Oh . . . but your tea?'

'Another time. I think you and Lily need to talk.' From her pocket Archer takes out a contact card. 'Call me later. I'll be waiting.'

Mrs Mercer's brow creases. She takes the card. Archer turns and meets Lily's gaze. 'Be brave, Lily.'

Chapter 43

THE WILTED ROSE IS SITUATED on the outskirts of the town centre, on a smart, trendy street lined with cafés and bistro restaurants. Its Victorian frontage is painted a tasteful dusty pink and stands out elegantly from its shabbier neighbours. In the window, blue, red and white hydrangeas are neatly arranged in glass vases alongside lilies of all colours and other unusual flowers that Mallory doesn't know the names of.

She pushes open the door. A bell pings, announcing her arrival. Behind a wooden rustic table is Eve Sommers, formerly Brunet, wrapping a bunch of pale blue hydrangeas for a customer. She smiles at Mallory. 'Be with you in a moment.'

Mallory smiles back at her. As Eve sees to her customer, Mallory pretends to look at the flowers, while sneaking glances at Eve, taking stock of her. She is a good-looking woman, elegant and well dressed in stylish casual trousers and a crisp white shirt. Her blonde hair is thick and wavy with threads of silver. If Mallory didn't know Eve's history then she might assume she was once a model for a glamorous European fashion house.

The customer leaves. It's just Eve and Mallory in the shop. Eve smiles warmly. 'How can I help you?'

'I'd like to send some flowers, please.'

'You've come to right place. What's the occasion?'

'Not a happy one, I'm afraid.'

'Oh, I'm so sorry to hear that.'

'It's a commemoration.'

'I see. I could do a bouquet or a wreath?'

'Probably not a wreath. Too funereal. A bouquet would be nice. Something colourful.'

'Did you have any particular flowers in mind?'

'I like the lilies, and the hydrangeas. Maybe some greenery, too.'

Eve is writing on a notepad. 'Sounds perfect. When do you need it?'

'How soon could you do it?'

'I have some time this afternoon.'

'Perfect.'

'How about a message?'

Mallory smiles warmly at Eve. 'Yes, please.'

Eve returns the smile.

'In memory of Elena Zoric. That's Z, O, R, I, C.'

'Got it. And who is that from?'

'There are some more names,' Mallory says.

'Oh, I'm ever so sorry.'

'That's OK. The next name is Sally McGowan. Then Hannah Daysy. That's D, A, Y, S, Y. Odd spelling, I know.' Mallory waits for Eve to finish writing. 'One last name . . . Star Royale.'

Eve freezes, her hand and the pen hovering over the notepad. She looks up, her expression one of hurt mixed with anger. 'It was you who called here earlier.'

'I need to talk to you—'

'Get out!' Eve says, firmly.

'Please hear me out.'

'I have nothing to say to you.' Eve strides from behind the table and opens the shop door.

'He's killing again. The man who murdered Star. He killed a young sex worker in London last week, and this morning another murder has been reported: an eighteen-year-old, Gemma McFadden. In 1991, Hannah Daysy was a mum trying to make ends meet for her son. He murdered her. In 1987, Sally McGowan was a teenager alone in London with no money. He murdered her—'

'And what am I supposed to do about any of that?'

'You're the only survivor of his attack. You could identify help him. The police have reopened—'

'I need you to leave. Now!'

'Eve, please. You could be a key witness in this investigation. You could help find the killer.'

'Do the police know you're here?'

'Yes, we're sort of working together.'

'Sort of? What does that mean?'

'It means I have given them vital information on a victim they knew nothing about, and I have now a new victim in Star. We also have you—'

'No, you do not! I can't imagine how you got my name, but I want nothing to do with this. I'm a married woman and respected in this community.'

Eve is trembling; her poised exterior is unravelling. In moments, her expression transforms. Mallory recognises the look. She has seen it in Bruce, and in many of the people she has interviewed for the podcast over the years. It's a haunted look of those who have survived death by violence. It's as if a switch has been flicked and Eve has become a different person. Mallory feels a surge of guilt. Only moments ago, Eve had seemed like the kind of person without a care in the world. 'I'm so sorry about what happened to you.'

Eve says nothing and huddles into herself.

271

'No one knows, do they?' Mallory asks.

Eve's shoulders sag. She shuts the door, locks it and turns the OPEN sign to CLOSED. She leans against the door. Tears fill her eyes. 'You know, the worst thing was not just the attack. It was dealing with the police. The men who are supposed to protect us – and by us, I mean everyone – not just . . .' Eve shakes her head, seemingly unable to verbalise what she once did to make a living. 'I remember them sitting opposite me, judging me with their cold looks. I heard them in the corridors whispering names about me and laughing behind my back.' Her eyes flare, her hands curl into fists. 'They even had the gall to ask me if I'd said anything to upset the bastard who tried to kill me. Can you believe that?'

Mallory feels a swell of anger. She imagines herself in that position and slapping the officer for saying it.

'They never asked me if I was OK, if I needed medical help or someone to talk to. None of that. God forbid. In their eyes, I was a "slag". A tart who upset a client who just wanted a bit of fun. I had it coming. I deserved it.'

'I can't imagine what that must have been like.'

'And the weird thing was, they almost had me believing it. Had it been my fault? Had I said or done something wrong?' Her jaw tightens. 'Bastards!'

'Star was murdered four weeks after the attack on you.'

Eve nods. 'Every day I wonder if I hadn't escaped, would Star still be alive?'

'You mustn't think that way. It will drive you mad.'

Eve narrows her eyes at Mallory. 'How did you find me?'

Mallory hesitates before answering. Should she give up Gwen's name? As if reading her mind, Eve says, 'Let me guess. Gwen Baker.'

Eve rolls her eyes and strides across the shop, and from the notepad tears out the page containing Mallory's order. She scrunches it and drops it into a wastebasket. 'I have work to do.'

'I met with Gwen this afternoon to talk about Star.'

'And of course she mentioned my name.'

Mallory shifts on her feet but says nothing.

'Gwen was always sweet, but she did like to gossip.' Eve sighs and looks blankly across the shop. 'I knew this would catch up with me one day.'

'I wouldn't have come here if it wasn't so important. He will kill again.'

Eve shrinks into herself and seems suddenly much smaller.

'Maybe no one needs to know,' says Mallory. 'Maybe the police will keep your name out of it.'

'If they bother to follow up. Their track record in these cases is beyond shitty. Even you should know that.'

'Things are different now. The detective leading the investigation is a woman. She's a strong person. A good person.'

A knock on the shop door. A handsome man with salt and pepper hair is smiling in. Eve's face pales. 'My husband. You better go.'

'But—'

'Just go, please.'

Eve forces a smile back at her husband and opens the door. She kisses him on the cheek. Mallory writes her number on Eve's notepad.

'Everything all right, darling?' he asks.

'Yes, all fine.'

'OK, I'll be off now,' says Mallory. 'I've left my number for you if you change your mind.'

Eve gives her a wan smile as her husband steps into the shop.

Mallory hesitates before leaving, a pleading look on her face. Eve's face flares with anger. Crestfallen, Mallory leaves the shop as Eve shuts the door and locks it once more. She understands Eve's reluctance and to a certain degree empathises. But that is not good enough. The victims need justice. Their stories need to be heard. Their names remembered. As a survivor, Eve has a responsibility that goes beyond protecting her reputation. Mallory has a responsibility too. She knows she should have done this sooner and is prepared to face the consequences. She's going to have to talk to Grace Archer. She glances back at the shop and at Eve Sommers, who is less than impressed that Mallory is still hanging around. *This is bigger than you, Eve. Sorry. This is for Elena, Hannah, Sally, Gemma and Star.*

Chapter 44

Star

Bridgwater, Somerset. 1988

STAR ROYALE SHUDDERS AS THE last of the whizz erupts through her body like glorious wildfire. With a freshly lit Marlboro Light dangling from dry lips, she leans against a lamppost, bathed in its warm glow. She exhales a puff of blue smoke and closes her eyes. The whizz – a restorative, a temporary fix – is a plaster for a wound she has struggled to heal. She needs proper meds and to get them she needs hard cash. So tonight, this girl has her work cut out.

She wears an oversized biker jacket, with bleeding hearts and daggers painted on the sleeves. She had stolen it from a trick who had sunk into a self-induced whisky, weed and skag coma some months back. She left him with her raggedy charity shop sheepskin coat in case he caught a chill. A rare moment of benevolence from her, despite the fact he'd never fit into it. She chuckles at the memory and fishes her lipstick from the jacket side pocket.

A Ford Cortina is parked by the lamppost. She crouches down, face in front of the wing mirror and teases her brittle, dyed blonde hair in an effort to give it some shape. She studies her face which is thin and angular with a strong jawline she detests. Sighing, she opens her mouth and applies the crimson lipstick. Cocksucker red, one client had called it. She had shrugged with a smile and proved him right, earning her a generous tip. She pouts and, satisfied with her artistry, lifts her head and frowns. Her neckband has slipped revealing her Adam's apple. Cursing under her breath, she pulls the band up concealing the offensive bump from view.

Time to get to work. Despite the evening gloom she puts on her statement sunglasses, perching them on her nose to give her a more feminine look. Like slutty Sandy from *Grease*, she drops the fag on the ground and extinguishes it with the sole of her peep toe heels. Sliding the leather jacket half off her shoulders, Star sashays like a supermodel up Market Street, her worn heels echoing across the narrow road.

A door creaks opens to her left. A thin, pinch-faced woman carrying a threadbare runner emerges from a tenement building and begins shaking the rug. Her eyes narrow as Star passes.

'Disgusting!' she hisses.

Star hesitates. With one chipped, purple nail she pulls the sunglasses down her nose, blinks at the shrew and flips her the finger. Star licks the finger suggestively. 'Swivel on this, bitch!' she coos.

The woman gasps, retreats inside, slamming the door shut behind her. Star laughs and continues up Market Street towards the Ship Afloat pub, a throaty cackle echoing in her wake.

Pulling open the door' she is greeted with the heady aroma of hops and cigarette smoke that hangs in the air like a bitter fog. There's a raucous hum from the clientele made up of the usual bull-necked local yokels from the surrounding coun- tryside. Correction: *cunt*ryside. They turn to look when she steps inside. With hands on hips, head up, all attitude and no knickers, she smiles as the catcalls and whistles come. *You better make this worth my while*, she thinks, taking them in one by one, searching for a target.

She catches a stranger watching her from the jukebox. He looks away when she meets his gaze. Definitely not from round these parts. He's inserting a coin into the machine all the while furtively side glancing at her. *Bingo*, she thinks.

Busty Gwen is working behind the bar tonight. 'What are you doing here, Star? You're barred. Bob'll do one if he catches you.'

'Pipe down, Gwen. I'm just meeting a friend.'

'You gotta go, Star. Now!'

Music from the jukebox thankfully drowns out her voice. 'Always on My Mind' by the Pet Shop Boys. She approves.

The stranger sits at the bar. 'Pint of bitter,' he says to Gwen.

'Comin' up.' Gwen smiles.

Gwen leans across to Star. 'We can't be having any of that funny business here, Star. Not after the last time.'

The 'last time' in question was when Bob caught Star in the toilets shooting up. He had wrenched her out of the cubicle and hauled her outside. Not her finest moment.

'Where is he tonight?' Star asks, a sudden wave of anxiety rippling through her.

'Dunno. Upstairs watching TV, I expect.'

Star looks at the stranger. 'Buy a girl a drink, sugar?'

'Don't mind her,' Gwen says to him.

He doesn't look up from his drink. 'Whatever she wants,' he replies.

Star smiles. 'Double G and T, Gwen. Easy on the T.'

'I'm not allowed.'

The stranger slaps a fiver on the bar top. 'Double G and T,' he says, his voice quiet but firm.

Gwen shifts awkwardly on her feet. After a moment she says, 'Just one. Then you leave.'

'Just one,' says Star.

She brushes past the stranger, caressing his shoulder, and perches on the stool next to his. 'I'm Star. Star Royale. At your service.'

Gwen places the pint in front of the man.

'And what service would that be?' he asks, eyes fixed on the pint.

Star smiles. 'Whatever you like, sugar.'

Busty Gwen arches her brows at Star as she places the gin and tonic and the change on the bar.

Star mouths a *Fuck off* at her.

Gwen mouths *Fuck you* at her and smirks.

Focusing on the stranger, Star says, 'Haven't seen you here before.'

'Just passing.'

'Where to?'

He shrugs and doesn't answer.

The music finishes, killing the atmosphere.

'What's your name?'

He hesitates before answering, 'John.'

'John, is it?' she purrs. 'Funny how all you out of towners are called John. I like it, though. It suits you.'

John takes a sip of his pint.

She leans in and squeezes his knee. 'I'll play a song. Just for you, John. It's a favourite of mine. Would you like that?'

He shrugs again.

Star reaches for the coins and takes one. 'Come boogie, sugar?'

He shakes his head.

She takes a large swig of gin. 'Then I will boogie for you.'

At the jukebox she inserts the coin and selects the track. He's looking back at her. She smiles coyly and begins to slowly gyrate her hips as the music begins. 'Private Dancer' by Tina Turner. What else? She watches him through hooded eyes as she lifts her arms and twirls her way back to the bar, edging her bony behind onto the stool.

A voice booms over the music. 'What the hell are you doing 'ere?' It's Bob, the landlord.

'Fuck!' she whispers, heart sinking.

He's tearing across the bar, face like thunder.

'Can't a girl just have a drink with a friend?'

Bob snatches the G and T from her hand and drops it behind the bar. 'Out. Now!' he says, pointing at the door.

'No need to be like that. We're just . . .' Before she can finish, his meaty paw closes over her arm. He hauls her off the stool. She hears laughter and feels a crippling shame. The whizz is still working, fizzling inside her, fuelling her confidence and anger. With all her strength she snatches herself away from his grip. 'Get your hand off me, you ape!' she snarls.

'Get out!'

Star's eyes slide to the bar and John. But he's not there. She scans the tables but he's nowhere to be seen. 'Fuck's sake!'

'Are you going to leave or am I going to make you leave?'

'Go fuck yourself,' she says, skirting round him and heading for the door.

Outside, she shivers in the cold night breeze, zips up her jacket and takes out her fags and lighter.

She blinks as a pair of headlamps flash, lighting the gloom. Looking down Market Street, she sees the Ford Cortina parked beside the lamppost. Sitting in the driver's seat looking her way is a silhouette. It's John. Star's heart lifts. She beams and hurries towards the car.

Chapter 45

LILY'S HEART IS POUNDING. THE police know it was
her that night with Gemma, dressed as a schoolgirl,
wearing a wig and a mask that clearly did nothing to
disguise her identity. Her head is spinning. Has anyone other
than the detective seen the pictures? Oh God, have Stuart
Vickers and his partner seen her naked and doing things with
Gemma? She feels nauseous at the thought and wants nothing
more than for the ground to swallow her up right now.

Mum is seeing the London police detective and Stuart Vickers
out of the house. Lily retreats quietly to the kitchen and out to
the back yard. She needs space. She needs time to think. If
Gemma was here . . . oh shit, but she's not! *Oh, Gemma!* The
grim reality of Gemma's murder and Lily's soon-to-be-exposed
shame rises like a tidal wave. She feels herself drowning and
desperately needs to escape.

Her bike is parked under the kitchen window. She grabs it
and pushes it to the side of the house. *Wait! My phone! Where
is it?* She has left it in the bedroom. *Shit! Too late now.* Besides,
she doesn't want it. The last thing she needs is her mum and
everyone else calling her. She needs time out to think. Lily
pushes the bike up the side of the house, treading lightly as the
front door closes. She hears Mum's voice calling for her inside.
She waits and watches the police car drive away. When it is

out of sight, she jumps on the bike and pedals furiously in the opposite direction to the police vehicle.

She doesn't know where she's going. Far away from here, that's all she can aim for. Far away from Mum, Dad and the confession that she has to make. Maybe she'll cycle to Berwick bridge, dump her bike and throw herself over the side, the tragic heroine in a shady story involving a seedy bloke, some drugs and, let's face it, two whores. That's what the world will call them. Isn't that what she is? Someone willing to sell her body, her soul, for a couple of quid. Her feet pound furiously on the pedals. She has to escape. Where can she go? Who can she turn to? There's only one person. One person who truly understands her. She turns right at the roundabout and makes her way out of town and up a country lane, unaware that a car has done a U turn and is following slowly, three hundred metres behind her.

Uncle Simon lives in a grey stone cottage on Springhill Lane, surrounded by fields like endless sweeping green carpets, and stunning 360-degree views of the Northumbrian countryside stretching for miles and miles. Horses graze in a nearby paddock. There is a stillness in the air that is almost too quiet. Back in East Ord the air is fairly clean, OK, maybe laced with the occasional tang of diesel, but here, it's almost pure. She smiles and feels calmer already. Pulling the brakes on her bike, she hops off and makes her way through the little gate.

'Uncle Simon! It's me, Lily!' she calls, knocking on the front door. She presses her ear against it but hears no movement inside. She knocks a second time and peers through the living room windows. Despite the day being sunny, the inside is dark and there is little to see. She raps at the window, and calls his name once more, but still, there's no response. She looks around. There's no sign of his car. He was supposed to be fishing with Dad but ended up cancelling. Is he unwell? Lily can't recall what Mum told her. She had other things on her mind. Where can he be? She walks around the cottage to the rear where there is a pathway lined with clipped tidy bushes leading to two outhouses fifty metres away. She walks towards them. In the distance she hears the quiet hum of a car but doesn't pay it much heed.

Both outhouses are shabby concrete buildings. She's never been inside either of them. They are always out of bounds when she'd come to visit. On one door is a rusted steel lock, heavily bolted. She wonders what's inside. A workshop and just some items to store, Simon had told her once: a freezer with meat and fish he'd caught, tinned foods, plus tools for looking after the house and the land he owned. She walks around it, idly enjoying her time alone and away from her mother's molly-coddling which would soon become harsh judgement, shouting, grounding and every other punishment under the sun. Dad would probably stop talking to her. No change there, then.

She notices a window at the rear. Why has she never seen it before? Mind you, it's been years since she visited the outhouses. There has never been any point. It's quite high up, too far for her to see on tiptoes, but she finds an old wooden bottle crate nearby and places it on the ground underneath the window. She steps up onto it but it's not high enough. She's able to stretch her arms to the ledge, though, and pulls herself up. The window is grubby, but the sun is shining and she can see inside. It looks like a workshop inside, neat and tidy, typical Uncle Si. There's a desk facing a wall, beside it is some sort of filing cabinet. Above the desk are photographs pinned to a corkboard. There are some of Simon and Mum when they were kids and a few of Lily through the years.

The sound of a car door closing jolts her; she loses her grip and slides down the concrete wall, her foot crashes through the weak wooden crate, and she lands on her ankle, turning it as her foot hits the ground. The pain is like an electric bolt, and she screams and loses her balance. Eyes wide, she scrabbles for purchase on nothing but clean country air as she falls backwards, hitting the ground with a thud, her head jerking back slamming hard against a rock. Her mind swirls and then everything goes dark.

Her eyes flicker open. She squints and groans, the light is blinding. She can see blue. Lots of blue. The sky. Her head throbs and begins to pound. She groans and feels herself floating. But she's not. It's as if . . . as if . . . she's being carried. She hears breathing. Heavy. Not hers. She feels herself slipping to the gritty hard surface and cries out. She smells rubber and thinks she can see a tyre very close to her head. A hand covers her mouth. Then a filthy towel that stinks of BO is wrapped around her head. She struggles to break free, but her captor slams her temple. Her head swims and then everything goes dark once more.

Chapter 46

ARCHER IS IN THE PASSENGER seat with Stu, approaching the Royal Tweed Bridge, one of the three grand structures spanning the River Tweed. Further down the river is the Royal Border Bridge, the immense and stunning railway viaduct. On the other side is Berwick Bridge, also known as 'the old bridge', DC Vickers informed her earlier, a smaller overpass built in the 1700s.

'For a relatively modest town, you have a lot of bridges.'

'We don't do things by half here,' he replies.

'It's a pretty town.'

'We like it.' He points across the river. 'That's Berwick Castle. She's twelfth century, and mostly a ruin, but still, I'm sure you'll agree, majestic, strong and beautiful.'

Archer smiles. 'I concur.'

As they drive across the bridge, Archer takes in the view of the town with its mix of medieval, Georgian and Victorian architectures. 'There's something very calming about this place.'

'I'm glad you think so.'

Archer's phone rings. To her surprise it's Mallory Jones. The podcaster is her usual perky self, full of energy and confidence, yet behind the effervescence something else is lingering. With the pleasantries over there's a hesitation.

'How can I help you?' Archer asks, breaking it.

'Are you in Berwick-Upon-Tweed?'

'Did you phone to ask me where I am?'

'No, it's just I saw the news.'

'Is that why you called?'

'No . . . listen . . . don't lose your shit . . .'

'Why would I lose my shit?' Archer replies, knowing she is probably about to do just that. Stu glances at her as he drives them across the bridge.

'I've found another victim.'

'What do you mean you've found another victim?'

'Someone listened to the Hannah Daysy podcast.'

'I thought you were going to take that down.'

'I don't recall saying any such thing.'

'I thought we discussed you not getting involved in this investigation.'

'We never discussed removing content.'

Archer is about to respond but Mallory interjects, 'You might want to listen to what I have to say before we go any further with this argument.'

Archer takes a breath. 'Who's arguing?'

'One of us is, and it's not me.'

'Fair comment. OK, I'm listening.'

'One of my subscribers, a woman in Somerset, emailed me after listening to the Hannah Daysy podcast. I spoke to her yesterday morning and thought it was a lead worth chasing.'

'Why are you only telling me this now?'

'I wanted to meet her and make sure it was legit. No point in wasting valuable police time.'

Archer notes the sarcasm in her voice. 'So you've met her?'

'I got the train first thing this morning. We met at lunch-time ...' Mallory lets that hang. She's clearly waiting for Archer to chase for the information. Silly game.

'And?'

She hears Mallory sigh. 'She had a friend. A sex worker. Killed and left for dead just like the others. Same injuries. Same situation with a lack of interest from the police. I'm positive it's the same killer, although there is a significant difference with this victim and the others. She was a biological male, who presented as a woman.'

'Interesting. What was her name?'

'Star Royale. Her real name was Kelvin Glover.'

'When did this happen?'

'Nineteen eighty-eight.'

Archer is processing what Mallory has told her. 'Did you talk to the police?'

'No. But Gwen and Eve did.'

'Who's Eve?'

'Sommers is her married name. Prior to that it was Brunet. I've just been to see her. It didn't go well. Eve was attacked four weeks before Star. She survived.'

Archer's mind races.

'I think you'll need talk to her. She won't speak to me about the past. It's something she doesn't speak about ever. Not even her husband knows about it.'

'Send me everything you have on an email.'

'Sure. Will do.'

'I'll review it and we can talk again.'

'Anytime.'

'And thank you. This is really good work.'

'That must hurt to say that out loud.'

'You don't know how much.'

287

Mallory laughs.

'I have to go,' Archer says.

Mallory had ended the call with Grace Archer, her mind turning over with questions. The detective was in Berwick-Upon-Tweed where another murder has been committed. Mallory shudders. Someone else she knows is in Berwick. Someone with skin in the game. Someone she had tried to help. Tom. *Oh God. Could he be involved?* She calls him. The phone rings five times and goes straight to voicemail. She tries again with the same result. She opens WhatsApp and drops him a message. She notices he has not logged in for two days and feels a twinge in her stomach. *Where are you?* Mallory types a message.

Hi Tom. Call me when you get this. Hope you're OK. M x

She presses *send* and waits, tapping the phone patiently with her finger to see if he opens the message. Moments pass and he doesn't. She types a second message.

BTW. I'm coming to Berwick first thing tomorrow morning.

When she has finished with the podcaster, Archer calls Quinn. Stu is driving them up Church Street. He turns left into the police car park. As they come to a stop, Quinn answers.

'Just had a call from our intrepid reporter,' she says, updating him with Mallory's news.

'Another victim?'

'Looks like it. And a survivor.'

'Gold star for Miss Jones.'

288

'Could you give her a ring and follow up with Eve Sommers?'

'Of course.'

'We'll need the reports on Kelvin Glover if they still exist. The murder predates our computer system, which means if we're lucky, they're languishing in a dusty cardboard box in the station's broom cupboard.'

'I'll call them after this. How's it going up there?'

'Making slow progress. Usual.'

'Understood. Anything comes up I'll give you a bell.'

'Talk later.'

Archer ends the call as she enters the station behind DC Stu Vickers. In the meeting room, DC Andy Ball is sitting alone. 'Where's Lee?' she asks.

'He's gone to check in to his hotel. Said he was tired after the journey.'

Archer clenches her jaw behind the smile she fixes at Ball. 'I see,' she says. 'It's getting to the end of the day. Let's have a recap. Stu and I just met with Lily Mercer. We had a few moments alone. In that time, I told her about the pictures we found and hinted that we know it's her.'

'Wow. How did that go down?' Ball asks.

'It was a gamble, but I think it was the right one. I want her to trust us. I told her to tell her mother and then we will talk to her again tomorrow. By winning her trust we should get more out of her.'

'What if she doesn't tell her mum? Lily's is not the easiest of people.'

'Then we go back and persuade her. She's a minor who's landed herself in a whole lot of shit. We need to tread carefully.'

'Remember both her parents are ex police. We might get some resistance.'

'I can deal with that.'

DCs Vickers and Ball exchange a look followed by a synchronised shrug.

'Any news on Townsend yet?'

'He used his credit card in Ayr and took out cash in Perth,' says Stu. 'He's all over the place, leaving a breadcrumb trail. We think he's heading to a family cottage in the Highlands. The family are keeping shtum about this despite it being featured on many of their Facebook profiles. I'm confident we'll pick him up soon.'

'Good. Anything else we need to cover?'

'Nothing from me,' says Stu.

Ball shrugs.

'OK. I'll head back to the hotel and catch up with some admin.'

'I can drive you,' Stu offers.

'It's a five-minute walk.'

'Give or take.'

'I fancy the stroll.'

They say their goodbyes and Archer makes her way with her bags down Church Street with Mallory's news and tomorrow's talk with Lily vying for space in her head. It's a warm, balmy evening as she makes her way down Hide Hill. On her left is an Italian restaurant with a buzzing front terrace filled with people drinking and eating. Out of the Northumbrian accents, and the Scottish accents, and those that are in-between, she picks up a Southern English accent and a voice she recognises. Peering through the entrance, she sees a smart–casually dressed Parry sitting at a table chatting to a woman at the next table. He's telling her he's a copper up from London working on a big case. Archer feels herself seethe. He asks the woman if she'd like another drink. She tells him she'd love one. He picks up their empty glasses and heads to the bar. For a moment, Grace thinks she'll march in there and ask what the hell he is doing but, with some reluctance, decides to rein her suspicions in, and give him the benefit of the doubt. Turning, she makes her way down the street to the hotel.

In her room that evening, Archer is sitting on the bed with her laptop, in the vain hope of searching the internet and HOLMES2 for any mention of Kelvin Glover AKA Star Royale. She knows the police database is a long shot because Star's case predated the inception of HOLMES, but it is worth a try. However, she does get a bite on the internet with a couple of obscure newspaper articles.

Her phone rings. It's Stu Vickers. It's almost 10 p.m. Late. She answers.

'Lily Mercer is missing,' he says.

Chapter 47

THERE IS NO RESPONSE FROM DS Parry's phone. She dials three times before making her way to his room and knocking on the door. She wonders if he is still in the Italian restaurant, drinking, chatting with women. Isn't he married? No answer. She knocks harder and listens at the door. She hears voices, closes her eyes and sighs.

'One moment!' Parry calls.

She hears shuffling, and whispering. The door opens, a half-dressed Parry peers through the crack, eyes squinting. 'Grace?' His breath reeks of cheap wine.

'Come back to bed,' a woman's slurred voice calls.

'Um . . . hi,' he says.

Archer feels her muscles tensing.

'Lee,' comes the woman's voice.

'Is your wife visiting?' Archer asks.

Parry looks away and rubs his neck.

Archer turns and leaves him.

'Grace . . . wait!'

Archer stops and, without looking back at him, says, 'I want you on the first train to London tomorrow morning.'

'Fuck!' he says.

Stu is waiting outside, the car engine rumbling. She gets into the passenger seat.

'Where's Lee?' he asks.

'Busy.' She pulls the seatbelt across.

'We have some news on Townsend.'

'He's been caught?'

'Not exactly. We have traced his credit card being used in St Abbs, which is spitting distance from here.'

'I thought he was in Scotland.'

'He was. He's possibly coming back or is constantly on the move to stop being caught. We also know he's been in touch with a mate in Fishwick asking for a bed for the night. Being on the run, he's out of his comfort zone and is making mistakes. I'm confident we'll pick him up in the next day or two, latest. Then we can sew this case up.'

'He's not the killer,' says Archer.

'Have you thought that Townsend could be a copycat? That maybe he read about the other murders and used them as a template?'

'My gut says no, but I could be proved wrong.'

'I was thinking . . . what with Lily missing . . . we should spill the beans to her parents on what she was doing with Gemma and Townsend.'

'It had crossed my mind, too. It could be that Lily has just run away to avoid the inevitable shame. But I'm inclined to leave it for now. See if she shows up by the morning. One other thing. The man who accused Barry Mercer of being responsible for various deaths. Do we know who he is yet?'

'We're still working on it.'

They arrive at the Mercers' within ten minutes. Outside their house is a marked police car, and on the driveway, a Škoda people carrier is parked.

'That's Simon Cooper's car,' says Stu. 'He's Isla's brother.'

A uniformed policewoman opens the door to them. They hear agitated voices coming from the living room. She recognises Isla's.

Archer greets her with a nod.

'This is DI Grace Archer,' Stu says to the constable.

The policewoman extends her hand. 'PC Anna Webb.'

'Good to meet you,' says Archer.

'How're they doing?' Stu asks the constable.

'Not great. Barry and Simon want to get out there and look for her.'

Stu sighs. 'Of course they do. Thanks, Anna. We'll take over.'

They enter the living room. Isla is sitting on the edge of the sofa, her eyes puffy from weeping, clutching a mobile phone with a garish pink cover. Next to her is a slim man in his sixties wearing a grey polo shirt. Sitting with hands gripping the rests of his armchair, is a second man with a slight build, possibly in his mid to late fifties. If she didn't know any better, she'd assume they were brothers. Archer detects a faint smell of whisky in the air. They're all looking at Archer and Stu as if they are the messengers of grave news.

'Have . . . have you found her?' Isla asks, her voice trembling.

'Not yet, Isla,' Stu answers.

'What're you doing here, then?' the man in the armchair asks. There's a slight slur in his voice. 'She isn't bloody here.'

'Let me introduce DI Grace Archer, from the Met.' Stu gestures to the man on the armchair. 'This is Barry Mercer, Lily's dad, and this is Simon Cooper, Lily's uncle.'

'What's this got to do with the Met?' Barry Mercer asks.

'We believe Gemma McFadden's murder may be linked to other cases.' Archer leaves it at that. No need to share any more details at the moment.

'What murders would those be?' Cooper asks, a confused expression on his face.

Archer is keen to press on with her own questions 'One in London last week. And two older cases. Possibly more.'

'I had no idea.'

'What about this Chris Townsend?' Barry interrupts. 'Have you caught him yet?'

'We're working on it,' Archer replies.

Barry snorts and shakes his head.

'Barry, you are a former copper. You know how these things work,' Stu says.

'You and Isla met working for the force, I understand,' Archer says.

'Back in the day, yes.'

A sob from Isla who can't help herself and starts to cry.

Cooper reaches across and squeezes her hand.

'If I could just ask you all a few questions . . .' says Archer.

Isla takes a moment and composes herself. 'Sorry . . . ask away.'

Archer turns to Isla's brother. 'Mr Cooper, if you don't mind.'

It takes a moment for Archer's hint to hit home. 'Yes, of course,' he replies, smiling politely. 'I've leave you to it, then.' He places his hand on Isla's knee. 'I'll see you in the morning.'

'Actually, if you could wait in the kitchen. We'd like to talk to you also.'

'Oh . . . Of course. I'll be in the kitchen,' he says, standing up and stretching stiff limbs. 'Isla, I'll be in the kitchen,' he repeats.

Isla nods and dabs her eyes with a tissue.

Archer takes his place on the sofa. 'Isla, did you speak to Lily after we left this morning?'

Her face creases. 'No, that's the thing! She disappeared at the same time as you did.'

'I'd like to know what you said to her!' Barry Mercer asks, gruffly.

Isla starts crying into her handkerchief.

'Mr Mercer, where were you today?' Archer asks.

He turns aways from Archer's gaze and breathes like a bull through his nose.

'I was fishing.'

'Where do you go?'

'The same spot I always go to . . .'

'On the River Tweed.'

'No.'

'He goes to Coldingham Loch,' Isla says.

'Oh . . . Where's that?'

'North. About thirty minutes' drive,' Mercer says. 'What has that got to do with anything?'

'How long were you there?' she asks.

'A few hours.'

'Three, four, more?'

'About four.'

'Did you drive?'

He frowns at the question and snorts once more. Silence fills the room.

'He lost his licence,' Isla says, breaking the quiet.

Archer suspects she knows the answer but asks anyway, 'Why was that?'

Mercer's eyes flare momentarily, his neck reddens. Isla is about to speak but her husband raises his hand, 'OK, I can answer for meself, thank you.' He takes a moment to compose himself. 'I was driving under the influence. Ridiculous, it was. I only had one extra and didn't even finish that.'

The smell on his breath might tell a different story, Archer thinks.

Isla sighs heavily, a look of vexation darkens her face. 'Thankfully, we have my brother here who can ferry us around.'

'How long have you been without a licence?'

'He had to surrender it last week,' Isla says.

'I see. Did Simon drive you to Coldingham Loch?'

Mercer answers with a single nod.

'And when was the last time you saw your daughter?'

'This morning, at breakfast.'

'And you've not seen or heard from her since?'

'No,' he replies frowning.

Archer turns to Isla. 'Do you have any idea why Lily left the house without saying?'

Isla shakes her head. 'Absolutely none. She was here, then she was just gone, like she'd vanished.'

'I assume she's not answering her phone?'

'That's the thing. She didn't even take it.' Isla holds out the pink device in her hand. 'She left it in her room.'

'Can I see it?' Archer asks.

Isla hesitates, frowning.

'It might contain a clue to where she's gone.'

'We've tried to access it, but it has a code that none of us know.'

'I can take it to the station and get one our tech guys to crack it,' says Stu.

Isla considers this and, after a moment, hands it across.

'We'll look after it,' Stu says.

'Has she ever been in trouble before?' Archer asks.

'What sort of trouble?'

'Perhaps at school, or at a youth club?'

'No, of course not. She's a good girl.'

Archer nods and turns to Stu. 'Perhaps we can talk to Mr Cooper now.'

'Excuse us,' says Archer, making her way into the kitchen. She stops and looks back. 'Just one more question, Mr Mercer. You were interviewed for a TV show recently at Berwick station.'

'That's correct.'

'There was an altercation.'

Mercer shifts uneasily in his chair. 'Aye.'

'A man accused you of being responsible for the death of some people.'

'A lunatic.'

'Why would he say that?'

'I have no idea. I've never hurt anyone, directly or indirectly. He's a madman. Nothing more.'

'Have you met him before?'

'No. Never.'

'Do you understand how this looks?' she asks.

He swallows. 'How do you mean?'

'It's an odd coincidence that a friend of your daughter is murdered, and then your daughter goes missing within days of a stranger accusing you of murder.'

His face reddens, he shakes his head and shrugs. 'I don't know anything about that.'

Archer studies him for a moment, unsure what to make of him. 'Thank you,' she replies, although she is utterly unconvinced.

Simon Cooper is sitting at the kitchen table, elbows resting on the surface, fingers entwined. Archer notices what looks like a wedding band on the ring finger of his right hand. He looks up when they enter.

'Thanks for waiting, Mr Cooper.'

'Call me Simon,' he replies. 'No need for formality.'

'Simon, it is. If you don't mind me saying, you and your sister don't have a Berwick accent.'

'That's right. We're from Liverpool originally.'

'You've lost your Scouse accent.'

'We both left when we were teenagers. There's a bit of every-where in our accents.'

'Where have you lived over the years?'

He looks away, his mind in thought as he ponders his response. 'Where haven't I lived . . . I was in the army for twelve years stationed all over the world. Did some time in Northern Ireland, got posted to Germany, then Somalia. Spent two years in Nevada and then came home.'

'How long have you been out of the army?'

'Twenty-three years now.'

'Do you miss it?' Stu asks.

'I miss being younger.'

'When was the last time you saw your niece?' Archer asks.

'This morning when I came to pick up Barry.'

'Did you talk to her?'

'No. She was in the hallway. I only saw her briefly. She didn't notice me. I was sitting in the car, you see.'

'I understand you drive the family around.'

'Not always. Isla does some of the driving, too. Barry should get his licence back . . . someday soon, I hope.'

'Do you live locally?'

'A little way out of town. In the country. I have a cottage in Springhill Lane.'

'Nice part of the world,' says Stu. 'Quiet. Remote.'

'Sounds idyllic,' says Archer. 'Are you married?'

'No.'

'Separated?'

'Single. At the moment, anyway.' He laughs.

'Is that a wedding band?' Archer asks.

'My mother's. It's all I have of hers.'

'Must be lonely living out in the countryside by yourself.'

'Not at all. I'm used to it.'

'What do you do for a living after the army?'

'Various jobs, I suppose. I worked in bars, restaurants, retail. I trained to become an accountant in my thirties and that became my career. I moved up here to be close to family. Isla and Lily, they're my only family.'

'Not Barry.'

He lets out a short laugh, 'Of course, Barry, too.' He leans across. 'Don't mention I left his name out. He'll never forgive me.'

Stu's phone buzzes, interrupting the interview. He takes it out and looks at the screen. 'It's Andy. Better take this.'

'I'll carry on,' Archer replies.

'Do you know why your niece might have left the house without saying anything to her mother? It's quite unusual, isn't it?'

'It's not like her. That said, she can be hot-headed.'

Stu's voice interrupts the questioning. 'Grace, a moment.'

Archer gets up from the table and joins Stu at the other end of the kitchen. 'Townsend just walked into the station and gave himself up,' he says.

Chapter 48

I N THE CAR ON THE way to the station, Archer thinks about the Mercers. An accusation of murder against Barry Mercer, the murder of a local woman, and their daughter, Lily, going missing. In her mind she can see the pieces of a vast puzzle floating away from each other, unable to slot together. Something else niggles at her. Something Isla said when they had spoken that morning. What was it?

With all of this churning over in her head she remembers the Parry debacle and decides to call Quinn.

'Hey,' he says, his voice sounds tired.

'Sorry, were you sleeping?'

'Just dozing. How's it going?'

'I'm sending Parry home.'

She notices Stu glance across at her.

'Has he been a naughty boy?' Quinn asks.

'I'll explain later. Can you come and take over from him?'

'Sure. What about Fletcher?'

'I'll deal with him. I need you here.'

'No worries. I'll book a red eye train and see you there.'

'Great. So, what's been happening?'

'Eve Sommers has proved difficult to talk to, as you said. I've asked Marian to go down to her neck of the woods, talk to her and explain she doesn't have much of a choice. While she's down there I've asked her to go to Bridgwater Police Station. They've given us the green light to go through their archives. We've been busy.'

'So it seems.'

'What's been happening at Berwick?'

Archer brings him up to date as Stu drives into the police station car park.

At the custody desk over one hour later, she waits patiently watching Stu preside over the formalities for processing the captured fugitive and suspect Chris Townsend. He's a tall man with a lazy posture. His shoulder-length blond hair is unkempt, he looks scruffy and unwashed, which is not surprising as he's been on the run for the last three nights. Townsend is agitated and not cooperating with the custody officer. When questioned, he responds with questions and demands in a loud posh accent that smacks of privilege.

'You can't keep me here! I haven't done anything,' he cries.

'Let's start with videoing underage girls for porn shoots,' Stu Vickers says.

Townsend flinches. 'I don't know what you're talking about.'

'We have some "interesting" pictures from one of your drives. And don't get me started on the Kitten Club live sex shows. We've had a few people calling in about those.'

'I'm not saying anything until my lawyer is here.'

'Then we'll all have to wait until tomorrow morning because that's when he arrives.'

'Please can I go home and come back with him in the morning? I did hand myself in, after all.'

Stu laughs. 'I don't think so, mate. Something about being a wanted fugitive and murder suspect might just stop that from happening. Don't despair. You'll spend the night in one of our finest rooms. We'll even throw in some breakfast.'

'You have rooms?'

'To be more specific, they're cells. Sparse but cosy.'

'Oh gosh!'

With Townsend locked up, and the search for Lily underway, Archer returns to her hotel for some much-needed shuteye.

At nine o'clock the following morning, Townsend's solicitor, Geoffrey Clarkson, arrives. Squeezed into a navy tailored suit, he's a large, surly man with a neck and head like a bull's. He doesn't acknowledge Archer, Stu Vickers or Andy Ball. Instead, he makes his way directly to the meeting room to talk with his client. They talk for thirty minutes, by which time Stu and Andy are granted an audience. Archer watches on a screen in the room next door. As the interview begins, she thinks of the Mercers again and quickly sends an email to Klara asking her to look up whatever she can about their background.

Twenty minutes into the interview, Townsend has become agitated, once again telling the story of how he had found Gemma in the cottage. The pictures of Gemma's dead body have tipped him over the edge. Clarkson is unimpressed and wants to call the interview off, but Stu tells them that as long as Lily remains missing he's going nowhere. Clarkson asks for proof and then out come the porn photos of Gemma and Lily and threats of going onto the sex register, which for some reason Clarkson finds amusing. To Archer, it seems the interview has become a pissing contest between Andy Ball and Clarkson, two alpha males, who seem to have forgotten that at the heart of this is the murder of several women. She feels a twist of anger and wants to kick her way in but decides she does not want to jeopardise her position here, especially with Fletcher looking for any excuse to nail her. To her relief, though, Stu brings it back on track and asks Townsend about Gemma.

'Did you love her?'

Townsend folds his arms and dips his head. He says something that is barely audible.

'Could you repeat that for the recording, please, Chris?' Stu says.

'Yes.'

'I know it hurts. Tell us about Lily.'

'What about her?'

'She's missing, Chris,' Stu says.

'I don't know anything about that.'

'Did you love her too?'

He frowns. 'No!'

'She was a commodity, then. Like Gemma. A way to make you some extra cash,' Ball says.

'No! It wasn't like that. They had cooked up this idea between them.'

'Can you elaborate on that?'

'Gemma had told Lily what she was doing with the live sex videos and the money she was earning. Lily wanted in on the action.'

'She's sixteen, Chris!' Ball says.

'Yeah, and she can act like a spoilt brat sometimes, but she knew exactly what she was doing. She's no innocent.'

'We know you spoke to her after Gemma's murder.'

'Did not!'

'The phone records say otherwise.'

Townsend sighs heavily and looks down. 'She called me.'

'Did you tell her that you killed her best friend?' Ball asks.

'My client did not kill her or anyone else!' says Clarkson.

'Chris, do you know where Lily is?' Stu asks, getting them back on track.

'No, of course not.'

'When was the last time you saw her?'

He takes a moment to reply. Archer bends closer to the screen to see his expression.

'The night of the shoot. I drove her home. Gemma stayed at the cottage, waiting for me. We had planned to spend the night there. Get high, and fool around.'

'So you dropped Lily off, drove back and found Gemma's body sprawled out on the bed?'

'Yes. That's exactly what happened. I swear to God.'

'Why didn't you call the police?' Stu asks.

He shrugs and shakes his head. 'I don't know . . . I panicked.'

'Panicked because you were photographing underage girls?'

'No! . . . yes.'

'So you ran?'

'Yes.'

'Did you take the camera equipment?'

He shakes his head. 'No. Whoever killed Gemma took it. He wrecked the place, took the cameras, and the spare drives.'

'You sure it was a he?' Ball says.

Townsend seems perplexed by the question. 'I don't know.'

'Do you know who did it?'

'For fuck's sake!'

'Let's say you're right—' says Stu.

'I am right!'

'You return. The equipment is gone, the place has been turned over. Lying on the bed is your dead girlfriend. The woman you love. Why leave her?'

'I told you, I panicked.'

'Is that all?'

'Is that not reason enough?' Clarkson says.

'I was high,' says Townsend. 'I'd taken a pill. My head was buzzing by the time I got back to the cottage. When I saw her lying there the drug just made it worse, almost unreal. But it was real. Her blood was on my fingers. I just ran out, got in the car, and drove.'

'Despite being high?'

'I wasn't thinking right.'

'I think we've heard enough,' says Clarkson.

'Wait. There's something else,' Townsend says. 'That night while we were filming, the bottles outside the cottage were knocked over. It freaked Gemma out. I thought it was a fox, but I don't believe it now.'

'What do you believe?'

'I think someone was watching us.'

Chapter 49

I T's 5.30 A.M. AND MALLORY is in King's Cross Station, which is bustling with the PPE masked, the semi-masked and the unmasked travelling out of the city. It's not unusual to see any of the capital's mainline stations busy at this time of the morning, even so soon after a pandemic, it seems. Mallory has purchased a Starbucks soymilk latte and has merged in with a swelling crowd watching and waiting for the platform number to appear on the digital board. The train journey from London to Berwick is approximately three and a half hours with one change at Newcastle. Mercifully, the train is on time. She hears children crying nearby and a couple arguing, and prays that she will not be subjected to any of that on her journey. That said, she is covered and brought her headphones for such emergencies.

The coffee is bitter, tasting more like a lukewarm chemical concoction. *Ugh!* Why did she buy it? She hates Starbucks, the McDonald's of coffee. She has a mind to take it back, but the platform number has been announced and the crowd moves towards it like unherded sheep, carrying Mallory with them. As they approach the platform, she notices a familiar head of neatly cropped dark hair, twenty feet or so ahead. Her heart sinks.

'Shit!' she whispers.

Harry Quinn is at the front of the crowd striding purpose-fully up the platform with a backpack over his shoulder. They're on the same train. What are the chances of that? He's the last person she expected, having assumed he'd be in Berwick already by Archer's side. She slows her pace and allows others to hurry past. He stops, climbs into a carriage, turning to look back as he does. Mallory gasps and dips behind the person in front. Did he see her? She can't be sure. She pictures the confrontation as he demands she leave the train and return home immediately. Fat chance. To the irritation of her fellow travellers, she cuts across them and scurries up the adjoining platform, keeping a watchful eye on the carriage Harry has entered. She sees him taking a seat. He wears his usual unfazed expression which, to her relief, suggests he hasn't seen her. She merges back into the crowd, joining the carriage at the front of the train, putting as much distance between her and Harry as she can. Mallory dumps her coffee into a wastebasket and searches for a seat. To her disappointment, there are none available. She heads back two carriages where she finds a spot at a table with an elderly PPE-masked couple opposite who nod politely at her.

'Morning,' Mallory says.

The whistle sounds from the platform and people hurry to board the train.

'Busy train,' says the elderly man.

'Yeah. People want out of London, I suppose.'

'It's the summer. Good to get into the country.'

The woman is staring at Mallory's tattooed arms. She leans across and says, 'If I was young again, I would get my arms painted just like that.'

Mallory smiles. 'Thank you.'

'They're very beautiful.'

'You could get my name tattooed on across your back,' the man says to his wife.

She laughs. 'I don't think so, dear.'

The train rolls forward and begins to gather speed. Mallory takes out her phone and checks the WhatsApp message she sent to Tom yesterday evening. There are two blue ticks, which means it's been received and read. And only five minutes back. She presses the dial and calls him. To her disappointment it goes straight to voicemail once more. This time she leaves a message.

'Morning, Tom. Please call me back. I'm worried about you. I'm on the train to Berwick and should be there before 10 a.m. . . . It's Mallory, by the way.'

She begins to scroll through the news and finds an article on Archer's investigation in Berwick. A suspect in the case, photographer Christopher James Townsend, is being questioned. There's breaking news. A young unnamed woman is missing. Mallory feels a knot in her stomach and hopes she's not another tragic victim.

'Tickets, please,' comes a voice.

Through her side vision she sees the guard standing by their table. 'I'll just get it,' she replies without looking up. She opens the ticket app and shows it to the guard. She narrows her eyes. It's not the guard. It's Harry. He's holding two hot drinks in a cardboard tray.

'Thought I'd get you a coffee before you get off. Latte, isn't it? Extra hot? None of that plant milk rubbish, though. Just cow cream. Yum!'

Mallory sighs heavily.

'Shift up.'

Mallory slides across to the window seat. 'What are you doing here?' she asks.

'Strangely, that question is on my lips, too.'

'Is everything all right, dear?' the elderly woman asks, eyes suspiciously watching the Irishman.

Harry takes out his ID. 'Detective Sergeant Harry Quinn. Thank you, ma'am. I can take it from here.'

'The police?' the woman says.

'In the flesh.' He nods at Mallory. 'We've been looking for this one for some time. She's in a lot of trouble.'

Mallory takes the coffee and rolls her eyes. She takes a mouthful. It's much better than the Starbucks, at least.

The couple are staring in silence.

Harry puts his finger to his lips. 'Keep it between us,' he says to them. Their eyes flare. Through their masks she can see their mouths open wide.

Mallory leans back into the seat, turns to look at Harry. 'Enjoying yourself?'

Harry smiles at her. She wants to laugh but refuses to give him the satisfaction. 'Before you ask, I'm not getting off,' she says. 'You can't make me.'

Harry takes a drink of his coffee. 'That's true. But neither the boss nor I will be best pleased.'

'Then just pretend I'm not there.'

'Hard to do that when you keep interfering in our investigation.'

Mallory notices the couple's eyes darting back and forth following her and Harry's exchange.

'I've just found two new victims, one of whom is a survivor. That's more than most of your team have contributed.'

'That's a little unfair,' Harry retorts. 'They've been working hard.'

'So have I.'

'I know you have, and I appreciate everything you do. Even Grace does. She's taking your calls and listening, which, to be honest, I never expected to see in my lifetime. You know she was never your greatest fan.'

'She should be grateful. I've told her story. She's become a cult figure in the world of true crime, all thanks to me.'

'Yeah, that's the last thing she wants, by the way. And it doesn't help that your listeners are writing to Charing Cross nick asking for signed photos. It's become a bit of a joke and some senior officers are mightily unimpressed.'

'Maybe she should learn to use that glory for her own good.'

Harry snorts a laugh. 'You can propose that one. Make sure I'm there when you do.'

Mallory turns and looks out the window quietly seething.

'All right, I'm sorry for being flippant.'

Mallory shrugs.

'So, tell me, considering we agreed for you to keep your distance, what is it you hope to achieve in Berwick-Upon-Tweed?'

Mallory finishes the coffee and thinks about what to say. Of course she's there to follow the story to make the best possible podcast that she can; however, she is also travelling to see Tom. She's convinced something is wrong and only she can help. Can Archer? Can Quinn? She turns to look at him and smiles. 'You know me. Just chasing a story.'

Chapter 50

WHEN THE TRAIN ARRIVES IN Berwick-Upon-Tweed, Mallory takes the opportunity to ditch Harry Quinn before he asks any more invasive questions. As much as she likes him, and she does *like* him, she is still smarting that he'd spotted her in King's Cross, despite her best efforts to be elusive and hide from him. That aside, she is also pissed that he'd had the nerve to come looking for her with a coffee in hand as if he'd planned the whole thing. Typically cocky. When the train stops, she makes a call to Tom, and hurries off the carriage with a thin goodbye smile at the Irishman. Moments later, she jumps into a cab outside the station with Tom still not picking up his phone.

She knows where he is staying. Bruce had pretended to be a delivery service and sweet talked the estate agent into revealing Tom's new address. Tom has recently moved to the town and rents a property somewhere. It wasn't difficult to hack into the local estate agents' systems and see who had rented which property. There wasn't a large selection, so the search was swift. Mallory gives the cab driver the address and is on her way to Tom's new home now.

'Here we are,' says the cab driver, ten minutes later, driving off the A1 and up a narrow country lane. 'The old Strother farmhouse. Never have much call to come out here anymore.'

It's an ugly property. A rickety grey pebble-dashed house that has seen better days.

'Who lives here?' she asks on the off chance he might have met Tom.

'I'd had heard a rumour in the village someone had taken it on but no idea who.'

Mallory pays the man.

'Do you want me to wait? Doesn't look like anyone's home.'

'I'll be fine, thank you.'

'Have a good day, then.'

'You too.'

Despite the warm temperature, there's something about this place that gives her a chill. A gravel path leads to the front door. Her feet crunch on the stones as she gingerly makes her way to the house. The windows are draped in dirty net curtains, making it impossible to see inside.

'Tom!' she calls. 'It's Mallory.' But there's no response.

She raps at the front door, gently at first, then harder. She waits, ear pressed to the wood, but no one comes. Crouching down, she peers through the letterbox. The hallway is sparsely furnished and looks as if it has not been updated in twenty years or more. The carpet is threadbare, the stairs are stripped wood. Underneath them is a doorway, a storeroom perhaps, or entrance to the basement. Her nose wrinkles at a musty, damp smell laced with cleaning fluid. She pulls away but stops when she hears something from inside. A thumping sound. She peers through letterbox again but sees nothing.

'Hello!' she shouts. That noise again but more urgent. 'Is someone there?' The noise of an approaching vehicle drowns out any sound. Mallory turns to see an old blue Land Rover Defender pull up outside the house. Tom Elston is at the wheel, his expression thunderous.

He climbs out of the car. 'What the hell are you doing here?'

Mallory is struck by his anger but also how unwell he looks. His face is gaunt and grey, like a corpse. His breath is laboured, his chest wheezing.

'I wanted to see you and make sure you're OK.'

'How did you know I was here? Is anyone else with you?' He's jittery and tense, his eyes scan the area looking for signs of other people.

'It's just me. I promise.'

His thick, bushy eyebrows are knotted into one, his eyes – although sunken – have a wildness about them. 'You need to leave. Now.'

'I came all this way to see you. The least you could do is invite me in for a coffee.'

He frowns and shakes his head. 'I won't ask you again.'

'But—'

'No buts!'

'Who's in the house?' she asks.

Tom flinches. 'No one's in the house. I live alone.'

'I heard someone.'

His eyes narrow. 'What exactly did you hear?'

Mallory shrugs. 'Just a noise. I called through the letterbox.'

Tom turns away and shakes his head. 'This place is overrun with mice and rats. In fact, I've just been to the landlord to discuss the matter.'

'There's been another murder, Tom. Here in Berwick.'

'What of it?'

'And a girl has gone missing.'

'And?'

'Why are you here, Tom? Why Berwick?'

He lets out a long breath. 'Don't you think I've suffered enough and maybe deserve to get away from all the shit back home and find some peace of mind?' A pained expression clouds his face. He closes his eyes, drops his head and folds his arms. 'I need to be alone. Please, just leave.'

Guilt sweeps through her. She has seen Tom like this before in the hours she has spent listening to him tell his story. Yet something is not quite right.

'I can help you,' Mallory says.

Tom laughs darkly. 'You know the problem with you is you just don't know when to give up.'

'Comes with the territory.'

Tom goes to the rear of the Land Rover and opens the back door.

'Let's go inside. We can talk some more. I really just want to help.'

Tom sighs and gestures towards the house. 'Lead the way.'

Mallory blinks and can't believe he's agreed. 'Really?'

'Really,' he replies, tossing her a set of keys. 'Open the front door. I need to carry some shopping in.'

Mallory smiles as she catches the keys. 'Wonderful!'

She turns and makes her way to the house, rifling through the keys. 'Which one is it?' She hears his feet crunching on the gravel, rapidly. In the downstairs window she sees a reflection. Something swinging through the air towards her. She gasps, swerves to dodge the blow but it's too late. The pain rings madly through her skull as she falls to the ground.

Chapter 51

ARCHER IS NOT IMPRESSED WITH Quinn's news that Mallory Jones has arrived in Berwick.

'I don't know why I'm so surprised,' she admits. 'I get the impression she thinks she's doing us a favour.'

'Where is she now?'

'Gone to see a friend, she said.'

'Convenient having a friend in the same small town where you're urgently "chasing a story".'

'That's what I thought. She's hiding something.'

'Any idea what?'

'We'll figure it out.'

They're driving through the countryside to Springhill Lane in a marked police car Archer had booked and borrowed for the day. Quinn had arrived just over one hour back and after introductions and updates from Stu and Ball, they headed out to talk to Simon Cooper.

'Makes a change from the big smoke,' Quinn says, admiring the scenery.

'Not missing all that lovely concrete back home?'

'In a few more days, perhaps. I like the countryside but it's all a bit too quiet for me.'

'I think that's it,' Archer says, pointing to the grey cottage almost two hundred metres ahead. She indicates left and turns into the drive, parking behind the Škoda people carrier. 'At least he's home.'

Quinn knocks on the front door. They wait but there is no answer. He knocks a second time as Archer peers through the living room and kitchen windows. There's a tray of cat litter on the floor and the remains of breakfast dishes on the kitchen counter but no sign of life or movement. She walks around the perimeter of the house. At the rear is a narrow pathway leading to two outbuildings. She hears a hissing and rustling at her feet and sees a fierce-looking black and white cat with a scarred face and a missing ear. It watches her suspiciously from the edge of path, and flinches when Quinn appears.

'Nice kitty,' he says gently, edging quickly past the animal.

'I think she likes you.'

'I think she might like to tear my face off and wear it for fun.'

They make their way up the path, stopping at the buildings – and the sound of shuffling noises from inside the first one. The door is ajar.

'Mr Cooper,' Archer calls.

The noises stop. Seconds later the door opens. Simon Cooper appears from behind it, a puzzled expression on his face. 'Detective Inspector Archer. This is a surprise.' He's wiping unclean hands with a rag.

'We were passing and thought we'd check in.'

'I see.' A concerned expression clouds his face. 'Is there news about Lily?'

'I'm afraid not.'

He sighs, sadly.

'This is my colleague, Detective Sergeant Harry Quinn.'

'Nice to meet you,' Cooper says. 'I'd shake but my hands are a bit grubby,' he adds apologetically.

'No worries. Have we disturbed you?'

'Is that a Belfast accent?' Cooper asks.

'One hundred per cent.'

'I spent some time there when I was younger.'

'Nice.'

Archer peers through the crack in the doorway. There's a bicycle inside, leaning against the wall. It looks clean and almost brand new. 'You like bikes?' she asks.

Cooper peers behind him. He smiles and pushes the door open. There are more bicycles inside. Around half a dozen in various states of repair. 'I'm the local bicycle repair man. It's my side hustle.'

'What's your main hustle?' Quinn asks.

'Being retired.' He gestures to the bike leaning against the wall. 'This one belonged to Gemma. Her mum asked me to fix it before ... before the murder. I was just cleaning it up, although I'm not sure what to do with it. I can't take it back. Not yet anyway.'

'No. I suppose not,' Archer replies. 'Did you know Gemma well?'

'I suppose as well as any of the other young people around town. I knew her parents better. Although I would occasionally talk to Gemma with Lily.'

'They were good friends.'

'Yes. Opposites, though.'

'In what way?'

'Gemma was more confident and outgoing. Lily would like to be but that doesn't come naturally to her.'

They look at the bike for a moment before Cooper breaks the silence. 'Come down to the house. I'll make us some tea. Or do you prefer coffee?'

'Tea for me,' Archer says.

'I'll have a coffee, thanks,' says Quinn.

They walk together back down to the cottage.

'Another beautiful day today. Unusual temperatures we're having. Warmer than we're use to up here. A consequence of us destroying our planet, it seems.'

'You believe in all that?' Quinn asks.

'Don't you?'

'Aye. I'm not far off believing the planet will burn in flames in the next few decades.'

'Then we are on the same page, detective. That's refreshing, is it not?'

Quinn raises an eyebrow at Archer. Her phone rings. It's Klara. She answers.

'Hi, Grace, I found some interesting info on the Mercers.'

Archer holds back and lets Cooper and Quinn walk on. 'We're with Simon Cooper at the moment. Can I call you back?'

'You might want to ask him what he and the Mercers were doing in London the same time Elena was murdered.'

'Are you serious?'

'I was looking through Isla Mercer's Facebook and found photos of Lily, Barry and Simon Cooper outside Buckingham Palace and various other tourist spots.'

The Mercers. In London.

'I have other info, too. Let's meet up when you're done.'

'I'll set a meeting for 2 p.m. with Stu Vickers and Andy Ball. Does that work for you?'

'I'll make it work,' Klara replies.

Archer ends the call and catches up with Quinn and Cooper, who is unlocking the front door of the cottage.

'How long have you lived here?' Archer asks, following him inside and into the kitchen. Quinn hangs back furtively, checking out the living room. The kitchen is small, sparsely furnished, devoid of any feminine touches.

'Around eighteen years,' replies Cooper, filling the kettle.

'Just before Lily was born?'

'That's right.'

'You two are close.'

'Lily and I? Yes, we are.' Cooper arranges three brown mugs. One is in the shape of an owl and chipped around the rim. 'Lily bought me this for Christmas a long time back.' He smiles.

Quinn enters the kitchen. 'You're an army man,' he says.

'Was,' Cooper replies.

'I noticed a picture in the living room. Black and white. Andy Town. That's how you know Belfast.'

'I served there for a few years during the mid-1980s.'

The kettle boils.

'That was a tough decade,' Quinn says.

'Indeed it was.' Cooper pours the hot water, finishes making the drinks, and offers milk and sugar. 'I'm all out of biscuits.' He leads them into the living room. Like the kitchen, it is sparsely furnished, with the exception of a few pictures, an old TV and some books. It's neat and tidy but seems a purely functional space for one man and his cat. Archer notices Quinn's lip curling. The cat is at his feet.

'You don't mind cats, do you?' Cooper asks.

'Nope, not me,' says Quinn, unconvincingly.

They sit at a small dinner table by the front window with views over the fields.

'Did you know Chris Townsend?' Archer asks.

'He's the photographer fella?'

Archer nods.

The cat jumps into Cooper's lap and purrs as the man strokes its fur.

'Not too well. He's not been here long, I understand. I knew him and Gemma were dating. I also knew Lily didn't like him much.'

'Oh, why was that?' Archer asks.

'She thought he was sly, and a bit full of himself.'

'Did you know what he was up to with Gemma?'

'How'd you mean?'

'Did you know they were making porn movies together at the cottage in Spittal?'

Cooper flinches. 'Making porn?' He shifts in his chair. 'Lily was right to be wary of him.'

'Indeed she was.'

Archer says, 'There was an altercation at the train station when your brother-in-law was being interviewed for TV. You were there, I understand.'

'That's right.'

'What can you tell us about it?'

'It was very odd. A man just barged through and began flinging accusations at Barry. He looked a little unwell. We didn't know what to make of it.'

'Unwell in what way?'

'Unhinged.'

'Did you recognise him?'

'No. I gave a description to Stuart and Andy.'

Archer nods. 'We appreciate that, thank you. As you're aware, he's a suspect.'

'The papers seem to think he's the prime suspect.'

'I don't know why they think that. Can I ask where you were the night Gemma McFadden was murdered?'

He smiles thinly. 'Ah. Am I also a suspect?'

'We have to ask everyone. It's routine.'

He places his mug on the table. 'I was here at home. Just me and Edwina.'

'Edwina?' Quinn asks.

Cooper nods at the cat. 'I'm afraid I don't have much of an alibi.'

324

'You were in London last week, with your sister and brother-in-law. Lily, too.'

'That's correct.'

'What took you to London?'

'Barry was invited to meet the TV production company. Isla decided it would be a good idea for us all to go for a few days.'

'Where did you stay?'

'We were in a hotel in Paddington. It was cheap. Not exactly three stars but it served its purpose.'

'Can I ask where you were on the evening of the twenty-third of July?'

He rubs his chin as he considers his answer. 'I'm not great with dates. My old man brain, you see. Let me just check my diary.' He lifts the cat from his lap, drops it to the floor and exits the living room. A few moments later he returns with a pocket diary. Sitting at the table he opens the calendar at the date and points. 'Ah, dinner at the Argentinian Steak House in Paddington. We had a table for four.'

'What time did you leave?'

'I can't remember exactly. Around nine thirty.'

He closes the diary.

Archer takes out her phone and shows him a photo of Elena. 'Ever seen this woman before?'

He regards the picture curiously for a moment. 'I don't think so.'

Archer pockets her phone. 'OK. Thank you, Mr Cooper.'

'Anything to help find my niece.'

'We'll be in touch.'

Chapter 52

MALLORY WAKES. SHE IS COLD despite a mugginess in the air. She can smell a musty odour like mould. What the hell? Her head spins and throbs but she takes a moment to gather herself. She is lying on her side on a hard slippery surface, her arms stiff and aching. What happened? She groans as her eyes blink open. It's gloomy wherever she is. Does she have a hangover? Her mind races and then the full horror sucker punches her. *Tom!*

She tries to get up, but her hands are tied behind her back. Her feet are also bound. In her mouth is a filthy cloth, taped to her face. *Oh shit!* Her eyes adjust to gloom. She winces at the stabbing pain in her head as she pushes herself up and takes in her surroundings. She's in a vast empty space with rows of tall, dirty windows obscuring the view outside, and in. At first, she thinks it's some sort of abandoned barn, but the walls are covered in filthy, broken tiles, the floor is stone and heavily stained. There are rusted animal pens lining the walls. Mallory feels nauseous. It's an old slaughterhouse. Her mind races. Tom's the killer? He murdered all those women, and his daughter, too? Mallory has spent so much time with him listening to his story, believing his lies. How did she not see through him? She had met him briefly in London around the time Elena Zoric had been murdered.

He had not seemed himself. How could she be so blind, so . . . stupid.

'Fuck!' she cries, wincing as the pain pierces her brain.

She tugs her wrists to try and free them from the ropes, but they are too tight. Nearby is a stainless-steel table. She hauls herself into a kneeling position. Her head spins. Narrowing her gaze at the tabletop she sees a roll of duct tape, a hunting knife with a serrated edge, a little box containing bullet cartridges and what looks like a handheld power drill. But it's not a drill. Mallory feels her spine icing over. It's a captive bolt gun. A device used for penetrating and zombifying the brains of cattle before slaughter, or in this case, a weapon used to murder women. Terror grips Mallory, her pulse races, sweat rolls down her forehead and into her eyes. She needs to get out of here and fast or else she'll end up dead, murdered by a cold-blooded killer just like the other victims. Just like her beloved Zach. The thought makes her want to weep, yet a fury ignites inside her. If it's somehow within her power, she will not let that happen.

She shuffles across the floor on her knees, ignoring the blinding pain in her head. It takes all her strength, and she sweats with the exertion. At the table, she notices a screw sticking out from the leg. An idea. Leaning across, she pushes the tape covering her mouth over it and hooks the flat end of the screw below the tape covering her chin. Carefully she pushes her head up and down until the tape begins to loosen. The screw is thankfully stable and after a painstaking ten minutes of uncharacteristic patience, Mallory has caught enough of the tape to slowly tear it from her hot, damp face. With a blessed relief, she spits out the filthy rag and takes in several glorious gulps of air.

She listens for signs of anyone nearby but hears nothing. The quiet is unnerving. This place, this filthy former abattoir is like something from a horror movie. The thought of all those animals, cows and pigs, being herded into this place to be killed and butchered for meat is terrifying. She swears if she gets out of this she'll become a vegetarian. The thought of dying here makes her pulse race and increases her determination to get away. Could she scream out and cry for help? Yes is the answer but Tom could be close by. Is it worth the risk? She can't have been out for more than five or ten minutes which means she must still be at the farmhouse and far from town. Maybe ramblers could stroll by. It's a fifty–fifty chance that someone could come to her rescue if she screamed. The likelihood is Tom would come and properly finish her off. That said, she's surprised he hasn't done it already.

Her eyes narrow at the knife on the tabletop. If only she can get it. She grits her teeth. She throws herself onto her back. It's painful with her arms tied behind her but needs must. Drawing back her legs she kicks out at the table dislodging the contents on top. Her head spins with the effort. She needs the knife but it's no good to her on the table. She takes a breath and kicks harder this time. The tape, the knife and the captive bolt gun fall to the stone floor with an echoing clatter. Not ideal. Mallory begins the arduous task of crawling towards the knife. Her head throbs. As she draws close, she spins her body around and uses her fingers to search for the blade but stops, gasping at the sound of a door opening. She turns to look in its direction. The missing girl, Lily Mercer, is sitting in a wheelchair, her hands and legs taped to it. Her mouth is also taped. Her eyes are red and puffy and widen when they see Mallory. Tom is wheeling her inside. He sees Mallory and her vain attempts to free herself. Parking the wheelchair, he makes his way towards her and lifts the bolt gun and knife.

'Tom, don't do this. Please. Let us go.'

'I can't do that.'

'Why kill us? What have we done?'

He is not listening.

'Tom, please . . .'

He sets takes the knife and slips it into the pocket of his trousers. 'You were always so resourceful,' he says. 'I liked that about you, Mallory. Truly, I did.'

His voice seems so cold. Not the Tom she is used to. She wants to kick herself. She was always such a good judge of character.

Mallory feels the tears coming. 'She's just a child, Tom.'

He closes his eyes, clenches his jaw and shakes his head.

Mallory feels a surge of anger and courage, too. 'I believed in you. I really did!'

'Shut up!' he cries.

'You can't face it, can you? You're a coward and a murderer!'

Tom swallows. 'It's time,' he says, lifting the bolt gun from the floor.

Chapter 53

ARCHER GLANCES AT THE CLOCK on the Berwick-Upon-Tweed police incident room wall. 'It's 2 p.m. Let's get Klara on the line.'

Quinn leans across and dials Klara's number on the video conference software. It answers within two rings. Klara appears on the screen, her orange hair almost glowing in the dimly lit room.

'Klara, it's Harry and Grace. We're with DCs Andy Bell and Stu Vickers,' says Quinn.

'Hi, everyone. I'm in my office with DC Marian Phillips.'

Phillips leans closer to the camera and smiles.

'Let's get started,' says Archer, says nodding at Stu.

'Townsend's alibi checks out,' he says as he pages through ANPR shots of the suspect displayed on a flatscreen monitor. 'This is footage of him in Edinburgh at the same time Lily went missing. And the rest are shots of him driving Lily home the night Gemma was murdered.'

Archer is not surprised. There was the slim possibility of him being a copycat killer but even then she was not convinced of that. 'The person we're looking for is older. Probably in their fifties or older,' she tells them. 'Someone unassuming, normal, an everyday person who you would not look twice at.'

'You think it's a Berwick resident?' Stu asks.

'Possibly. Or the man who levelled the "death" accusation at Barry Mercer. He's the right age bracket and is a stranger in town.'

'We have a name for you,' says Stu. 'He's just moved to town in the last month and has rented the old Strother Farm. He's called Thomas Elston. He's retired, is all we know.'

'Good work. Harry and I can pay him a visit later.'

'Townsend is no longer a suspect, although he will face charges of underage pornography and a spell on the sex register,' says Stu.

'Tragic,' says Ball.

Stu continues, 'We managed to access Lily Mercer's phone. Seems she been sexting with an anonymous ripped dude. We tracked the number down to a skinny, spotty kid at her school who looks nothing like his alter-ego.'

'He practically shat himself when we showed him what we had from Lily's phone,' Ball laughs. 'His alibis check out, so nothing to follow up on there.'

'OK, thank you,' says Archer, keen to move on. 'So, to summarise, we have a string of murders dating back to the 1980s: Sally McGowan, murdered in London, 1987; Star Royale, AKA Kelvin Glover, murdered in Bridgwater, 1988; Angela Bailey, murdered in Warfield, 1989; Hannah Daysy, London, 1991; Elena Zoric, London, 2022 and Gemma McFadden 2022, Berwick-Upon-Tweed. Lily Mercer remains missing. There is a chasm of a time gap between Hannah's and Elena's murder. However, I believe we have barely scratched the surface. So many people – women on the fringes of society, like our victims – have gone missing over the years. I expect our killer has chalked up many more names that we have not found yet.

'What do we know about the victims? All women, or in Star Royale's case, a man who presents as a woman to get clients.

All have been involved in some capacity in the sex business. From what we can gather, the majority of the victims are estranged from family or friends. Not all, but some. Historically, these are people no one has much cared about. Not even the police. All have been brutally murdered, like cattle, with a captive bolt gun and a single penetrating 5mm puncture wound, pretty much like a stake to the heart.

'What picture does all of this paint of our killer? We know from witnesses he's male. Given the date of the first recorded murder, he is at least in his mid-fifties. He dislikes women, in particular, sex workers. He doesn't rape his victims; he just murders them. Maybe he's single or married. Maybe he gets sexually aroused by the murders; maybe he doesn't. The use of the captive bolt gun is curious. Does he see sex workers as cattle or lambs to the slaughter. What is going on in his twisted mind? I think it's fair to assume this man lives among people without being noticed. He has been doing his thing for many years. He understands his true nature and has learned probably from a very young age how to hide. He knows how to behave like everyone else. He is a chameleon among neighbours and family. We are certain he takes souvenirs. This seems to be jewellery but might be other personal items. Any questions so far?'

Silence from the room. DCs Vickers and Ball look perplexed. Archer is aware this is new territory for them, unlike her immediate team.

'OK, let's start off with an update. Marian, what do you have?'

'I got the green light to search the Bridgwater archives. It took some hours, but I found the incident reports for Star Royale and Eve Sommers, or Brunet as she was then. It may come as no surprise that the reports were sketchy and unkind, practically laying blame with the victims for the choices they had made. As you mentioned, the police didn't seem to care too much. Eve's report was the most insightful. She gave a description of her attacker. This is what she said: *He was a quiet man, dressed smart-casual with short, cropped tidy hair. Ordinary looking, about five foot eight. He was polite enough, and nervous, which is not unusual. We drove to a quiet spot near the harbour. He then suddenly punched me in the head. Of course, I panicked and fought my way out of his car. My head was spinning as I tried to get away. I cried for help, but we were out of earshot, or so I thought. I tripped and fell. He came at me then with this weapon, pinning me down with his knees on my arms. I didn't know what it was. It looked like a heavy black metal baton. It was around a foot in length. I thought he was going to beat me with it. Instead, he ripped my blouse open and pressed it hard into my chest. He pressed a button and it made a clicking sound but nothing happened. It confused him. He started trying to fix it. By this time, I was screaming for help. Then I heard voices. He looked so angry he raised the weapon and hit me on the head with it. Then I woke in hospital.* That's Eve's story. A grim tale. One she was lucky to survive.'

'Did you talk to her?'

'I did. I showed her the statement and it seem to trigger something in her. She's going to come forward. She needs to talk it over with her husband and family.'

'Of course. Excellent work, Marian,' says Archer. 'Klara, I updated Harry, Stu and Andy with the news on the Mercers' trip to London. You mentioned you had other info?'

'I do. And this is where it gets interesting.'

'How so?'

'There is one single person, or persons, linking the murders in Bridgwater, London and Warfield.'

'Barry Mercer?' Archer says.

'And Isla Mercer, too.'

'Isla?' says Stu.

'Isla worked for the Met back in the late eighties. It's where she met Barry. Sally was murdered in London. Isla then shifted to Reading, which is a forty-minute drive to Warfield where Angela Bailey was murdered. Barry had a spell working in Taunton. Bridgwater is close by and as we know Star Royale and Eve Sommers worked there.'

It's like the pieces of a puzzle are slowly falling into place.

'Then who is this Thomas Elston?' Stu asks.

'I can answer that,' Klara says. 'While you were talking, I ran a search. Thomas Elston is the biological father of Hannah Daysy. Which means—'

'Which means he blames Barry Mercer for his daughter's death,' Quinn says.

'Why don't they have the same surname?' Stu asks.

'According to Mallory Jones's research, she was estranged from her father. She took her mother's maiden name.'

Archer feels her heart racing. They're getting close. 'Let's get him in right away.'

'Stu and I know the Strother Farm. We can head there now,' says Ball.

'Good. Harry and I will pick up Barry. Let's call it a meeting for now.'

Chapter 54

ISLA MERCER HAS NOT SLEPT since Lily went missing three nights ago. In the shadow of the murder of Gemma McFadden, Isla can't help but fear the worst. It is all so overwhelming. Her anxiety levels are through the roof, alongside her blood pressure, which has become dangerously high. She has always been a fidgeter and finds the tiniest of solace in pottering around the house, aligning ornaments that don't need to be aligned, cleaning cupboards and surfaces that have already been cleaned or puffing cushions that do not need to be puffed. The list goes on, but it helps keep her mind off the creeping dread that her wonderful, beautiful Lily might be . . . She shakes her head, unable to finish her train of thought.

Lily's fine. She's OK. She's just upset. Why wouldn't she be? Her best friend has been murdered and now all those awful rumours are being whispered around town. Vile, disgusting, horrible, untrue rumours!

Barry and Simon have just returned from another fruitless search for Lily. She won't admit it but she resents them for failing to find her. They can't be trying hard enough.

'Come and sit down, Isla,' says Simon, his voice calm and soothing. 'I'll make us a nice cup of tea.'

But Isla can't bring herself to talk to either of them. Barry is sitting in his armchair, drinking whisky and shifting constantly, making grunting and puffing noises as if he wants attention, but he won't get any from her. Not when he's drinking. His behaviour has been strange since Lily left. He's moody and hasn't washed in two days. He's been out every day with Simon visiting Lily's favourite spots in the hope she might be there, waiting to be found. Yet each time they have returned without her. She knows Barry can sense her disappointment, her blame. He turns from her and closes in on himself. Isla doesn't know what to make of that. It might be nothing. For all she knows, he might think she's behaving strangely. Why wouldn't he? They may have both worked for the police but this experience as the mum and dad of a missing teen is just so . . . raw and uncharted.

Isla is standing at the living room front window, peering up the street, hoping beyond hope that Lily might appear and make her way down. *Please, please, please come home to me.* She is idly dusting one of the Royal Doulton figurines, a porcelain dancing lady. Her eyes drop to the statue. She is beautiful with tumbling red hair, just like Lily's, and is dressed in a flowing crimson frock. Isla trembles. She's so delicate. Her eyes begin to water and sting. She glides the duster over the glossy ornament, her mind spinning and confused, her heart at the point of splitting in two.

'You cleaned that damn thing ten minutes back!'

Isla flinches, the figurine slips from her fingers, tumbling from her hands, it falls, its pretty head slams against the edge of the sill and snaps off at the neck. She gasps and chokes out a sob.

'Now look what you've done!' he hisses.

The head clangs off the radiator and rolls across the carpet, stopping at Isla's slippered feet, the porcelain face smiling up at her as if decapitation was her party trick. Isla crouches down and scoops the head gently into her hand.

'Let me help you,' Simon says, but Isla doesn't want help. With her free hand she picks up the body, tears pricking her eyes. She looks from one piece to the other and wonders where the superglue could be.

Barry's phone rings. They all turn to look at it sitting on the coffee table, glowing and vibrating like some sort of alien object.

'Answer it! Quick, it could be Lily!' says Isla, her heart racing.

Barry is slow, seemingly unable to move. Isla slips the figurine's body into the crook of her elbow and dashes across the room, snatching the phone from the table. She doesn't recognise the number. Her heart in her mouth, she presses the green button to answer.

'Lily, is that you?'

Silence for a moment. Only breathing. Isla feels her pulse racing.

'Mum, is that you?'

'Lily? Oh my God! Oh my God! Where are you?'

'Mum ...' she replies, her voice quivering.

'Lily?'

Barry stands and reaches for the phone but Isla backs away from him.

A stranger's voice, a man, comes on the phone. 'I have your daughter,' he says, coldly.

Isla feels her world spiralling away from her. 'Who is this? Why do have my daughter?' The phone is wrenched from her hand.

'What the hell is going on?' Barry shouts into the phone.

Isla is terrified. She edges closer to her husband and listens to the caller.

'Barry Mercer,' the man spits. 'This evening there will be a reckoning.'

'Where's my daughter?'

'If you want to see her alive again you will listen very carefully to what I say. Do you understand?'

Barry's face pales. He scratches his head. 'What do you want?'

'I want you, Barry. Just you.'

'What do you want with me?'

'All will be explained. Just do as I tell you and she won't be hurt. Understand?'

Isla's hand is squeezing the figurine's head. There's a sharp pain, and a warm wetness but she ignores it.

'But—' protests Barry.

'Do you understand?' the man demands.

Isla is at the point of exploding. 'Yes! Yes!' she cries. 'He understands. He will be there if I have to drag him there myself.'

'Just Barry. No one else.'

'Where?' Barry asks.

'The Strother Farm abattoir. I'm waiting.'

'Please let me speak to Lily.'

The phone goes dead.

'No!' Isla's heart sinks. She wants to scream and weep but she turns to her husband. 'You get out there. You do whatever he asks.'

Barry's eyes dart from Isla to Simon. 'We should call the police, no?'

'Oh my God! Did you not hear what he said? He will hurt our daughter if you do not go there alone.'

'But—'

'Where is he, Barry?' Simon asks.

'He's at the Strother Farm in the old abattoir.'

'Then we go together. You and me.'

'Simon, no!' Isla protests.

Simon reaches out to his sister and gently squeezes her shoulders. 'It's the only way. I know the area. Barry will go in

340

alone. I will check the place out. There is more than one entrance to that building.'

Isla trembles in his grip. She trusts Simon more than her husband. 'Bring her home to me.'

'I promise, I will.'

Chapter 55

THERE'S NO ANSWER AT THE Mercers' door. Quinn presses the bell a second time and raps his knuckles hard on the door. Archer peers in through a crack in the living room window. The room is empty, neat and tidy, the only thing that seems odd is a headless figurine lying on top of the coffee table. Quinn is looking through the letterbox. A response vehicle, requested by Archer, pulls up outside the house. Two female uniforms get out.

'Give us a moment,' Archer says to them.

'I just saw Isla Mercer,' Quinn says, rapping the door. 'She darted into the kitchen.'

Archer makes her way to the rear of the house. 'Why is she hiding?'

'Mrs Mercer, I just saw you!' Quinn bellows into the letterbox.

Archer is looking through the kitchen window. There's no sigh of Isla Mercer. She stands on her toes and, looking down, sees the grey middle parting of her hair. She is crouched on the floor, her back pressed against a cupboard.

'Isla, it's Grace Archer.'

But Isla doesn't respond.

Archer tries the back door which is surprisingly unlocked. She steps inside. The woman is cowering, fists bunched, one with blood dripping from it.

'Isla, are you hurt?' Archer says, crouching in front of her.

Isla doesn't answer. She is pale and unwell-looking, which is not surprising, considering what she has been through. At the same time, she seems distant, as if she's not fully switched on. Archer wonders if she has taken something for her nerves.

Quinn is outside instructing the two officers. He enters the kitchen, skirts around Archer and makes his way into the house, looking for Barry.

Isla opens her bloodied hand. Inside is the head of the broken figurine. The porcelain neck is jagged and has pierced her skin. Isla stares at the little head and still has not acknowledged Archer and Quinn's presence in her home.

Archer reaches for the head. 'Isla, has something happened?'

Isla's lips tighten. She folds in on herself, her hand covering the broken ornament.

'You know you can talk to me,' Archer says. She can hear Quinn's footfalls upstairs but no voices. 'Where's Barry?'

At the mention of his name Isla stiffens and slides away from Archer.

'I need to find the superglue,' she says.

Quinn arrives at the kitchen entrance and shakes his head. 'Where's Barry, Isla?'

Isla begins opening the cupboard doors and drawers, rifling through the contents. 'I need to fix her.'

Archer places her hand on Isla's arm. 'The glue can wait. Come and have a seat,' Archer says gently, gesturing at the table.

Isla pauses, eyes down, uncertainty clouding her face.

'There's been some developments in the investigation. We need to talk to your husband.'

Isla sets the figurine's head on the worktop. 'I cut myself,' she says, looking down at her palm. There are two small but deep gashes.

'You might need a stitch for those.'

She frowns sadly. 'Oh . . .'

Archer finds a roll of kitchen paper, tears off a sheet, folds it and places it over the wounds. 'That'll do for now.'

Isla smiles weakly. 'Thank you.' She sits at the table. Archer sits beside her.

'Shall I make us some tea?' Isla asks.

'Would you like one?' Archer replies.

Isla nods her head.

'I can do that,' Quinn says, reaching for the kettle and filling it.

'Is everything OK?' Archer asks Isla.

She nods and smiles. 'She's coming home.'

Archer narrows her eyes. 'Do you mean Lily?'

Isla's smile widens. 'She's coming home,' she repeats.

'Have you spoken to her?'

She looks at Archer, holding her gaze momentarily, and biting her lip. She nods her head, her expression lightening.

'Where is she?'

'He's bringing her home?'

'Barry?'

'Her dad. Her dad is bringing her home.'

She catches Quinn's eye as he pours boiling water into a teapot.

'But Barry is her dad, isn't he?' Archer asks.

Isla folds her arms and doesn't reply.

'Who's Lily's father, Isla?'

Archer looks across at the refrigerator. There are photographs on the doors, pictures from holidays, pictures of Lily as a baby and Lily growing up through the years. There's a shot of a younger Isla, dressed in her police uniform. She looks smart. Standing beside her with an arm around her shoulder is a younger Barry, smiling and proud. Archer narrows her gaze. Wait, that's not Barry. She had noticed before that there was a slight resemblance but thought nothing of it as it was mainly height, body, dress sense. They were both just two unassuming, ordinary men.

'It's Simon. Simon is Lily's father?' Archer says.

Isla's eyes widen and Archer realises this is a long-buried secret.

Archer's phone rings. It's Stu. She swipes to open the call.

'I just had a call about a sighting of Barry Mercer and Simon Cooper racing out of town. Looks like they're driving to Cooper's house. We're not far from there now.'

'OK. Go there and see what they're up to. We'll join you shortly. Keep me updated.'

'Will do.'

'Is Lily at Simon's?' Archer asks Isla as she ends the call.

She doesn't respond.

'Why would Lily be at Simon's, Isla? Please help me understand.'

'She's coming home. That's all you need to know.'

Archer is getting nowhere. She meets Quinn's gaze. He shrugs. Archer nods at the two policewomen to come inside. 'Can you please stay with her? If anyone else comes here, family or friend, then call me immediately.' Archer hands her contact card across.

They hurry to the car and with the siren and blue lights flashing, make the journey to Simon Cooper's house.

Archer's phone rings once more. A number she doesn't recognise. She answers, 'This is Detective Inspector Archer.'

'Hello, you don't know me. I'm a friend of Mallory Jones. Bruce Radley is my name.'

Archer sighs. 'That's nice for you. I'm a little busy right now.'

'I'm worried about her.'

'She is a worry. Listen, call me later—'

'She's missing. I've been calling her all day and she's not answering.'

'She's chasing a story, apparently.'

'No. It's not like her. She always takes my calls whatever the situation. She and I, we're—'

'Mr Radley, I would love to chat about Mallory—'

'I know she's in Berwick and I know you're there, too. Please help her.'

'What makes you think she's in danger?'

'She's visiting someone. A man we interviewed for a podcast.'

Archer frowns. 'What man?'

'His name is Tom Elston. He's the father of Hannah Daysy, a victim of the captive bolt gun killer.'

'When did you last talk to her?'

'Last night.'

'Did she say where she was going?'

'We found his address at a place called the Strother Farm in Belford. I've done a trace on her phone. She's definitely there. It hasn't moved in four hours.'

Chapter 56

MALLORY'S HEAD IS STILL THROBBING from the clobbering it had taken that morning. Breathing steadily through her nose, she tries to calm herself and think. She is inside one of the animals' pens at the rear of the abattoir, sitting against the mesh of a filthy, rusted animal cage caked in mould and, she's certain, ancient dried blood. *Ugh!* It smells so bad she has gagged three times already but is gradually getting used to the stench. It's early evening and still light outside, the sun not due to set until after nine or so. Despite that, in this place, in this godforsaken pen, it's dark, shadowy, and damp, too. She shudders. Is this where she's going to die? Is Tom going to slaughter her with that bolt gun in the same way he has killed the other women? If so, why hasn't he done it already? She has to do something. Reason with him at least, beg if she has to.

Tom is back in the centre of the building with Lily. He has just finished a call to someone. She had heard Lily's voice crying for her mum. Then Tom had spoken. The exchange had been tense; he had raised his voice. She'd heard him spit Barry Mercer's name. Why him? The call had ended, and she could hear Lily crying hysterically. And then it was quiet. For a moment Mallory thought he'd finished her off but then she heard muffled cries. Thankfully, she is still alive.

Mallory needs to move. She needs to get out of here and take Lily with her. She has to try. 'Tom,' she calls. 'Tom, please.'

His boots echo in the cavernous space as he slowly approaches. She hears his laboured breathing. They had spoken before of his health problems. His 'dodgy ticker', as he called it. He appears at the gate of the pen and pushes it open. His face is gaunt and grey. He's not carrying the bolt gun.

'You look worse than I feel,' Mallory says.

'I've had one of those days,' he replies. Shuffling inside, he leans against the cage and slides himself down to the ground.

'Where are we?' she asks.

'Not far from the house.' He looks around the grim space. 'An appropriate place to end all of this.'

'Are you going to kill me?' she asks.

Tom closes his eyes and drops his head as if resting. After a moment, he says, 'I've never killed anyone in my life. Not directly, that is.'

Mallory frowns. 'What does that mean?'

'It's my fault Hannah is dead.'

'So you did kill her?'

'In a way, I did. If it wasn't for me, she'd still be alive. I was a terrible father, and a worse husband. Growing up a strict conservative Christian does not always equip you with the tools to be a good man. When Hannah became pregnant, I tossed her out into the street.' A desolate expression clouds his face, which morphs into a wince. He jolts and clutches his chest.

'Tom, you need a doctor. Please phone an ambulance.'

But he's not listening. 'What kind of man does that to his own flesh and blood?' Tears fill his eyes. 'Every day, every hour, every minute, I think about her, the grandson I lost, and what could have been if only I'd been a better man, a better father.

But I wasn't, and she died, murdered in the most savage and cruel way. So, you see, Hannah did not die by my hands but it's because of me she died.'

'I'm so sorry about Hannah, Tom. But Lily doesn't deserve to die. She's an innocent. As am I.'

He sighs. 'I'm sorry that I hurt you. I'm sorry that you're in this position now, but you just couldn't keep your nose out.'

'Tom—'

'I have no intention of hurting you, Mallory. You're in here for your own protection.'

'What do you mean?'

'Just keep quiet and out of sight, and you will be fine.'

'I don't understand.'

'He is coming, and he will answer for what he's done to my Hannah and the other women he has murdered.'

'Do you mean Barry Mercer?'

With a pained effort, Tom slides onto his knees and pulls himself up using the bars of the cage to support himself. 'If anything goes wrong, it would be best for you to keep out of sight.'

'What do you mean, if anything goes wrong?'

'He will arrive soon.'

'Mercer?'

'One of us will die. I'm not intending it to be me. But if it is, then I suggest you stay quiet and out of sight.' From his pocket, he takes out the knife with the serrated edge, and places the grip in Mallory's hands. Her fingers wrap tightly around it. 'It won't be easy, but you should be able to saw through the rope and free yourself.' He looks to the rear of the abattoir. 'There's a back door should you need to make a quick exit.'

'Why not let me go now?'

'I wish I could but I can't risk you calling the police only for them to interfere. I want Mercer. I want him to die like my Hannah died. I want him to bleed and to suffer.'

'What about Lily?'

'Don't worry about her.'

'Are you going to kill her, too?'

Tom turns and makes his way out of the pen. 'I haven't decided. Take care of yourself, Mallory,' he says.

Mallory feels her blood pumping. Could she really be in danger from Barry Mercer? If Tom kills Lily and Barry kills Tom then Mallory's options are limited. Mercer won't want any witnesses and he'll pin her murder on Tom. She can't let that happen. Turning the knife carefully with her fingers, she points it downwards and begins awkwardly sawing at the rope.

Quinn has punched in the address of the Strother Farm in Belford and is speeding down the A1, lights flashing, siren wailing.

'Nice to have a relaxing drive in the country,' he says.

Quinn is a good driver, she trusts him, but the constant swerving and overtaking is making her a little anxious. She grips the door handle with one hand and the edge of the seat with the other. 'Edge of her seat' is an understatement. Her phone rings. She's popular today. Or so she thinks. It's Fletcher. She swipes to answer.

'Chief Inspector Fletcher,' she says, as yet unable to bring herself to address him as 'Les', which he would prefer, of course, but considering he remains a massive douche, she prefers to remain on formal terms.

'DI . . . I hear the sirens. Have I interrupted something?'

'Yes, sir. We are heading to the location of a possible missing person.'

A pause, then Fletcher clears his throat. 'OK. I'll make this quick. What the hell is Parry doing back in London?'

'I sent him back, sir.'

'I know that but on whose authority?'

'On mine.'

'You can't make those decisions without my say so.'

'Parry was compromising the investigation. I had no choice.'

'You do have a choice. You call me and I make that decision.'

'I'm assuming Parry didn't tell you why I sent him home.'

'I know he's making a formal complaint.'

Archer laughs. 'Of course he is.'

'This is not a laughing matter, Grace.'

'We're almost there,' Quinn says.

'I have to go, sir. Work is calling.'

'Now, just you wait one—'

Archer ends the call.

Quinn indicates left and drives up a narrow lane.

'What was that about?'

'Just some bullshit.'

Quinn kills the siren as they approach. Ahead they can see a rundown grey pebble-dashed house. Parked outside is an old blue Land Rover and Simon Cooper's people carrier.

Chapter 57

MALLORY PUSHES HERSELF INTO A standing position, the knife gripped firmly in her fingers. Hot, dirty and clammy, with sweat running down her back and chest, she saws carefully at the rope around her wrists and stops when she hears a scraping noise from beyond the cages. Narrowing her gaze through the mesh and the gloom, she sees Tom dragging the table across the floor, the bolt gun rattling noisily on the stainless-steel surface. He stops at the centre of the vast space next to where a fretting Lily sits tied to the wheelchair.

Mallory jumps at a rustling sound behind her and holds her breath. She squints into the rear of the abattoir but sees nothing. Did she imagine it? She looks back towards Tom and sees him stiffening as the front door creaks open. Swiftly, he grabs the bolt gun from the table, points it at Lily's head and waits. Mallory feels her pulse racing. The silhouette of a man appears dwarfed in the frame of the large entrance. Lily tries to shake herself free from the chair, her cries muffled behind the tape covering her mouth.

'Come in and close the door,' Tom says, jabbing the bolt gun against Lily's temple.

The man steps inside, his hands raised in a placating fashion. Mallory recognises him from his picture.

'Let my daughter go,' says Barry Mercer.

'You want me to spare your daughter after what you did to mine?'

'I don't know what you're talking about. I've never met your daughter.'

'You murdered my daughter. Shot her in the heart with a bolt gun. Just like this one.' Tom grabs Lily's hair and presses the barrel of the gun hard into her head.

Mallory gasps the knife slips from her fingers and falls to the floor with a clatter.

'Please don't,' cries Mercer.

'Stay where you are!' Tom commands Mercer before he quickly darts a look behind him.

Mallory crouches to the floor. The knife is a foot away from her and she has to awkwardly manoeuvre her feet to slide it across the floor, as Tom and Mercer's voices murmur in the background.

She hears the soft padding of feet nearby. Her stomach clenches. Looking up, she sees a slim older man with grey hair. He is barefoot and crouching down to pick up a stray brick lying on the floor. She has no idea who he is. She is breathing too heavily and stops. His eyes narrow, his head turns slowly in her direction. He sees her and frowns. She swallows. His grip tightens on the brick. He raises a finger to his mouth to shush her before treading rapidly like a ballet dancer across the abattoir. Who the hell is he? For the second time, she hauls herself up. The man is running at Tom with the brick raised high. Mallory is frozen, unsure what to do. Her heart is pounding. Something is just not right. 'Tom. Behind you!' she cries.

Tom turns just as the second man swings the brick at him, striking him hard on the face. At the same time she hears the bolt gun crack and sees Lily's head snap to the left. Tom's legs give way and he falls to the floor as the two men cry out Lily's name. Mallory's pulse is racing, her eyes on Lily. She is slumped in the chair, dead or unconscious, she cannot tell.

Barry Mercer is shaking, unable to move. The second man is crouching in front of Lily, pulling the tape and cloth from her mouth. Barry Mercer is sobbing. 'Is she . . . Is she . . . Oh God, my Lily . . . We need an ambulance, and the police, Simon,' he says, fumbling a phone from his pocket.

The man called Simon prises the bolt gun from Tom's hand, takes a cartridge from the box on the table, and loads it into the gun. 'I know who you are, Elston. After your little outburst, it was easy to ask around and find the name of the new man in town. A quick internet check and I discovered you were Hannah's father.'

'Do you know him?' a puzzled Mercer asks.

Tom is lying on the ground, staring up at Simon. 'It was you?'

'Hannah was delightful. She was a credit to you. You should be proud, Tom.'

'You bastard!' says Tom. He winces and clutches his chest. Mercer looks at him with a confused expression. 'Why?'

Simon holds the gun with both hands. 'Because I could. And I wanted to. Because it was easy. Because no one cared about them. They were insects.'

'No!' says Tom, his voice broken. 'No!'

'I know it's very sad,' says Simon. 'But I had no choice.'

Tom's body goes rigid. He trembles, clutches his chest and lets out a cry before lying deathly still.

'Oh, Tom!' Mallory whispers, as she desperately tries to cut through the ropes.

Simon crouches down and feels his pulse.

'Simon, what did you mean just now?' asks Mercer.

Simon stands, lifts the gun, points it at Barry's forehead and presses the trigger. The crack echoes in the vast room as Barry Mercer falls backward like a felled tree, blood spraying from his head.

Mallory stifles a shriek. Simon turns to look her way as he loads another cartridge into the gun. 'Hey, little rabbit, caught in a trap,' he says, mockingly.

Terror floods every fibre of Mallory's being, but she has mercifully freed her wrists. She is hot and thirsty and panting like a dog, and begins to cut into the bonds on her ankles.

With the greatest of efforts, Mallory cuts through the single rope around her ankle. Pushing herself up she runs for the cage exit, but it's blocked by Simon. He looks at her with cold, hungry eyes and levels the gun at her chest. Mallory still has the knife and – knowing she has nothing to lose – swings it at Simon's face, slashing his cheek open.

'You bitch!' he cries, stumbling backwards.

Mallory wastes no time and bolts across the abattoir, drunk on adrenaline. She can hear him close behind, inches away, but she runs, leaping over Tom's body. She lands badly on her ankle, twisting it, pain shooting through her leg like a knife. Desperation claws at her. 'Help me!' she screams. She hears voices, urgent tones. The abattoir doors swing open. Mallory could cry. Grace Archer and Harry Quinn are running inside. Harry calls her name. Mallory slows her pace. 'It's him! He killed them all. He killed Barry Mercer, too.' Mallory feels something hard press against her head. Her heart sinks. Simon's arm reaches around her neck and squeezes. *This is it.*

'Put the gun down, Mr Cooper, please,' says Archer, her eyes darting to Lily. 'Back-up is on the way.'

Mallory can feel Simon's hot breath on her neck. Quinn hurries over to Lily. Archer's gaze meets Mallory's for a moment. In that brief second, she knows Archer will do everything she can.

In the distance, the police sirens sing their song.

'It's over,' Archer says.

Mallory feels Simon trembling, the barrel of the gun shakes precariously against her temple. Tears fill her eyes. *I can't die like this. There's so much I want to do.*

'Let her go. Please.' Archer says.

'Uncle Simon. Do as she says, please.'

Mallory remains still but slides her eyes to the left. Lily has a bloody gash on the side of her head but is at least alive. Harry has freed her from the chair and she is shuffling slowly towards them. She reaches across and gently takes the gun from him, which he surrenders without question. Mallory breaks free of his grasp and hurries to Archer who puts her arm around her. Outside the police vehicles have arrived.

Simon Cooper smiles at Lily and opens his arms. She regards him for a moment before turning away and kneeling beside her dead father.

'Lily . . .' he says.

But she is stroking the hand of her dad and ignores him.

Chapter 58

THE OLD ABATTOIR AT THE rear of the Strother Farm has become a bustle of activity since the police and ambulances arrived. Simon Cooper has been arrested and is on his way to Berwick Police Station for processing. Lily Mercer lies in the back of an ambulance being attended to by a paramedic. Quinn is overseeing the crime scene, barking orders to the local uniforms. Archer has taken Mallory outside and listened to her account. Despite the trembling, the podcaster, who is still in shock, manages to keep it together.

'I should go back inside and make sure Tom's OK,' Mallory says, turning to go back.

Archer leans across and gently takes her hand. 'Tom's gone, Mallory.'

'Yes, he has.' Mallory Jones's shoulders begin to shake as she begins to sob. Archer wraps her arms around her. 'I'm sorry.'

'Room for one more,' comes a voice. The paramedic from Lily's ambulance is looking at them. 'Let's get you to the hospital,' he says gently.

'I'm really fine. Honestly.'

'You may have a concussion. You should go,' says Archer. 'Harry and I will come and see you later.'

Mallory rubs her arms, a blank look on her face. 'I need to call Bruce.'

'I'll do that. I have his number.'

'Make sure he's taking his tablets.'

'I'll remind him.'

The paramedic gently guides the podcaster away and into the ambulance.

Quinn is approaching. 'All squared up here for the time being. Shall we go?'

'Let's do it.'

On Simon Cooper's arrest, DC Stu Vickers had gained entry to his house and outhouses. He had called Archer. 'You might want to come and see this,' he said.

Archer calls Bruce Radley on the journey to Springhill Lane. She gives him a potted summary of what happened, reassures him that Mallory is being seen to by a doctor, and that she and Quinn will call in to see her later.

'Thank you so much for calling me and letting me know,' says Bruce.

'You're welcome.'

'Listen, I know you're not our biggest fan, but we really appreciate and are in awe of everything you do.'

'Thank you.'

'I'd like to meet you one day.'

'Me too, Bruce. Oh, before I forget. Have you taken your tablets? Mallory asked me to remind you.'

He laughs.

They arrive at Simon Cooper's house ten minutes later. Several police vehicles are parked off the road. Stu and Andy are waiting for them outside the outhouses. Stu leads them into Cooper's bicycle workshop where a tall shelving unit containing tools has been shifted to another part of the space. There's a doorway in the wall.

'We found this behind the unit.'

Archer steps into a room. It's an office space with a desk, a lamp and photos from over the years of Cooper, Isla and Lily. None of Barry Mercer. In fact, there are two with Barry Mercer cut out from the picture. To the left and just below a grubby window is a glass display cabinet. Archer feels her blood go cold. Inside are a dozen or so neatly arranged items of jewellery: women's rings, bracelets and necklaces. Each of them has a small tag tied to it with a date and a first name inscribed. She recognises one: a fine gold chain with half a heart attached to it. Archer swallows. She doesn't need to look at the tag to know this belonged to Elena. She scans the objects, searching through the names. There's a pair of gold hoop earrings that had belonged to Hannah; a silver ring that was Angela's; a *Choose Life* badge that belonged to Sally; a toe ring belonging to Gemma; and a set of thin gold bracelets that had belonged to Star.

'We counted thirteen items,' says Stu.

'Sick bastard,' adds Ball. 'And to think he's been living here right under our noses all this time.'

'We have six victims accounted for,' says Quinn. 'Who are the other seven?'

'We should beat it out of him and find out,' says Ball.

'Not sure that would cut it,' Quinn says.

The men are talking, their voices seem to meld into a monotonous hum that Archer zones out of. She wishes she could find some relief in Cooper's arrest, but she can't. Yes, he will go down, but he has killed thirteen women. Cooper had been stationed abroad with the army. Has he left a trail of bodies spanning the globe? Some of the names suggest that might be the case. The missing seven they know nothing about other than the type of jewellery they wore, the date they were killed and their first names. *It's a start, at least.*

Chapter 59

MUSIC to fade

Mallory Jones (voiceover): Dear listeners. My final thoughts. In the weeks following his arrest Simon Cooper pleaded guilty to the murders of Sally McGowan, Star Royale, Angela Bailey, Hannah Daysy, Elena Zoric, Gemma McFadden and Barry Mercer. After his performance in the abattoir, he had little choice, never mind the collection of victim souvenirs he curated and displayed in his creepy cabinet. From that evidence, the police have deduced that a further eleven victims remain unaccounted for. Judging by the names inscribed on the tags of each souvenir, at least five of these murders are believed to have occurred in other countries.

Cooper was an army man stationed at various British bases across the globe. A partnership initiative led by a newly formed Interpol team has been set up to investigate what happened to the remaining unidentified victims. Rest assured, I will be keeping a close eye on developments and will broadcast my findings as they come. So do make sure you have subscribed to the *Mallory Jones Investigates* podcast.

From the transcripts of the police interviews, it has been revealed that Cooper on occasion returned to the UK on leave to visit the only family he had: his sister Isla and her husband, Barry Mercer. No one could have known the secret history of the siblings' relationship. With different fathers, Isla and Simon had the same mother. A troubled woman who died from an overdose when Cooper was eleven and Isla, seven. It's believed, but not confirmed, that their mother was a sex worker. Read into that what you will, but could he have harboured some sort of trauma and resentment from his childhood?

Isla Mercer and Simon Cooper grew up in care together. They became lovers as teenagers and into their mid-twenties. Witnesses who knew them from back then had no idea they were siblings. But Isla desperately wanted a normal life and broke away from the relationship. Simon was devastated. He joined the army, maybe to run away and forget her. Isla joined the police, met Barry and lived and worked in different locations across the country. She remained close to her brother but their relationship, she maintains, stayed platonic.

Hannah Daysy's estranged father, Tom Elston, had found a common thread among the victims: Barry Mercer. Barry had worked on his Hannah's case. He had even spoken with Tom all those years back and from what we now know, reading Barry's police report, he was less than kind about Hannah. Tom discovered Barry had worked indirectly on Angela Bailey's case and had come to the conclusion that Barry was the killer. When Tom learned that Barry was in London at the same time Elena Zoric was murdered, his mind was made up. But Tom was wrong. We now know that during Simon Cooper's leave, Cooper stayed with the Mercers and would take himself off into the night looking for his next victim.

For years it seemed the Mercers were never going to have children. Despite several rounds of unsuccessful IVF for Isla, Barry had contented himself with a future without kids until Isla suddenly became pregnant in her mid-forties. But this was not a successful IVF procedure. This was the result of an afternoon with her half-brother rekindling a long-hidden love and desire.

Cooper claims that he stopped killing when his daughter, Lily, was born. It seems that while she was growing up he may have not killed, but that as yet remains to be proven. The reality is a leopard cannot change its spots. As we know, he killed again twice, and would have killed me had Lily not stepped in and asked him not to. Lily, I am forever grateful.

So, who is Simon Cooper, and should we care? The answer is both yes, and no. If you saw him in the street you would not give him a second glance. He is the epitome of ordinary. A sixty-one-year-old white man who dresses in beige and greys. He's of medium build, average height, with nondescript features. To those who knew him they say he was polite, friendly, a pillar of the community. Others say he was a man of few words with no personality. To his victims, however, he was a monster. A violent murderer stalking his victims with stealth. He preyed on the vulnerable: women living in poverty, trying to make ends meet in the only way they could; women that he believed the police – or anyone, for that matter – would not care about or miss. Should we care about him, and people like him? Absolutely, not! After what he did to those women, and how close he came to killing yours truly, he can go straight to hell and burn for eternity as far as I'm concerned. That said, we must learn from people like him. We must educate ourselves and others and, God willing, this understanding will perhaps contribute to the prevention of similar murders in the future.

As for Detective Inspector Grace Archer, she returned to London to face off against her chief inspector who had had a complaint raised against him about his conduct as a constable during the disgustingly brief investigation into the missing teenager, Sally McGowan. He has been suspended from duty while the investigation is in progress. In other happy news, Grace Archer has been promoted to DCI. Congratulations, Grace! I hope we can have a drink together soon.

Finally, this show is dedicated to DCI Grace Archer but, more importantly, it is in memory of Sally McGowan, Star Royale, Angela Bailey, Hannah Daysy, Elena Zoric, Gemma McFadden and the as yet unnamed eleven victims. May they rest in peace.

EXIT MUSIC

Chapter 60

52 Roupell Street, London. Four weeks later

THE ALEXA ALARM BEGINS TO chime the 7 a.m. wake-up call. Archer is curled up under the duvet, warm, safe, and in a state of bliss that she has not experienced in a long time. Her eyes open as the alarm rises in volume.

'Alexa, stop!' says Liam, his voice sleepy.

'Good morning, Grace!' says Alexa. 'Today will see a high of twenty-one degrees with blue skies and sunshine. Is there anything else I can help you with?'

'Make us some breakfast!' says Liam.

'I'm afraid I didn't get that,' replies Alexa.

'Alexa, shut down,' Liam says.

Archer rolls onto her back. Liam pulls her to him, nestling his face into hers. 'Morning.' He kisses her cheek.

'Morning.'

She melts into him, their eyes meet. He smiles and kisses her gently on the lips. Pulling back, he says, 'Should I be offended that your Alexa cannot tell my voice from yours?'

Archer chuckles. 'She's still learning. I wouldn't take it personally.'

He leans in and kisses her once more. 'Big day today.'

'It'll be the same as any other.'

'Yeah, but detective chief inspector. That's some awesome shit.'

'We'll see.'

'I'm sensing some reluctance to embrace your new role.'

'It's not that. I'm just not sure I want it, or any role within the Met.'

Liam pushes a strand of hair from her face. 'You might need a holiday.'

'I wish.'

'When was the last time you had one?'

'Eight years ago, maybe. A rainy week in Spain. We weren't so lucky with the weather. Since then, a couple of weekend city breaks.'

'Shit. That's tough. Listen, no obligations, but how about we take my campervan and drive to France for a week? Somewhere south where the sun is shining and the wine is on tap. What do you say?'

'I'm not sure.'

'Tell me you'll think about it?' He's nose to nose with her, smiling that winning smile again.

She laughs. 'OK, let's do it.'

Acknowledgements

Thank you, David Headley, as always. The world is a better place with you in it.

Thanks also to the team at Zaffre: Ben Willis, Georgia Marshall, Kelly Smith and designers Nick Stearn and Dominic Forbes for the stunning cover.

Finally, thank you to all the readers, bloggers and reviewers who have continued to support and shout about these books. You are unsung heroes.

If you enjoyed *A Violent Heart,*
why not join the
DAVID FENNELL READERS' CLUB?

When you sign up you'll receive an exclusive deleted scene,
plus news about upcoming books and exclusive behind the-
scenes-material. To join, simply visit:
bit.ly/DavidFennellClub

Keep reading for a letter from the author . . .

Hello!

Thank you so much for picking up *A Violent Heart*.

The first three books in the Archer and Quinn series are unconnected mysteries with different killers each with their own modus operandi. You could consider them a trilogy. The main story in each one is the hunt for a killer but there are also two separate and important plotlines that conclude in *The Silent Man*. If you've read all three, you'll know one plotline tells the story of Grandad Jake, his declining health through dementia and the emotional impact this has on Grace. You'll also be aware of the second thread that tackles vengeful gangster, and let's be honest, utter douche bag, Frankie 'Snow' White. The devastating fallout of his revenge on Grace, her family and colleagues was challenging to write but I hope made for good reading.

A Violent Heart is the fourth in the series and a reset for our heroes. A standalone mystery, it reintroduces Mallory Jones, the True Crime Podcaster from *See No Evil*. Mallory becomes an asset to Archer in the hunt for a killer who for decades has flown under the radar leaving a trail of murdered women who were addicts or sex workers, surviving on the fringes of society. Women that no one, especially the police, cared for. This is a work of fiction but has been inspired by real events in the UK and the USA.

If you would like to hear more about my books, you can visit www.bit.ly/DavidFennellClub where you can become part of the David Fennell Readers' Club. It only takes a few moments to sign up, there are no catches or costs.

Bonnier Zaffre will keep your data private and confidential, and it will never be passed on to a third party. We won't spam you with loads of emails, just get in touch now and again with news about my books, and you can unsubscribe any time you want.

And if you would like to get involved in a wider conversation about my books, please do review *A Violent Heart* on Amazon, on Goodreads, on any other e-store, on your own blog and social media accounts, or talk about it with friends, family or reader groups! Sharing your thoughts helps other readers, and I always enjoy hearing about what people experience from my writing.

Thank you again for reading *A Violent Heart*.
All my best,
David Fennell

Don't miss out on Grace Archer's other thrilling cases . . .

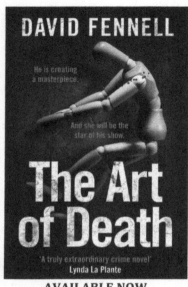

AVAILABLE NOW

AVAILABLE NOW

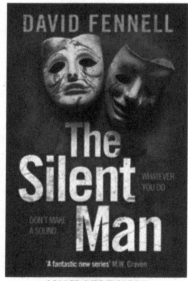

AVAILABLE NOW